The Road To Oblivion

THE ROAD TO OBLIVION

"EVEN WITHIN THE CHAOS, YOU CAN STILL FIND SOMETHING DEVASTATINGLY BEAUTIFUL"

Jessica Voll

Copyright © 2022 Jessica Voll

All rights reserved. No part of this book may be reproduced or used in any manner without the prior written permission of the copyright owner,
except for the use of brief quotations in a book review.

To request permissions, contact the publisher at
AuthorJessicaVoll@Hotmail.com
Harcover: ISBN 9798847621243
Ebook: ISIN B09X3TCTB
Paperback: ISBN 9798847620536
The Road To Oblivion Second Edition

Edited by Twisted Alder Designs
Interior Design by Twisted Alder Designs
Cover art by Adrian Păsărin (Adrian Dsgns)

Dedication

To *the ones who* love *so much it hurts.*
"*Behind every beautiful thing, there is some kind of pain." -* **Bob Dylan.**

Contents

Dedication
Contents
Playlist
Acknnowlagements
Prologue 16
Chapter 1 29
Chapter 2 49
Chapter 3 57
Chapter 4 69
Chapter 5 81
Chapter 6 87
Chapter 7 93
Chapter 8 105
Chapter 9 117
Chapter10 131
Chapter 11 136
Chapter 12 145
Chapter 13 149
Chapter 14 157
Chapter 15 163
Chapter 16 171
Chapter 17 187
Chapter 18 193
Chapter 19 209
Chapter 20 219
Chapter 21 227
Chapter 22 245
Chapter 23 251
Chapter 24 261
Chapter 25 271
Chapter 26 279
Chapter 27 291
Chapter 28 297
Chapter 29 305
Chapter 30 311
Chapter 31 319
Chapter 32 329
Chapter 33 341
Chapter 34 355
Chapter 35 365
Chapter 36 379
Chapter 37 387
Chapter 38 393
Chapter 39 402
Chapter 40 411
Chapter 41 421
Chapter 42 433
Chapter 43 441
Chapter 44 453
Chapter 45 461
Chapter 46 465
Chapter 47 471
Chapter 48 479
About Author
More books

Book 2 Sneak Peek

Chapter 1 01
Chapter 2 09

Playlist

- ♡ Paradise by Coldplay
- ♡ Earned It by The Weekend
- ♡ Love by Lana Del Rey
- ♡ Say Something by A Great Big World
- ♡ Green Eyes by Coldplay
- ♡ The Mess I Made by Parachute
- ♡ Strip That Down by Liam Payne
- ♡ Up Down (Do This All Day) by T-Pain
- ♡ Gangsta by Kehlani
- ♡ Between The Raindrops by Lifehouse
- ♡ Kiss Me by Ed Sheeran
- ♡ 8TEEN by Khalid
- ♡ When You Were Young by The Killers
- ♡ Imagination by Shawn Mendes
- ♡ Electric (feat. Khalid) by Alina Baraz
- ♡ Pursuit Of Happiness by Kid Cudi
- ♡ Just A Lil Bit by 50 Cent
- ♡ You and Me – Acoustic Version by Matt Johnson
- ♡ High Hopes by Panic! At The Disco
- ♡ Sexy Bitch (feat. Akon) by David Guetta
- ♡ loving you by Mahogany Lox
- ♡ Car Wash by Rose Royce
- ♡ I Ain't Ever Loved No One – Acoustic by Donovan Woods, Tenille Townes
- ♡ Young Forever by Jay-Z
- ♡ Sweat by ZAYN
- ♡ In Your Arms (with X Ambassadors) by ILLENIUM
- ♡ Best Friend (feat. Doja Cat) by Saweetie
- ♡ Yeah! By Usher
- ♡ Iris – Acoustic by The Goo Goo Dolls
- ♡ Wait by M83

The Road To Oblivion Spotify Playlist.

Acknowledgments

Out of this long and tedious process, thanking those who were there for me from the beginning is the easiest. This is the first book I have ever attempted to write; trust me; it was quite the ride! I poured everything I had into this story, so a huge thank you to the man of my dreams and high school sweetheart Cody for holding down the house and picking up my slack (even though you like to complain about it) while I spent months and many, many sleepless nights engrossed in this story.

Angela, my sister-in-law, soulmate, sister from another mister, and many more titles, thank you! You have no idea what you did for me in this book. Reading every chapter that I sent to you, staying up with me till the early hours of the morning shooting ideas off each other, answering my calls just for me to rant some more about this book, the characters, the process, and everything in between. Your honesty and feedback had such a huge impact that I can say without a doubt that this story or this process wouldn't have been the same without you! You went above and beyond, and I can never thank you enough. I will forever be grateful for your support and endless hours of intervention when I felt I was in over my head.

Alyssa, my sister, my best friend, thank you for listening over facetime as I read you random chapters of this book. For encouraging, believing, and supporting me through it all. Most importantly, thank you for just being there. I'm so happy to have you as my person. Sorry I tortured you with a couple of chapters at a time and made you wait weeks, sometimes months, before you got another one! LOL.

Emily, thank you for picking up my call when I first had this dream and answering my hypothetical question that started it all. You were one of the very first people I told my idea to, and at the time, I wasn't sure I even had it in me to write a book. It was you that convinced me otherwise and gave me the encouragement and reassurance that I needed. So, a big thank you to you because without you; I don't know if this book would have ever happened.

Arc Readers! You guys are such a vital part of the process. Life is unexpected and crazy, so thank you for taking time out of your busy schedules to meet Rayne and Christian and thank you for taking a chance on me. I'll remember you forever.

Adrian, thank you for taking my vision and bringing it to life with this fantastic book cover!

Anna, my editor, teacher, and friend. Thank you from the bottom of my heart because, honestly, I would not have been able to do any of this without you! From the endless number of questions (because we both know I have plenty) to the hours of conversation and more! Thank you. You have taught me so much throughout this process, and I feel like I can never repay you. Thank you for your patience, understanding, knowledge, advice, help, encouragement, and much, much more! If I could do this all over again, I'd choose you every time. Thank you for working with me. I can't wait to get to work on future projects with you.

And lastly, to my readers! Thank you so much for following me along this journey! I'm so honored that you chose to read my words and hopefully fell in love with the world I created. Rayne and Christian are my first fictional babies, and now I hand them over to you. I promise I will always give my all and put 100% into any book I decide to release because you guys deserve nothing but the best! This may be my first book, but I can assure you that it will not be my last. I can't wait for you guys to continue this journey with me! I owe it all to you. Thank you!

With so much love, Jess.

xoxo

Rayne ♥

I have always been a hopeless romantic who can't help, but love the idea of love it is rare, but I believe that it does exist. I have experienced it first hand by watching the love my parents share toward one another. I find love very intriguing; did you know that your brain releases intensely-euphoric hormones when you are in love So much so that it can make a person addicted to love and the person they are in love with. Interesting, right?

The thing that is so fascinating about love is it's the one thing that can make someone feel complete; The one thing that can make someone feel so high and unstoppable. However, it is that exact thing that can flip someone's life upside-down -- bringing it to a crashing halt. The one thing that can completely destroy someone and forever change them. Love can be so beautifully devastating.

I enjoy watching romance movies, you know the kind where the bad guy meets a good girl, they are totally opposite from each other, but you know the saying "opposites attract?" well yeah, there is an attraction between the two. Bad boy does something horrible, good girl is devastated, bad boy grovels, and gets good girl back. Then they live happily ever after, blah, blah, blah. isn't that what we all want though?

A movie kind of love-- a love that consumes you, a love that sets your skin on fire. The only difference between movies and reality is that movies are planned and written out, whereas life is unpredictable, and you should expect the unexpected. Everything can change in the blink of an eye, and in life, our happily ever after doesn't always turn out the way we expected.

My name is Rayne Davis and this is my story.

xoxo

Prologue

Rayne

"What do you think of this?" Laynie asks, looking down at her outfit. She is wearing skinny black jeans with tears on the knees, a white Adidas shirt and black and white slip-on vans. Laynie always comes to me for advice on clothing, and I love it. It gives me practice for when the day comes, I'm styling A-list celebrities.

"Simple, but cute. It's chilly outside, so I would pair it with this." I remove a denim jacket from the hanger and hand it to her. From her jewelry box, I grab a silver pair of hoops. "Wear your hair in a messy bun or ponytail and wear these hoops." I love how a small piece of jewelry can make such a big statement.

"Good call! Thanks, babe."

"Welcome!" I shout over my shoulder, walking back into her closet to find a shirt.

Still only wearing my blush lace bra, black skinny jeans, and my favorite doc martens, I raid her closet. I grab a ribbed black crop top matching it with a plaid black and white cropped jacket and a simple gold chain from her jewelry box.

"Can you help me with this, please?" I ask Laynie, holding out the gold necklace. She takes it from me, and I hold up my hair, so it's not in the way.

"I wish I had amazing tits like yours." I giggle at her straightforward comment.

"Please, your boobs are way bigger than mine! Trust me, they are amazing." I'm not lying either; Laynie is a total bombshell. She has a killer body, an impressive bust, and mile-long legs.

"I do have some good tits." She admits clasping the ends of the necklace.

I giggle and playfully roll my eyes as I finish getting dressed. Since I spent the night at Laynie's after school yesterday, I grabbed my backpack and threw my school uniform inside before misting myself in my favorite lavender body spray and heading to the living room with Laynie.

"Hey, kiddo," Laynie's dad Charlie says, ruffling my hair.

I smile, using my fingers to brush my long, dark hair back into place. "Hey, Charlie."

"You ready to get going, girls?" Laynie's mom, Stacey, asks, taking a sip of her coffee.

Laynie and I both nod and follow her out the front door. About twenty minutes later, we arrive at The Hideout, Laynie and I's favorite coffee shop. It sits on a busy street corner in Los Angeles, close to our school. We always sit back in the corner where they have the most buttery leather loveseat and an industrial coffee table to sit our stuff on. They bathe the area in natural light from the tall windows that line the front of the shop. The rest of the shop has trendy brick walls to pull its look together. The ambiance is intimate with chill background music and a diversity of unique individuals. Los Angeles can be so hectic, with all the people and the constant noise, which is why I love coming here. It is the opposite of the chaotic streets just outside.

"Have you heard? Gretchen Adams is dating Chase Mathews!" Laynie exclaims, hot on my tail as we walk through the large glass doors. "Rayne! Did you hear what I said? Gretchen Adams is dating Chase Mathews."

How could I forget him? The notorious Chase Mathews was a senior and the star quarterback at our school two years ago when we were freshmen. He was my first and only crush. Since then, I haven't had time for boys, focusing on my future instead. Gretchen Adams is in a grade above me and is the head cheerleader at my school. She is gorgeous and very outgoing, and she is everything I'm not.

"Isn't she a senior this year and isn't Chase like a sophomore in college?"

"Yes! how the hell did she get so lucky to bag Chase?" That lucky bitch.

"Because she's hot as fuck, of course," I tell her, standing in line.

"That's true, but you're hot too, and you never got him." She blurts and grimaces, realizing how it sounded.

"Jeez, thanks."

"Sorry... you know I didn't mean it like that."

"Well, if you remember correctly, someone kind of messed that one up for me." Laynie rolls her eyes.

"That's true... I can't believe he did that! He's such a little shit."

"I can believe he did that because he has done it most of my life, and he is at least six feet, so that would technically make him a big shit."

Laynie bursts into laughter, which causes me to join her. The tall guy in front of us, hearing our giggles, turns his head to look. I can only make out his side profile, but I notice the slight smile on his face, and the way his lips twitch like he's trying not to laugh.

Laynie sits in our usual spot by the fire, and I wait in line to order our drinks. Now that Laynie isn't here keeping me company, I have no choice but to admire the guy standing before me. His shoulders are broad, causing his black t-shirt to hug his muscles. The shirt was loose around his narrow waist and hips. Something about his herculean shoulder's screams masculine. He steps up in line to order, and I can't keep my eyes from traveling down to his round, defined ass. Shit. His ass is perfect. Even better than Chase's.

Eyes up, Rayne... stop looking at his ass.

Instead, I force my eyes away and stare at the back of his sun-kissed sandy-blonde head. His shoulders tense as he pats his pockets, then subtly shakes his head at the Barista, and that's when I realize he must have forgotten his wallet. Without hesitating, I walk forward and stand next to him.

"You can add his order to mine," I say and feel him looking at me. Ignoring it, I give her my order, making sure she adds his to mine.

"I don't need your handouts." He says to me harshly. His voice is smooth like velvet, even with the bite behind his tone.

I don't know what the hell this guy's problem is, but I was expecting something more like a thank you. I hand over my cash and turn to face the asshole next to me. I'm about to give him a piece of my mind, but stop dead in my tracks. HOT. SO HOT. *Is he real?* My fingers tremble, wanting to reach and touch him to make sure, but that would be super weird. He looked pretty damn good from the back, but from the front, oh my god!

His eyes, golden like melted honey, penetrate my emerald - green ones. Our gaze fixes and his eyes widen just a smidge. He parts his lips, shakes his hair out from in front of his eyes, then presses his lips tightly together, furrowing his brows. I mirror his expression, no longer blinded by the beautiful body in front of me.

"A thank you would be nice." I scoff. "Nobody is giving you a handout. It's called being a decent human, and you should try it." I brush past him, my shoulder lightly grazing his arm, and tingles ignite up and down my entire body. *What the hell was that?*

He follows me, standing off to the side as we wait for our order.

"And how do you imagine I do that?" he asks, crossing his arms over his chest, looking annoyed and unmovable. His chest looks firm, and the veins in his arms bulge. *Why are the hot guys such assholes?*

I lift my chin, trying to seem confident and not look like I'm totally shaking in my boots. He's hot as hell, strong, and a jerk. Usually, that combination would be intimidating to me, but something about his rude remark and the smug look on his face got under my skin, and I couldn't hold my tongue.

"You can start with a thank you."

His smug smirk drops, and he stares intently at me, and I stare right back.

"You're serious."

"No. I'm joking." My tone is full of sarcasm. The corner of his mouth twitches as it did earlier, and I know he's trying to keep from smiling.

"Thank you."

"You're welcome," I say, more like a question. I'm shocked that it was that easy and expected him to argue.

"Sorry, I'm new around here and have been driving for almost fourteen hours."

"Explains the attitude." He chuckles, and I feel it all the way in my toes.

"I'll be good once I get my coffee."

I nod in agreement. "So, where are you from?"

"Oregon." His response is short as he crosses his arms and shuts down. Any sliver of emotion he was showing vanished.

Oregon must be a touchy topic. Noted. I don't know this guy, and I'll probably never see him again, but I find him intriguing with his gruff responses and sly smirk. He is tense, but something about him makes me want to look past his hard exterior to see why he's so guarded.

"Why LA?" I ask. His brows scrunch, and he brings his full, soft lips between his teeth, thinking. I can't help wondering how they would feel against mine.

"Opportunity." He responds, and my eyes snap away, causing the corner of his mouth to twist. Smug bastard. I roll my eyes.

"Man of many words, I see."

"You know… sometimes people say the most when they aren't saying anything at all." I'm not sure what he means by that. *How can somebody say so much without saying anything?* I'm about to ask him, but I don't get the chance to.

"Why help me?" he asks. "Why pay for my order when you don't know me?" his question confuses me. *Has no one ever done anything nice for him?* I didn't think paying for someone's drink was a huge, grand gesture. My parents do things like that, and I've thought nothing of it. It's what a nice person does, and when I can help someone out, I do.

As I look up at the stranger standing in front of me, I can't help all the questions swirling through my mind. *Who is this guy? Why does he look sad? What's his story? And why do I care to know?* I smile at him genuinely, and his eyes drop to my mouth.

"There are good people in the world, ya know?" I shrug. "And I choose to be one of them."

He doesn't respond and studies my face like he's unsure about me. Or maybe he's staring at me the same way I did him, wondering if I'm real or not. All I know is I like the way I feel when he looks at me and how every hair on my body reacts to him. While he studies me, I study him. His nose comes to a perfect point, and dark eyelashes guard eyes of honey. He's fucking gorgeous, and I have to fight to pull my eyes away.

He finally goes to speak. "I'm Chr—" the barista calls out our order, startling me.

We both reach for our coffee, our arms crossing over each other, touching at our forearms. Jolts like electricity shoot to my fingertips, and I instantly pull my arm back as his eyes widen. *Did he feel it too?*

I quickly grab mine and Laynie's coffee, unsure how to respond to what happened.

"Um, nice meeting you... I should get back to my friend." I hold up the coffee and gesture to Laynie over my shoulder. He nods his head with a puzzled expression.

"Nice meeting you."

"Welcome to LA."

"Thanks." He gives me a small smile that doesn't show his teeth, and I turn around and walk toward Laynie. I don't look back, but I hear him say, "See ya."

Laynie's mouth is hanging open when I approach her. "Wow... who the hell was that?"

How could I forget to get his name? I frantically turn around, hoping to catch him before he leaves. He's already gone, without a trace of him ever being there. He was beautiful, wrapped in a mystery, and I felt inexplicably drawn to him. I'm so pissed off at myself for not getting his name: way to go, Rayne... way to go.

Handing Laynie her white mocha cold brew, I sigh. "I don't know who he is because I didn't get his name."

"Rayne!"

"Laynie!"

"You guys talked the whole time, and you're telling me you didn't even get his name?"

"That's exactly what I'm telling you." I take a sip of my iced coffee to avoid her gaze.

"We come in here all the time. Maybe you'll see him again?"

"Yeah... maybe."

"I couldn't get a good look from over here, but he oozed sexy." I sigh, reminiscing about how sexy he was. His tan skin against his light hair and those honey-colored eyes... chef's fucking kiss.

"He was sexy, Laynie! You have no freaking idea. Damn, I really blew it." She giggles.

"It's so good to see you reacting this way over a guy Rayne! I thought you'd end up being some gray-haired old lady who owned thirty cats." I playfully flip her off.

"I'm shocked I'm reacting this way! It's not like I had a choice… he was… he was dreamy."

"Well, babe, if it's meant to be…"

"It will be." I finish her sentence, smiling.

Christian

I pull up to a gas pump, opening and closing my hand to get the feeling back into my fingers. I've been gripping the steering wheel for what feels like an eternity. I'm still adjusting to all the bustling energy and chaotic noise L.A. brings. It is fucking gigantic compared to where I'm from and can swallow my small town, Baker City, whole. Fuck, it feels great to be out of there.

Arriving at the house, we are now calling home; I slowly come to a stop. It's a beautiful two-story house, light grey, aside from the oak garage door. I back the U-Haul into the driveway and park next to my car that my mom drove here. As I roll down my window, my mother walks to the driver's side door.

"This is it." She says with glistening eyes and looks toward the house, taking it all in. It wasn't an easy decision for her to uproot our life, but it was time.

"This is it," I smile, and she nods, bringing her attention to me.

"I'm going to call your uncle Maverick and tell him we've made it. I'll be back out to help bring everything in."

"Tell uncle Mav I said hi." She smiles and heads inside.

After an hour, I took a break. I use the bottom of my shirt to wipe the sweat coating my forehead. Damn. It's September, and it's warm. The weather is very different here from what I'm used to in Oregon. I sit on the back of the U-Haul, taking everything in as I chug some water. I've unloaded half of the truck already, and I'm beat. The suburban neighborhood looks nice. Large houses fill the street, kids ride bikes, and neighbors walk their dogs. They all seem very friendly, waving as they pass.

"God damn it!" someone shouts in frustration to my right.

Following the outburst, I see the sexiest car I've ever seen... well, aside from my classic Mustang. It's a Camaro z28, and my fingers twitch to see what's under the hood. The hood is lifted as the guy under it comes into view. He's around my height, maybe a little shorter, but not by much. His eyebrows are scrunched in concentration as he grabs a rag and wipes his hands. I contemplate going over there and offering him some help, but I already have a shit ton of stuff to do. Plus, I'm used to the assholes in Baker City who weren't as welcoming as the people here seem to be, which doesn't help with my apprehension about approaching him.

The last thing I need is for this guy to be a dick and piss me off. I don't need beef with my neighbor on my first day here. His frustration grows along with a tirade of cuss words as he throws down the rag he used to wipe his hands. Amused, I chug the remainder of my water.

"Fuck it," I mutter to myself. Hearing me approach, he brings his head up to look at me. "What's up, man?" I say, and he gives me a welcoming smile. Thank fuck.

"What's up, bro? You're our new neighbor." he nods his head at the house behind me. "That your car?" he gestures to my Mustang.

I follow his line of sight, "Yeah, just getting in today," then I look back at him, unable to contain my grin. "Sure is."

"Fuck, she's sexy. You from around here?"

"Na, I'm from Oregon."

"That blows. You'll like it here a lot better."

"Yeah, I'm sure you're right about that."

"Ooo, not so good in Oregon?"

"Something like that."

"I'm Ryker," he holds out his hand, "but you can call me Ry." I try not to stare at him for too long, but he looks oddly familiar. It's impossible to know him since I just moved here, but I feel like I've seen him before.

"Christian," I shake his hand. "You need some help?"

"Yeah, I can't figure this shit out. My car randomly won't start, and I don't know why."

"Mind if I look at a few things?"

"Be my guest."

Under the hood, I inspect his battery, which seems new, so I doubt that's what is causing his car to stall. Walking over to the driver's side, I get in. With his keys already in the ignition, I start the car. When I turn the key, a clicking noise follows, and the engine doesn't start. I try again, and this time it turns on, but I notice the dim interior lights.

"Does your engine stall if you don't get the car moving?" I ask.

"Yeah, sometimes." I nod, leaning back under the hood. I check the battery terminal, which is slightly loose, but can make a huge impact on the car and affect the flow of electricity.

"Your battery's terminal is loose and is most likely causing a connection block. It's a simple fix. Just tighten it, and you should be good to go." I grab the rag, using it to wipe my grease-stained hands.

"Fuck, I feel like an idiot. I work on cars. It's literally my job, and I couldn't figure out a loose wire."

I chuckle. "You work on cars? That's cool, man, me too. I have to find a job out here first, but it's what I love doing."

"Yeah, my pops owns Davis automotive. Why don't you come for breakfast tomorrow, and I'll introduce you?"

"Your serious?" I eye him skeptically, unsure why'd he'd do that for me. He doesn't even know who I am.

"Serious as a heart attack." He gives me a mischievous smile. "Is it just you and your…"

"My mom, yeah. It's just us."

This is when the question "where's your dad?" happens. I don't want to talk about my father right now. I love him, but I don't need Ryker to know me as the guy who lost his dad. That's all I've ever been known for. Just this once, I want to be known as Christian, and that's it. Thankfully, Ryker doesn't ask.

"For sure. Well, you helped me out. What do ya say I give you a hand and help you guys move in?" I nod my head, holding out my knuckles.

"Sounds fair."

We spend the next hour and a half unloading boxes and carrying them into the house as we talk and shoot the shit. He's the same age as me and has a younger sister and parents that have been together since high school. He seems like a good dude that comes from a good family. We have a lot in common; we both love cars. His dad owns his own auto shop just like mine did, and we both have no problem with women. However, nowadays, I'm steering clear of females. I had enough of them back home, and the last thing I need is some girl drama. I don't have the time or the patience for that shit. I never have.

I may not have time for girls, but it doesn't stop the girl with the piercing green eyes from flashing through my mind. She was fucking beautiful, and there was something angelic about her. I noticed her the moment she walked into the coffee shop with her friend, but I quickly turned to face forward, not wanting even to entertain the idea of chalking up a conversation with her. That plan ultimately went to shit when she stepped forward and paid for my order because my dumb ass forgot my wallet inside the truck. Who just pays for someone's order? Oh, that's right. A decent human being... something I've got to learn, clearly.

When her eyes connected with mine, I felt lost for a second and almost forgot we were standing in a crowded coffee shop. Sounds corny, I know and trust me, I'm no romantic, but there was something about her I can't quite explain. Her laugh was contagious, and her smart mouth was surprising.

Girls back home were whiny, annoying, and had no backbone, but this girl was quick-witted and kind, and how she didn't back down from my dickish behavior was refreshing. I don't always like being an asshole, but it was so damn easy with other girls. It was fucking pathetic. They didn't care and let me walk all over them, but that was before, and this is… now. This is a fresh start and a new beginning.

Fuck. I can't get her out of my head, though. All rational thinking flew out the window the moment she looked at me. I was about to ask for her number, but before I could, she was walking away from me and back to her friend. *It's for the best.* That would have opened a realm of things I'm not looking for. If I had her number, I wouldn't have been able to stay away. I wouldn't have *wanted* to stay away. It sounds crazy because I don't even know this girl. Standing next to her was like standing next to a gigantic orb, just waiting to suck me in. I've never experienced anything like it. Quite the opposite, I wanted to stay the fuck away from everyone in Baker City. Still, with her, I wanted to stand there and continue to talk to her. I wanted to know the pretty girl with a smart mouth.

When she looked at me, she really looked at me like she had one hundred questions and wanted to get to know me… all of me—which is a scary fucking thought. When we touched, it sparked something and ignited me at my core. Just a simple and innocent touch almost brought me to my damn knees. *Fuck, do you hear yourself?* Whoever she is, is long gone by now and nothing but a memory.

"I'm gonna head out," Ryker says, setting down the last box. "I'll see you tomorrow morning, right?"

"Yeah, I'll see you tomorrow."

Chapter 1

Rayne

"Baby girl," Dad said, brushing my hair from my face. "Wake up." I groan, rolling over, tossing my pastel pink comforter over my head.

"Ten more minutes."

"It's Sunday and you know we have breakfast as a family on Sundays. If I let you sleep any longer, I can't guarantee anything will be left. You know how much your brother can eat."

Flipping onto my back, I drag the comforter from my face, popping one eye open. "What is on the menu today, pop?"

My dad uses his index finger, pushing his reading glasses further up on his nose, smirking at me. "Get up and come find out. I promise it won't disappoint."

I don't know if it's because I'm more awake than I was two minutes ago, but I notice the smell of syrup as it enters my nose and my mouth waters.

"Mmm, pancakes."

"And bacon." My dad adds with a wink as he stands up and heads for my door.

"Let me brush my teeth first, then I'll be down. Oh, and please don't let Ryker dig into the food until I get down there."

My brother, Ryker, is one hundred and eighty pounds of pure muscle. He eats anything and everything but never gains a pound. I'm incredibly jealous. He doesn't even work out like I do! He chalks it up to a fast metabolism and 'good genes,' Which I must constantly remind him we share.

Shaking his head, my dad smiles. "Five minutes, and then it's fair game."

After quickly getting out of bed, I grab my phone and head to the bathroom, and put on 'Paradise by Cold Play' and washed my face to help wake me up. As I stare at my reflection in the mirror, I can't help but notice I look so much like my mother. It's almost eerie. I have her deep brown hair, except mom's is now shoulder length, whereas mine falls halfway down my back. She is five-six, and I'm five-three. We share the same round-shaped face, full lips, and button nose. Besides our height, the only difference is that she has porcelain skin and sea-blue eyes, whereas I inherited my dad's olive skin tone and emerald green eyes. My mother, at my age, was gorgeous! I hope to look half as good as she does when I get older.

"Rayne! I'm going to eat the last of the pancakes and bacon if you don't get your ass down here." My brother, Ryker, shouts from downstairs, breaking me free from my daze.

I roll my eyes at his threat. Taking my time, I turn off my music, brush my teeth, then throw my nest of hair into a messy bun on top of my head and make my way toward the kitchen. My mother's voice drifts up the stairs as she asks my dad if he would like another cup of coffee, but I also notice the sound of another voice that sounds familiar, and I can't think of where I heard it before.

"Sure thing, just up the stairs. First door to the right." Ryker says.

I'm looking down at my feet, trying to figure out who he's talking to, as I step off the last set of steps and smack straight into something solid.

"Ouch!" I squeal as my hands fly up and grab a set of powerful arms in front of me.

Instantly, I get a whiff of a citrus aroma that smells heavenly and doesn't help with my unsteadiness. I'm still looking down at my feet, covered in my favorite fluffy pink socks, then notice another pair of feet. This other set is large compared to mine, covered in all-black Converse. I slowly drag my eyes up his skinny denim jeans that hug his thighs like they were made solely for him. I note the black AC/DC shirt and smile as my eyes track higher. *He has good taste in music.*

The skin on his neck looks as smooth as silk, and *I wonder if it feels as soft as it seems.* My eyes finally avert to his, and I suck in a sharp breath. Eyes of golden honey... eyes I'd recognize anywhere stare down at me.

Holy shit! I blink, unsure if he is even real. Maybe, dad never came up and woke me this morning, and this is all a dream. He is a dream.

His eyes widen slightly, causing his eyebrows to rise. He pulls the right side of his beautiful mouth into a smirk, shooting tingles straight to my core between my thighs, and I must fight the urge to squeeze my legs together.

I realize in a state of shock that I am still holding onto his arms. "Shit, sorry." I quickly drop my hands, and they instantly feel cold, the opposite of what they deemed a few seconds ago, and I already miss the warmth. *Jeez, Rayne, get a grip.* The boy from the coffee shop is here in front of me in my living room! How is this possible?

He goes to speak at the same time I ask, "What are you doing here?"

His mouth shuts before transforming into a wide smile. The kind of smile that's so big it reaches his eyes, and I can tell it's genuine. He seems to be in a better mood than he was yesterday. His teeth are white and straight, except the bottom two are somewhat crooked, making his smile even more perfect. When I realize I'm staring at his mouth, my cheeks flame, and I gaze back to meet his honeysuckle eyes.

He chuckles, not answering my question. "You must be Rayne?"

"How do you know my name?" his lips twitch at my shocked expression, shaking his head to get his messy sandy hair that hangs slightly in his eyes out of the way.

"Your brother helped me move in next door yesterday and at some point mentioned he had a little sister, which I am assuming is you, no?"

Wait, Ryker helped him move in yesterday, and he's my neighbor? *Yeah, I'm definitely dreaming.*

"I didn't realize anyone moved in next door. Then I smacked right into you, and you caught me off guard." I awkwardly lean back on the heels of my feet. "Sorry if I came off rude. Let's just start over. Hi, I'm Rayne Davis." I stick my hand out for him to shake. "Welcome to the neighborhood."

Oh my god! A handshake? So lame, who sticks out their hand to give a handshake, especially to a boy their age? Well, not totally my age. He must be closer to my brother, who is two years older than me. He once again does that sideways smirk and stares at my extended hand. He slowly takes my hand in his, and tingles shoot up my arm, traveling to my toes. His eyes widen a fraction before returning to normal so quickly that I might have imagined it.

"I know your name, Rayne Davis, but thank you for welcoming me to the neighborhood." He pauses, roaming his eyes over my face, "I have a feeling I'm going to like it around here."

My cheeks instantly heat again. Why the hell does that keep happening around him?

I clear my throat. "Since you know my name, I think it's only fair to know yours."

The corner of his mouth twists up in that sexy way he seems to do. Does he realize what that does to me? I'm going to need a new pair of underwear at this rate.

"I'm Christian."

"Christian..." I repeat, still not believing the guy from the coffee shop is standing here in my house. "I better get in there before Ry eats it all." I nod my chin toward the entryway of the kitchen behind him, and his lips do that sexy tilt again. *Damn him.*

"Better hurry."

We stand there for a second, not saying anything, before I finally will my feet to move, walking around him.

As I pass by him, he says, "Hey, Raynie." Butterflies dance in my stomach at the nickname.

"Yeah?"

Staring right at me, he says, "Nice shirt."

Confused, I look down at my oversized blink 182 tee and see my nipples are hard enough to cut glass. I quickly cross my arms over my chest, embarrassed, and hurry into the kitchen.

"Good morning, mama." I lean over the kitchen island and give her a quick peck on the cheek.

My brother snorts and mimics, "Good morning, mama." I turn my gaze to him and scowl.

"Oh, big brother, don't get jealous that I'm the favorite of the two of us."

"Pshht, who's told you such lies?" I look between my dad and my mom, who is now returning to her seat at the table. My dad laughs and shakes his head.

"We love you both equally." My mom ruffles my brother's hair. "My first baby," then looks at me, "And my youngest baby."

Ryker fixes his now disheveled hair. "Love you too Ma, but there is nothing like the love you have for your first child, am I right?" he gives her a massive grin.

Ryker is such a mama's boy. For as long as I can remember, he has always been. Even now, at eighteen. He has absolutely no shame about it either. They share a close bond that I honestly think is cute. My brother and I share a similar relationship as well. We are close in age, so we always did things together growing up. He was kind of stuck with me, but he never seemed to mind. Ry took me wherever he went, like the proud big brother he has always been. He is a massive pain in my ass most of the time, but I love him. He's always been extremely protective of me, which is admirable and annoying! Now that I'm older, he has finally realized I don't always need his protection, so he's backed off a little. I can't believe I'm admitting this, but I will miss him when I go to college. Yes, he is a bit over-the-top protective, but I always feel safe with him.

We share similarities, but mostly, we are opposites. He is outgoing, loud, and popular, especially with the ladies. Before he turned eighteen and started stepping into the family business, Ryker was known for getting wild and partying hard. On the other hand, I am shy, except with the people I'm most comfortable with. Then I am very outgoing, like with my best friend, Laynie Mae or Jamie. I have never partied, and I'm definitely not loud. My preference is to be a wallflower standing on the outside looking in. Also, I'm highly inexperienced in the dating department. I've never even had a boyfriend. Having Ryker for an older brother has not made dating easy. He's scared off every guy who might have been interested in me. He claims they aren't good enough for me. I've never really been interested in anyone, anyway. Even so, he is a cock block. I love the idea of being in love, and I can't wait to be in love one day—everyone deserves to be loved.

Under my breath, I murmur, "Kiss ass."

Ryker's eyes dart to mine at the same time both my parents say, "What was that, Rayne?"

"What was that, baby girl?" I smile at them sweetly, taking a seat across from my brother.

"Oh nothing, I'm just curious how Ry would know the love a parent feels toward their first-born child." I smirk and shrug my shoulders. "I mean, is there something you would like to tell us, big brother? Perhaps a baby we don't know about?"

My mom chokes on her coffee but coughs to play it off. Ry may be my brother, but there is no denying he is attractive. It's apparent by the number of girls dropping to their knees for him. He stands six feet tall, with dark brown hair that is shorter on the sides and longer on the top: porcelain skin, and sea-blue eyes like our mother. I cringe internally just thinking about him and his extra-curricular activities. My brother may sometimes be a douche with a capital D, but he isn't stupid enough to go without protection.

"Relax, Ma, Rayne here is just trying to give me shit." He glares at me.

"Language, Ry," my dad says impatiently.

"Besides, I go by the motto—no glove, no love. So, you know I'm always safe."

"You're disgusting!" I gag at the same time as my mom says with wide eyes.

"Okay, okay, enough of this topic. You guys may grow up, but you're still my babies, and I don't want to hear about any sexual experiences of yours. Either of you."

Now it is my turn to choke. "Mom! I'm sixteen and have never even had a boyfriend. No sexual anything is going on." My dad's eyes dart to mine with a stern look. The kind of look fathers give their daughters when they aren't messing around.

"Damn right, no sexual experiences are going on with you, and it better stay that way until you're at least thirty."

Not that I plan on having sex soon, but what a double standard. Ry is over here talking about some no glove, no love, bullshit, and it's no big deal. I mention I've never had a boyfriend, and my dad looks at me as if I'm having sex on the table. I understand he's highly protective, especially with me being his only daughter, but he can't possibly think I will be an inexperienced virgin forever. Nothing is wrong with being a virgin, and I'm not the type to hook up with just anyone, but I am curious about sex and would like to have it one day with the right person.

"Dad, there is nothing to worry about, but isn't that a little unfair? Ry here is talking about no glove, no love. I know he is eighteen but let's be honest, he isn't a saint, and we all know he hasn't been for a while now, but I'm expected to wait till I'm at least thirty?" I say a little louder than I intend to.

My mom is smirking at my dad, waiting for his reaction.

"I don't want to talk about this right now, and I don't even want to think about my baby girl growing up." He huffs, still scowling. "Besides, that should never even be considered unless it's with a man you love and most certainly a man deserving of you. As far as I'm concerned, no man could ever be that."

"Yeah, I agree with dad." Ryker follows up. And I dramatically roll my eyes at him. I'm surprised they didn't get stuck in the back of my head. Hoping she will intervene, I look at my mom, but she smiles, shaking her head. *Come on, us girls gotta stick together.* I want to punch Ry and wipe that smug look off his face. I have my doubts about going to college so far away, but in moments like this, I can't wait to be out on my own and not under the microscope of them. Come on, let a girl live a little. This conversation isn't going anywhere, so I lean over and give my protective father a quick peck on the cheek, then change the subject.

"I'm starved, and breakfast smells amazing."

My stomach growls as I stack two pancakes on my plate, two pieces of extra crispy bacon, just the way I like it, and a ton of syrup.

"So, Ry, it was nice of you to help Christian move in yesterday." My dad says as he grabs the napkin resting on his lap and wipes the corner of his mouth.

At the mention of Christian's name, my heart rate speeds up. I guess Ryker was out front messing with his car per usual, and Christian came over to help him. It turns out he knew a lot about cars and figured out the problem. I don't know much about cars, but I can change a tire and check the oil, thanks to Ry and my dad. That's about it, though. Once they were done working on Ryker's car, Ryker offered to help Christian move in. I still can't believe he's my neighbor! He moves into the only house available in my neighborhood, out of all the places he could have moved to in Los Angeles. Crazy. I'm not mad, though. He's smoking hot, and the thought of seeing him around doesn't seem like a bad idea. My stomach flips at the thought. Just as I'm about to ask more about the unfamiliar boy, he walks in.

Christian strolls into the kitchen, smiling as he sits next to Ry. "Yeah, man, I know I already said this, but thank you for helping us unload yesterday. It took half the time it would have if it were just my mom and me."

Ry puts his knuckles out, and they fist bump. "No problem, bro. Glad I could help."

Before I even have time to think, I blurt, "Where is your dad?"

Shit.

Shit.

Shit!

Me and my damn word vomit. When something pops into my head before I can even think it through, it pours out of me. I can't help it. Ryker looks nervous, and both of my parents look slightly disappointed at my rude question, making me instantly regret asking.

"I'm sorry. What a rude thing to ask, and it's none of my business." Christian stares at me for a second as something I can't decipher passes through his eyes before he quickly returns to normal and smiles at me.

"No worries, don't be sorry. My dad passed away in an accident when I was ten, and it's been just my mom and I."

My heart instantly hurts. I could not imagine losing either of my parents. I'm close with both and could never picture a life without them. Growing up, I had girl nights with my mom, where she would sleep in my room. We would do each other's hair, eat our favorite snacks until we were almost sick, and watch movies until we couldn't keep our eyes open. Dad and I would do father-daughter dates once a month, which was such a big deal for my five-year-old self. Mom would do my hair and let me pick out a pretty dress. My dad would get dressed up and leave. Then come back and ring the doorbell. I would answer the door with the biggest smile, and he would stand there with a bouquet of light pink roses and lavender, mirroring the same smile as mine. We would go to the backyard and have a dinner date, and he would tell me all about how my mom and I were the most special girls in his life. Seeing how my dad still treats us has taught me how I deserve to be treated and what to look for in a man one day.

A lump forms in my throat. Why couldn't I keep my mouth shut? Why did I have to ask such a stupid question? I need to apologize for being so insensitive.

"And before you try to apologize again, don't. Although it hurts like hell, I like to think I'll be okay. No need to be sorry."

I sit there, stunned and feeling guilty. I avert my gaze down to my lap and nervously play with the nails of my fingers.

"Well, Christian. I am sorry my daughter here asked such an intrusive question, but don't take it personally. For as long as I have known her, she has always been brutally, blunt which is a blessing and curse. It will probably get her into trouble one day." I meet my dad's eyes, and he winks. "Anyway, we are glad to have you over for breakfast. You are more than welcome to come over at any time."

"If you or your mother ever need anything, please don't hesitate to ask." My mother adds.

"Thank you. I'm sure I will see a lot more of you." He looks at me as he says it.

My cheeks once again heat under his stare. He tilts his head a little, noting the effect his simple words have on my body.

"Ryker told me you helped him with his car battery and that you are quite knowledgeable." My dad says.

"Yeah, my dad was a mechanic. I guess that's where my love for cars started. It was a way for me to feel closer to him, even though he was no longer here. I like to think he's there with me when I'm working on them and that he would be proud seeing me follow in his footsteps."

The table is quiet, and my eyes water. *Don't you dare cry, Rayne.*

"That is beautiful, dear. I am sure your dad is very proud of you. I know I would be." My mom says, eyes glistening.

He smiles. "Thank you, Mrs. Davis."

"Oh, please call me Olivia."

"You know I own Davis Automotive, and we can use another mechanic at the shop if you're interested?" My dad tells him.

Ry interjects, "Yeah, man, as you know, I work there too. I hope to take over the family business one day once this old man retires." He flicks his thumb in dad's direction.

My dad scoffs as he pushes his glasses further onto his nose. "Son, I'm not old. I'm forty-four, for crying out loud, and still have some years left on this engine." *No pun intended.* I think to myself. My mother laughs, and my dad's eyes light up at the sound.

"I was going to put in some applications tomorrow. Are you sure? I'm extremely grateful for the offer, but I expected to put in a day's worth of applications before I even got an interview, and I feel like I have to prove myself at least."

"Life doesn't always have to be so damn hard. We all deserve breaks now and then." My dad leans back in his chair, staring directly into Christian's eyes, letting him know he's serious. "I don't want you thinking this is a handout. We need help at the shop; you have experience and are looking for a job. You can start on Wednesday. Look around the shop and see if it's even something you want to do."

He leans forward and interlocks his fingers, resting them on the table. "If it makes you feel more comfortable, we can start you on a probation period, and you can show me your skills. Once your probation period is up, we can discuss pay and go over all the paperwork required. How does that sound?"

Christian reaches over the table and shakes his hand. "Thank you, sir. I don't know what to say." He pauses, "Just... thank you."

My dad gives a curt nod. "So, we're all set, then. I will see you on Wednesday at eight-thirty a.m. Sharp."

Vzzzt, Vzzzt, Vzzzt. My phone vibrates on the table.

"May I please excuse myself so I can take this?" I ask, looking at my dad.

"Go ahead, just put your dishes in the sink if you're finished eating."

I smile and grab my plate with my free hand. The whole time I walk to the sink, I feel eyes directly on my back. The hairs on my neck stand up, but I swiftly shake them off and head out of the kitchen without making eye contact with the culprit.

"Laynie Mae," I say as I walk up the stairs to my bedroom.

"Rayne Davis, long time no talk."

I roll my eyes, smiling, "We just talked last night."

"Really, and here I thought you forgot all about me," Laynie says, and I can tell she is smiling too.

"Never."

"Promise?"

"Always." I put my phone on speaker and make my bed.

"Have you heard about the party Jackson Reed is throwing this weekend?"

It's the only thing everyone seems to be talking about lately. Just the thought of Jackson Reed has my skin crawling. Jackson is a senior this year but gives me the total creeps. He doesn't have the best record at school and has had his eyes set on me since I was a freshman. Although it was flattering initially, it rubbed me the wrong way when he wouldn't take no for an answer and accept that I wasn't interested.

"You know how I feel about him, Laynie."

"I know, I know, but it's after the homecoming game and it's going to be epic! There will be so many people there we won't even see him."

Laynie does have a point. I'm sure it's going to be packed, and it wouldn't be hard to steer clear of Jackson. Fuck it. Why not?

"You're lucky I love you." She shrieks, and I pull the phone away from my ear. "Let me check with my parents and make sure it's okay with them first. If it is, then fine, I'll go."

"Don't sound so excited. It is going to be epic. We are going to dress up and look hot as fuck. Then we're going to dance our asses off." I smile at her excitement.

"Okay, when you put it that way, it sounds fun. Let's talk more about it at school tomorrow."

"Sounds good. I'll see you tomorrow, babe. Love ya!"

"Ditto, Laynie Mae."

After I got off the phone with Laynie, I changed out of my pajamas and took a shower. If I could live in an oversized tee and spandex shorts, I would. I applied some mascara, light blush, and lip gloss while letting my hair air-dry into its natural loose waves. Once I was done getting ready, I did some homework, studied, and read a few chapters of the current romance book I'm stuck on. It's so easy to get lost within the pages of a book, and I wasn't aware a couple hours had passed since I'd been downstairs. My stomach growls, and that's my cue to put my book away and get something to eat.

As I make my way toward the stairs, I hear Ryker shouting at the TV. Let's just say he takes Sunday football seriously. He was good enough to make the football team in high school, but never tried out. Ryker told me he enjoys watching it more than he does playing it, but I think he was having too much fun doing what he wanted after school and partying on the weekends. It's crazy to see how much he's grown up since graduating just last year. I think working Monday through Friday at dad's shop had a big part in that. It hit him pretty

Chapter one 41

hard when all his friends were going off to college after graduation, and he didn't have any plans to. That was a pivotal point for him and really made him question what he wanted to do for a career.

I wonder what that was like? I've known what I wanted to do since I was a little girl, but I can't deny the feeling of dread now that it's so close that I can almost touch it. The thought of being alone in New York is terrifying, but I am excited and happy. Everything I have ever done in my life, everything I have ever worked for, was for New York.

Stepping down the stairs, I expect to see Ryker and dad. Ryker is leaned forward with his elbows propped on his knees as he stares intently at the TV. Sitting next to him, I see the back of Christian's head as he sits casually leaned back with his arms propped on the couch, looking a lot more relaxed than Ry. I'm surprised to see him still here. I guess he and my brother are really hitting it off. *Great.*

It's not that I don't like them hanging out, but after meeting him at the coffee shop yesterday, I didn't think I'd ever see him again. Now, he's been over for breakfast, met my parents, and is now chilling watching Sunday football with my brother. I really thought I blew it when I didn't get his name or his number, and now he's here in my house and in my life. I can't help but feel like this was fate. *What are the chances?* He's my freaking neighbor! Yeah, that's going to take some getting used to. I can't lie and say I'm not happy to see him and get a second chance at getting to know him, but I kind of wish we met again under different circumstances and not through Ryker. Christian is hot as hell, but he's no longer a stranger in the coffee shop. He's now my brother's friend and a possible employee of my dad's. *Things just got complicated.*

"Scoot a little closer to the TV, Ry. I don't think you can see from where you're at." I tease.

Rykers face is a foot away from the screen, and I don't know how he isn't blind yet. His attention drifts to me as he dramatically rolls his eyes.

"This is some serious shit, sis." He quickly brings his attention back to football like he's scared he will miss something if he doesn't.

"Global warming is some serious shit. Not football."

Christian stifles a laugh, bringing my attention to him, and I smile. At least he thinks it's funny. When there is a commercial break, Ryker leans back, returning to regular proximity from the television, and scowls at me.

"Take it back."

"Make me," I smirk, crossing my arms over my chest in defiance.

"Take it back... or else." He stands to his full height as Christian's eyes ping-pong between us, completely amused.

"Or else what?" he holds up both hands, wiggling his fingers. *Oh. Shit.* I hate being tickled because it's the worst kind of torture, but I'm also too stubborn to back down.

"One." He counts. "Two..." I slowly take a step back.

"I'm not taking it back."

"Three!" he shouts, and I turn, making a run for it. He's much faster than me because I don't make it three steps before he grabs me in a bear hug and throws me over his shoulder. I yelp as he tosses me on the love seat and starts tickling me.

"Stop, stop, stop," I plead in between laughs. My eyes are squeezed shut as I flop on the floor like a fish out of water. "Okay... mercy." I laugh, barely getting the words out.

He releases me as I lay there trying to catch my breath. I open my eyes, meeting his piercing gaze and smug look. "Take it back."

My eyes narrow, and he holds up both hands again, challenging me. Fine. He wins.

"I take it back," I mumble. He grins, holding his hand out in a truce, and I slap it away and stand up on my own, brushing my now wild hair out of my face. On instinct, my eyes move to Christian, who wears a lopsided grin, taking all the oxygen out of my lungs. Suddenly, I feel very hot. Damn him. Why does my body react like that?

Chapter one 43

"I'm going to the kitchen to get something to drink and snack. Do you guys want anything?" I ask, avoiding their gaze. I don't want Christian to notice my reaction to him, and I certainly don't want my brother to see.

"Water, please," Christian says.

"Me too," Ryker adds. "Oh, and popcorn with that cheesy powder stuff."

I make two popcorn bags for Ry and me, and I pour them into bowls as my mom walks into the kitchen with a smirk on her face. She rests her elbows on the island as she leans close to me like she's about to spill some juicy tea.

"He's cute." She whispers, then looks over her shoulder out into the living room.

"Who?" I whisper back, pretending I don't know who she's talking about. She rolls her eyes, knowing I'm full of shit.

"I may be old, but I'm not blind. You're telling me you don't think he's cute?" she wiggles her eyebrows, and I blush, avoiding her question as I turn around to grab water bottles from the fridge. "That's what I thought."

"What." I shrug. "I'm sixteen, but I'm not blind." I throw her words back at her, grabbing our snacks and drinks. My lips twitch at her laugh as I exit the kitchen and walk back into the living room.

Ryker moved to the love seat, getting closer to the television, leaving the middle and end seat next to Christian open. Shit. Do I sit in the middle next to him? Or do I sit at the far end of the couch? If I sit in the middle, it might seem too eager. Deciding to take a seat at the far end of the sofa, I pass Ry his bowl of popcorn and water bottle, and he takes them without looking at me, his eyes still focused on the football game. He mumbles thanks under his breath, and I roll my eyes at how consumed he is. I turn to Christian, and he whips his head to the TV.

"Here's your water." My voice cracks and my cheeks redden in embarrassment. He turns to look at me, and his crooked smile returns. As he takes the bottle from my hands, his fingertips graze against mine, sending a shiver through my body. I draw in a sharp breath as my heart pounds inside my chest. *What. The. Hell.*

"Thank you." He swallows, throat bobbing.

Still holding in my breath, unable to form a sentence, I smile instead. For the next hour and a half, we all sit silently watching the football game with an occasional outburst from Ry. I stare at the TV, but I'm not paying attention and have no clue what's going on. I'm too lost in thought about the boy sitting an arm's length away, and I don't dare look in his direction, afraid my body will betray me because it seems to have a mind of its own whenever he is around.

The jolting electricity that takes place at the simplest touch has stunned me silent. I have never had a reaction like that toward anyone, and I don't know what the hell it means. My response to him confuses me, and I can't help but wonder if he feels it, too? When he grazed my fingers, it felt intentional. Did he do it on purpose? *Is that flirting?* Honestly, I don't know, which only makes me more puzzled.

Ryker gets up to use the restroom during a commercial break, leaving Christian and me alone. My beating heart thumps wildly, and my palms get clammy. This is the closest to alone we've ever been. Christian looks entirely at ease with his arms spread out along the back of the couch, and his long legs stretched out in front of him. Laynie is right... he oozes sexy, and he doesn't even try. His presence is intense and intimidating, but I'm shockingly not intimidated; I am completely captivated.

"Tell me a secret." He says, interrupting my thoughts.

I look at him as he stares at me studiously. Tell him a secret? No one has ever asked me such a question. I don't even know him, but for some reason, it doesn't stop me from wanting to tell him one.

I think you're so damn hot, with the most beautiful eyes and a lopsided smile that makes me feel things completely inappropriate.

"You go first." I gulp nervously, fidgeting with my fingers.

"I asked you first." He shifts his body to face me. "Tell me something you've never told anyone."

"Um…" I pause. It's hard to think of anything with him looking at me. "Late at night, when I can't sleep, I climb out of my window and onto the awning. I like to lay and look up at the stars."

Not a fascinating secret, but still something no one knows. It's the perfect place to go and think. It's my junior year, and my counselor is hounding me about college choices and wants me to start the application process early. Since I was a little girl, I have wanted to do something regarding fashion, and New York has a great fashion school. It should be an easy choice, but it's not. I'm scared to leave everyone I love behind and go off on my own. It's all happening so fast, and I feel I need to have all the answers when I don't.

Christian smiles wide, showing me his perfect teeth. He doesn't often smile, so it catches me by surprise when he does. I take mental pictures hoping to burn them into my memory.

"Your turn."

"Whatever I tell you stays between us, okay?"

"Scouts honor," I say, holding up three fingers.

"I never was a boy scout."

"And I never was a girl scout." The corner of his mouth lifts and my eyes drop to his lips.

"Let's see…" His tongue traces his bottom lip, causing heat to swirl in my stomach. *Now is not the time to be fantasizing.* He looks at me, but his eyes are no longer bright. "Every year on the day of my dad's death, I write him a letter. It's stupid because it's not like he will ever read them, but it makes me feel good."

Turning my head, I close my eyes, so he doesn't see my eyes water. What am I supposed to say? *Sorry?* Sorry, won't bring him back. I don't want him to think I pity him either because I don't. I admire him and his strength. If I ever lost someone I loved, I wouldn't want to hear how sorry everyone was. I don't think I'd want to hear anything at all.

Not giving it much thought, I scoot closer to him, our thighs touching, and goosebumps break out like hives at the contact. I rest my hand on his leg, trying to comfort him.

"It's not stupid, Christian… It's sweet. And I think you are wrong." His eyes focused on my hand that rested on his leg dart to mine, waiting, almost pleading to hear what I had to say. "I think your dad is right there with you every time you write him a letter, and I think he's smiling."

Christian's throat bobs as he swallows. His eyes turn glossy, but before I can really look, he quickly turns his head so I can't see. Did I say the wrong thing? I'm about to apologize for upsetting him but stop when he places his large hand on top of mine, engulfing it completely.

"Thank you." His voice trembles.

I want to ask more about his dad and more about him, but it doesn't seem appropriate to ask now. I get the feeling talking about his father is hard for him, and it means a lot to me he felt comfortable enough to tell me this secret. We hardly know each other, but as our eyes are connected in this vulnerable moment, an unspoken word is passed between us—trust. He trusts me, and I trust him. That's when I understood what he meant: *"Sometimes people say the most when they aren't saying anything at all."*

"You're welcome." I squeeze his hand and smile.

Neither of us attempts to move our hands. I like the way his hand feels on mine, and I want to savor this moment and enjoy the warmth he brings me. I can tell he is guarded by massive walls with tiny windows only allowing me to see parts of him, but the little pieces I have seen are beautiful, and something that beautiful should never be hidden.

We don't say anything as we sit in silence. Our thighs were still pressed against each other, and his hand was still on top of mine. I don't know why I felt the strong need to get closer to him, more than I already was, but I lay my head tenderly on his shoulder, letting him know that his secret was safe with me. I feel him tense. And for a moment, he stays just like that body, rigid and unmoving. Then he moves his hand, and

I cringe, regretting getting so comfortable. He surprises me when he flips it over in an open invitation for mine. My head is still resting on his shoulder, so he doesn't see the massive grin on my lips as I set my hand in his, and our fingers intertwine.

The moment is short-lived when the toilet flushes upstairs. Before I can react, Christian's body turns tight, and he urgently lets go of my hand. I recoiled, immediately backing away from him and returning to my seat on my side of the couch. My eyes scan Christian's face. I'm not sure what I'm looking for *reassurance?* His armor is back in place, void of all emotion.

Ryker returns to his seat just as the commercial ends. I glance at Christian a few times, trying to get him to look at me, but he never does. Shortly after, he announces he has to go home and leaves without glancing in my direction.

What just happened? We had a moment, right? I don't know… maybe it was just me comforting him and nothing more. Perhaps I pushed too much too soon. I probably freaked him out. He was being friendly, and I got way too comfortable. I've never felt that way with someone before. He's a stranger, but it doesn't feel like it. Whatever, no big deal. I wouldn't consider us friends yet, so who cares if I scared him away?

Lies.

I fear I just messed up any possibility of getting to know him more.

Chapter 2

Christian

It is six a.m. on Wednesday, and today I start my first day at Davis Automotive. I tossed and turned all night and couldn't sleep because my mind was too active. Instead, I daydreamed about my new job and the girl with sea-foam eyes. It's been three days since our *moment* on the couch and I still can't get her out of my head.

When she crashed into me at the bottom of the stairs, I thought I was hallucinating. To say I was dumbfounded would be an understatement. She looked fucking good when I saw her at the coffee shop, but seeing her fresh out of bed and still in pajamas was something else entirely. Her natural beauty nearly took my breath away. In a world full of fake appearances, she was so real.

Now I know why Ryker looked so familiar. He's her fucking brother! I can't believe I didn't put the two together because they look so much alike. What the fuck are the chances of me moving into a house and meeting Ryker, who just so happens to be related to Rayne? It was bad enough to meet her at Hideout and force myself not to run after her and get her number, but now she's my neighbor, and how the hell am I supposed to stay away from her now? *You have to stay away! You'll ruin her. You will ruin everything.*

I don't know what I was thinking, asking her to tell me a secret. Since when do I like sharing secrets? I'm a calculated person for the most part, but I feel impulsive and can't think straight with her. She has this ability to pull things out of me without even meaning to. Telling her about my secret letters to my dad honestly shocked the hell out of me. I expected the same automated response everyone gave. *Sorry.* I didn't expect her to tell me she believes my dad is right there with me and that she finds my letters sweet. I didn't expect her to scoot closer to me and bravely place her hand on my thigh in comfort, and I didn't expect it to work.

Initially, I tensed at the contact. There was a couple of reason why, for one, I don't like anyone touching me unless I allow them to, and two, her touch caused tingles that shot straight to my dick. I know, I know, highly inappropriate, but my dick has a mind of its own. Sue me.

When she laid her head on my shoulder, it was the cutest thing. *Cute?* Oh, God. I want to slap the shit outta myself right now. Still doesn't change the fact that I enjoyed it, and I liked having her close. She probably didn't think so by how I reacted once we heard Ryker upstairs. Fuck. I'm an asshole. I felt her staring at me, but I wouldn't look in her direction... I couldn't. If I had looked at her, I would have seen her face and wanted to comfort her or tell her something that would give her some false hope.

She's perfect, and I'm so far from it she deserves better. I got caught up in the moment, and things aren't that simple. She isn't just a stranger in a coffee shop. She is... I'm not sure what to call her. *Are we friends?* I've never had any of those. The bottom line is she is Ryker's little sister and my new boss's daughter. My mother and I just moved here. This is our fresh start, and I wasn't always the best person. I can't afford distractions or the possibility of fucking everything up because I'm pretty good at that shit.

So much has happened within the past five days, and I'm

still trying to wrap my head around the fact I found a job so quickly, made a friend... *and met a girl that invades your thoughts and makes you feel things when you didn't believe you were capable of feeling at all.* Stop thinking about her, I mentally tell myself. I have a job! And I'm doing what I've always loved to do... work on cars.

I have been working on cars since I was seven. When I was ten, before my dad died, we would work with his brother, my uncle Maverick, on his classic Ford Mustang GT500CR. I loved doing everything with my dad, but working on cars with him was my favorite. The mustang was a project he surprised me with and was something I looked forward to everyday after school. I knew I wanted to be just like him when I got older. I learned how to change oil, a flat tire, car battery, and replace wipers and air filters by ten years old. It probably sounds boring to you, but to me, it meant everything. I was determined to absorb and learn all there was to know, and I knew it was possible because I had the best teachers. I remember the look on my dad's face when we were working on the mustang, and I handed him a tool without him asking for it because I already knew what came next and what he needed. A smile graces my lips at the memory.

"*Look at that, son. I don't need to point to the tools anymore or tell you what comes next. You are so smart, and you make your daddy so proud. Keep watching me and Uncle Mav, and you will work on cars of your own one day.*" I give him the biggest toothy smile.

"*I want to be just like you. Do you really think I can do it?*"

"*Son, you will be better than your uncle and me.*" The corner of his mouth hooks up, glancing at Mav. My uncle smiles widely and nods his head in agreement. "*I believe you can do anything if you want it bad enough. I will always believe in you. No matter what, all you need to do is believe in yourself. I will always be by your side, buddy.*"

As I lay there staring up at my ceiling, I whisper, "I love you, dad. I hope I'm still making you proud up there." I wait, hoping for a sign or response but get nothing.

Sighing, I swing my legs over the side of my bed and sit up, heading to my bathroom to take a quick shower before I head to work, but hear a faint sound coming from outside my window. Curious, I follow it.

I'm facing the upstairs window of Rayne and Ryker's house. The window is open, giving me a clear view of the bedroom. I can hear the soft hum of music, so I crack open my window, and I can hear it more clearly.

'Earned It by The Weekend,'
"You make it look like it's magic (oh, yeah) 'Cause I see nobody, nobody but you."

At first, I laugh a little to myself, thinking of Ryker listening to this song or worse, his father Jack, but then I see her. Rayne Davis in front of a long mirror that stands caddy corner in her bedroom. She is only wearing short black spandex shorts and a pink sports bra. Her hair is in a messy bun on top of her head as she stares at herself in the mirror.

The Weekend's voice penetrates my ears just as Rayne sways her hips to the song's slow beat. I know I should look away, and my mind is telling me to move, but my body has a mind of its own because it stays rooted in place. From what I can see, her legs are toned and tan, just like the rest of her body. She has a perfect hourglass figure with thick sculpted thighs, slightly wide hips, a small tight waist, and full perfect sized breasts that would fit perfectly in the palm of my hand.

She slowly runs her hands up her thighs, then further up the front of her stomach, over her breast, and into her hair, and continues to sway her hips hypnotically back and forth. When she removes her hair tie, her deep brown hair comes crashing down her back in thick waves. The thought of my hands running through her hair causes me to harden, and now I feel like a creep. My mind is fighting with my body to move. Just as I am about to, her emerald green eyes pierce mine in the mirror. I hurry away from the window, leaning against my wall, breathing hard.

Fuck.

Fuck.

Fuck!

I'm such an idiot. Not only do I feel like a total creep, but now she probably thinks I'm one, too. I am confused at this foreign reaction because my body has never responded to any girl the way it responds to Rayne. It's as if I have no control over my own body. Hearing the music stop, I close my eyes, sighing as I run my hands through my hair, brushing it back away from my eyes. I stand there for a few seconds to get my breathing under control and then head to the bathroom to take my shower.

I dress in denim jeans, a plain beige t-shirt, and my Timberland work boots. As I reach the bottom of the stairs, there's a knock at my front door, causing my heart to beat rapidly. I pause, thinking it's going to be Rayne coming over here to tell me the fuck off for being some weird ass peeping tom.

Reaching the door handle, the person on the other side knocks again. I look through the peephole, relieved it is only Ryker. Then another thought occurs to me. What if Rayne told Ryker that I was watching her this morning? Fuck. He is probably coming over here to kick my ass, and I would let him because I deserve it. I don't have any siblings, let alone a little sister, but if my mom told me some perv was watching her, I would do the same thing. I let out a breath I didn't even realize I was holding and opened the door.

"What's up, bro?" Ryker says with a huge smile. I feel slightly hopeful he isn't here looking for trouble. "You gonna invite me in?"

"Shit, man, sorry, of course, come in. I was just about to pour myself a cup of coffee. Would you like one?" shutting the door, I head toward the kitchen.

"Fuck yeah. I hate mornings." he takes a seat on the stool at the kitchen island. Laughing, I shake my head, grabbing two coffee cups from the cupboard. "Sorry for stopping by unexpectedly like this."

I finish adding a slight dash of creamer to my cup, and I'm about to do the same to Ryker's cup.

"Bro, you might as well drink your coffee black. I'll take a lot of creamer in mine, please." I pour more creamer into his cup, which is now half coffee, half cream, then turn around, setting it in front of him.

"Thanks." He takes a sip. "As I was saying, sorry for stopping by unexpectedly like this, but I forgot to get your number on Sunday when we had breakfast. Did you want to catch a ride with me to the shop for your first day?"

"Actually, yeah, that sounds good. Thank you." I set my cup of coffee down. "Let me see your phone, so that I can add my number." He takes his phone out of his jeans, unlocks it, then slides it over. And I add my contact, then text myself, so I have his number too. "I sent myself a text, so I have your number."

"Sweet." He chugs the rest of his coffee, using the back of his arm to wipe off his mouth. "You ready to get going?" I finish the remains of my coffee, grab his cup along with mine, and set it in the sink.

"Yeah, let's go."

We hop into Ryker's 69 Chevy Camaro. It's a stick shift with a black interior, and a billet polished wood steering wheel with a bowtie horn. I look over at Ryker from the passenger seat.

"I forgot to mention it, but what a classic." I run my hands over the dashboard. "This car is a real gem." Ryker's eyes light up as a knowing smirk tugs on his lips.

"I know."

"Ahem." Someone clears their throat from the back seat. I turn slightly in my seat, locking eyes with Rayne. My eyes widen slightly before I quickly mask it. After this morning, I feel awkward. She can easily tell Ryker about this morning and that would be awkward as fuck!

"We're giving Rayne a ride to school." Ryker says.

My eyes trail over her doc martens, dark green and black

plaid skirt, white knee-high socks, a crisp white button-up shirt that squeezes her body like a glove, and a dark green tie. She looks like every guy's fantasy. The right side of her button-up shirt says Huntington Prep, which explains a private school's attire. Her hair was pulled back in a high ponytail, with a few pieces framing the front of her face. The green in her uniform makes her green eyes stand out against her deep brown hair.

"Are you guys done drooling over cars?" she smiles, and my heart does this weird flutter thing. *What the fuck?* "We need to get going so I can meet Laynie at the coffee shop before school."

"You really don't realize the true beauty of classic cars, sis, and it breaks my heart." He places his hand over his chest. Rayne rolls her eyes, trying to hide her smile.

As Ryker drives, I pull my eyes away from her pouty mouth and face forward. Rayne leans forward between the driver and passenger seat, grabbing a slim CD case that is resting between the seats. She smells of lavender, and I can't help but breathe her in. Leaning back in her seat, she flips through the options in the case before settling on a CD. This must be a routine for them, because without looking, Ryker holds his hand back behind him, and she sets the disk into his palm. He inserts the disk, and the beautiful melody escapes the car speakers.

<u>'Love by Lana Del Ray,'</u>
"Back to work or the coffee shop. Doesn't matter cause it's enough to be young and in love, ah, ah."

Enjoying the music, I observe the pedestrians, track homes, businesses, and restaurants we pass, still not believing I live in Los Angeles. I look into the rear-view mirror and catch Rayne in the back seat. Her eyes are closed, her head leaning back, and she is swaying to the music. As if she senses my eyes on her, she brings her head down and opens her eyes, connecting with mine. I don't move, and neither does she.

Chapter two

I nearly jumped out of my skin when she caught me watching her dancing this morning, but I won't be the one to break eye contact this time. My eyes drop to her mouth, and she unintentionally sweeps her tongue along her bottom lip; her cheeks turning a light shade of pink. I love how her body reacts to mine. The feeling is certainly mutual if my shallow breaths and slight chub are anything to go by.

Trailing my eyes back up her face, I meet her eyes, the corner of my mouth lifting into a half smile. I note her chest movement as she inhales and exhales. She breaks eye contact, looking down shyly at her lap.

"We're here." Ryker's voice breaks my contact as he pulls up next to the curb. It's a two-door car, so I unbuckle my seat belt and step out onto the busy sidewalk in front of the coffee shop. Rayne pushes the seat forward, and I extend my hand to her. She looks at it, then up to me, and arches a questioning eyebrow.

"I don't bite Raynie."

Hesitating, she grabs my hand, letting me help her out of the car. She pulls her cross-body bag over her shoulder and stands to her full height. Her head reaches my chest, making her tilt her head up to look at me.

"Well, aren't you such a gentleman?" she teases.

I am no gentleman.

A light gust of wind hits us, blowing some of Rayne's hair into her face. Without thinking, I brush the hair behind her ear, and her body trembles under my touch. Her cheeks redden as she stares up at me with innocent eyes. Fuck, she's beautiful. A car honks, snapping me out of my dream-like state. I take a step back, clearing my throat, putting my hand into my pockets to refrain from touching her anymore.

"Sorry." I murmur, "I didn't mean to do that."

Rayne frowns, as if she is disappointed. Without saying another word, I get into the car. As Ryker drives and leads us to the shop, I look in the rear-view mirror and see Rayne still standing on the sidewalk, staring back at the car as we drive further and further away.

Chapter 3

Rayne

I stand on the sidewalk, still staring in the direction Christian went long after Ryker drives off. I'm so confused and can't quite read him. On Sunday, before and during breakfast, I thought I caught him looking at me on more than one occasion, but thought it was just my naïve mind making something out of nothing. Then he purposely brushed his fingers against mine. He could have easily taken the water bottle from my hands without touching me. We had a real conversation, and he opened up to me before he ran out of there like his ass was on fire once our moment was interrupted. Since then, he and Ryker hung out a few times but never at our house, only at his. I felt he was trying to stay away from me. But why?

Then this morning, he watched me while I danced in front of my bedroom mirror, and I know I didn't imagine that. I felt his gaze on me in the car. He stared at me attentively, and I thought he was flirting with me. I was wrong to think an eighteen-year-old, someone who looked like him, who I'm sure has plenty of experience, would be interested in me.

His delicate touch made me weak in the knees when he

brushed my hair behind my ear. I felt like we had a moment until he took it back, saying he didn't mean it. It's okay to feel that way, but if that's the case, he shouldn't touch me, even if it's innocent. My feelings are hurt, to be honest, and I scowl at the sky for feeling that way. I hardly know him.

"Rayne Davis, you've got some explaining to do." I jump at the sound of Laynie's voice, putting my hand over my heart.

"Jesus, Laynie Mae, you almost gave me a heart attack." She stands, arms crossed over her chest.

"If you weren't so distracted by that fine piece of ass, you would have noticed me standing here like I said I would be." She takes a step closer to me. "Seriously, Rayne, who was that guy? He is a total snack! A snack I wouldn't mind getting a taste of." Jealousy surges through my veins at the thought of my best friend touching him, and she must notice because she says, "Whoa!" holding her hands up in surrender. "I'm only kidding, babe. Well, not about him being a total snack, but the part about me getting a taste."

I sigh shamefully, "Sorry, Laynie Mae, I didn't mean to react that way, especially toward you." I wrap my arm around her shoulder. "Let's go order our coffee, and I will explain everything."

After grabbing my usual vanilla iced coffee with half and half and an everything cream cheese bagel, Laynie and I grab our usual spot by the fireplace.

"Okay, spill!"

"Truthfully, there isn't much to tell." She rolls her eyes, not believing what I'm telling her.

"Oookayyy, well, let's start from the beginning. Who is he?"

"You really don't recognize him?"

"Um, no. Should I?" she is going to flip when I tell her who he is.

"His name is Christian, and he moved in with his mom next door," I smirk and pause dramatically, making her wait. She squirms in her seat, barely able to contain herself.

"Out with it already! I'm dying over here."

"He's the guy from the coffee shop Laynie!" My mouth spreads into a massive grin. Her eyes scrunch in confusion, then widen when she realizes who I'm talking about.

"No. Fucking. Way!"

"Yes. Fucking. Way!"

If Laynie's gaping mouth is anything to go by, I would say she is just as shocked as I was. She just about lost her shit when she found out he moved in next door. She couldn't believe it. *You and I both girl... you and I both.* I thought she might have a heart attack when she heard Ryker offered to help him move in, making a comment about how "he might just have a soul after all." My brother is a good guy, but her statement doesn't surprise me because they always give each other shit.

I tell her how I bumped into his chest and almost fell on my ass because he's rock solid. Yeah, she laughed at me for that one. She gasped when I told her I felt like I got the wind knocked out of me when our eyes connected as if I lost all oxygen to breathe.

"Rayne, this is a huge deal. You are beautiful. You never even give a guy a second glance. Then you bump into that fine piece of ass and lost the ability to breathe."

"What do you mean, I don't even give guys a second glance?" she tilts her head and looks at me with an *are you serious right now* expression.

"You're hot babe. You walk into a room and every guy turns their head, but you never even give them a chance."

"I never noticed because I always thought they were staring at my gorgeous best friend."

I figured the guys were staring at Laynie. Besides her physical traits, she is outgoing and confident. I'm also confident and have a good sense of who I am and who I'd like to be. I know my worth, and I'll never settle for less than I deserve, but it's the outgoing part I am trying to work on. At almost seventeen and just about finished high school, I've worked hard to get to where I am, and all that hard work is paying off. I think it's time to take my head out of the books and start living. To really look around and enjoy these moments because this will all be over before we know it. I don't see how Laynie does it, but she can balance good grades and still make time to party and have a social life. I'm so far ahead with my grades and schoolwork that it's the perfect time to open myself up.

"Well yeah, I'm hot too." She winks at me. "But seriously, babe, you never mentioned a guy before. Not ever! Then Christian has you all flustered, and all he had to do was look at you." My skin warms at the thought of his golden honey eyes.

Laynie was in a fit of laughter when I told her how Christian complimented my shirt and how embarrassing it was when I realized my nipples were rock hard. I've never had a reaction like that to a guy, and it was interesting, to say the least. Now, whenever I'm around him, I glance at my nipples to ensure they aren't trying to cut through my top. Laynie is laughing so hard tears are forming in her eyes.

"Fuck. I swear shit like that could only happen to you. It is kind of hot though. Your tits are amazing, and no one should get to see those for free."

I scoff. "Laynie Mae you are so bad."

"Never claimed to be good."

That statement couldn't be truer. She is a lot more experienced than I am in many aspects and she owns it. It's one of the many things I love about her.

"There's more…" I tell her.

"Omg, what else could possibly have happened?"

You have no idea. "Well… this morning I woke up early, so I could get in a quick workout. I put on Earned It by The Weeknd and I was feeling myself. I opened my window and turned the music up and stood in front of the mirror dancing." Laynie's eyes open wide with surprise, but before she can say anything, I continue.

"As I'm swaying my hips to the music, I can feel the hairs on the back of my neck stand on end and I just knew my plan worked." Laynie scrunches her eyebrows.

"What plan?" I still can't believe I did it, but as I was working out, all I could think about was the boy next door.

"On Sunday, when I bumped into Christian, I felt this connection between us, but I thought I was being foolish and imagining it. He is eighteen. Why would he be interested in me? You saw him... why would he be interested in an inexperienced sixteen-year-old?" Laynie goes to speak, but I hold up a finger. "I wanted to test that theory. If he weren't attracted to me, he surely wouldn't watch me, right?"

"Watch you?"

"Since he is my neighbor, I figured if I turned up my music loud enough, he would hear it. Then I walked over to my mirror and waited to see if he showed up at his bedroom window. Once he did, I began dancing sensually. I could feel him watching me, and I enjoyed his eyes on me. I kept dancing like I had no idea he was there, and toward the end of the song, I looked into the mirror right at him and stared him right in the eyes." Laynie gasps. Her eyes are so wide I think they might pop out of her head.

"What did he do?"

"He looked like a deer caught in the headlights. He bolted so fast out of the window I couldn't see him anymore. I waited a minute to see if he would return, but he never did. So, I turned the music off, jumped in the shower, and got ready for school."

I don't tell Laynie about his dad. We tell each other everything, but this is different. He trusted me, and it's not my story to tell. I didn't tell her how he held my hand, then freaked out and left because that was embarrassing. She wouldn't judge me, I know that, but to keep my pride intact, I left that piece of information out.

"Wait, why do you seem disappointed?"

"Because he didn't come back. What if he didn't like what he saw, and I looked stupid?" I clearly didn't think my actions through or think about making a fool of myself. I felt confident and wanted him to see just how sexy I could be. A completely different girl than he met in the hallway with her oversized band tee and fluffy socks. I felt something I thought only existed in movies and romance novels I've read. Maybe it is my foolish, fickle heart talking, and I imagined it all.

Laynie gets up, takes a seat in the lounge chair beside mine, and grabs my hand. "Rayne, are you kidding right now? He liked what he saw, all right! You're fucking hot. Anybody with eyes could see that. I bet you turned him on, and he was embarrassed."

Hmm, I didn't think about that. Just maybe, she's right, and it is not just me. Could he be interested in me?

"You think so?"

"I know so, babe." She squeezes my hand. "Fucking hell, Rayne, that is the hottest thing I have ever heard. My innocent Rayne might just have a little bad in her after all." She smirks, and so do I.

"What was that I saw outside of Ryker's car?"

"Honestly, I do not know. I caught him staring at me through the rear-view mirror. We had some sort of stare-off. Like he was almost challenging me to see if I would be the one to break eye contact. He looked at my lips, then gave me a panty-dropping smirk, and I lost it. I broke eye contact because I couldn't handle how I feel when his eyes were on me, how something, as simple as a smirk, had my panties soaked." My best friend chokes on her coffee.

"What has gotten into you? Just when I think you can't do anything else to surprise me, boom! You hit me with something else."

I tell her how he helped me out of the car, and my hair blew in my face, but before I could even reach for it, he beat me to it and gently brushed it behind my ear.

"Okay, that is cute as hell, also kind of intimate." I nod my head eagerly.

"That's what I thought! Then, before I could even say anything, he said he didn't mean to do it and shut down. He got back into the car without saying bye and left."

"Well, that's weird?" Laynie frowns. "There has to be

more to it based on what you've told me and what I saw. Something is going on between the two of you. Why don't you ask him?" I shook my head back and forth so fast I could get whiplash.

"No. No way. I barely know him, and it's probably all in my head."

Laynie disagrees with me and thinks I should play it cool and see how he acts the next time we hang out. I told her how it was all confusing and messing with my head. She knows I have zero experience with guys and warned me to be careful and never be afraid to communicate what I'm feeling. She is right. I shouldn't be scared to speak my mind and voice how I feel. However, it's complicated with Christian because my feelings scare me; I feel stripped bare and vulnerable. I'm still trying to figure out what it all means to tell the truth.

I lean over and hug my best friend. "I love you, Laynie Mae."

"Ditto, babe."

Sometimes *I feel as if my life is on a constant loop.* It's the same shit every day. School, study, homework, workout, read, hang out with Laynie, and repeat. *Blah. Blah. Fucking blah.* Life usually isn't this boring, right? God, I hope not. I'm craving more... I need more. What that is exactly, I'm not sure. Adventure? Excitement? Romance? All the above!

Thankfully, today, I'm doing something a little different. It's Thursday, and Laynie and I got our nails done after school. I'm leaned back in a comfy leather chair as I soak my feet in heavenly suds. Laynie is in the seat next to me, groaning now and then when the lady squeezes her foot in just the right spot. I would think something entirely different and inappropriate if we weren't in the middle of a nail salon.

"Mmm, this feels so good." She groans.

"I can see that." I giggle. "Guess what?" She opens one eye and looks at me.

"What?"

"Mom and dad said it was okay to go to Jackson's party."

Dad gruffed and said no right away, but mom told him I was old enough and that they should trust me. Whenever it involves my mom, it doesn't take much persuasion, so he caved and said it was fine.

"Hell yeah. Oh my god, your first party. I can't wait!"

"I know! We're going to look good."

"You know it! You're helping me choose an outfit, right?"

"Of course." She claps with excitement.

"Yay! So, have you talked to you know who?"

Nope. Yesterday after school, Laynie's mom Stacy gave me a ride home, and when I got there, Christian was chilling on the couch with Ryker, looking relaxed and sexy as hell. Ry said hi, and Christian didn't say anything besides give me an awkward wave. A freaking wave! Shortly after, he left and went back home. I don't know what his deal is.

"Nope." I say, popping the 'P.'

"Well, have you seen him since the incident in front of the coffee shop yesterday?"

"Yeah, after you dropped me off, he was over at my house, hanging with Ry. I walked in, and he gave me a lame-ass wave and left."

There isn't anything wrong with a wave, but the way it was all forced and awkward bothered me. Plus, we went from telling secrets to not even speaking. I'm noticing a pattern. Sunday, when he came over for breakfast and football, everything was good and normal between us until I laid my head on his shoulder. After that, he avoided me like the plague. I noticed his lights on in his room every night, but he closed his blinds. Then he finally talked to me outside Ryker's car on Wednesday before he freaked out and left with Ry, not even saying bye. Once again avoiding me later that day when I got home.

"He didn't say hi?" I shake my head. "Well, maybe he had something important to do," Laynie suggests, trying to make me feel better, and I love her for it.

"Yeah, maybe..."

We spent the rest of our time at the spa talking about what we would wear to the party on Friday and how our friend Jamie might go. A night out with my girls is exactly what I need. Laynie told me a senior named James asked her out on a date. She kindly told him no, and when I asked her why, she paused for a moment before saying she wasn't looking for a relationship; she was trying to have fun. I'm not mad at her for it, but I am a little jealous. Not of her, but of the fact a guy asked her out. It would be nice to experience what that is like.

We finished getting our nails and toes done. I went with a pretty pink color that stands out against my tan skin, and Laynie went with white. With everything on my mind and the chance of going home and seeing Christian there only for him to avoid me didn't sound very pleasing, so I went to Laynie's house. We did some homework and watched a movie. It was, of course, some chick flick. The movie was great, and I can't wait until I find a love like that one day. Someone willing to put me first, love me wholly, and fight for me always.

Stacy made a fantastic lasagna with buttered garlic toast. She dropped me off at home later that night, around nine, and my parents were already asleep by then. Ryker was sitting on the couch watching reality TV. We usually watch it together, but I'm not feeling it tonight.

I shower, change into a light pink satin Cami pajama set that matches my nail polish, and climb into bed. I snuggle into my thick comforter, waiting for sleep to take over. It feels like hours have passed since I've gotten into bed. Tossing and turning for the first thirty minutes and staring blankly at my ceiling for the last twenty. Sighing, I pull my comforter off and stand up. Grabbing a throw blanket, I walk over to my window and open it before stepping out onto the awning. The chilly air lightly flutters through my long hair strands, scattering them in different directions.

Sitting on my smooth blanket, I grab my phone and play 'Say Something by A Great Big World,' making sure the volume isn't too loud. Leaning back, I gaze up at the stars that glitter in the night sky. It's breathtaking out here tonight. The sky is clear, and the stars are vibrant. Staring up at the vast canvas makes me feel hopeful about my future, reminding me of the endless possibilities.

Branches crack, and leaves rustle down below—damn cats. Letting out a long sigh, I close my eyes and focus on the melody playing softly in the background. I feel a presence beside me, and I'm about to freak the hell out, but the smell of citrus drifts around me, and I smile. *Christian.*

"How did you get up here?" I ask keeping, my eyes closed. He lays down next to me, putting a little space between us.

"I climbed the wooden panel with all those vines."

"Oh, the wooly?" I try to hide my smile.

"Yeah, that." I can't hold in my laughter, and I all but snort.

"What?" my head rolls to face him.

"Wooly is a sheep, Christian. You just agreed to climb a sheep to get up here." His eyes widened before he burst into laughter with me.

"You tricked me."

"The thing you climbed is called a trellis, and I did not trick you. You agreed to something you didn't know."

He pulls out his phone, looks up the definition of trellis, and confirms that I'm telling the truth.

"You learn something new every day. Now, I know to fact check before I agree to things." I giggle. "Oh, you think it's funny, huh?" I nod my head, still laughing. He puts both hands up and wiggles his fingers.

"You wouldn't dar—" his digits go to my belly, cutting me off before I finish my sentence.

I'm laughing the hardest I think I've ever laughed as I wiggle like crazy with him on top of me. He hits the spot right below my ribs, and my stomach tightens, and my head launches forward, connecting with his.

"Ow!" we both say in unison.

"Oh my god! I'm so sorry. That's my weak spot."

"It's just a concussion, no big deal." He says, rubbing his head.

"A concussion? Oh my god, do you need to go to the hospital?" I brush his hair out of the way, trying to examine his head. Now, it's his turn to burst into laughter.

<u>'Green Eyes by Coldplay,'</u>
"The green eyes... Yeah, the spotlight shines upon you."

My eyes widen in shock because I fall for his trick, but I end up smiling because of how playful he is being. It's a bit confusing because of how he's been around me, but I don't question it. I like being around him. He stops laughing abruptly, and that's when I realize the position we're in. His entire weight is on me, caging me in. His minty breath fans my face as his chest rises and falls. My heart beats wildly, and I hear he is in sync with mine.

"What's going on in that pretty little head of yours?" he whispers.

"Y... You think I'm pretty?"

"Pretty isn't a good enough word." My cheeks flush, and my breaths become shallow. Christian inches close as condensation drifts from his mouth when he says, "Tell me a secret."

Is he going to kiss me?

Please kiss me.

Our faces are close. I can feel the mint of his breath trace over my lips. My eyes drop to his tongue, which softly glides his bottom lip. I swallow, pulling my eyes away, and let them roam the entirety of his face… his defined jaw and the day's worth of stubble on his chin. I slowly bring my hand up, tracing the coarse hair against my smooth fingers. He groans, biting his bottom lip, and my stomach flipped like I was on a rollercoaster at the sound.

My eyes skate back to his and they hold me captive like a prisoner. His eyes have a deep, earthy glow, the perfect reflection of the sun, encompassing me in their warmth. We are just a tiny speck in this universe, but I feel big under his stare… I feel powerful.

"Tell me a secret, Raynie." He rasps.

"I want you to kiss me." I lean closer to his mouth, and he follows. "I've never been kissed before." And just like that, the warmth was gone, and his golden eyes were no longer on mine. He jumps to his feet, and I scramble to my knees, looking up at him.

"C… Christian…"

"I have to go."

What is happening?

"O… Okay… but…"

"It's late, and I have work in the morning."

What the hell? I am so embarrassed. Absolutely humiliated. I have never felt like this before. My stomach hurts, and I think I might puke the moment he leaves.

I nod and stand to my feet, grabbing my blanket and phone. I mumble about not realizing it was so late and how I should get to bed too. I step back into my bedroom and shut my window, not sparing him a glance.

Curling into bed, I throw the blanket over my head and cry into my pillow. Sleep never came.

Chapter 4

Christian

After Sunday I did my best to stay away from Rayne, but it didn't stop me from thinking about her every day. When I'm in my room, I'm tempted to look at her window, hoping to catch a glimpse of her, but instead, I keep my curtains closed.

Then Wednesday came around, and after getting caught watching her, I stupidly agreed to carpool with Ry for my first day of work. I had no idea Rayne would be there, or I would've declined his offer. With one glance at her, I was sucked back into Rayne's orbit. I couldn't keep my eyes off her. When she stepped out of the car and was close to me, I had to touch her. The wind blew her hair across her face, causing it to stick to her glossy lips. The pull was too strong, so I reached up and delicately brushed it behind her ear. I should have kept my hands to myself, but it was already done.

Rayne has this effect on me that causes my body to react independently. I thought it would be better to keep my distance from her because it would be easier that way. She is like forbidden fruit and my greatest temptation. It's always the things you shouldn't have that you crave the most. She is pure

and innocent and deserves more than what I can offer.
She's also too fucking good for you.
You don't respect women.
What makes you think you won't ruin her too?

Wednesday was my first day on the job, so I didn't do too much hands-on stuff. Ryker gave me a tour of the place and when the shop got a little busy, I did three oil changes, but other than that, I shadowed him for most of the day, watching how he interacted with customers and how the shop ran.

The shop is friendly and well maintained. I can tell Jack put a lot of time into it. The front of the building says Davis Automotive, and directly underneath, you have six large steel garage doors that, when opened, have connecting stations for auto body mechanics. To the left of the garage, you have two tall glass doors that lead you to the customer waiting area and the front desk. I'm already in love with the atmosphere and can see myself fitting in perfectly. I feel more at home here than I ever did in Oregon.

There are two other mechanics besides Ry and me, named Liam and Derek. They are both older and in their thirties. Liam has been working here since my age, and Derek started five years ago. I know I can learn a lot from them and plan to soak up all the information I can while I am here and strengthen my skills. This is the perfect stepping stone, and it gets me one step closer to my ultimate dream—a shop of my own.

After work on Thursday, Ry sent me a text asking if I wanted to help him add some new headlights to his car and stay for dinner. Although it makes avoiding Rayne a lot more complicated, he's still my only friend, and I enjoy hanging out with him. I should be relieved she never came home and wasn't there for dinner because I planned to avoid her, but I caught myself glancing at cars hoping to see Rayne step out, but it was only neighbors getting home from work, school, and sports, and I found myself disappointed every time. The Davis's are great, but not having her around was different. It didn't feel the same with her absence. I glanced at her empty seat many times during dinner, searching for her eyes or smile. I sound fucking pathetic.

Later that night, as I lay in bed blankly staring up at my ceiling, I heard a window open, and I knew it was her, which is why I ended up pulling back my curtain just enough to see her. One look was all it took; I couldn't avoid her anymore. We're like two magnets, with a strong pull toward each other. The closer we are, the more forceful the pull becomes.

As I approached the side of her house, the low hum of music filtering through the air, I observed the side of her house, figuring out how the hell I was going to get up there. There was a wooden panel full of vines, and I decided that's how I would climb. I sent a silent prayer that nobody caught my ass. Dressed in all black, ascending the side of a house isn't my best look. Fuck. What a stupid idea.

I didn't say anything to Rayne as I lay beside her. She smiled, knowing it was me. I don't know how she knew, but she did. She kept her eyes closed, and I took the time to look at her.

So. Fucking. Perfect.

We joked, teased, and laughed, and it felt good. Hearing her laugh is addicting; all I wanted to do was hear it again. Thanks to Ryker, I knew being tickled was her weakness, so I did that as payback for her teasing, or maybe it was an excuse to touch her. She laughed and squirmed underneath me, and I stopped my innocent assault and looked at her, and she froze under me. At that moment, I wanted to kiss her.

Her mouth inched toward mine, waiting for me to close the distance, and I was going to. She whispered she'd never been kissed before, and that knowledge slapped me in the face, almost knocking me off balance. How has nobody ever kissed her, and what the hell was I doing? I don't do shit like this with girls. She has no idea how I treated people in my past and who I was. I don't deserve to be her first kiss. She'd probably think it would mean something, and it would, but it couldn't. We could never be anything more, and she deserves more. The problem is I'm not capable of giving it to her.

It has been nonstop at work today, but I'm not complaining because I love what I do. I don't want to be stuck in the office when I have my shop one day. I want to be out with the boys, getting my hands dirty. Despite it being busy, today has been an easy workday. I have done six oil changes, a check engine diagnosis, replaced a headlight bulb, a tire rotation, and car service. I'm washing my hands at one of the cleaning stations at the garage when Ryker approaches.

"Hey, Bro."

Looking back over my shoulder at him, I continue to lather the soap over my hands. "What's up, man?"

"I wanted to ask you for a favor."

"What kind of favor?" I arch my eyebrow suspiciously.

"I had a customer call asking if I can squeeze him in. His check engine light is on, so I'm going to run a diagnostic test and, depending on what we find, schedule the appointment for tomorrow. I'll probably run a little late on closing shop. Can you pick up Rayne from school on your way home?"

Shit! "Yeah, sure. No problem."

Ryker smiles, holding out his fist. "Thanks, bro. I owe you one."

"Don't worry about it." I shrug, letting him know it's no big deal to me, even though it is. I can't even look at her.

"Have you met our receptionist yet? I know she wasn't here Wednesday and had an early day yesterday."

I shake my head. "No."

He walks toward the front desk and moves his hand, gesturing me to follow. "Come on. I'll introduce you before you go get Rayne."

Ryker swings the front door open, causing the bell above

the door to ring, notifying the front desk someone is here. The woman behind the desk smiles when she sees Ryker.

"Hey, Ryker. What can I do for ya?"

"I wanted to introduce you to our newest employee." He indicates to me by extending his arms in my direction.

"Well, not an official employee just yet," I say, resting my elbows on the high front desk counter.

"You know your shit. You'll be off the probation period in no time, and we'd be lucky to have you as part of the team."

I smirk at him, then flick my eyes to the woman standing there listening to our conversation.

"Hi, I'm Christian Hayes."

Smiling sweetly, she shakes my hand. "Aubree, O'Connor, nice to meet you."

"Nice to meet you."

She is an attractive woman, a couple of years older than me, with fair skin, auburn hair, and deep brown eyes. Her nose kissed with a few freckles. Aubree is pretty. I am surprised when I realize I'm not attracted to her. When I look at her, I can't help but compare her to Rayne. They are completely opposite. Aubree has red hair, whereas Rayne has long, dark hair that looks black. Aubree has milk chocolate-colored brown eyes. Rayne's eyes are a striking green that I can't seem to get out of my head. I pull out my phone and check the time. Four-thirty p.m.

"What time does Rayne need to be picked up?"

"She does after-school classes a couple of days out of the week to earn college credits. Her class today lets out at five. You can leave now since you finished with your last appointment."

I'm supposed to be avoiding her, but here I am about to pick her up from school. Ryker asked me for a favor, and what the hell was I supposed to say? No? Then he would ask why and how could I answer that? I had no choice.

It will be just us alone, and I am unsure how I feel about it, but that is exactly the problem. I shouldn't *feel* anything at all. How am I supposed to look at her after what I did last night?

Waiting for Ryker's text with directions to Rayne's school, I get into my classic Mustang GT500. When my dad passed away, my uncle Mav and I continued to work on his car. Once it was all fixed up, my uncle Maverick stored it at his house because my mom said it was too hard to see, knowing my dad wasn't around to enjoy it. On my sixteenth birthday, she surprised me with the ultimate gift.

"Make a wish." *My mother says. Closing my eyes, I wish to see my dad one more time, blowing out the candles in one try. When my eyes open, my uncle and mom stand at my side, smiling at me.*

"What?" *I ask. My mother's eyes fill with unshed tears, but her smile remains.*

"I can't believe my boy is sixteen already. It feels like yesterday you were running around in a diaper and playing with your little toy cars." *My uncle Mav smiles, rubbing her back in comfort.* "We have a surprise for you."

"What is it?"

"Well, it would no longer be a surprise if we told you now, would it?" *Uncle Mav says.*

I follow them to the front of the house, my veins surging with anticipation. We reach the driveway, and I see what looks like a car covered by a tarp with a huge red bow on the top of it.

"No way. You got me a car!" *I beam, rushing over to pull off the cover.*

"Wait," *my uncle says, placing his hand on my shoulder, bringing me to a halt.* "I just want you to know that I love you and that I'm so proud of you, Christian. I know your dad would be too. You are turning into such a brilliant young man, and you deserve this." *His eyes water as he takes a step back.*

I quickly remove the cover, and a lump forms in my throat. Sitting in my driveway is my dad's Ford Mustang GT500. White exterior with a black pinstripe going down the middle of the hood. Black tinted windows and black rims. It's just the way I remembered it. My eyes sting as I gradually run my fingertips along the exterior of the car, admiring the beauty in front of me. Stopping, I hang my head as I choke out a sob. All the memories we had come rushing into me.

"I miss him so much! I wish he were here. I wish that I could feel him one more time." The sound of my mother's choked cries rattles me. Turning around, I wrap my arms around her. "I love you, Mom. Don't cry. This is the perfect gift I could have ever received. I just miss him, that's all." Leaning back, I bend my knees a little to look her in the eyes.

She brings her hand up to my face and caresses my cheek. "I know, sweetie, it's okay to miss your daddy. You'll always miss him." She glances at my uncle Mav, then looks back at me. "I know I do every day. We will never forget him. I am so thankful he gave me the most precious gift—you. You are so much like him, you know? And because of you, I will always have a piece of him. The car is yours. He would have wanted you to have it. I know it won't replace him, but I hope it makes you feel you have a little piece of him, too." She says as she sniffles, hugging me again.

"Thank you, mom." I squeeze my eyes shut. "It's perfect."

A light breeze came out of nowhere and in that moment, I felt my father there with us—and I smile.

I pull up the directions Ryker sent me and head toward Rayne's school. The streets of LA are jam-packed. The traffic is terrible, but when you live in the entertainment capital of the world, it's to be expected. Los Angeles is the home of the rich and famous, the glitz and the glam bullshit.

Due to traffic, I'm running about twenty minutes late when I finally pull up to Huntington Prep High school. The campus hides in the hills of Hollywood. Reaching an open iron gate, I drive through and notice this high school looks more like a modern palace. There is a massive round building at least four stories tall with a dome top. Glass windows surround the building, making it look translucent. To the left, a connecting building is made of glass with a round, arched roof.

I'm unsure where I am supposed to meet Rayne, so I park in front of the school and pull out my phone to call Ryker. Just as I'm about to hit the call button, the school's front door opens, and Rayne steps out. Just like on Wednesday, she has her school uniform on, but instead of her hair being up in a high ponytail, she is wearing it down in thick waves. The first couple of buttons of her shirt are unbuttoned, hinting at what they hide underneath. I feel the charging magnetic pull, which intensifies with every step she takes toward me.

I am so busy admiring her I didn't notice she wasn't alone. A guy is walking next to her, and without knowing who he is, I find myself feeling overwhelmed by a rush of envy and frustration. He looks like a typical jock you see in those teenage romance movies. Tall but not as tall as me, and slim with light blonde hair. He is wearing a dark green football uniform with tight black pants that slightly cover his long white socks, meeting at the calves. White writing displayed the last name Reed across his shoulder blades, with the number one underneath it. I roll my eyes.

Who is this guy? A total fuck boy, I'm sure. Trust me, I would know. I saw plenty of them when I was in high school. He is the type of boy that acts like his shit doesn't stink, and he's god's gift to women. The kind that doesn't like being told no and has a little bitch fit when he doesn't get his way. I can spot boys like him a mile away.

Rayne walks around him, and he puts his hand on her shoulder, stopping her. She stiffens slightly, and it's only because I'm aware of every part of her I notice the tenseness in her shoulders. He's talking to her with a flirtatious smile and animated hands. Whatever he is talking to her about, he seems excited.

She stares at him as if she would rather be somewhere else. He reaches to push a piece of hair behind her ear just as I did the other day, and I want to break that fucker's fingers. Rayne takes a small step back as I step out of the car.

They still haven't noticed me as I lean against the driver's side door, arms crossed. My eyebrows scrunched up, and my jaws clenched so hard I could crack my teeth.

Rayne glances in my direction, and her eyes pop open. Reed notices her surprise and follows her line of sight... his eyes landing directly on me. He is trying to prove his dominance by challenging me with a look. His look doesn't bother me; it's hardly a threat. *Little boy, don't be stupid. I'll mop the floor with your ass.*

Rayne walks toward me, and the dipshit follows her.

"Hey, Raynie," I smirk as she approaches.

"Hey, Christian." She says, looking down at her booted feet, and I don't miss the way fuck boy squints at me before quickly returning to normal.

"What's up? I'm Jackson." I look at his offered hand and don't uncross my arms to shake it. The tension between us is so thick it's nearly suffocating. I don't like him, and I hope he fucking knows it. He looks at Rayne, but he doesn't see her as a person and certainly doesn't deserve to be in her presence. He is looking at her like she's nothing more than an object. Stripping her clothes off in his mind, looking at her like a predator stalking its prey.

"I'll see you tomorrow Jackson at the party," Rayne says, looking at me and dismissing him.

What party? Is this dude her boyfriend? Jackson drops his hand, looking pissed the fuck off, which only makes me smile sadistically.

"Yes, you will. Wear something sexy." He says impertinently, and before anyone can respond, he walks off. Clenching my fists, still looking in fuck boy's direction, I debate on laying his ass out and teaching him a thing or two about how to speak to her.

'The Mess I Made by Parachute,'
"I'm staring at the mess I made as you turn, you take your heart and walk away."

"What are you doing here, Christian? Where is Ry?" Rayne says, putting her hands on her hips. She is so cute when she's irritated.

There's that fucking word again. *Cute.*

"He added a customer to the schedule last minute and had to stay late, so he asked if I could pick you up and give you a ride home."

"Figures." She scoffs, rolling her eyes.

"What's that supposed to mean?"

She crosses her arms. "You're a runner."

"A runner?" I repeat, copying her stance.

"Whenever anything happens between us, you run!" she throws her hands up. "I figure you're only here because Ryker needed you to be, or else you'd be as far as you can be from me after that shit you pulled last night." Her cheeks turn red, and this time it's not from desire; it is out of anger. She steps toward me with fire behind her eyes and confidently lifts her chin. "I can't figure out what the hell you're running from but what I do know is if you push away those around you the same way you push me away, you're not going to have anyone left, and what a lonely world that will be."

Her words hit me straight in the core, knocking the air right out of me. Everything she said was accurate, and I hated it. I would have never given a single fuck if these words were spoken by anyone else, but hearing it come from Rayne's mouth fucking hurts. I knew I'd probably end up alone, but I never gave a shit until now.

She stares at me, waiting for me to respond, and when I don't say anything, she huffs, walking around to the car's passenger side. Her words, *"You're not going to have anybody left, and what a lonely world that will be,"* play through my mind on repeat, getting louder with every step she takes away from me. For the first time in the last eight years, being alone doesn't sound so appealing.

As we drive, I look over and see Rayne isn't wearing her seatbelt.

"Put your seatbelt on."

"Who do you think you are telling me what to do?" she snaps. "What if I don't want to wear my seatbelt?" I tighten my hands around the steering wheel.

"My dad died in an accident, remember? Put your damn seatbelt on."

The sound of a *click* fills the car.

I don't know how long we drive in silence. Rayne is clearly pissed at me, and I want to demand her to talk to me, yell at me, anything. Music lightly plays, doing a shit job at breaking the tension in the car.

"How long have you guys been together?" I glance at Rayne, and she looks confused, so I add, "You and whatever his name is."

Realization dawns on her face.

"His name is Jackson, and he is not my boyfriend." She grits. I feel relieved even though I have no right to be. She isn't mine. "Why do you even care?"

This is what I was afraid of. I shouldn't care, and now I'm put on the spot, not knowing how to respond to her question. So, I don't.

"You're unbelievable!"

"I don't know, okay? I shouldn't... but I do." I turn up the music, confused with my feelings ending the conversation. She looks out the window for the rest of the way home. I pull into my driveway and before I can turn the car off, she gets out, slams the door shut behind her, and crosses the yard, entering her house without ever looking back.

Chapter 5

Rayne

I walk into my parent's house, slamming the door behind me, so infuriated with Christian and with myself for letting him get to me the way he has. I'm pissed with Christian because how dare he act all possessive and jealous, as if I was his when he saw me with Jackson. Everything that has happened between us from the start, the lingering stares, flirtatious grins, the intentional touching, and the almost kiss. Now, the annoyance he showed toward Jackson after seeing us together. It is all a bit much for my mental state.

If he wasn't playing so many games with me, I would probably be flattered by his territorial behavior. Because of my lack of experience with guys, I don't know if his reactions are normal. When I asked him why he cared, he could not give me a straight answer. "I care about you, but I don't know why." What does that even mean? It is confusing. He has some nerve pulling the shit he did yesterday out on my roof and showing up at my school as if nothing had happened.

I'm leaning against my front door, trying to calm down, when I notice another presence in the room. Looking up, I see my parents sitting there staring at me.

"What is going on, honey? Are you okay?" my mom asks me, wearing a worried expression.

"Yes, mama, I'm fine, just dealing with some stuff." My dad sits there looking uncomfortable, totally out of his element.

"Okay…" my mom says, uncertain if she should leave it alone or not. "If you need to talk about anything, you know you can come to me, right?"

"I know. I promise it's nothing, and I will be fine."

Still unsure, she gives me a hesitant nod as I head upstairs to my bedroom. I huff and plop face down onto the bed. When my phone rings as my face hits the mattress, I groan, rolling over to answer it.

"Laynie Mae."

"Who pissed you off? And don't you dare blame it on shark week because we're in sync, and I'd know."

"Who do you think?" I groan in annoyance.

"What did that fine piece of ass do this time?"

"He is messing with my head, and I don't like it. Is this normal?"

"Relationships of any kind are complicated, babe, especially when feelings are involved. You are allowing yourself to be vulnerable, and by doing so, you are opening yourself up to the possibility of getting hurt. However, some guys play mind games, but is it okay? Absolutely not. If he is messing with your head, you need to be upfront about it and nip it in the ass before it carries on too far. You know the saying, can't teach an old dog new tricks and what not?"

I take in her words. I don't know what it is exactly I feel for him. It's apparent that I'm attracted to him, but everything else is uncharted territory, and I don't know him enough yet to say that I like him. Maybe if he weren't so back and forth, I'd be able to decipher through these feelings and figure it out. I don't understand his behavior. One minute I think he feels the same attraction, and the next, he throws me for a loop, making me question everything.

"Look, you don't have to have all the answers right now.

You will figure it out. I told you the other day, don't be afraid to communicate what you're feeling. This isn't a one-sided thing; it takes two to tango."

This is why she is my best friend. Laynie gives me the best advice and never sugarcoats anything. She's always honest with me, no matter the circumstances.

"You're the best, Laynie Mae, and I love you."

"Ditto, babe."

"What is the plan for tomorrow?" I ask.

Laynie informs me she will meet at my house tomorrow around eight, since the party starts at nine after the football game. I asked her why we would meet only an hour before the party, but she told me nobody arrived early to parties, and we would be arriving fashionably late. I don't go to parties, so I'm still catching on to the social scene, and I guess showing up late is the *cool* thing to do. It doesn't make any sense, but again, what do I know?

"Sounds good." I yawn.

"See you tomorrow, babe. We're going to have so much fun!"

"Can't wait," I say, my eyes feeling heavy, and Laynie hangs up.

Sometime later, the sound of knocking wakes me up. What time is it?

"Coming." I groan, half awake.

My father stands there casually leaning against my door frame when I open the door. "Hey, baby girl, just checking on you. You didn't come down for dinner last night, which worried me, but I wanted to give you some space. You know I'm bad with these things."

Smiling, I think what a daddy's girl I am. I go to him for everything; he always makes me feel safe. As I've gotten older, I don't go to him as much as before because certain topics are more comfortable discussing with my mom. He understands, and I think he prefers it that way.

"I'm good, dad. I was exhausted yesterday. I must have passed out after talking to Laynie."

"Yeah, I can see that." He chuckles, eyeing my school attire. "I'm glad to hear everything is okay. Go shower. You look awful." He says with a wink.

I slap his arm and smile at his teasing. "Thanks for checking in on me, pops."

"Anything for my baby girl."

I finish showering and lather myself in lavender body cream. I throw on an oversized hoodie twice my size and some yoga pants.

"Good morning, little sis," Ryker says with a mouthful of cereal when I enter the kitchen.

"Morning," I grumble, opening the pantry and pulling out a loaf of sourdough bread.

"I already made you a cup of coffee. It's in the fridge and cold, just how you like it."

"Aww, thanks, Ry."

He rolls his eyes. "Don't thank me. Only did it, so I didn't have to deal with you without it."

"Whatever makes you sleep better at night, big brother. You so love me."

He mutters, "Yeah, yeah, whatever. So, what are your plans for today?"

"Laynie's coming over later, and we're going to get ready for the party tonight."

"What party?"

"Jackson Reed's party."

"Why the hell are you going to Reed's party?" he asks, his voice laced with displeasure.

"Because," I drawl. "I've never been, and Laynie convinced me to go."

"Do you listen to everything Laynie says?" frowning, I look over at him.

"No... I'm going because I've never been to a party and it's sad. I think it's time to step out of my comfort zone. Plus, it's going to be epic! It's right after the homecoming game, and I think it will be fun."

"Does mom and dad know?"

"Yes, Ry. Chill."

He sits there in silence, with a worrying impression.

"I've been to his parties, and even though he was a sophomore at the time, they got wild. You and Laynie need to stick together and don't accept drinks from anyone."

"Yes, dad."

"I'm just looking out for you. You aren't used to that scene and need to be careful. I'm not fucking around!" He exclaims, clenching his jaw. His seriousness makes me feel uneasy. I'm used to him being overly protective and dramatic, but something about his tone and the look in his eyes. Usually, I'd give him shit or have something clever to say in response, but this time I don't.

"Stay with Laynie always and don't accept drinks from anyone. Got it."

"And call me if you guys need anything and I. Mean. Anything. Rayne." He adds, looking at me with such intensity.

"Okay, Ry. I promise."

Chapter 6

Rayne

Later *that night,* as Ry and I are sitting on the couch watching The Challenge, there is a knock at the front door. When I answer it, Laynie is standing there wearing black leggings with a sheer cut-out running along the sides. I grin at her shirt because it fits her perfectly. Her cropped white shirt says, "Women don't owe you shit," spread across the chest. Laynie and I are all about women's empowerment, and I'll have to ask her to borrow it.

"What's up bitch!" She grins.

"What's up, Laynie Mae."

She picks up her duffle bag and grunts as she struggles to lift it.

"Do you need help with your bag?" Ryker asks, joining us at the door.

She looks up through her eyelashes and, with an innocent tone, says, "Yes, please."

"Where do you want me to set it?"

"Up in Rayne's room."

"How did you carry the bag to the door, anyway?" Ryker asks her as he carries the bag effortlessly up the stairs. We're following behind him when she looks over, smirking at me.

"I carried it."

"Wait? Weren't you struggling to lift the bag at the door?" he lifts an accusatory brow.

"Oh, that? I just wanted to see you get off your ass and carry my bag as you should for all the shit you've put me through since knowing you." She pats his shoulder as she saunters past him with an extra swing to her hips.

Ryker's mouth is gaping open in shock as he stands there, dumbfounded. I take Laynie's bag from his hands now that I know it isn't as heavy as she made it out to be.

"Wow, big brother, someone has actually made you speechless."

"Tell Laynie we can play games all day, and I'll be the one coming out on top." His tone is challenging as he spins on his feet and storms off.

I stand there staring at the stairs, wondering what the hell happened. I'll leave it alone, but I'll mention it to him again another time. Tonight is about enjoying myself with my bestie and having no regrets. After everything that happened between Christian and me these past few days, this party is the perfect way to clear my head and forget.

I enter my room and shut the door, setting Laynie's bag on my bed.

"Let's get this party started, baby!" she says with so much enthusiasm I can't help but get pumped up for what the night may bring. She walks over to her duffle bag and unzips it. I'm watching her debating on bringing up the incident between Ry and her. I don't want to ruin the mood, but I'm missing something. Ry has always messed with Laynie, but lately, I can't help but feel something has changed between them. I just can't put my finger on precisely what's different.

"What was that all about between you and Ry?" she shuffles through her bag, pulling out her makeup bag and clothes.

"I don't know what you're talking about, babe." She replies without looking at me. I know my friend, and she is a horrible liar, especially regarding me. She isn't making eye contact with me, which is a dead giveaway, and I don't believe her for a second, but for the sake of tonight, I'll drop it.

I pull out a glass bottle sticking out of her bag. "What is this?"

"This, my friend, is our best friend for the night." Grinning, she takes the bottle from me. "Tequila, meet Rayne, Rayne, meet tequila."

Besides sneaking a sip of my mom's wine during family gatherings, I have never drunk before. I'm a mixture of nervousness and anticipation.

"I don't drink. You know that."

"Exactly! Tonight is all about stepping out of your comfort zone, and we won't go crazy." She pauses. "Unless you want to?" She wiggles her eyebrows.

"You are so much trouble, Laynie Mae," I say, shaking my head.

"I think what you meant to say was I'm so much fun. Besides, you will try alcohol sometime in your life. Might as well try it with me, someone you trust." She has a point. It's not that I'm opposed to the idea; I've just been so caught up with school I never cared to try. There was never a suitable time to do it, anyway. Laynie has drunk alcohol many times, and I trust her with my life.

"Touché," I say, and she claps her hands in excitement.

"Let's get some music going and get ready."

An hour and a half later, Laynie is standing in front of my full body mirror, fluffing her hair. She's wearing a black leather skirt that stops a little above mid-thigh. Her long legs make the already short skirt appear even shorter. She borrowed my red corset top that hugs her curves and makes her bust look phenomenal. I paired the outfit with black knee-high boots that tie in the back. Her icy blonde hair is in messy curls, bringing her hair up to her shoulders with a ruby red lip. She looks hot!

Aside from the skirt I wear to school, I enjoy wearing them. I'm always trying new things and turning something simple into something magnificent. It really depends on my mood or the occasion when deciding what to wear. I can live in leggings and hoodies, but I also enjoy wearing skirts and bodysuits, cropped tops and shorts, and tight bodycon dresses. I love dressing down, but still looking cute. When styling clothes, the possibilities are endless, and you can really tell someone's character by what they wear.

Laynie was set on wearing a leather skirt, so I made it the centerpiece and styled her outfit around it. Her outfit displays confidence, sexiness, fearlessness, and power. Everything Laynie Mae represents.

"Oh my," I fan myself bringing her attention to me. "You look so hot, Laynie! Damn."

"Thanks, babe." She eyes my attire. "Is that what you're wearing?" I look down at my oversized hoodie and leggings that I'm still wearing from this morning.

I playfully push her, rolling my eyes. "Obviously not. I'll be out in a moment."

Usually, Laynie and I change in front of each other, but I want to see her reaction after I have everything on. It's a bolder choice, and I know she will love it. I walk out a few minutes later as Laynie pulls two shot glasses from her duffle bag.

"So watcha think?" I ask, giving her a little spin.

"Oh. My. God. Who are you, and what have you done with my best friend?"

"You like it?" she slowly walks around me, observing me from head to toe.

"No. I don't like it. I love it! I always knew you had a rocking body, but damn, Rayne, the way you look right now is making me question my sexuality."

"Tell me more. Your compliments are appreciated and totally boost my ego."

I wear skintight black leather pants with flare bottoms and black strappy heels. My top is a long-sleeved, sheer black cropped top with a sparkly lace bralette underneath. I'm wearing my hair in a messy bun with hairpieces framing my face. My makeup is a light smoky eye with my natural long dark lashes held in place with mascara and my signature blush pink lip gloss bringing the look together. I feel fucking sexy!

"Seriously, Rayne, your boobs make my mouth water and your ass in those pants..."

"Okay, okay," I say, waving my hands.

"Here, you can wear these. I brought an extra pair just in case I didn't feel like wearing these hoops." She gestures to her ears. I take the box from her hands and gently open it. I gasp, bringing my hand up to my mouth.

"These are beautiful. Are you sure?"

"Positive. I know you own every piece of clothing in the world, but not a single piece of jewelry. These are perfect for you!"

I lean in, kissing her on the cheek. "You're the best, thank you."

"You can make it up to me by taking a shot with me." She pops the cork out of the Patron bottle and pours us each a shot that is filled to the brim, spilling a little as she hands me one. "What should we make a toast to?" Laynie says, tapping her index finger against her chin as she thinks.

I feel very nervous, and I don't know what to expect. I don't want to get sick like I've seen Ry get a few times when he would attend these parties in high school. Ryker's warnings about not leaving my drink around or accepting drinks from anyone and staying with Laynie at all times have alarm bells going off inside my head. Instead of overthinking, I decide to make a toast.

"Here is to stepping out of our comfort zone and having no regrets." I hold my shot glass up, rattling it with Laynie's.

"Cheers bitch." Laynie says.

The instant the liquor hits my tongue, my throat feels instantly on fire, like rubbing alcohol on a wound. I cough as I use my fist to tap on my chest, as if that would help ease the burn.

"That was awful," I tell her through a coughing fit.

She informs me that with each shot we take, it only gets easier. My eyes bulged at her comment. How many shots does she expect me to take? I asked her if she was trying to get me drunk, and she smirked at me mischievously and reminded me of *no regrets*. So, for that reason, I agree to do another shot.

Chapter 7

Rayne

After that second shot, I'm feeling fantastic. Despite the disgusting taste, drinking doesn't seem to be that bad. I feel happier, confident, and way more excited about tonight. Based on the way I currently feel, I get the appeal.

"Let's take another!"

"Easy, tiger, you already had two. You want to pace yourself. We haven't even made it to the party yet."

"You're no fun," I pout, even though she is the best and I always have the most fun with her.

"Babe, we both know that isn't true. Is Ryker giving us a ride?"

"Hell no. I was hoping you had the ride situation figured out. I don't want my brother dropping us off at my first party, knowing Ry he would be overbearing, and I wouldn't put it past him to try to come into the party with us."

"True." She hums. "I'll send Jamie a text and see if she can pick us up on the way."

Jamie is our friend we met freshman year. We went to different elementary and junior high schools. She got into a fight with some girl in eighth grade and got expelled, which is how she ended up at Huntington Prep High. She is outgoing like Laynie and has quite the temper, nothing crazy, but she "doesn't take bullshit from anyone and will put a bitch in her place." Her words, not mine.

She has a petite and athletic build, five feet exactly and one hundred and twenty pounds. Natural curly brown hair with hazel eyes, bronzed skin, and voluptuous. She may be small, but she is fierce. We don't hang out with her a lot outside of school because she lives outside our school district. Now that she's saved up and bought a car, I hope we all can hang out more, outside of school. Especially once Laynie and I start driving.

"Let's take another shot before Jamie gets here," Laynie says, handing me a shot glass.

Raising an eyebrow, "What happened to pacing ourselves?"

"One more before we go, and then we can pace ourselves on the ride over."

I don't argue. "On that note, cheers!"

We clink our glasses, knocking them back. I scrunch my face and shiver at the harsh taste, instantly covering my body in gooseflesh. A rush of warmth spreads throughout me, and I already feel lighter.

"Wooooooo!" I shout, throwing my hands up.

"Although I am loving buzzed Rayne, let's keep it down before your parents come up here." Giggling like drunken idiots, we drink water before heading out front to meet Jamie. As we were walking to Jamie's silver Honda Civic, a car door slams in the distance.

"Where the hell do you think you guys are going dressed like that?" Ryker shouts.

"Dressed like what? We look fucking fantastic." Laynie says, placing her hand on her hip in defiance.

"Yeah, Ry, we look fucking fantastic," I agree. I'm definitely feeling the liquor. I'm about to laugh at Ry's shocked expression when I notice Christian standing next to him with his hands in the pockets of his black jeans. His jaw clenched, and he looks just as pissed off as Ry does, but damn, he looks good. His hair is messy, like he has been running his fingers through it. His white t-shirt is tight around his chest with a black leather jacket and all-black high-top Converse.

"You guys are leaving very little to the imagination, and there is No. Fucking. Way. I'm letting you go to Reed's party dressed like that." Ry says.

"I agree with Ry." Christian takes a step forward and crosses his arms, standing united with Ryker.

Now I am pissed. The nerve they have telling us what we can and can't wear. I'll be damned if I ever let a guy dictate what I wear. I take a huge step forward, doing my best not to wobble.

"Good thing I'm not asking for your permission, big brother." I slowly look Christian up and down and add, "Who do you think you are? You don't get a say in what I choose to wear." Giving them my back, I look at Laynie, who is gaping at me. "Let's go, babe. We have a party to get to."

"You are amazing!" Laynie says when she gets into the car. "You should have seen their faces! Ryker went from taken back to full-blown pissed, and Christian... well, Christian just looked pissed. I swear his fists were clenched, and he looked like he wanted to yank you out of the car and throw you over his shoulder."

I wouldn't mind that at all. The thought of him throwing me over his shoulder makes me want to clench my thighs together.

"Well, good! I understand Ry is only looking out for me, but what the hell was that about? Leaving little to the imagination and not letting us go out dressed like this. Have you seen the girls he usually shags? They are practically naked!" Laynie scoffs, rolling her eyes. "Besides, it's one thing to feel that way about me, but why does he care what you're wearing?" heat creeps into Laynie's cheeks.

"I don't know, babe, probably because he looks at me like his little sister."

"Yeah, you're probably right. As for Christian, we hardly even know each other. He gives me one ride home from school, and suddenly he thinks he has a say in what I wear and do. Did you see the way he was looking at me? He was staring at me like I was naked or something. I don't know who he thinks he is or why he thinks his opinion has any validity."

Having enough of this conversation, I lean forward and give Jamie an awkward hug from the back seat.

"Hey, Jamie, sorry about all that. Thank you for picking us up and taking us to the party."

"I have three big brothers, so I know all about how they can be."

"I only have one, and I can't imagine dealing with three."

She chuckles. "It's not that bad. Well, it can be, but I promise you will learn how to deal with it. Sometimes it takes them a while to realize you don't always need protection. Are you and your brother close? Do you have a good relationship?"

"The best. Even though he drives me nuts half the time, I can't picture my life without him."

"How does it feel to be driving?" Laynie asks, changing the subject.

"Amazing! I can't wait until you guys finally get behind the wheel."

Laynie and I explain our driving excitement, and Laynie promises that we will pick her up at the next party we attend. I can't wait to start driving. This reminds me I need to start looking for a job to buy a car. I'm sure my parents would help me out, but it would be nice to do it on my own. I can already picture the late-night drives with the music on full blast and the wind in my hair. Freedom.

Jamie winks at her through the rearview mirror. "I'm holding you to it. Until then, take a shot with me because we're here bitches!" she says as she drives her car up the long driveway and parks.

The driveway is jam-packed with vehicles. Most are luxurious Mustangs, Mercedes, BMWs, Cadillacs, and other cars I don't know the names of. Ryker and Christian would be drooling right about now. I shake my head, trying to remove Christian from my mind.

Now that I have some alcohol coursing through my veins, my nervousness is replaced with full-blown excitement. I'm at my first party, and I'm with my girls. For once, I'm experiencing it for myself and not having to imagine what it would be like. From the number of stories I've heard from Laynie and Ryker, you would think I wouldn't be as excited as I am, and I'd know exactly what to expect by now, but it's not even close to how it feels to be here for real.

I feel good, look good, and the night has just begun. What could possibly go wrong? I'm so pumped I can hardly contain myself. I am a massive ball of energy, and all I want to do is get in there already. I wonder what it's like on the other side... the boys, the drinking games... the experience. I have a feeling there's going to be a lot of firsts tonight, and I am so ready!

"This place is un-fucking-believable." Laynie says, astonished.

"So, this is what it's like growing up in the hills of Hollywood." Jamie examines the mansion in front of us.

"Trust me, there are some real nasty parts, and it isn't all what it seems," I tell her.

"I'm sure you're right, but it's got to be better than my side of the tracks," Jamie says, with a sad look in her eyes. Before I can comment, she continues. "Let's go inside. I'm freezing my tits off."

Jamie looks phenomenal. She is wearing a tight black dress that stops mid-thigh with thin spaghetti straps and black suede platform heels. All of us are wearing black besides Laynie's fire red corset. Standing side-by-side with Laynie, we resemble Lucifer and his Lilith. We look sexy, and I'm feeling bad.

"We are the three hottest best friends I have ever seen," Laynie says, hooking her arm through mine. I smile and link my arm through Jamie's.

"Let's do this, babes."

You can feel the vibrations from the music trembling through the floor as we walk to the door. My heart begins to race. You can tell the place is cram packed from all the cheers, laughter, and roaring voices.

When we reach the door, it swings open, and a tall, dark man with a bald head dressed in black stands there, taking up the whole entryway.

"Hello, ladies. Are you on the guest list?" Guest list? I nervously look between Jamie and Laynie.

Laynie scoffs, rolling her eyes, "What is this? Dinner with the damn president? There is no guest list. Stop giving us shit and let us in."

"Feisty, I like it." He reaches for her cheek, but it all happens so fast. Jamie has his fingers bent and his arm twisted behind his back.

"Didn't your parents teach you not to touch a woman without her consent? In fact, you shouldn't touch anyone without their permission."

He grunts, "Y... You b-bitch."

Using her platform heel, she shoves it into the back of his knee, causing him to drop. "Now that's not very nice. Do you talk to your mother with that mouth? You owe my friend here an apology."

"S... Sorry." He hisses in pain. She lets go of his fingers, and he collapses to the floor, groaning.

"Let's get this party started, shall we?" Jamie says, casually stepping over him. Laynie and I stand there, mouths open, not believing what we just saw. Holy shit. We quickly step over the guy on the floor.

"Jesus Christ, Jay, thank you, but was that really necessary?" Laynie asks.

"Yes, it was. He needs to learn to keep his hands to himself, and now he will think twice before touching another female."

"Where did you learn how to do that?" I ask her. That sad look in her eyes returns before it quickly vanishes.

"Where I live, you need all the protection you can get."

"What do you mean, where you live? Are you okay? Is someone hurting you?"

"I meant where I'm *from*; you need all the protection you can get. Not the best neighborhood and all." She quickly recovers.

"Oh. Okay? Well, damn, remind me never to mess with you. I'd love for you to teach me sometime."

"Yeah?" she beams at me.

"My god, yes!"

"Don't leave me out of this. Me too!" Laynie adds.

"Fuck yeah! Now let's go before people notice big man on the floor. I need a drink."

Jackson's house is massive! White marble flooring throughout the house and high ceilings make the massive house feel enormous. We walk toward the kitchen as we pass a spiral staircase, all white aside from the gold railing. It has caution tape on the bottom to keep people from accessing the upper level. The living room has panoramic windows giving a clear view of the backyard and the city lights of Los Angeles below. 'Strip That Down by Liam Payne' is booming throughout. Despite being inside a mansion, it's hard to maneuver throughout the place because there are many people. It feels like the whole student body is attending this party.

Many students wear school spirit to support our football team's homecoming game early tonight. I see a few football players wearing their jerseys, and others either didn't go to the game but dressed for the party or got ready after the game to come here. Laynie warned me tonight would be epic, but I did not expect this. It is insane.

They converted the living room to a dance floor with multicolored lights and bodies grinding together. Girls are sensually dancing with guys as if they are having sex; a thin layer of clothing is the only thing separating them. Some girls are grinding on each other as the guys stand around ogling, and there isn't one person here who doesn't have a red solo cup in their hand.

Every kind of alcohol imaginable litters the kitchen countertops. I don't know how Jackson is underage with access to this much liquor, but it's a party, and I am not complaining. Even the kitchen is packed full of people drinking and chatting. In the center of the kitchen is an island with ten red solo cups in the shape of a triangle at both ends. Two guys on each side throw a ping-pong ball back and forth, trying to make it into the cups. Interesting.

"What's that?" I ask Laynie, pointing towards the guys throwing balls back and forth.

"It's a drinking game called beer pong."

"What are you guys going to drink?" Jamie asks us.

"We already started drinking tequila, so we should stick to that," Laynie replies.

"Tequila it is. Let's take a shot, and then I will make us a mixed drink."

Jamie grabs plastic shot glasses and fills them with tequila. There is a bowl of cut-up limes and several jars of salt. She hands us our shot with a lime, and I look at the lime, confused, unsure what I need lime for. Jamie must see the confusion on my face because she giggles.

"Here, like this." She turns my free hand over, rubbing the lime back and forth on the top of my hand, then grabs the salt jar and pours it on top. The juices from the lime make the salt stick.

"Before you take the shot, lick the salt, take your shot, then bite into your lime. It helps the burn, trust me."

I hesitantly nod my head. Who knew there was so much involved with drinking? Jamie and Laynie do the same to their hand, and then we all raise our cups to the ceiling.

"To an epic night. Cheers bitches!" Jamie shouts over the blaring music. I lick the salt off my hand, shoot my shot, and instantly bite into the lime. Jamie was right. It immediately takes away the burn.

"Wow…"

Jamie grins. "Good, right?"

"Yes! I can take another one right now."

"Be careful. It's smooth, but can easily sneak up on you." Laynie tells me and I make a mental note.

While Jamie works on our mixed drinks, I turn around, taking everything in. I catch one of the guys playing beer pong looking at me. His eyes drag up and down my body before meeting my eyes. Without looking at the cups across the island, he holds up the ball and throws it, still holding eye contact with me. I follow the ball he just threw, which lands directly in the cup. Impressive.

I drag my eyes back to him, my lips tugging at the corners, and slowly clap my hands.

"That was hot as fuck." Laynie and Jamie both say, breaking our stare off.

"It was, wasn't it?" I say as both of their eyes shift over my shoulder.

"What are we drinking tonight?" a voice says from behind me. They both move their eyebrows up and down at me, smirking. I slowly turn around, and the guy with the impressive beer pong skills stands there. He's good-looking, about seven inches taller than me, so probably around five feet eleven, with brown wavy hair that falls in his eyes.

His lips are nice, his bottom lip slightly more prominent than his top. He has a skater style dressed in an army green windbreaker jacket left unzipped and opened, showing his black t-shirt underneath. He has on black jeans folded at the bottom with old-school black and white vans. Cute.

Laynie steps next to me on my left as Jamie stands to my right, handing me my drink.

"Were drinking tequila with sprite," Jamie says.

"Tequila, huh? You ladies have good taste in liquor. Tonight, I stick to beer." He says, grabbing a Bud Light from the metal bucket filled with ice. "Would you guys like to play a game of beer pong with my friend Daniel and me?" he nods toward his friend, who is still standing at the island setting up the cups for a new game. "We can do teams."

"Sure," I say before either of my friends can respond. "After you." I gesture my hands toward the beer pong set up.

Chapter seven 101

"Ladies first." I giggle as Laynie, Jamie, and I walk to the kitchen island.

"I'll sit out for this game," Jamie says as she takes a large gulp from her mixed drink.

"What? Are you sure? I can sit out, and you can play."

"Don't be silly; I've played beer pong with my brothers many times. You play."

I'm thankful she is okay with sitting out. I wouldn't mind sitting out, but I've never played beer pong, and it seems really fun. I'm so focused on school and getting good grades, I never really felt like I was missing out on much. Being here, I'm feeling differently about that, not the drinking or smoking aspect, but just spending time with my friends and letting loose. All of us being here together is a first for us. It's nice being here with my friends, and I hope to do more things like this.

"So, you're my partner, Laynie Mae?" I lightly bumped my hip with hers.

"I was thinking you can be partners with..." she pauses, looking over at the guy who offered us to play. "What's your name?"

"Sorry, I'm a little buzzed. I'm Tyler."

"Laynie." She says, "I was thinking you can be partners with Rayne." She smirks at me mischievously.

"I like the way you think." He smiles at her before averting his eyes to mine. "You okay with that, Rayne?"

"Uh, umm, yeah, sure. I've never played before, so I'm probably not any good." I take a large sip of my drink.

"Well, I just happen to be the best, so you're in expert hands."

Based on the shot he made earlier, I believe him. I look down at his hands and the way his long fingers tap rhythmically on the side of his beer can and can't help but think about all the things those hands can do. More specifically, all the things they could do to me. I wonder what his touch might feel like against my skin.

The alcohol coursing through me, mingling up all my thoughts, has me thinking about things I shouldn't be. Ever since I met Christian, I've realized how my body can physically react to a boy, and now I am noticing things that never even occurred to me to notice before. As quickly as the thought enters my mind, I take another sip to get rid of it. Tyler still has his eyes on me, just as he did earlier, causing my cheeks to flush. Thankfully, he can't read my mind, *or can he?* No. Nope. I'm buzzing. Of course, he can't.

"Perfect. You can be partners with Rayne, and I'll be partners with your friend Daniel." Laynie says, walking over to Daniel. "Hey, Daniel, I'm Laynie. Your friend Tyler thinks he's the best, but he hasn't seen me play yet." Daniel laughs, tilting his beer to connect with Laynie's cup.

"Well, this is going to be interesting." He looks at Tyler, then gulps the rest of his beer before opening another.

"Let the games begin," Laynie says, gulping her drink.

Chapter 8

Rayne

Tyler wasn't lying when he said he was the best. We are halfway through our first game, and he has made every single one of his shots, except one. I, however, have only made it into one cup. Tyler is super sweet and doesn't make me feel bad for being horrible at this game. Daniel is pretty good, too, same with Laynie. It's a close game, and we have two cups left, and they have three. I've been chugging my drink for every cup they've made, and I'm feeling well over buzzed at this point.

"It's anyone's game at this point. Focus on the cup you want to hit and shoot. You got this. Don't overthink it." Tyler says.

Now I'm overthinking it. I've only made one cup, but I'm determined to make this shot. Shaking out my hands to loosen up and calm my nerves, I take a slight step back so I can focus better on the front middle cup. Holding up my right hand, I close one eye, trying to focus and keep from swaying and carefully aim and shoot the ball forward. It sinks right into the cup.

Jumping up and down in excitement. I look at Tyler, and

his grin matches my own. I don't know if it's the alcohol or the adrenaline pumping through my bloodstream, maybe both, but I turn and jump on him, bringing my arms around his neck and wrapping my legs around his waist. He's laughing as he holds me up just under my ass and spins us around.

"I knew you'd make it." He breathes into my neck before pulling back. We are smiling at each other, his gaze falling to my lips, and suddenly I feel hot all over and am very much aware of our position, where his hands are resting, and how close our faces are. He slowly leans in to kiss me, and I get invaded with a musky spice mixed with beer. I instantly compare it to Christian's citrus smell and hate how it doesn't make my stomach flip like his. Moments Christian and I have shared flood my mind making me dizzy. I panic as his lips are about to touch mine, and at the last second, I turn my head—his lips connecting with my cheek.

"Erm, sorry. I don't know why I did that." *Yes, I do.* I came here to loosen up and try things I wouldn't normally do. Although he's cute, and I wouldn't have minded kissing him. It just felt wrong. The boy with the eyes that remind me of the sun just had to pop into my head and ruin what could have been my first kiss.

Get out of my head.

"Um, I never, I—"

"Don't worry about it. No need to apologize, and I shouldn't have tried to..." He pauses. "You know."

"Kiss me?" he runs his hands through his hair, blowing out a breath.

"Yeah, I shouldn't have tried to kiss you. I read that all wrong."

"No, you didn't." I place my hand on his arm, my cheeks turning pink. "I, um, I just don't have much experience with guys, and I panicked." I cover my face with my hands. "Besides, when I was eight, Toby Rodgers awkwardly kissed me on the playground."

He laughs, making this ten times worse. His hands gently wrap around my wrists, pulling my hands away from my face.

"You're cute when you're embarrassed." I look at him through my eyelashes and see he is still smiling at me.

Laughing awkwardly, I ask, "So, you don't think I'm a total loser?"

"No, of course not. If anything, I'm jealous of eight-year-old Toby Rodgers."

"Oh," I say shyly, avoiding eye contact. He tilts my chin, so I am forced to look at him.

"I would like to try this again, but not like this. Your first kiss shouldn't be like this." A wave of relief washes over me. Just then, a ping-pong ball hits Tyler in the head.

"Any day now, love birds," Daniel says, swaying a little because of the alcohol.

"Let's make this quick," Tyler whispers in my ear. My body doesn't ignite in goosebumps like they do with another guy I can't seem to get off my mind. Tyler stands in place, lining up his shot. He flicks his wrist and sinks it into the same cup I made previously.

"And that, my friend, is how it's done." He raises both his hands, looking at Daniel, and he rolls his eyes.

"GG." *Good game.*

"Well, that was fun. Let's go dance." Laynie says, stumbling into me, and because of my drunken state, I almost fall over but quickly catch myself.

"Wait," Tyler says, looking nervous. "Let me give you my number, and you can text me sometime." I flush, pulling out my phone. "I hope to hear from you soon," he says.

I smile shyly, tucking my phone into my back pocket.

"Aww, man, I missed the end of the game. Who won?" Jamie asks when we approach her.

"Yours truly. Although Tyler did most of the work."

"A win is a win." She says.

"You're right. That wasn't the only win tonight." I wink at Jamie.

"What else did I miss?"

"Oh, nothing. Tyler just gave me his number before we left." I say like it's no big deal.

Jamie squeals and smacks my ass. "That's my girl. Are you going to text him?"

"He's really nice. I might text him."

"You better text him!" Jamie and Laynie both say in unison.

"We'll see," I smirk.

"Playing hard to get, I see." Laynie bumps me with her shoulder.

"Just keeping it cool and not looking too much into it."

We all step outside in the backyard, and I can't help but pause and admire my surroundings. Like the house, the backyard is gigantic and has a vast infinity pool that overlooks the city. A fire pit sits to the left, surrounded by many people drinking, smoking, and talking. The bonfire was a flower of flame that reached toward the sky, generous in shades of red. Something about the blazing fire has me captivated. Looking at it, I am reminded of Christian; he is warm and ignites my bones whenever he is near—drawing me to him like a moth to a flame.

The pristine grass is littered with people dancing, girls shaking their asses as guys watch; a DJ in the yard's corner. He wears enormous headphones and is bopping his head to the music as he twists a bunch of nobs. Off to the far left is a pool house, a very nice pool house, almost as big as my parent's home. It's dark, showing no one is inside.

Many howls and hollers start when the DJ changes the song.

'Up Down by T-Pain,'
"She a bad bitch, and she already know it (yeah, she know it) Yeah, she know it. Yeah. Yeah, she know it."

"This is my song. Let's go!" Laynie shouts, grabbing hold of my hand.

I chug my full drink in one go, tossing it into the trashcan as I pass on our way over to the DJ. I reach for Jamie, and she interlocks her fingers with mine. When we get to the makeshift dance floor, she slowly spins me around, pulling me into her at my hips. If I was sober, I would freak out right now because I am not used to dancing unless it's in front of my mirror in my bedroom where no one can see me. *Besides him.*

Why am I thinking about him right now? I'm doing a shitty job at keeping him out of my head. No matter what I do, he seems to have a permanent spot in my mind. Thank God for Tequila, because I can easily push the thoughts of him out of my head—for now.

This is the best I've felt in a long time. My mind feels free, and my body feels loose. A part of me I didn't realize I possessed enjoys the eyes I feel on us from other partygoers.

With my hand on top of Jamies, I move my hips, rotating them in small circles as I lower myself to the floor. She follows my lead, grinding against my ass, lowering herself with me. Slowing, making our way up, I turn to face her. Jamie's eyes are glossy and dilated, mirroring my own, and I know she is feeling just as good as I am. We drunkenly giggle, as I run my fingers through her silky curls, and down the front of her killer body, moving my hips in a figure-eight as I lower myself back to the floor, dragging my hands down her legs as I go.

I'm completely losing myself in the music, the beat pulsating through my veins. I hear howls and whistles behind me, but I feel too good to care.

Making my way back up her body, she smiles as she leans into my ear and whispers, "You look so hot. Keep going. The guys look like they're about to explode just from watching you." I panic just a little, but I stop when Jamie wraps her arms around my shoulders and tells me, "Relax."

Laynie comes up behind me and grinds on my ass. I'm sandwiched between them as they both drag their bodies along mine. We look seductive and powerful out on the dance floor.

I feel warm, a light layer of sweat forming between our bodies. We continue to dance for a few more songs, entirely engrossed in each other. Jamie signifies she will get us another drink while Laynie and I continue to dance carefree.

"I have to go pee so bad. Time to break the seal, babe." Laynie says.

"Go ahead. Go. I'll wait here unless you want me to go with you?"

"No, I'm good, but I don't know how I feel about leaving you here."

"Go, go. I'll be fine. I'm going to be dancing right here when you get back." She waits, contemplating for a minute, and I roll my eyes, shooing her away with my hands.

"Fine. Stay here. I'll be like five minutes. Jamie should be back any second." She hurries off, and I lose her in the crowd.

The DJ switches the music to a slower song, 'Gangsta by Kehlani.' I close my eyes, tilting my head toward the sky, running my fingers up my stomach and over my breast. I sway my hips to the beat and pace of the music, rolling my body in perfect rhythm. A cool gust of wind blows, drying the damp skin of my exposed neck as I bring my hands up toward the heavens as if I could reach the stars.

I feel the perfect amount of intoxication and euphoria as I dance as if no one is watching. My eyes are still closed, and I'm still lost in the music when I feel a pair of hands grab my waist. At first, I thought it was Laynie or Jamie, but these hands aren't delicate. They are rough and slightly demanding. For a beat, I have a simmer of hope it might be Tyler until I turn around, open my eyes, and stand face to face with Jackson Reed.

This entire time I have been feeling beyond amazing and had completely forgotten I needed to keep an eye out for him, so that I could avoid a situation like this.

"Hi, gorgeous." He smirks, but he doesn't fill my stomach with butterflies or make my toes curl like someone else I know.

"Hi, Jackson," I say flatly.

"I'm glad to see you listened and dressed sexy for me." He undresses me with his eyes.

Ew. "I didn't dress for you. I dressed up for myself."

"You wound me." He places one hand over his heart,

pretending to be hurt, before resting his hand back on my hip. "In all seriousness, you look sexy as hell, and the way you were dancing had me mesmerized." Well, that's... nice?

"Thank you." I gently remove his hands from my waist. "Nice party." I glance over his shoulder, hoping to see my friends.

"It's epic, isn't it?"

"I wouldn't go that far," I say, not wanting to boost his ego more than it already is naturally. This party is epic, and he knows it.

He chuckles. "Want a drink?" he holds out a red solo cup.

"No, thanks. Jamie should be here any minute with our drinks."

"Why wait when you can have one now?" I don't answer. "Suit yourself," He goes to take a sip.

"Wait." I hesitate to think about what I should do. I am hot and thirsty from all the dancing, and I'm feeling good. Another drink sounds perfect and just what I need right now. "Fine. I'll take this one." He gives me a wicked smile as I take the cup. I take a sip, and my face instantly scrunches. "What is this?"

"Jack and Coke." He says, laughing a little at my reaction.

"I don't know how I feel about it."

It doesn't taste very good, but it also doesn't taste disgusting. If I wasn't already tipsy, I would probably think otherwise.

"Drink some more and find out. It's not that bad."

I take another sip while someone from behind me bumps into me, and half my drink spills down my sheer crop top.

"Shit!" I hiss at the cold liquid against my blazing skin.

"Sir... so... sor... sorry." The drunk guy who knocked into me slurs. Clearly hammered.

"Here, let me get that." Jackson takes my drink. "Let's get you cleaned up."

The state of my shirt doesn't give me much choice, and I

don't have anything else to do but follow him. He guides me to the pool house that I noticed earlier.

"Where are we going?"

"The pool house. I have some spare clothes in there, and I'm sure I can find you a shirt to change into, or at least a towel to dry you off." He opens the door, and we step in.

It's pure blackness in here, with a tad bit of light sneaking through the blinds from the moon. I feel a little dizzy from the alcohol and stumble into Jackson.

"Woah, easy there. Wait right here while I look for a shirt or towel."

"Okay, thanks." I watch Jackson take off, disappearing into the darkness.

The pool house has an open floor plan with an enormous kitchen to my right, but I can't make out anything else because it is so dark. My eyes slowly adjusting to the dark, I walk over to the kitchen in search of a light switch.

Feeling even dizzier, the alcohol from the night finally catching up to me, I lean my hands against the countertop, trying to keep the room from spinning.

"Jackson!" I call out, but get no response. "Jackson?"

I am feeling a little uneasy, but not from the alcohol. Anxiety is creeping in as I realize I'm all alone in an unfamiliar dark pool house with Jackson Reed. He hasn't given me any reason to feel uncomfortable, but something feels off.

Ryker's warnings flash through my head, making me feel sick because I ignored every single one. I turn around and head toward the door we came in from. I don't care about my soaked shirt anymore. I just want to find my friends. As I'm about to grab the doorknob, a pair of hands grab my waist.

"Boo!" Jackson shouts behind me.

"What the hell, Jackson!" I shout, leaning over to catch my breath, and he laughs at my expense.

"Chill, I'm just messing with you. Relax." He says as he rubs my tense shoulders. "You can be so uptight sometimes."

"Don't touch me," I tell him sternly. My eyes have finally adjusted, allowing me to see his face. He has a serious look in his eyes, cold and unfeelingly.

"You're such a fucking tease!"

I flinch, and my stomach coils. His sudden mood change is making me uneasy.

"W... What do you mean? How am I a tease?"

"Don't play dumb, Rayne. Nobody likes a stupid girl." He spits. "You are a fucking tease, and you know it! You're always walking around campus flaunting your sexy little body, giving all of us a show. You act like some virgin Mary with a stick up her ass. Like you're too good for me." He steps toward me, and I step back, bumping into the door.

"I... I... I don't k...know what you're t...talking about." I stammer, so terrified I can barely speak.

"Yes. You. Do. Stop fucking lying to me!" he says, punctuating each word, and I flinch, fear showing in my eyes.

"You're scaring me, Jackson. Let's go back out to the party. You're drunk."

"Drunk? I'm not drunk. I have had nothing to drink tonight, not even a sip. I was waiting for you to show up. Then I see you walk in with your two slutty friends dressed like this." He eyes me up and down in disgust. "Flirting with that guy you played beer pong with, then you dance like a whore giving every guy here a fucking show. You act like you're so innocent, like you're too good to be touched by anyone, but let's be honest, we both know with a body like this." He grabs my hips, grinding himself into me. "Those legs of yours have been spread plenty of times."

Completely paralyzed with fear, I don't even realize I'm crying until Jackson lifts his fingers and brushes my tears away.

"Don't cry and mess up that pretty face. I'm going to make you feel good and give you what we both know you want. Isn't that why you dressed sexy like this, because you wanted this to happen?"

He did tell me to dress sexy, but he can't seriously think that's why I dressed like this tonight. He must realize I dressed for myself to feel sexy like every other girl here. Did he not believe me when I answered this question earlier? I didn't do this for anyone other than me. Jackson is in such a manic state right now I don't want to say or do anything to make things worse. I quickly think about what I should do.

"You're right. I'm sorry. I always thought you were sexy and wanted you to notice me tonight."

He smiles. "Now, was that so hard to admit? I always knew you wanted me. Well, baby, you can have me." He roughly kisses my neck, and I feel like I'm going to vomit. I have so much adrenaline convulsing through me that I no longer feel drunk. I feel completely sober and know I need to get out of here. "God, you're sexy, and you make me so hard. I have imagined this day since I first laid eyes on you." His fingers go to the button of my leather pants, and he tugs them down my hips. He pushes against me forcefully, and I can feel his hardness pressing firmly against my abdomen as he reaches around, grabbing my slightly exposed ass to pull me closer. Squeezing my eyes tightly together as tears run down my face, I bite my lip harshly, trying not to break down.

My heart is beating at an unhealthy speed, crashing into my chest. How am I going to get away and out of here? His fingers go back to my pants, and I urgently grab his hands, stopping him. He tenses, his eyes vacant as they stare into me. I look up at him and paint on the biggest fake smile I could muster.

"No, not like this, Jackson… kiss me first?" He shrugs like it's a waste of time but leans in anyway, pushing me into the wall. Grabbing my chin, he viciously kisses me on my mouth, biting my lips like a starved animal. He groans into the kiss, enjoying the assault. His lips feel like sandpaper as he forces my lips apart and crams his tongue down my throat, almost making me throw up.

Now that he's distracted, this is the perfect time for me to make my move. I place my hands on his shoulders, grabbing onto them in a death grip. Squeezing as hard as I can, I dig my nails into him and bring my knee up as fast as possible, connecting with his balls perfectly. He falls to the floor with a grunt, and I waste no time lifting my pants, turning around, and bolting out of there.

I'm running so fast that everything around me is a blur as I smack straight into a body, both of us tumbling to the ground.

"Get off me, get off me, get the fuck off me!" I shout in panic.

"Rayne, it's me," Laynie says, and I instantly feel relieved at the sound of my best friend's voice. I open my eyes and see her straddling me with watery eyes. She stands, pulling me with her, and wraps her arms around me like a safety blanket shielding me. She squeezes me tighter, and a sob escapes my lips.

I'm crying in fear and relief because I made it. For a moment, when Jackson had me pinned against the wall and my pants halfway down my ass, I didn't think he would stop, and I knew if he successfully removed my bottoms, making it out of there wouldn't have been possible. I would have been stripped bare with my dignity left on the floor.

"What happened? Did Jackson do something to you?" She whispers in my ear, her voice cracking.

I can barely speak when I say, "How did you know it was Jackson?"

She squeezes me tighter. "I should have never left you. I'm so sorry. When I got back from the bathroom, you weren't there. Some drunken idiot said he bumped into you and spilled your drink all over you. Then he told me Jackson took you to get a change of clothes. I panicked, and Jamie and I rushed to find you, and when we couldn't, I called Ryker."

"You what!" I shout, finding my voice as I break free of her hold.

She cries, mascara running down her cheeks.

"I was so scared. I'm a horrible friend. I... I should have never left you, Rayne. If something happened to you, I could never live with myself. I could never... I could never—" I cut her off, embracing her in a tight hug. I'm hugging her as if I will never see her again.

"Stop it!" I pull away, looking her straight in the eyes as tears run down our cheeks. "You did nothing wrong. This is on me, and I really don't want to talk about it right now. Can we please get out of here?" she sniffles, nodding, using the back of her hand to wipe her tears.

I notice a few bystanders standing around, staring at us. Most people here are too drunk to notice anything going on. Thankfully, there are only a few who saw me crash into Laynie. I'm sure we both look like a mess with our mascara-stained cheeks. Jamie stands next to me.

"Nothing to see here, people! Get back to the party and mind your fucking business." She shouts, and the few people watching quickly turn around and return to what they were doing.

We get to the front of the house and sit down on the curb as we wait for Ryker.

Chapter 9

Christian

I'm hanging out with Ryker on his living room sofa, watching a movie I can't seem to focus on. I was too distracted thinking about how good Rayne looked when she left the house. It has been almost three hours since she went with her friend to a party. I really should be heading home, mainly since I can't focus on the movie or anything Ryker says to me. Still, I sit here impatiently, checking my watch and hoping she will return before I leave. Just one more glance at her tonight, and I would welcome sleep, just for the dreams.

I feel anxious waiting for her to get home. Tonight, she looked fucking stunning in those black leather pants that fit her like a second skin, hugging her curves perfectly. It turned me the fuck on, and all I could think about was slowly stripping them off her while trailing my tongue down her bare skin as I did. Her sheer long-sleeved crop top with her sparkly bra underneath was beyond sexy. Her body is a treasure from head to toe, and I want to explore every part of her. Fuck. I'm getting hard all over again, making it awkward as fuck to sit here with Ryker. I adjust myself and glance at him. Yup, that did it. No more boner.

It's becoming a challenge just being around her at all. This sexual tension building up inside me makes me feel like a ticking time bomb getting ready to detonate. No matter what she is wearing or where she is, she will always catch the attention of others. Thinking about her being at that party tonight, oozing sex, makes me want to break things. Ryker told me this was her first party, and I couldn't help but worry about her. She is innocent and naïve, but it's what I find the most attractive about her. I don't want some douchebag like Jackson fucking Reed, who does not know her value tainting her. Knowing he will be there makes me jealous, and it's clear he is into her. Who wouldn't be? It makes me sick thinking of him touching her. She deserves more; Rayne deserves everything. I'm not even worthy of her, which is why I've been trying to keep my distance.

It's a constant battle within myself, and I'm constantly fighting what my mind is telling me is right and what my body is craving. I am a little older and a little wiser, and I need to be the better man. Easier said than done when it comes to her.

Ryker's phone rings. He scrunches his brows at the screen, then answers.

"Laynie?" he says, more like a question. Ryker abruptly stands up. "What the fuck do you mean she's missing?" he paces back and forth. I lean forward, resting my elbows on my thighs, trying to listen. *Who's missing?* I think to myself, a knot forming in my gut. "Well, fucking find her. I'm on my way!"

He rushes to the door, grabbing his keys off the hook on his way out, and I rapidly follow him out the door. He is already swinging his car door open when I get to the passenger door and hop in right as he takes off.

"What's going on?"

"Rayne." Is all he says, and my heart sinks to my stomach.

"What do you mean, Rayne? What happened to Rayne?"

"She's missing." His hands grip the steering wheel so tight his knuckles turn white.

"What the fuck do you mean she's missing?"

"What the fuck does missing mean, Christian? Lost. Stolen. Disappeared. Gone. Fuck!" he shouts, slamming his fist against the steering wheel, causing the car to swerve and jerk me to the side.

My heart thumps wildly as I grab my seatbelt with sweaty palms clicking it into place. He is speeding well over the speed limit, and I am freaking out internally—flashes of news articles from my dad's accident flood my mind. I squeeze my eyes shut, trying to remove the images from my head and regain my composure.

"Calm the fuck down!" I say through gritted teeth. "We will find her, but driving like a lunatic and killing us both before we can even get to her won't do us any good." He slows down a tad, allowing me to relax a bit. "We will find her, man. I promise."

He side-eyes me and nods his head, not saying a word. We pull up a long driveway leading to a mansion. *Fucking rich pricks.* We see Laynie, Rayne, and some other girl sitting on the curb huddled together. Ryker pulls the car into park and hops out, leaving the car idling. I rush out, slamming my door behind me.

"Oh, thank God!" Ryker says, kneeling in front of Rayne, holding both sides of her face with his hands, "I freaked the fuck out when Laynie called me, saying she couldn't find you." I stand back, giving them space even though all I want to do is bring her into my arms and selfishly carry her far, far away from here. "Where the hell were you? I told you to stay with Laynie!" His voice rises with each word, and Rayne's shoulders shake as she sobs.

"Not now, man. This isn't the time." I know it isn't my place to get involved, but seeing her cry is hard to witness. Rayne is upset, and Ryker shouting at her isn't going to help the situation.

He shoots daggers at me with his eyes, but doesn't fight me on it. He stalks back to the car, pissed off.

"So, are you guys covered for the ride home?" the girl

sitting on the other side of Rayne asks.

Rayne let her friend Jamie know they're riding back with us and apologizes profusely for ruining their epic night. What happened? How did Rayne ruin the night? Jamie reassures her, telling her not to apologize. She looks at her with intense eyes as she tells Rayne she did nothing wrong before pulling her into a hug and whispering something I can't make out into her ear.

They all have a group hug, telling Jamie to text them when she makes it home safe.

Laynie stands awkwardly next to Rayne, wrapping her arms around herself. "Well, um, I'm gonna wait in the car." She flicks her thumb toward Ryker's Camaro, and Rayne gives her a small smile.

I'm thankful now that it's just us as I watch her pick at her fingernails.

"Please look at me, Raynie." She lets out a long breath and looks up at me. The headlights from Ryker's car are shining on us, illuminating Rayne and her emerald green eyes. Even standing here with her lashes clumped and mascara-stained cheeks, she is still the most beautiful girl I have ever seen.

I am sure Laynie and Ryker can see us and are probably watching our interaction, but right now, I couldn't care less. With the back of my index finger, I wipe away a tear resting under her eye, and she flinches. My muscles go tight, and I grit my teeth. If someone hurt her, I will end them. The extreme need to protect her is overwhelming.

I rest the palm of my hand on the side of her face, and she closes her eyes, leaning into my touch.

"Are you okay, Rayne? If anyone hurt you, I swear..."

She rests her hand on top of mine. "No one hurt me, Christian," she whispers so softly I can barely hear her. Rayne slowly opens her eyes, rimmed in red from crying, and they look as if they are glowing. "I'll be okay." She wraps her delicate fingers around my hand, dragging it away from her face. "We should go," she says, letting go of my hand, and walks away.

The drive back home is silent, and Rayne and Laynie disappear upstairs when we get there. I sit on the sofa I was sitting on not even an hour ago, and Ryker takes a seat next to me. I can feel his eyes burning a hole in the side of my head, and I already know I can't avoid the conversation that's coming.

"Is something going on between you and my sister?"

"No," I blurt.

It isn't a lie. I have this intense, unexplained pull toward her, and the attraction is a given, but is there anything going on between us? No. He stares at me fiercely, and I stare back at him, holding the same intensity.

"It's been a long night," he huffs out. "I'm going to head upstairs. You can stay and finish the movie. Crash on the couch if you want. It's whatever. Goodnight."

"Goodnight," I say with a nod in his direction. I should call it a night, but I'm wide awake after tonight. Deciding to stay and finish the movie, I grab the remote and press play. For the past fifteen minutes, I've been trying to pay attention to the movie but still can't seem to focus. Something happened tonight, but I can't figure out what. I had never seen Rayne so upset, and it bothered me to see her that way. I'm lost in thought, my mind reeling with everything that had happened tonight as I stare blankly at the television.

"Ahem." I turn around and see Rayne standing at the bottom of the stairs. Her hair is down and wet from a shower, and tiny pink spandex shorts peek out from underneath the same blink 182 t-shirt she was wearing when she crashed into me. "Do you mind if I join? I can't sleep."

"You don't have to ask Raynie. It's your home, but I don't mind if you join me." She says nothing, giving me a small smile in response. "We can turn this off and watch something else?"

"No, this is fine. I like this movie." She walks over, taking a seat next to me on the sofa. My eyes flutter shut, taking in the lavender scent emanating from her as she passes me. When she sits, my eyes trail down her silky-smooth legs resting on the coffee table, and my fingers twitch, wanting to reach out and touch her. I cross my arms in refrain. We watch the movie in silence, but it isn't awkward. It's nice and comfortable. I do my best to focus on the movie, but I am so aware of her next to me that it is almost impossible.

When I sneak a glance, it's like coming up for a breath of fresh air. She is free of makeup and looks completely at peace, much different from how she looked earlier tonight. Not knowing what happened is driving me insane. Despite wanting to find out, there is a small part of me that is afraid of it. If someone hurt her, I don't know if I can just sit here and do nothing about it.

"You just going to sit there and stare at me the whole time, or are you going to watch the movie?" she teases.

"What happened earlier tonight?" her smile drops as she shifts on the couch, clearly uncomfortable with the reminder.

"Nothing happened."

I turn to face her fully. "Bullshit. Something happened." I go to reach for her, then think better of it and pull my hand back. "Please tell me. You can trust me. I would never hurt you."

"I can trust you?" she scoffs.

"Of course you can trust me. What makes you think you can't?"

"Hm, let's see." She holds up her finger. "One, you are constantly hot and cold with me. I swear you give me whiplash every time I'm around you. Two," she holds up another finger, "You touch me, something as innocent as brushing the hair out of my face, then take it back as if touching me is a sin. Don't even get me started on how you almost kissed me, only to humiliate me by stopping the kiss from happening. Three," she adds another finger. "You act dominant and possessive, basically having a pissing match with a guy you don't even know, as if you have that right. I'm. Not. Yours. And you have made that perfectly clear." She catches her breath, then continues, "Do you like playing games with me? Am I just some innocent, naïve girl you get your kicks off by fucking around with?"

I have been trying to do the right thing by keeping my distance, but I didn't realize that doing so was making her feel this way. Now I feel like a dick, and I'm angry at myself for even being in this situation.

"No, of course not!" I run my fingers through my hair in frustration. "Of course, this isn't some twisted game. I'm not trying to mess with your head, Rayne. I didn't even realize I was doing it."

When she doesn't respond, I lean back against the sofa with my eyes closed.

I don't know how much time passes when she whispers, "At the party..." she pauses.

I say nothing, letting her have this moment. Turning my head to face her, I open my eyes, giving her my full attention.

Rayne finally speaks, telling me she's never drunk before, aside from sneaking sips of her mom's wine on special occasions. She fidgets with her fingernails, which I noticed she does whenever she is nervous or uncomfortable. I want to reach over and cover her hand. Provide her comfort, letting her know she doesn't have to be either of those things.

Her eyes light up when she tells me how much she enjoyed drinking for the first time. She smiled when she told me she won her first game of beer pong with some dude named Tyler. It was the first time I had seen her really smile tonight, and I couldn't help but feel jealous. *Get the hell over it.* This isn't about you.

After the game, they all decided to have another drink and hit the dance floor. Fuck! I wish I could have seen her dance. It pissed me off when I found out Laynie and Jamie left her alone on the dance floor, regardless of whether she insisted. Rayne said she had no control over her body as the music invaded her senses, but I can only think about how I have no control over my body when I'm around her. My mind drifted, imagining my hands and how they would squeeze her hips as she sexily ground into me. I jolt out of my dream-like state as it quickly emerges into a nightmare when I find out Jackson grabbed her hips.

I had a bad feeling about him from the moment I met him. He reminds me of people from my past, automatically making me feel sick. I'm trying my best not to be that person anymore, but these feelings that emerge at the mention of his name make it hard not to. Old habits die hard it seems.

"Promise me, Christian, that after what I'm about to tell you, you won't do anything stupid? Not because I want to protect him, but because I want to protect you."

"What, you think that fuck boy can kick my ass or something? You don't need to protect me from him. Trust me." I say a little louder than I expected.

"No." She deadpans. "I want to protect you from doing something you might not be able to take back, something that can get you in trouble or, worse, arrested. You're eighteen, Christian, and you aren't some minor who will get a slap on the wrist. It's just you and your mom, right?" She sets her hand on my thigh, causing goosebumps to spread across my body. I don't answer her, and she takes my silence as an answer.

"Right. Your mom needs you, and I don't need something happening to you at my expense, especially over some fuck boy like Jackson Reed." She remarks.

Is she trying to joke with me? Using my fuck boy description of him. God, she's so damn cute. Everything she said is true, though. What I want to do to him, I could get myself in trouble. Being eighteen makes me an adult, and that's exactly how the justice system would treat me. I know for a fact Jackson fucking Reed wouldn't handle it like a man and instead would handle it like a little bitch, and probably press charges.

What really gets me is that she knows it's just me and my mom, and she needs me. It would destroy her if anything happened to me because I'm all she has left. My heart does a little flip in my chest because Rayne cares not only about me, but about the most important woman in my life, my mom. She wants to protect me just the way I want to protect her.

I set my hand on top of hers, resting on my thigh. "You're right." I say, "Thank you. It means more than you can imagine that you care about my mom like that." I pause, trying to find my voice. "And for caring about me."

Besides my uncle, I am the only one who looks out for my mom, and my mom and uncle Mav are the only ones who ever look out for me. It's weird having someone care for me that isn't my family. I am not used to it, but I already like the feeling.

"Promise me you won't do anything if I tell you, Christian." Her voice is stern, and her eyes intense, showing me how serious she is.

I can't sit here and not do anything. I know what I have to lose if things go south, but this wouldn't be my first rodeo. I've dealt with bitch boys like Jackson before. If I don't promise her that I won't do anything, she won't tell me what happened, and I need to know. For the first time, I lie to Rayne.

"I promise that I won't do anything to Jackson."

She searches my eyes, seeking truth. I feel like shit knowing I'm looking her in the face and telling a lie, but this is to protect her. I don't want her to worry about me.

When Jackson approached her, it caught her off guard. She explains how she was caught up in the moment that she forgot to try to avoid him. *Why would she need to avoid him? Aren't they friends? I thought she was going to his party to hang out with him. That's the impression I got when I picked her up at school.*

I scrunch my eyebrows in confusion. "Why would you avoid Jackson? I thought you were going to his party to hang out with him."

"No, I was going to have fun with my friends and for the experience. I was hesitant about going because he's always given me the creeps. The party was after the homecoming game, and Laynie said it would be packed, and I didn't think it would be hard to avoid him."

Okay, well, I guess that makes sense. When Jackson approached her, he was kind to her, so she thought she may have misjudged him. He offered her a drink, and she accepted.

No, no, no, please don't tell me he roofied her drink. Why the fuck would she accept a drink from him? Because she's good, that's why, and she has no idea how awful people can be. I wanted to be frustrated with her, but how can I be? She was drinking for the first time and having fun with her friends. Why would she possibly worry about accepting a drink from someone she's familiar with? When I used to get drunk, I did many things I wasn't proud of, and I have made a lot of mistakes. I drank whatever the hell was available, not giving a fuck who it was from.

Some drunk asshole stumbled into her, and she spilled her drink down her shirt. Jackson, of course, was the fucking hero and offered her some clothes to dry off. Taking any opportunity to get her alone, and brought her to his pool house. Yes, a pool house... fucking rich pricks.

As she continues her story, her eyes fill up with unshed tears, almost making them sparkle. Based on her reaction, I know this is going to be wrong. My stomach aches just thinking about what she might tell me.

I sit and tentatively listen to her as she tells me everything that went down in that pool house. I absorb her words even if what I'm hearing makes me feel sick.

I'm going to kill him!

That bitch has another thing coming his way. I'm clenching my fist so hard together my knuckles are white, and my nails are digging into my palms, cutting skin. I have the burning rage of a thousand suns pulsating through me. I'm so angry it's practically consuming me.

Rayne sobs as she tries to get through the horrific events. Tears are streaming down her face, now soaking her shirt. I scoot closer to her and open my arms up, giving her the option to embrace me or not, careful not to make her feel uncomfortable. She leans into me, and the fury I feel eases up by having her in my arms. We sit there for what feels like hours as she cries into me, and I stroke her long damp hair, trying to calm myself down and bring her comfort.

It breaks my fucking heart seeing her like this. The beautiful girl so full of life looks defeated, and I don't know how to help her. Nothing I do will take away what happened. When she told me Ryker, and I were right, and she should have never gone to the party dressed the way she was, and it was her fault, my heart went from broken to fucking shattered. Fuck! I shouldn't have said anything earlier. She was beautiful, sexy, and hot as hell. I only agreed with Ryker because I was envious of every other guy who would be laying eyes on her.

Closing my eyes, ashamed of how much of a prick I am, I kiss the top of her head. "No. We were wrong… I was wrong. Don't you dare think you asked for this because of what you were wearing. Do you hear me, Rayne?" I squeeze her tighter. "God, you're so damn beautiful, Raynie. I was being a jealous prick because you looked sexy, beautiful, and perfect… you looked fucking perfect. I was jealous at the thought of other guys witnessing it. I was wrong and had no right feeling that way. I'm so sorry."

She doesn't say anything and sobs harder. "Shhh, you're okay. I got you." I say, whispering into her hair and rubbing her back.

I'm trying to hold it together for Rayne, but my body is surging with anger. I'm doing my best to not leave right the fuck now. I want to drive over to that fucker's house, kick his god damn doors in, and beat the shit out of him. I have only ever felt this protective of my mom. This anger that's building up inside me is terrifying. I have never gotten so infuriated in my life. I have never been on the verge of breaking, not for anyone… not ever. But somehow, Rayne has this effect on me, and I don't understand it.

My arms are already wrapped around her, but I need her closer. I lift her up with ease, setting her on my lap in a straddling position. She exhales, closes her eyes, and rests her head on my chest.

With the movie long over, I turn off the tv and pull my phone out, selecting shuffle on my Spotify playlist.

Chapter nine

"Between The Raindrops by Lifehouse,"
"There's no one but you and me... Right here and now...
The way it was meant to be."

I am relieved that nothing else happened, but I'm heartbroken for Rayne. I'm heartbroken that she had to go through this traumatic experience. From this moment on, I will do everything in my power to always protect her.

"I am so proud of you. That took a lot of courage, Raynie, and you are stronger than you realize."

She pulls back, looking at me with puffy eyes and swollen lips. "Thank you, Christian." She smiles sadly as she brings her palm up, caressing my cheek as I did to her earlier.

I tense, not used to being touched this way.

"I'm lucky, you know? I got away before anything too bad happened. Not many people can say the same, and for that, I'm grateful." She rubs her thumb up and down my jaw. "I know it's just a silly kiss, but a part of me is sad that my first real kiss was tarnished. It was forcefully taken from me, and that is something I won't ever get back."

"You're right; you can't ever get that back, but with the right person, that one moment he took from you won't matter. It will be replaced with something." I pause, the side of my mouth hooking into a smile. "Something epic."

The light I'm used to seeing returns to her eyes. "Epic, huh?" both of her hands glide to my shoulders.

"There is a lot of dark in the world, and I like to believe that with the right person, anything they do together will overshadow the darkness." I drag a piece of her hair, brushing it behind her ear. Her eyes drop to my mouth, her tongue wetting her bottom lip. "You once told me you didn't trust me because when I touched you innocently... something as innocent as brushing your hair out of your face, I took it back." I lean in and kiss her forehead as she closes her eyes.

I slowly pulled back a tad; our faces were so close we're

breathing each other's air.

"You said I took it back as if touching you was a sin." I lick my bottom lip as her eyes follow the movement.

"Do you trust me now, Raynie?" I bring my hands up, cupping both sides of her face, looking her directly in those mesmerizing green eyes. She nods. "I need to hear you say it."

"I trust you," she says, full of conviction, not breaking eye contact.

My gaze zeros in on her full lips, and her breath catches. "You may be my biggest sin, but I'd gladly walk through the gates of hell for you." And I kiss her.

Chapter 10

Christian

"Kiss Me by Ed Sheeran plays in the background as my lips gently connect with hers. This is the most passionate kiss of my life. Entirely different from any kiss I've ever experienced. I'm not rushing, wanting to take my time and savor every second. I need her lips on mine like I need oxygen to breathe.

Tenderly, our lips meet. Her lips are soft, lush, and warm. If I could stay in this moment with her forever, I would. If I ever lose my memory, I swear I'll never forget this moment; I will never forget her. She is like a drug, and I'm fucking addicted. I can't get enough.

I teasingly lick the bottom of her lip, and she murmurs. It's the most beautiful sound. Her sighs of pleasure are music to my ears, and I want to hear them over and over again. She parts her lips, giving me access to her plump bottom lip. I nibble at it, tenderly sucking it into my mouth. She squirms on my lap, causing my hardness to throb. Noticing, she let out a deep sigh, and I dragged my hands through her hair and tenderly pulled her head back, breaking the kiss. We're both breathing heavily, our chests rising and falling rapidly. I kiss her jaw. Then work my way down her neck.

"You," I kiss her collarbone, "Are," My lips skate up, kissing the pulse in her neck. "So," I kiss the corner of her mouth. "Perfect."

"Christian," she breathes into the kiss.

Fuck. I love how my name falls from her lips like it's the most natural thing. It's as if she's said my name thousands of times.

I wrap my arms around her, picking her up, gently laying her down on the couch, her legs locked around me. I used one hand to balance my weight above her. Our lips join, and she runs her fingers through my hair, tugging at the ends, and a moan escapes my lips.

Kissing along my jaw, she works her way up, licking around the rim of my ear, suckling on my ear lobe until I almost cum in my pants. *Holy shit!*

"Fuck, Rayne, that feels good."

"Yes," she moans in response.

Leaning back, I grab the hem of her t-shirt and look at her questioningly. "Is this okay?" she nods. "I need to hear you say it, Raynie," I say, kissing her lips.

"Yes, please, Christian."

Tugging her shirt, she lifts her arms, allowing me to remove it fully and toss it to the floor. Drawing in a breath, I admire how she looks in her white lacey bra and how her full breasts almost spill out of it. *Fuck.* Everything about her is angelic. She looks beautiful, laying beneath me, her dark hair fanning across the couch pillow. She looks so pure. Knowing I'm the only one who has ever touched her this way does things to me. I want to mark her, claim her the same way she has marked me without even realizing it. I am hers.

Placing feather-light kisses on her collar bone, I draw my tongue down the valley of her breast, watching her eye my every movement. With a squeeze at her breast, I bring her perfect tit to my mouth. Through the lacey material, I feel her nipples harden.

"Oh," she gasps.

"Do you like that?"

"Oh, God, yes," she moans, throwing her head back.

Kissing and suckling my way down her stomach, I'm uncomfortably hard. My dick is tightly pressed against my jeans, begging to be released. Rayne is soaking through her tight little spandex shorts, and I can smell her sweet juices turning me on more. All I want to do is taste her, drink her in.

"What do you want me to do, Rayne?"

She leans up on her elbows, looking down at me. "What do you mean?"

"This is about you. What do you want?"

"I, um, I, don't know what I want. I've never done any of this before."

"What is the first thing that pops into that pretty little head of yours?"

"Can you take off your shirt?" she says shyly. I smirk, grabbing the back of my tee with one hand. "Wait." I stop and look at her with concern clear on my face. "I want to take it off you," she says nervously.

Grinning, I sit up, letting her know she is in full control. She meets me, coming up onto her knees. Face to face, she uses both hands to grab the hem of my shirt and slowly brings it over my head. Then discards it on the floor next to hers. Her eyes widen as she takes in my bare chest, licking her bottom lip.

"C... Can I touch you?"

God, yes! I want her to touch me, never to stop touching me, and it scares the shit out of me.

"You never need permission to touch me."

Rayne bites back a smile, spreading her fingers over my chest and bringing them down, tracing my abs. Her eyes follow her hands as if she is studying every part of me. With every trace of her fingers, jolts of electricity radiate through my body.

Grabbing the back of my neck, she smashes her lips against mine, and my arms engulf her, pulling her closer. We are now kissing in a frenzy. Hands and mouth all over each other, biting, nipping, and devouring. She breaks the kiss, bringing her mouth straight to my chest, kissing her way down to my belly button.

I would have never expected her to take charge the way she is. It is such a turn on. This is about her; I want her to feel in control and have all the power.

She reaches to undo the button of my pants. God, I want her. I want all of her. Seeing her this vulnerable and needy, wanting me as badly as I want her, is everything. Having her on her knees in front of me and picturing her mouth wrapped around my fullness is the ultimate fantasy.

Thud! We both pause, startled by the sound that came from upstairs. Shit. Her parents or Ryker may come downstairs. I was so captivated at this moment that I lost all consciousness. We're in an open living room where anyone can walk in on us.

Rayne resumes unbuttoning my jeans and pulling my zipper, relieving some of the restriction going on in my pants.

What am I doing? What the fuck Am I doing? I just told Ryker nothing was going on between us. Jackson tried to take advantage of her tonight, and now here I am doing the same thing.

She was vulnerable tonight, and I feel like I took advantage of that weakness. I can't do this, shouldn't do this, but I want her so fucking bad. It's difficult to think straight right now. It's like I'm being pulled in two different directions. My mind pulled me one way, and my body tugged me the other. I know how I feel about Rayne in this short time. Nobody has ever made me feel like this, not even a little.

Fuck! How could I let things progress this far? I grab her hands, stopping them from unzipping me fully.

"Did I do something wrong?" she panics, scooting away.

I hang my head, not able to look at her. "No, you did everything right." I pause. "It's me. I... I..."

"You coward!" she shouts.

I look up and see her eyes brimmed with tears. She rapidly gathers her shirt off the floor, flipping it right side out.

"Get out!" she shouts again, throwing her shirt on and covering herself from me. I have never seen her this pissed, and I want to go to her and rewind and take back my words.

"Raynie."

"No." She shakes her head, "No! don't you, Raynie me. Get the fuck out!" she points to the door as the tears in her eyes finally fall.

My heart aches knowing I caused this, and my throat feels tight, as if I'm being strangled by an invisible noose.

"I'm so sorry..."

"Go!" she yells. "Please just leave," she chokes out.

Hanging my head, I grab my shirt and leave the house, not bothering to put my shirt back on or button my pants.

Chapter 11

Rayne

I wake up the following day with puffy red eyes from crying myself to sleep. Today is Sunday, which means our weekly family breakfast. We all get together in one place to bond and talk about our week, but I really don't feel up to talking about mine. What would I say? Hey, mom and dad, I got drunk for the first time and almost got taken advantage of. My first kiss was stolen from me, but Christian made me forget all about that when his lips collided with mine. His lips were so soft, a complete contrast to his rough hands, and I can still feel them there—his lips on mine. Our kiss was delicate as rose petals and demanding like ocean waves. Kissing Christian made me feel drunk all over again.

He asked me if I trusted him right before he kissed me, and I answered truthfully. At that moment, I did. I felt so safe with his arms wrapped around me, the rhythmic beat of his pulse as I rested my cheek on his shoulder, the pounding of his heart against my own. His hands rubbing up and down my back, cocooning me in a safety net. That beautiful, unexpected moment went up in flames the second he got in his head. I knew what he was about to say before he could even speak the words. My safety net broke, and he pulled away from me again, leaving me to crash and burn in the aftermath.

I am tired of this game he plays with me. I may be sixteen, but he shouldn't mistake naivety for being stupid. I understand the battle that must have gone on in his head. My brother is his best friend, my dad is his boss, and just because I understand where his mind is at does not mean I agree with his actions. I've already told him how he confuses me with his hot and cold mood swings. He knew I was vulnerable last night, yet he asked me to trust him and kissed me breathlessly. He knew how big of a deal that was to me. The instant things got hot and heavy; he backed out like a coward! What really hurts me is this wasn't the first time he stopped an intimate moment between us. I couldn't even hold my tongue last night. I was a mixture of so many things. Confused, vulnerable, hurt, embarrassed, and, most of all, livid.

I wasn't sure if he was interested initially, but now I know he wants me. The way his body reacts to me is a dead giveaway. I'm young, but I know what I want, and if he can't step up and say what he wants, then hell with him. I deserve better, and I won't be a ball in this back-and-forth tennis match he seems to play. Two can play this game. If he wants me like I know he does, then he needs to prove it. If he thinks it's best to keep his distance, I'll make it hell for him to try.

I roll over, groaning because my head is killing me. I don't know if it's from the alcohol I had last night, the lack of sleep, or all the crying I did. It's likely a combination of it all. Laynie walk's out of the bathroom looking refreshed; she even has a glow to her.

"Good morning, sleeping beauty. You look like shit." She says, jumping onto the bed next to me.

"Thanks, Laynie Mae. You're a real peach to wake up to."

"I am, aren't I?" she sits up. "Seriously though, your eyes are red and puffy like you've been crying all night."

"I have been crying all night."

"Is this about Jacks—?"

"I don't want to think about him right now." My body shakes, trying to rid of the chill at the mention of his name. "I was crying because of Christian."

"What the hell did he do? Do I need to march to his house and kick him in his goods?"

Laughing, I say, "No, Laynie, but thank you for the offer. I'll save that for another time." I bump into her with my shoulder. "We kissed last night." I blurt.

"You what!" she shouts, getting on her knees.

"Calm down, will you? It was just a kiss."

"Don't tell me to calm down and stop downplaying this. You and that fine piece of ass kissed!" she shrieks.

"Shhh, keep it down. The entire house can probably hear you, and the last thing I need is Ryker knowing."

"Girl, he is passed out."

"How would you know that?" I look at her suspiciously.

"Umm, I don't know. I just assumed he would still be asleep after last night." My eyes widen. "No, no, God, no!" Her cheeks heat. "I'm talking about after everything that happened with you. He was clearly worried sick. He pulled up to the party like a bat out of hell."

"Oh…" I look at her, but she quickly looks away. "Yeah, probably."

"Why were you crying? Was the kiss horrible? Damn, that sucks. He's hot, and I totally had faith in his kissing skills. Looks can only get you so far. What a bummer." She says all in one breath. She yelps when I push her and almost falls off the bed.

"No, the kiss wasn't horrible. It was…" images of last night flooding my head. "It was epic."

"Well, what's the problem?"

"The problem is, he stopped it. It was getting intense. Something just came over me, and I just took charge. I wanted him." My cheeks heat pink.

"Atta fucking girl, babe!" she punches the air.

"Did you hear me, Laynie? He stopped it. It was so embarrassing."

Chapter eleven 139

"Right. Sorry!" she grimaces. "I was having a proud bestie moment of you taking charge. I always knew you had it in you. Why would he stop?"

I feel guilty for never telling her about how we almost kissed before, but it was too humiliating to admit. Imagine if I told her, then I'd have to explain how he did the same thing. The fact that he kissed me is so much worse, and I would have rather he had not kissed me at all.

I groan, shoving my face into the pillow and telling her how he wasn't in his head for once and was completely in the moment. We were in our own bubble until something fell from upstairs. Laynie's eyes widen before she puts on a neutral face. She doesn't understand why that would cause him to stop. I tell her how once our moment was interrupted, it was as if a rush of things came charging into his stubborn ass head, and I instantly knew I was losing him. It was like he was in a daze and then snapped out of it once he realized what we were doing.

"What's the big deal? What's stopping him? He clearly wants you. That much is obvious."

"I don't know. He's never actually come out and told me. If I were to take a guess, it would be because I'm his best friend's sister, and my dad is his boss. Those are the only things I can think of."

She rolls her eyes. "He needs to get the hell over it. Who gives a shit what Ryker thinks! He will get over it. As far as your dad goes, I don't know about that one. I'm sure it would take some convincing, but Christian is a good guy, from what I can tell. I think he would come around."

"I don't know, but honestly, I don't care. If he can't own up to his feelings for me, then he doesn't deserve me, anyway." I shrug.

"You're such a boss." She replies, leaning her head on my shoulder. "An independent boss ass bitch who needs no man, especially one who won't fight for what he wants." I chuckle, shaking my head. "What? I'm serious."

"I love you, Laynie Mae."

"Ditto, babe. Let's eat. I'm hungrier than a six-month pregnant woman with weird-ass food cravings."

I burst into laughter. God, I love her.

After cleaning myself up and applying some concealer to the bags under my eyes, I look a lot more presentable. I didn't want to go downstairs looking the way I did earlier this morning. They would have asked a hundred questions I don't want to answer. Changing out of my pajamas and into a dress, I leave my hair down and spray some lavender body spray.

In the kitchen, my dad is in his usual seat at the end of the table, with my mom and Ryker.

"Good morning, mama," I say, giving her a peck on the cheek before turning to my dad and doing the same. "Good morning, pops."

"Good morning, baby girl." My parents respond.

"Good morning, Jack, good morning, Olivia," Laynie says, taking a seat across from my mom.

"What about me?" Ryker scoffs.

"Oh," she slaps her forehead, "Good morning, Ryker." He scowls at her as my parents and I all chuckle. "Mmm, French toast, my favorite," Laynie says, adding an unhealthy amount of powdered sugar to her toast.

"Ryker requested French toast this morning," Mom says. Laynie looks over at Ryker as he sinks a little into his seat. "How was the party last night, girls?"

Even though the question was directed toward Laynie and me, I feel all eyes are on me. Ryker is staring at me intensely. He still doesn't know the full story. Laynie looks at me with empathy, and my parents look at me with curiosity burning in their eyes.

"It was good." I take a bite of my French toast.

"That's vague, sis. Anything worth sharing?"

"Umm, not really. It's just like any other party you've been to, I'm sure."

"We danced all night. Rayne here has quite the moves." Laynie interjects, saving the day.

I squeeze her thigh under the table, thanking her. Ryker's

phone vibrates with an incoming text, and he quickly replies before putting his phone back into his pocket. I hear the front door open and close, and Christian walks in, pausing awkwardly at the entrance.

"Hello everyone," he looks at everyone but me as he rubs the back of his head. "Ryker invited me over for breakfast, but I had a few things I had to do at my house first. Sorry, I'm late."

"Don't be silly. You're just in time. Please, take a seat." My mom replies as she stands up, grabbing another plate. Christian hesitates before walking over and sitting down next to me, the only seat available. *Great.* "Help yourself. There's plenty." She says, setting his plate in front of him.

"Thank you, Mrs. Davis."

"What did I tell you about calling me Mrs. Davis?" she teasingly tells him. "Makes me feel old."

He gives her a cheeky smile. "Right, my apologies Olivia."

My mom blushes.

Why does he have to be so damn perfect? My mom even takes a liking to him. Why couldn't he be some rude ass jerk with no manners? It would make things a lot easier.

"Did you finish the movie last night?" Ryker asks, and Christian's gaze snaps to mine.

His cheeks tint pink, definitely thinking about everything other than the movie. My foot brushes his under the table. His eyes widen, and his mouth opens before quickly closing it. Moving his attention to Ry, he answers, "Yeah, I finished the movie. It's one of my favorites."

"Mine too," Ry says, adding more powdered sugar to his French toast.

"Do you mind passing me the sugar?" I ask Christian.

"Sure." I intentionally brush my fingers along his as he passes it to me and feel nothing but satisfaction at the noticeable shiver that rakes through him.

"Thank you," I smirk.

"No problem," he clears his throat.

Laynie pinches me under the table, causing me to jump. I look at her, and she widens her eyes at me in a *what are you doing* kind of look. I grin, shrugging my shoulders. Cutting into my French toast, I grab the small piece with my hand and dip it into the puddle of syrup on my plate. I can feel Christian's eyes on me. I can feel him everywhere, taking me back to when I was straddling him on the couch.

My eyes hold his as I bring the toast to my mouth, wrapping my lips around it and slowly sucking off the sticky mixture of syrup and powdered sugar.

He closes his eyes, taking a deep breath. When he opens them, still looking at me, I grin, arching my brow at him. I turn my attention to the table, grabbing my cup of orange juice and taking a sip.

"I'll be right back," I announce. "We are going to Laynie's house after, so we can study for our upcoming driver's test. Laynie's mom is picking us up soon, and I forgot to get my things together." Laynie looks at me questioningly, but I ignore it.

The moment I'm in my bedroom, I exhale a deep breath and quickly gather the practice test we are using to study. I didn't have to come up here right away, but teasing Christian was hard for me to do. His presence affects me just as much as mine does him.

I stuff the paper into my bag, stopping at the window that faces Christian's room. It feels like yesterday I was dancing in front of my mirror, knowing he was watching. I remember the goosebumps that coated my arms at his gaze. At the time, I thought I imagined everything; the tingles my body ignited with when we shook hands, the longing stares at the kitchen table during breakfast, and his flirtatious panty-dropping smirk. It feels like so long ago when so much has happened since then. He kissed me.

I smile, bringing my fingers up to my lips.

"Do you like teasing me?" Christian whispers in my ear from behind me. His breath fanned my neck, making me shiver.

I was lost in the memories of everything that had taken place between us. I didn't even notice him walk into my room.

"I don't know what you're talking about," I say, still gazing out the window.

"Oh, but I think you do." he grazes his fingertips down my arms, and I close my eyes, leaning into him. "I think you know just how much you affect me and how much my body responds to you." He adds, grinding into me from behind.

I can feel his hard length pressing up against my ass. Tilting my head back with my eyes still closed, I sigh, breathing heavy.

"Fuck, I love the way your body responds to me." he groans, resting his hands on my hips. "I bet you would be soaked if I were to slide my fingers inside your panties right now."

Damn him. He's right. I'm drenched and achy. I don't care how turned on I am right now. I will not be made a fool. I will no longer put myself in a situation where I give myself to him for the taking just for him to grab on, then let me go. As I said, if he wants me, then he has to prove it.

I turn to face him, leaning in, my lips ghosting his. He closes his eyes in anticipation of a kiss, but before our lips connect, I dodge his mouth, whispering in his ear.

"There's only one problem… I'm not wearing any panties."

Gently bumping his shoulder, I grab my bag and leave the room.

Chapter 12

Rayne

The rest of the day was spent studying with Laynie. We quizzed each other at least twenty times, and I felt confident about our test in two weeks. I'm exhausted beyond belief and ready to go to bed. Walking into my room, I get hit with citrus, making me feel dizzy. Leaning against my bedroom door, I breathe it in. My room smells just like Christian, and all it makes me want to do is touch him.

Huffing, I change out of my dress from earlier and get ready for bed. My body betrays me when it involuntarily stops at my window. His lights are on, but I don't see him. Deciding not to stand there like some creep, I lay down.

For five minutes, I just lay there, staring at the ceiling, letting my mind wander. The little teasing act I did earlier today got me all worked up, and I need some sort of release. All it took was one taste of him, and I'm addicted. I want his rough hands on my body and his lips on mine.

Interrupting my thoughts is a feminine giggle outside my window. Curiosity getting the best of me, I get up to see where it's coming from. *I swear if Ryker is outside putting the moves on his flavor of the week, I'm going to throw up.* I can't keep count of how many girls he goes through. I can't even be mad at him, though, because he tells them he isn't a relationship type of guy, but they each think they will be the one to change his player ways. It always ends the same: heartbreak; or a really pissed-off chick.

At the window, my heart nearly stops, and my legs almost give out from under me. Ryker isn't outside with a girl... Christian is. They are leaning against his Mustang, and his broad back is all I see. She is giggling at something he said, with her hand around his bicep.

I'm frozen, watching their interaction as my blood boils. She is beautiful with long dark red hair and a dancer's body. Seeing her wrap her dainty fingers around Christian's arm makes me want to break every one of them. The girl has done nothing wrong; she is just caught in the crossfire.

How can he go from making out with me on the couch and grinding into me earlier today to being with another girl outside his house where I'm sure he knows I would witness it? This beauty looks a little older than Christian. She is probably way more experienced than I am. Is that what this is about? I'm too inexperienced for him? Would he rather be with someone like her? *Oh. God. What is happening to me?* I have never been insecure in my life, yet here I am. He brings out the worst in me and might just be my biggest downfall.

He walks her to her car and opens her door. *What a gentleman. (insert eye roll here).* She pauses, looking at him, putting the ball in his court to see if he will make a move or not. I feel sick. I don't want to look, but I can't pull my eyes away. He leans in; I hold my breath. He only hugs her; I breathe a sigh of relief.

He waits for her to drive off before turning around and walking toward his house. Sensing me, he looked up at my window, catching me before I even had the chance to move. He stops dead in his tracks. His eyes widen in guilt. I stare at him for a few seconds, eyes glistening, and nod once before turning around and returning to bed.

I can't believe I'm on the verge of crying again. How can

someone make you feel like you're floating one minute but don't exist the next? In those moments where it's just us, I feel important, and cherished even. He touches me like he wants to explore every surface of my skin; then, there are those moments where he closes himself off, and he can't even look at me.

If I'm not enough, then that's his problem. He is clearly moving on from whatever this is, and I should, too. He has made it clear that regardless of this attraction we share, it can never be anything more. *What would Laynie Mae do?*

Smiling, I grab my phone off my nightstand.

Me: Hey, it's Rayne (:

Text bubbles appear as my heart accelerates. *Ugh, why am I nervous?*

Tyler: Hey stranger... I was starting to think I gave you the wrong number.

Me: Nope, you gave me the correct number. Sorry it took me so long to text you.

Tyler: It's okay I'm just glad you did (:

Me: Me too!

Tyler: Anything planned this weekend?

Me: Not at the moment. What about you?

Tyler: I have a date this weekend, and the girl is out of my league! I need all the luck I can get, so I don't mess this up.

Me: Oh, a date?

Tyler: Yeah, are you free?

Wait, is he?

Me: Tyler... Are you asking me out?

Tyler: If I say yes, will you?

Me: Yes (:

Tyler: It's a date!

I'm extremely nervous. I have been preoccupied with Christian that I didn't think about the possibility of anyone else. He is the first guy I have met that I was instantly drawn to. It's as if invisible ropes were intertwining us, tethering us together.

From what I have seen, Tyler is a nice guy and cute. Yes, I may not have a magnetic pull with him, but that could change if I just moved on from Christian and gave him a chance.

Unlike Christian, Tyler is upfront with me; for instance, he wanted me to text him, so he gave me his number. He wanted to take me on a date, so he asked. I like that about him. He isn't scared to go after what he wants, which is the type of guy I want. Not someone who will touch, kiss, tease, and convince me to trust him, only to reject me in the end. *It's time to move on, and going out with Tyler this weekend is the perfect way to do it.*

Chapter 13

Rayne

All week has been nothing but prepping for finals, and I'm over it. If I have to go over the four states of matter one more time, I might just bang my head into the desk.

Tomorrow I'll be going on my first date, and I'm on edge. What if we have nothing to talk about? Our date is awkward as hell, and we have nothing in common, or he tries to kiss me? Do I kiss him? Am I even ready for that? Ugh, so many questions that I don't have the answers for.

My after-school class is over, so I'm putting away my books that I won't need this weekend when my locker door gets slammed. Startled, I shriek, and my eyes shift, landing on Jackson. A gasp flies from my mouth at what I see. His left eye is damn near swollen shut, and a deep cut engraves his bottom lip, making it completely busted. His nose is bruised, split, and almost looks broken. I'm met with his icy glare and am immediately thrown back to Saturday night in the pool house. His eyes are just as cold and distant, causing the hairs on my arms to rise as I stand frozen in place by fear.

"Jackson! W... What happened?"

"Don't act like you don't fucking know what happened!"

he shouts, and I flinch in response to his raised voice and anger.

"I... I don't know what you're talking about."

"Stop. Fucking. Lying!" he screams, slamming his hand against my locker.

"Please calm down!"

"Don't tell me to fucking calm down. Look at my face! I can't even play at the next game because of *you*! You wanted me, and you fucking know it. Why did you have to run and tell your friends something different?"

What? I didn't tell my friends anything. I lift my chin, attempting not to cower.

"I didn't run and tell my friends anything. They saw me running out of your pool house! And something *did* happen! You have it in that sick fucking head of yours that I want you." I poke him in the chest. "And you would not take no for an answer! I was too scared even to speak that night, let alone move, but I won't be afraid of you anymore. Get this through that thick head of yours. I. Do. Not. Want. You. I never did! So, leave me the fuck alone, and don't ever put your hands on me again!"

Unfazed, Jackson maniacally laughs. "Or what? What is sweet little Rayne Davis going to do? Nothing, you scared little bitch!" He steps toward me, backing me into my locker, and rests his hands behind me, caging me in. "Listen to me and listen good. You will regret this. I'll sit and wait for the perfect time you'll never see coming. I'm going to drive you mad. You will be terrified watching over your shoulder every day, not knowing where or when I'll be there, but remember this... I'll always be there." He leans only centimeters from my face, forcing me to turn my head away from him. "This isn't a threat. It's a fucking promise," He whispers, his tone cold, sending chills down my spine.

I close my eyes, trying to get my breathing under control. When I open them, Jackson is gone, and I'm left alone in the school hall, on the verge of tears. I have no idea what to do. Should I tell Ryker? No, I can't do that because I don't want him involved. He still doesn't know exactly what happened, and if he finds out, he will kill him. I couldn't live with myself if something happened to him because of me.

I can't tell anyone about this. It is my problem to fix. I wouldn't be in this mess in the first place if I didn't get drunk and end up alone with Jackson. I've succeeded at avoiding him all week, but that doesn't matter now because he found me, and everything is far worse than I could've imagined. What is Jackson planning on doing to me? I believe in his threats, and whatever he has planned will not be good. He's already in my head.

I'm shaking with nerves. Tyler will be here any minute to pick me up, and I feel like I might vomit. I'm looking at myself in the mirror for the hundredth time, contemplating if I should change or not. I'm not sure what Tyler has planned for our date, so I dress casually in jeans and a bodysuit. My hair is braided, and I wear only a touch of makeup.

Vzzzt.

Vzzzt.

Vzzzt.

My phone vibrates on my vanity, and I quickly rush to grab it.

"Laynie Mae."

"Rayne Davis, long time no talk."

"We talked last night," I say, laughing.

"And here I thought you forgot all about me."

"Never."

"Promise?"

"Always."

"I'm just calling to check on you. Knowing you, you're probably freaking out for no reason." I walk back over to my

Chapter thirteen 151

mirror.

"You know me so well," I say, looking at my ass.

"I'm going to switch over to FaceTime. Let me see what you're wearing."

"I've been looking at myself for the last thirty-five minutes, debating if I should change or not," I say, angling the camera down so she can fully see my outfit.

"No! Don't change. You look perfect. Tyler is going to be in awe when he sees you!"

"You think so?" I question, more at ease with my outfit choice.

"Yes! Trust me. You're gorgeous."

"Thank you, Laynie Mae."

"You're welcome, babe. Have fun tonight, okay? Try not to be so in your head. Go with the flow and enjoy yourself. Text me your location, so I know where you're at."

"Sending it now," I say as my doorbell rings, and my steady heart starts to beat rapidly. "Tyler is here. I got to go! I'll text you later. Love you!"

"Ditto, babe! Don't do anything I wouldn't," she says, smirking at me.

Grinning, I say, "That isn't much."

"Exactly! Now go answer the door." she blows me a kiss and hangs up.

I take a deep breath with one last glance over at the mirror. Descending the stairs, my dad opens the front door, giving me a clear view of Tyler. He looks really good, like mouth-watering good! His eyes connect with mine before sweeping over my body in approval. My dad notices, clearing his throat, and Tyler quickly averts his eyes.

"Hello, sir, I'm Tyler" he holds out his hand. My dad stands, arms crossed. This being a date, my dad wasn't thrilled about it. After some convincing from my mom, he eventually agreed.

After a moment of awkward silence, he gruffs and takes it. "I'm Jack Davis. I can't say if it's nice to meet you or not because that depends entirely on how this date with my daughter goes." He drops his hand, returning to his crossed arms stance, and Tyler shifts uncomfortably on his feet.

"I can assure you Rayne is in great hands."

I smile at him, giving my dad a quick peck on the cheek, "Bye, pops, I'll see you later!" I hurry onto the front porch, joining Tyler.

"Not so fast." I pause, turning around, but he's looking at Tyler. "She is to be home by ten tonight, not a minute later."

Tyler gulps, nodding his head. "Ten. Got it."

My dad gives a curt nod, then looks at me. "You are beautiful, baby girl. Have fun."

"I will. Love you."

"He's right, you know?"

"What do you mean?"

"You are beautiful."

"Oh…" I flush, "thank you."

We continue toward his car, but I stop short, spotting Christian to my left.

He is out front in his driveway, shirtless, working on his car. His chiseled and sun-kissed stomach glistens with sweat, and my fingers involuntarily twitch, begging to touch him. I follow his sculpted abs that lead to his deep V. Naturally licking my bottom lip as I take in his grease-stained denim jeans tightly wrapped around his muscular thighs. His white Calvin Klein's are peaking out of denim that hangs dangerously low on his hips, making me ache to see what lies underneath. The sight of him ignited something low in my stomach, a fluttering spreading to my chest.

Then he turned, and his eyes found mine immediately, as if he was drawn to me. His golden eyes widened before darkening into a beautiful shade of whiskey as he trailed my body, gently brushing his bottom lip with his tongue. I can feel his gaze searing into my skin, causing me to feel hot all over. He brings his eyes back to mine, and they hold such an intensity that he is speaking to me without having to say a word. We are practically stripping each other naked, and I can only imagine all the dirty things going through his mind. He likes what he sees just as much as I do.

"Did you hear me?" Tyler says, placing his hand on my shoulder, bringing my attention back to him.

Shit! I was under his spell again. In our little bubble that we seem to live in whenever we are in each other's presence, I became completely unaware of Tyler. He is the guy I need to be focusing on! Tyler looks good but not Christian good. Damn it. Now I'm comparing them. This is so messed up! He crawled his way in without me even noticing, apparently having some vice-like grip on my heart and mind.

I can't think when he is near. He must have been lost in the moment with me, because he didn't see Tyler standing beside me. I can tell the exact moment he notices him because his expression and demeanor instantly change. He went from looking like he wanted to rip my clothes off me to wanting to rip Tyler's head off instead. Christian clenches his hands into a fist, his knuckles white, looking as if they are about to burst through his skin. The tick in his jaw was prominent.

Shaking my head, snapping myself out of my ogle fest, I bring my attention back to Tyler.

"Sorry, I spaced out for a second. What did you say?"

"I said you're cute when you're nervous. You don't need to be nervous around me."

Tyler is sweet, and he should be the one holding my attention, not the boy next door. Turning to face him fully, I place my hand in his.

"Thank you, you're right. I don't need to be nervous around you. You're awfully cute when you're being sweet," I say, looking down at our interlocked fingers.

"You ready to get out of here?" I nod, and we hold hands as we walk to his car.

Before opening my door, he pulls me into a hug, and I lock eyes with Christian over his shoulder. His chest is rising and falling at a rapid pace as he takes a step toward us. My eyes widen. He stops dead in his tracks, his nostrils flaring as he pierces me with a ruthless glare. Tyler's hands move to my hips, and I swear Christian stops breathing.

"Thank you for going out with me tonight."

"Thank you for taking me out tonight." I look back to Christian as I place my hand on Tyler's bicep the same way the redhead previously did to him.

Christian's eyes narrow at the contact as he clenches his jaw. He takes another step toward us, his chest heaving, our gaze fixed on each other, but then he stops and shuts his eyes, letting out a deep exhale. Then he turns around, slams the hood of his car shut, and stalks off.

Tyler looks over his shoulder. "Do you know him?"

Shit! "Yeah, he is my brother, Ryker's friend."

"Is there anything going on between the two of you?"

I chuckle nervously, "Why would you ask that?"

"He looked like he wanted to wring my neck."

"He seems to be moody these days. Pay no attention to him."

"Noted," he says, opening my door.

What the hell was that about? For a second, I thought Christian would come over to us, which would have been very awkward. Why did he seem so pissed off? He was just with another girl. He can be with someone, but I can't. He is out of his damn mind, if that's what he thinks.

Chapter 14

Rayne

I'm having a fantastic time on our date. He is the perfect gentlemen, opening doors for me, attentive, flirty, funny, and conversation is easy. As the sun sets, we walk with our hands intertwined along the Santa Monica pier.

"Want to play a game?" he juts his chin toward a game called roll a ball.

"It wouldn't be like me to back down from a challenge."

"Let's make this interesting, shall we?" I arch my brow at him, fully aware of what I'm getting myself into.

"Define interesting."

"Let's make a bet. Whoever wins gets to choose a dare for the other person to do."

"Sure… why not?" he smiles at me, walking over to roll a ball.

"Welcome to roll a ball, folks!" the worker greets us with enthusiasm. Tyler holds up his arm to show her our unlimited ride and game wristbands. Smiling, I hold up mine too. "Alright, lovebirds, the object of the game is to roll the balls into the holes!"

"Ready, love bird?" I wink.

"Ready, baby."

The whistle blows, signaling the game has started. I grab onto a ball and roll it straight into a hole. Yes! I grab another, pushing it forward, but miss my target. Quickly looking up, I see my horse in the lead, but not by much. Catching another ball, I slide it into my target.

"He is hot on your tail, sweetheart." The announcer says. I look over at Tyler. A smile teases his lips, his focus on the game. He grabs two balls at a time and rolls them, making double the points.

I steal his technique and grab two balls, rolling them both. I make one but miss the other. I reach for another ball, moving it just as the bells ring, announcing we have a winner. Looking up, I see he crossed the finish line before I did, making him the winner of this game and the bet. Pouting my bottom lip, I look at him.

"Aww, don't be sad, baby."

"I totally thought I was going to win!"

"What can I say?" he holds up his arms.

"Wanna know what I think?"

"Absolutely," he smirks, putting his hands in his front pockets.

"First, it was beer pong, then this," I gesture my hands to the game we just played. "I think you're really good at playing with balls." His jaw drops, and his eyes expand.

For a second, I feel nervous, thinking maybe I took it too far with my joke, but then he throws his head back and laughs. A full belly chuckle that makes me smile.

I like the sound of it.

"Want to get some ice cream?" he asks, after picking a light pink elephant as his prize and giving it to me.

"First, winning me a prize and now, offering me ice cream. You sure know the way to my heart." I watch his throat as he swallows; a light blush graces his cheeks. He looks at me for a moment as if he wants to say something but doesn't. He takes my hand instead.

We eat ice cream as we walk to the end of the pier, watching the sun that falls just below the horizon. The sky looks majestic. It's a conflagration of yellow, orange, and red. Something about sunsets brings me peace. Life is so full of distractions, but as I stand here looking at the natural beauty earth offers, I have none.

"So beautiful." I sigh.

"Yes, you are."

"Smooth… real smooth," I giggle.

"It was kind of cheesy, but it doesn't make it any less true."

"I think I owe you a dare."

"That's right," he taps his finger against his chin. "I dare you too…" he pauses, and I hold my breath in anticipation. "Eat the rest of your ice cream in one bite."

"I have almost a full bowl left. How do you expect me to do that?"

"A dare is a dare." I scoop up the remaining ice cream in my bowl.

"Here goes nothing," I say before shoving it into my mouth. My cheeks are stuffed full, and I have to breathe through my nose. I know I must look ridiculous.

Tyler puffs his cheeks out, mimicking me, making me lose it! I laugh hard as ice cream drips down my chin and onto the floor, causing him to double over in a fit of laughter.

"No fair, I had that, you cheater!" I push him lightly.

"I guess we'll never know," he puffs his cheeks again.

"Har-har," I say as he hands me an extra napkin.

"All better?" I smile, and he stifles a laugh. "What?"

"You're just very cute," he takes a step closer. "You also missed a little." I pause, looking at him as he wipes off the ice cream I missed from my face. The simple touch makes me smile. I can't get over how sweet he is.

I was shocked at his dare. I was sure he was going to dare me to kiss him. The fact he didn't do such a cliché dare makes me respect and appreciate him so much more.

Tonight has been a perfect date, and I feel foolish for being nervous about it. He has done nothing but treat me with respect. He has been patient and kind in every sense of the word. My eyes fall to his lips, making him pause his movement, and he swallows. Without stopping to consider, I put my hands on his chest and kiss him.

His eyes widen in shock before slowly closing. The kiss is gentle and nice, the complete contrast of urgent. He slowly opens his mouth, and I follow his movement. His tongue tenderly sweeps along mine in a slow dance. As we kiss, I wait for the tingles that reach my toes, the spark that ignites my bones, and a magnetic force that brings me to my knees. When it never comes, I can't help the disappointment I feel. It has nothing to do with Tyler and everything to do with me. I'm searching for a familiar feeling that I'm aware of thanks to Christian. *Here I am, thinking of Christian as Tyler kisses me. No, no, no, this is all wrong.*

Placing my hand on his chest, I push away. "Stop. I can't." He looks taken aback and hurt. The hurt I see clearly on his face makes me want to cry. "I'm sorry Tyler." I look down, wiping under my eyes. "I'm confused."

He wraps his arms around my shoulders, and I can't hold my tears back anymore. I cry.

"Let's get you home, okay?"

"Okay," I sniffle.

The drive back to my house is filled with awkward silence. I feel like a horrible person for unintentionally playing with his emotions like that. *I don't even recognize myself right now.* I stare out the window the entire drive home, unable to look in his direction. He puts the car in park when we get to my house, but neither of us moves as the car idles.

Unbuckling my seatbelt, I turn to face him. "Tyler... I don't know what to say. Anything I say will sound like an excuse, so the least I can do is be honest with you." I fiddle with my fingernails. I'm aware of him looking at me, but I don't meet his eyes. "Let me start with you did nothing wrong, absolutely nothing. You're good to me, and I have had so much fun with you, so if you think you did something, I promise you didn't."

"Hey, yes, it sucks how the night ended, but I had no expectations going out with you tonight. I still enjoyed every minute of our time together, Rayne." With his thumb, he brushes a tear that escaped. "I can't compete for your heart when it already belongs to someone else," he smiles sadly, leans over the console, and hugs me. "If it's any consolation, from what I saw, you aren't the only one who is feeling screwed up. He is too." Sniffling, I squeeze him a little tighter.

"Thank you, Tyler," I whisper.

"You don't need to thank me. We can still be friends, and you can call me Ty," he pulls back, smiling at me.

"Ty." I smile, repeating his nickname.

"Thank you for today. Don't be a stranger. Call or text me anytime, alright?"

"No, thank you for everything. We will talk soon."

He gives me a small wave, driving off into the night as I stand there watching his taillights until they become nothing but a distant memory.

Chapter 15

Rayne

It has been one hell of a week, and I'm exhausted in every way imaginable. After my date with Tyler, the realization that Christian has a tighter hold on me than I like to admit is exhausting. Thankfully, I haven't seen him since my date last week. He didn't come to Sunday breakfast, which made me feel disappointed and relieved. If I want to move forward and away from his grip on me, he's right. It's best if we keep our distance.

In order to keep Christian out of my head, I've been keeping myself busy, and my mind occupied with studying and homework. Mostly it's working. I don't think about him as often when I'm constantly focusing on other things, but nights seem to be the hardest for me when I'm in my room late at night, knowing Christian is just across the way. My mind runs wild with things that have happened and the possibilities of what could happen if he gave us a chance.

With everything going on, all I want to do is get away from here. Over breakfast on Sunday, we discussed how to celebrate my birthday this weekend on October sixteenth, and

I know the perfect place. My parent's cabin in Big Bear, California.

"**It's** *your birthday weekend, bitch!* What are we doing?" Laynie wears a smile that tells me she's up to no good.

"I can't believe I forgot to tell you; we're going up to the cabin in Big Bear. Please tell me you can come."

"Babe, do you not know me at all? I have a free schedule just for you," she grins. "Of course, I'm going. Whether you invite me or not. Who's all going?"

"The usual. Ryker, mom, dad, and you. Hopefully, Jamie can come too."

"What if your parents don't come and it's just us and… maybe a few friends?" she says with a scheming look in her eye.

"My parents would never let us go to the cabin alone."

"Ryker is eighteen. What if we can convince them? You've been so stressed out lately. What if you tell them you don't feel like doing much and want to have some girl time?" she air quotes. "Ryker can drive us, and we will be back Sunday in time for a family brunch."

"Hm, I don't know if they'd go for that. Who would we invite anyway? I don't have the biggest group of friends."

"Leave the party guest to me," she pats my shoulder. "I'll talk to Ryker. We can figure something out. You know he's a momma's boy and can get your mom on board, and once she agrees, it will be easier to convince your dad."

"I don't know if this is a good idea," I tell her as we walk over to Jamie.

"Rayne, what's the worst thing that can happen? If your parents say no, then it will only be us as planned, no big deal." She shrugs.

She can be so convincing when she wants to be.

"Okay, okay, I'm leaving the convincing to you and Ryker. I don't want any part of it."

Laynie squeals as she takes her seat at the lunch table. She tells me how excited she is and fills Jamie in on all the party details.

Jamie eagerly nods her head, telling us she needs a break from this place, anyway. I told her not to get her hopes up because Laynie still had to convince my parents to let us go alone, but Jamie says she doesn't give a shit if we are alone or not. She wouldn't miss my birthday for anything.

I smile. I may not have the most friends, but I have the only ones I need and that's what really counts.

"Let's go shopping tomorrow! I can drive once we pass our driver's test in about…" she checks the time on her phone. "Four hours. I can't wait to drive my car. She's been sitting in the driveway looking all sad and dusty."

"She?" Jamie and I question at the same time.

"Yes, my BMW is too pretty to be a he. Her name is ladybug." I almost choke on my sandwich.

"Ladybug?"

"She's red, duh, and you know I've had a weird thing for lady bugs ever since we were little."

"It's kind of perfect for you."

"I know," she winks.

As I go to take another bite of my sandwich, I stop midbite when I catch sight of Jackson on the other side of the cafeteria. My blood runs cold as he stands casually leaning against the wall, staring directly at me. Laynie is talking, but I have no idea what words are coming out of her mouth because I hear nothing, only the thumping of my heart in my ears and the blood whooshing in my veins. He smiles at me in a murderous way. The more uncomfortable I get, the more sadistic his smile becomes.

"Rayne!" Laynie says loudly, snapping me out of my paranoia.

"What?"

"Are you okay? I was talking to you and all the color drained from your face as if you've seen a ghost. You weren't listening to a thing I said." I draw my gaze to where Jackson was standing, but he's no longer there. It's as if he disappeared into thin air.

Did I imagine it? I seriously might be going crazy.

"Sorry. This sandwich and my stomach aren't mixing so well."

She looks skeptically at my barely eaten sandwich.

"I'm good. I'll stick to my apple."

Wednesday *quickly came and went.* Laynie and I passed our driver's test with an almost perfect score. We are officially license holders in the state of California, and I'm on cloud nine. All I need is to save up and get a car.

Thursday *after school,* Laynie and I are walking to her car and since she is officially a licensed driver, we both agreed she can take us to the mall to go shopping for this weekend. Technically she isn't supposed to drive with anyone under the age of twenty-five for at least six months, but Laynie, being the rule breaker she is, doesn't think it's a problem.

"Are you sure it's a good idea for me to drive with you? I don't want us getting in any trouble," I say anxiously.

"Babe, will you relax? Everything will be just fine. No one will know. Plus, I'm an excellent driver."

"I don't really have a choice, do I?"

"No. You really don't."

A rumbling engine catches our attention, and Ryker pulls his Camaro into the empty parking spot next to us.

Unbelievable.

"Going somewhere?" Ryker says, exiting the car with Christian.

"What the hell are you doing here?" Laynie crosses her arms.

"Do you think I'm going to let a brand-new driver drive with my sister... illegally, I should add?" The corner of his mouth lifts in arrogance.

My eyes meet Christians, and he quickly whips his gaze to Ryker and Laynie's standoff. I've been doing so well, not thinking about him and avoiding him at all costs. Why the hell does he have to show up with Ryker right now?

"If you think you guys are coming with us, you're crazier than I thought," Laynie says, not breaking contact with Ry.

"Do you really have a choice? You either let us come with you or I tell your parents that you were going to drive illegally with Rayne."

"Wow, I never took Ryker Davis for being a fucking snitch," she spits, clearly pissed off. He doesn't say anything; he stands there staring at her before shrugging his shoulders.

Turning around, "Get in!" she shouts over her shoulder.

He smiles smugly and I push him. "Why do you have to be such a dick, Ry?"

"You love me," he says, getting into the back seat.

"Debatable!" I turn facing Christian as he stands with his hands in his front pockets, smiling. "What are you smiling at? You think you guys showing up here is funny?" he stares at me before dragging his eyes down my body, causing goosebumps to crawl up my arms.

"No, I just think you're fucking cute when you're mad," he says before joining Ryker in the back seat.

Ugh! He is so damn frustrating!

An hour and a half later, with a shopping bag full of clothes, we reach our last store. Ryker and Christian left after following us into the first one. I guess they're tired of us going through each rack of clothes trying on option after option. Good! They shouldn't have come in the first place.

Laynie and I rake through clothing racks, picking up and putting things down. I need to find an outfit for my birthday and a new bikini for the Jacuzzi. I was shocked my parents agreed to us going to Big Bear without them. Laynie said it took them a little convincing, but they did it on two conditions: Ryker has to be with us at all times, which only seemed to annoy Laynie, and we must check in twice a day. I was already excited about this weekend, but now I can hardly wait. An entire weekend with no parents. Hell yeah! This weekend is going to be insane.

After looking around the store, we didn't find much; however, I found a sexy mauve pink spaghetti strap mini dress with diamond tassels cutting across the left side. It's a tad risqué and something I wouldn't normally wear, but it's my birthday, so why not? I also grabbed a bikini set for the Jacuzzi that was to die for.

"I'll be right back. I'm going to try this dress on," I inform Laynie, walking over to the fitting rooms.

Slipping on the dress, I can't help but smile at my reflection because it fits my body like a second skin. It shows a lot of leg, but I love it. With a pair of sparkly heels to really bring out the diamond tassels, it will be perfect.

"Do you have the dress on? I want to see it on you."

"Coming." I step out of the fitting room.

"Holy shit!" Laynie shrieks, at the same time something crashes to the floor behind her.

Turning our attention to the noise, "Shit!" Christian says, standing behind her as he takes me in.

His eyes travel from my face down my body, leaving a blazing trail with his heated gaze. I hate that I flush under his stare, and goosebumps break out amongst my skin, but what I hate the most is that I can't pull my eyes away from his no matter how much I want to.

It's such a bittersweet situation to hate how my body reacts to him, but love the way it makes me feel.

He breaks our stare, grabbing his phone that had fallen to the floor. "Yeah, I'm here. I'll let them know," he says into his phone and hangs up. He looks back at me, swallowing hard. "Um, that was Ryker. He has a customer at the shop that he needs to meet with. It's urgent. He's waiting at the car." He stands there awkwardly, running his fingers through his hair.

"We were just finishing up here. Let me change and pay for this, and then we can go."

"Okay, cool." he nods as he backs up, bumping into a rack of clothes. He turns, holding his hands up to stop the rack from rolling, then turns back, looking at me. "I'll... I'll, um, go wait out front for you guys to finish." he turns around before either of us can respond and leaves the store.

What the hell? I have never seen Christian act so nervous before.

"Hot! So hot! You had that poor man all flustered." Laynie laughs. "He couldn't even concentrate on seeing you in that dress." I ignore her comment because I don't want to go there.

"Yes, to the dress, then?"

"Fuck yes! If you don't buy it, I'll buy it for myself."

"I love this dress." I grin. "I'm buying it."

Laynie drops Ryker off back at our school so he can get his car before heading to the shop. Ryker insists Christian drives with us, dropping us both off at home.

"Love you, babe. See you tomorrow! This weekend is going to be one for the books." Laynie says, pulling up to the curb in front of my house.

"Ditto, can't wait." I give her a quick peck on the cheek.

"Thanks for the ride," Christian says, getting out of the car as I follow.

Laynie drives off, leaving us standing on the sidewalk. I shift awkwardly on my feet as Christian places his hands in his pockets. It bothers me that things have to be like this between us. I wish we could go back to talking and telling each other our secrets, but too much has happened, and I don't think we can be just friends anymore.

"Well, bye." I turn and walk away.

"Wait!" his plea stops me in my tracks, but I don't say anything.

"Can we talk?"

"No."

"But wait," he places his hand on my shoulder, and I hate the zap I feel from his touch. I freeze, and my body goes rigid.

"Can you stop doing that? Stop touching me whenever you feel like it. What is there to talk about? Will this conversation change anything between us?"

Please say yes. Tell me I'm not the only one who feels this connection between us, and it's not all in my imagination.

He looks down, running his fingers through his hair, not saying anything.

"Thought so. We have nothing to talk about."

I walk to my front door, leaving him on the sidewalk.

He lets me go.

Chapter 16

Rayne

My *birthday weekend is finally here!* The drive is about three and a half hours without traffic, so we should arrive in Big Bear around seven p.m. Ryker plays '8teen by Khalid,'. I roll my windows down, taking in the crisp air and the smell of fresh-cut grass. Our neighbors have pumpkins lining their steps, emphasizing the feeling of fall. I'm not sure when I dozed off, but I stir to the sound of Laynie and Ryker's voices.

"Can you please not act like that? You drive me mad, woman."

"Act like what, Ryker? What exactly am I acting like?"

"A jealous girlfriend."

Laynie scoffs. "I would never be your girlfriend, and I am certainly not jealous of any bimbo you decide to play with! I have plenty of options, and if I didn't, and you were the last person on earth, I'd rather be celibate."

Not sure where this conversation is heading, I stretch, slowly opening my eyes, letting them know I'm awake. I can tell they are both getting worked up, and I don't want them at each other's throats on this trip.

"How much longer till we get there?" I ask, looking between Ryker and Laynie in the back seat. His jaw is tight as Laynie gains her composure before smiling.

"We're about thirty minutes away."

Pulling up to the gas pump, Ry gets out, slamming his door. We sit in silence before I turn back in my seat and face Laynie.

"Can I ask you something and promise to be honest with me?" she closes her eyes before they open, meeting mine.

"I'll always be honest with you, even if it hurts, remember?" she holds out her pinky, and I wrap mine around it.

"What is going on between you and my brother?"

"There isn't anything going on between us," she pauses, unlocking our pinkies. "But something *did* happen."

"Okay... well, what happened?"

"The night after, you know whose party," she pauses as I shiver at the thought of that night. "I went to use the restroom, and Ryker's room was opened. I went in there to check on him because he was so upset that night."

"Did you two have sex?" I gasp.

"What the hell, Rayne? We had a moment, a heart-to-heart, I guess you can call it, and I thought... well, it doesn't really matter what I thought. Your brother is an asshole."

"Do you like him?"

"No," she quickly says... too quickly. "There isn't anything going on, okay? If there is, I promise, I'll tell you."

"Okay..."

Ryker approaches, pumping gas before getting back in the car, still pissed off, and he remains that way for the rest of the drive.

"When is Jamie going to get here?"

"She will be here first thing in the morning. She had some family things she had to deal with." Laynie replies as she steps out of the car.

"Is she okay?"

"You know how Jamie is. She never really says much when it comes to her home life."

"That's true… I worry about her sometimes." I grab my suitcase out of Ryker's trunk.

Something in my gut tells me something is going on in her household, but she never talks about it, so it's hard to know for sure.

"Me too," Laynie says.

Ryker and Laynie grab their bags, and we all walk to the cabin. He unlocks the door, and my eyes bulge. The cabin has been kept up and looks exactly how I remember it. Being here brings back memories of when I was a little girl, and I had absolutely no worries or care in the world. Life was so much simpler then.

We came out here every Christmas, just Ry, mom, dad, and I. I can't help but smile at the memory; my mom would cook a huge turkey dinner with mashed potatoes and gravy, mixed vegetables, buttered rolls, and pecan pie. We decorated our tree together and made a new ornament every year, adding it to the tree. We would play board games by the fire and sip on hot chocolate. My parents would wear a matching pajama set, and so would Ry and me. It's very cheesy, but we loved it. My mom and I would bake cookies and peel carrots, leaving them out for Santa and his reindeer.

"Wow," I gasp, taking in the cabin. Even though I haven't been here since I was ten, my parents still come out here a couple times a year to get away and enjoy some alone time. I have never seen two people so in love with each other; my mom told me the secret to a successful relationship is to never stop dating each other no matter how long you are with that person. They radiate love, and I can only dream of having a relationship like their's. A man who loves me like my dad loves my mom, to be so utterly in love with one person the way my mom is with my dad.

"It's been so long since we've been here. It feels good to be back," Ry says.

Laynie dives face-first into the gray sectional, "This place is fucking phenomenal! I don't remember it being like this."

"I'm going to head upstairs and put my things away. I call dibs on the master bedroom, since it's my birthday."

Passing the loft, I head to the master room at the very end of the hall. I open the door and sit on the edge of the king-sized bed. The huge space has high vaulted ceilings, but my favorite part is the view. The windows allow you to look at the serene lake, massive mountains, and the towering pines surrounding us.

"Get your bikini on! We're hitting the jacuzzi!" Laynie says, walking into my room with a bottle of Patron in her hand, already strutting her black and cheeky swimsuit.

"First of all, how the hell did you get into a bikini so fast, and secondly, Patron already?"

"I wore it under my clothes, and it's your birthday weekend. Of course, we're already going to start drinking. Chop, chop, Ry is already in the jacuzzi waiting for us."

"Touché, Laynie Mae." I quickly change into my new bikini, eager to start the night.

Ryker has his eyes closed as he casually leans back with both arms propped on the rim of the jacuzzi. 'When you were young by The Killers,' flowing through his Bluetooth speaker.

"Hold this for me, please?" Laynie passes me the Patron. "The party has arrived!" she shouts, hurdling over the edge and into the water, soaking Ry.

"Damn it, Laynie! This is a jacuzzi, not a god damn pool," he says, startled.

"Here, Ry, take a shot. It might loosen you up a bit," I say, stifling a laugh.

"That's a great idea, little sis," Ry says, uncorking the bottle and taking a large swig.

It feels incredible outside. The air is crisp with a slight chill. Ryker has a fire burning off to the side, its blaze coaxing my skin in warmth. The night sky is astonishing; I can see every star clear as day, way different from the skies you see in Los Angeles. Depending on where you are, the smog from the city barely allows you to see stars at all.

"Ooo, that's hot." I hiss, stepping into the hot tub.

"It feels so good, Rayne. This is exactly what I needed," Laynie says, snatching the Patron from Ryker's hand, "and this, of course," she takes a shot straight from the bottle.

"Ahh, this feels nice," I groan as my body adjusts to the hot water. "My turn," I reach, grabbing the bottle from Laynie's hand.

"Look, I know it's your birthday weekend, and all, but it's weird as fuck seeing my baby sister drinking," Ry eyes me.

"Ry, you've been drinking since you were a freshman in high school."

"Exactly, but you're not me, Rayne."

"Are you going to stop me?" I challenge.

"No, but I'm not babysitting either, so drink with caution," he warns.

"Jeez, Ryker. She's taking a shot, not downing the bottle," Laynie says, annoyed. "Take a shot, babe. It's your birthday weekend and I will be here if you need me." I look at him, gauging his reaction, but all he does is roll his eyes.

"Cheers to the two people I love most in this world!" I shout, looking between them, and take a long gulp.

"Damn little sis, I never thought you had it in you."

"I'm full of surprises."

The sliding glass door opens, and Christian walks out. *Are you kidding me? No matter how hard I try, I can never get away from him.* Why the hell is he here? Coming here was supposed to get me away from confusing feelings.

On the other hand, I can't help the little skip my heart does at the sight of him. I enjoy being around him, just not the tension it causes. My want for him intensifies whenever I'm near him, but if he can't return those feelings, it's pointless.

"What are you doing here?" Laynie blurts, "I mean... I just thought it was going to be us?" she says awkwardly, glancing at me.

"I invited him. I didn't want to be the only guy on this trip. Is there a problem with him being here?" his eyes land on me.

Yes. "Nope."

Christian walks toward us. His swimwear is simple, but somehow, he looks anything but; he looks sexier than ever. He reaches the edge of the hot tub, raising his hand behind his back and grabbing onto his shirt. The action causes his shirt to rise, showcasing his deep V lines. My throat goes dry, and I curse at myself for reacting to him.

Quickly peeling my eyes away, I knock my head back, taking another large gulp of liquor as Christian steps into the water. I squeeze my eyes shut partially from the burn of the alcohol, but mostly because I'm mentally preparing myself for spending the whole weekend near him.

I avoid Christian and pass Laynie the bottle as she suggests playing a game called Truth or Drink.

This should be fun.

She explains everyone goes around asking someone a question of their choice, and they can either answer it honestly or drink if they don't want to.

"I'm game," Ry says, rubbing his hands together.

"You start," I tell him, and his eyes immediately land on Laynie.

"Laynie bug, what is your biggest secret?" *Laynie bug?*

"First of all, don't call me Laynie bug, secondly…" she takes a drink, not answering the question.

"Ry, what's one thing you secretly want that you're too chicken shit to admit?" she counters.

"I'm not scared to admit anything."

"Bullshit," she coughs.

"Okay, okay," I say, interrupting their charade. If I didn't, they'd go back and forth for hours. "Laynie, why does Ry call you Laynie bug?" her cheeks turn a light shade of pink at my question.

"Ryker likes to give me shit for liking ladybugs, which is why he calls me Laynie bug." she rolls her eyes.

Hmm… I never heard him call her that before.

"Christian, do you currently have feelings for anyone?" Laynie asks, and I shoot her a death glare.

Why would she ask him that?

"Yes." My gaze snaps to Christian and he's already looking at me.

"Oh. Shit." Laynie mumbles, so only I can hear her.

"Hell yeah, bro! I see you've been holding out on me. How come you haven't told me about her?" Ry says. "Wait... do you have feelings for Aubree?"

"Who's Aubree?" Laynie interjects with a slightly defensive tone.

"She's this redhead from work," Ry says, unknowingly causing an ache in my chest.

So, the beautiful redhead I saw Christian with last week was Aubree. He works with her, and they spend hours together daily. Who knows how often they hang out after work? I'm so damn stupid. I feel Christian staring at me as my eyes fill with tears. I urgently wipe my eyes before my tears can fall, because I will not let him see me cry.

Christian doesn't confirm or deny anything. I knew it was a possibility he was on a date the night I saw them, but it still didn't make me feel any better about the situation.

"What is your aspiration in life?" he asks me, and I can feel all eyes on me.

I'm silent for a few seconds, thinking of my answer, avoiding looking in his direction.

Slowly looking up, peering into his golden honey eyes, I say, "To be happy."

Silence...

"Well, on that note, cheers to happiness," Laynie salutes the Patron bottle, taking a shot and breaking the awkward silence. She passes the bottle to me.

"Cheers to happiness," I drink, passing the liquor to Ry.

"To happiness and great sex," he knocks it back.

"Seriously? Ry?"

"What?" he shrugs. "I like sex. Sex makes me happy." Christian laughs, and I can't help but giggle. However, Laynie doesn't even smile.

"Cheers to whatever makes you happy," Christian says, taking a sip.

What makes you happy, Christian?

"Well, ladies and gents, it's been a great night," Laynie pauses, glancing at Ry. "With great company," she says sarcastically, "I'm beat from the drive, and we have big plans tomorrow. I need my beauty sleep."

"Goodnight, Laynie Mae."

"Night," Ryker and Christian say in unison. The rest of us relax in the hot tub listening to music and playing truth or drink for the next hour. Christian and I stopped drinking once Laynie left; however, Ry continued to drink, almost finishing the bottle himself.

"I lava you gays," Ry slurs.

"Alright, man, let's get you to bed," Christian lifts Ry's arm over his shoulder.

"Um, such an id... idiot. I miss... I mess everything up."

"What are you talking about, brother?" I ask.

"Bug," Ry says as Christian practically carries him to the sliding glass door. Bug? *What is he talking about?*

"You're going to feel like shit in the morning," Christian says.

"Do you need help with him?"

"No, I'm good. I know where his room is. I'll lay him down and set him up with some water and a trashcan."

"There is some Tylenol in the medicine cabinet in his room."

"Good call. I'll be back."

I lean back against the tub, mesmerized by the night sky. The steam from the hot tub rising and evaporating in the air. I need to go to bed, but I'm not at all tired. Being here alone in a hot tub with Christian probably isn't the best idea. The rational part of me is screaming to get to my room before he returns. However, the irrational side of me is begging me to stay. Despite how angry I am with him, it doesn't change the fact that I like how he makes me feel.

Still surveying the night sky, I hear the sliding glass door open, announcing his arrival. Great, I guess I'm staying.

Bluetooth connected.

'Imagination by Shawn Mendes,'
"You don't know it, but it's true. Can't get my mouth to say the words they wanna say to you."

Closing my eyes, I draw in a sharp breath because of the emotions this song evokes. I've listened to this song countless times when lying in bed at night thinking of my neighbor next door. Why is he playing this song right now? Out of all the songs he could have chosen, why did he choose this one? The words to this song do nothing but remind me of him. *"In my dreams, you're with me. We will be everything I want us to be...."* Do these words speak to him too? Without saying anything, Christian joins me in the hot tub sitting where Ryker once was.

I know he is looking at me; I can feel it. I always feel him everywhere, searing me with his gaze, lighting my body on fire with his closeness. I decide to ignore him because anytime I've put myself out there, it does nothing but backfire in my face, and I don't know how many more times I can take the burn.

"Can we please talk?"

Keeping my gaze above, I say, "We've been over this. There isn't anything to talk about, Christian. Nothing is going to change."

"Everything has changed," he whispers under his breath.

"Like what?"

"Everything..."

"You were just on a date last weekend! I can't do this." I rise to my feet.

"Wait! Please just hear me out," he says urgently.

"No."

"Damn it, Rayne! Would you please just listen to me?" I spin to face him.

"What do you want from me?"

"I want *you*!" he shouts. "I want you, okay?"

I'm stunned at his admission. For the first time, he admitted he wants me. I want to be excited, but how can I trust him? I'm scared to be vulnerable and get my hopes up just to have him push me away again.

"Yeah, for how long, huh? Until you get in that head of yours and change your mind?"

"Don't you see? I've wanted you the moment I laid eyes on you inside a coffee shop, and I didn't even know who you were. I tried to forget you. I tried telling myself you were just some stranger, and I'd never see you again. Then you quite literally came crashing into me with your messy bun and oversized blink 182 t-shirt, and it was game over for me. I knew then I'd never be able to forget you."

His confession causes me to lose all ability to speak. He's wanted me that long? I knew we had an undeniable attraction, but to hear him confess to it is something else entirely. My feelings that I wasn't aware of started to grow with each encounter we had. It took me a while to realize it, but when I did, that's when I knew I had to stay away from him in order to move on and save myself from this back-and-forth match we seem to always be in.

"My mom and I came here for a fresh start. It took her a long time to let go of the house after my dad died. We moved here to let go of him." He pauses, and I don't miss the crack in his voice. "Not forget about him because that isn't possible, but to move forward and start over. Then, my first day here, I met you." The saddest eyes I have ever seen search out mine. "You surprised me. I had no idea who you were, but I wanted to get to know you for some reason that I can't explain. Then I met Ryker, and he said he had a sister, and I didn't think anything of it. Moving here wasn't to find someone. A relationship was the last thing on my mind. Then you crashed into me, and I couldn't believe it was you standing in front of me. Your eyes drew me in; it was as if they could reach the depths of my soul. The more I was around you, the more you intrigued me. You are so pure, innocent, and oblivious to how fucked up life can be. Being around you is a breath of fresh air. It's as if I was suffocating these last eight years, and I could finally breathe."

His eyes filled, and a lone tear escaped from mine. I want to go to him. I want to wrap my arms around him and tell him everything will be okay. Tell him he doesn't have to suffocate anymore. I will breathe oxygen into his lungs even if I lose the ability to breathe in the process.

"I fought so hard to stay away from you, not because I wanted to hurt you or mess with your head, but because I was trying to protect you."

"From what?" my voice shakes, and I hate it.

I have never seen him so vulnerable. He's usually guarded, only allowing me to see parts of him, but right now, he's showing me everything. I want to wrap my arms around him in comfort and remove the pain, but I know he needs to do this. He deserves to tell his story, and I know it's not easy, but I deserve to hear it... I deserve the truth.

"My mom was going through her own issues with losing my dad. When she thought I was asleep, I'd hear her painfully sobbing through her bedroom door. Moments when she didn't think I was looking, I would see her happy façade crack and see the broken woman she was. I just wanted her to be happy. I didn't want to bring any of my shit to her, so I hid who I was; an angry and distraught kid. I got into trouble a lot. Whenever trouble came, I took the opportunity to fight, to release all of this built-up anger. It's how I learned to cope with life's disappointments.

"I was different, Rayne. I was a dick to everyone, and I didn't respect girls. They were just another notch on my bedpost, and I treated them like objects. You are the first person I've allowed to truly see me, not the guy who was pissed off at the world with daddy issues. I was trying to protect you from me." He pauses to look at me. "I don't want to lose you."

"Oh, Christian," I choke, my voice unrecognizable.

His words cause flutters to emerge in my stomach. He said he didn't want to lose me, which means he claims to have me already. The thing is, he does. I want to kiss him fiercely. With a kiss, I want to tell him everything I am too afraid to speak. This is all I've ever wanted, and yet I feel panicked. A part of me wants to run from him and protect my own heart. Can I trust him?

Silence overcomes us as we're both deep in thought. A million things are running through my head. The guy sitting before me, I could never imagine doing those things. When I confessed to him about what happened at Jackson's party, he was caring and patient. He was protective. Christian rubbed me tenderly, comforting me, and made me feel completely at ease. And yet he ran and abandoned me, twisting me with so much confusion.

"What do you mean, you treated girls like objects?" I nervously ask, unsure if I want to hear what he is about to tell me, but I need to know.

"I would use them. They were just a way to pass the time," he shrugs his shoulders as if washing off the memory. "I was miserable back home, and girls meant nothing to me. I would have sex with them or use them for my own personal pleasure and never talk to them again. I had rules." He pauses with a distant look in his eyes, looking lost in thought. "I never hooked up with the same girl more than once, and I never took a girl out on a date. Staying overnight with a girl after sex wasn't an option. I got what I wanted and left before they could even get dressed." He looks at me and quickly averts his shameful eyes. "When I knew a girl was interested in more than just a casual hook up, I'd lead her to believe there was a chance we could be more, and then I'd purposely invite them somewhere, knowing they'd see me with someone else."

"What?" my voice breaks. "How could you do that to someone?"

"I was fucked up, okay? There is no excuse I could give that would justify my actions. I'm ashamed of them, and I regret it every day. I hate that guy and don't want to be him anymore. I tried avoiding you because you deserve someone better than me, but I can't be around you and not want to touch you. I can't be around you and not wonder what's going on in that pretty little head of yours. All I want to do is know everything about you, Rayne."

Am I just one of his games? I can't tell what's true and what's not. I would have never imagined Christian being that kind of guy. Truthfully, I couldn't picture anyone doing such cruel things. Everything he is saying is difficult to comprehend, but I'm sure of the way I feel when I'm around him. My heart dances when his eyes meet mine, and my body vibrates when I feel him near.

I've been sheltered my whole life and being around him is freeing. When he looks at me, I feel sexy; when he holds me, I feel safe, and when I'm around him, I feel unstoppable.

"But what about Aubree?"

"I don't have feelings for Aubree. She's just a girl from work." He affectionately rubs his thumb up and down mine.

"But I saw you with her outside of your house?"

"It wasn't what you thought. That morning, you teased me at the table during breakfast." He squeezes my hand, making my stomach somersault. "I was so turned on by you and your teasing, but I was angry and frustrated with myself, so I went home and drank some vodka." Shame washes over him, but he continues. "The alcohol wasn't working, so I went to the shop to let off some steam and check who was on the schedule for the week."

"You idiot," I say.

He looks taken aback, his mouth open.

"Never drink and drive. I don't care how upset you are. You could have seriously gotten hurt or hurt someone else!" I take a deep breath, trying to calm myself down. "Promise me never to be that stupid again? I don't want anything to happen to you." He slowly nods with a particular look in his eyes that I can't read.

I wouldn't want anything to happen to him just because he's done some terrible things. He was a boy who lost his father at a young age and grew up in a town where no one took the time to get to know him. He was alone, and nobody gave him a chance. I don't want to be like those people. Looking at him, I can see nothing but remorse and regret; I believe he means everything he's telling me. I can feel his guilt and know

Chapter sixteen 183

he wants to change. Right now, Christian is showing me much more of who he was and who he wants to be than he ever has before. I refused to judge him for his past or be like the others; I decided to give him a chance.

"I'm sorry for yelling at you," I apologize, feeling guilty.

I didn't mean to yell at him, but someone needed to talk some sense into him. I don't want him ever being reckless and getting behind the wheel under the influence. If something happened to him, I couldn't bear it. If he hurt someone else, the guilt would eat him alive.

"No, you're right. I deserved it, and I was being stupid and wasn't thinking." He pulls in his bottom lip. "It's hot when you put me in my place like that." He teases, and the tension in my shoulders disappears. "Aubree was there, and she could tell I was upset. She was on her way out but could smell the alcohol on me. She insisted I go home, but I didn't listen. I continued to work on my car for hours. She questioned me repeatedly about why I was so upset. It got annoying, but I gave in and talked after a while. I didn't tell her about you, but she knew there was a girl. She wanted to follow me home to make sure I made it back safely, and that's what you saw."

Well, now I feel like a bitch for misjudging her. All she was doing was looking out for Christian, but could you blame me for thinking otherwise? Anyone with eyes would be attracted to him, and anyone who got to know him would fall for him just as quickly. This is the deepest conversation we've had, and I already care about him. My suppressed feelings finally blossoming.

I'm so screwed.

"I'm sorry for upsetting you."

"You didn't upset me, Raynie… I was upset with myself because you were right that night. I was a coward and have been for a while now, but I don't want to be a coward anymore." he pulls me into him. "Can I ask you something?"

"Of course."

"Who was that guy you went out with?" I slightly pull back, looking up at him.

"That was Tyler."

"The guy from that party? The one you played beer pong with?" I nod, surprised he remembered. His jaw hardens. "Did you kiss him?"

"Why does that matter?" I say defensively.

"It doesn't," he says through gritted teeth.

"Doesn't seem that way."

He is just now admitting his feelings to me. What was I supposed to do? Sit around and wait for someone I wasn't even sure wanted me. How could I sit around and wait for someone who did nothing but push me away?

"Did you kiss him, Rayne?"

"Yes."

Christian scoots away from me as if I burned him. "How could you? I was your first kiss, and that meant something to me. Did it not mean anything to you?"

"How could you say that? It meant everything to me until you took it back! What did you expect, Christian? You hurt me, and I was trying to move on. I—"

"Why isn't he here?"

"I... I couldn't do it. It felt wrong, and he didn't make me feel the things I felt when kissing you."

"This is all my fault. If I were honest with you about my feelings, you would have never gone on a date with him in the first place."

He's right; I wouldn't have, but there isn't any point in saying that because we both know it.

"Can we please just start over?" he pleads.

It's hard to forget everything that's happened and be so quick to jump into trusting him again, but I can at least try.

"Yeah, I'd like that."

Chapter 17

Rayne

We are lying on a thick blanket with mountains of pillows surrounding us in the living room. After being in the jacuzzi for so long, I felt like a prune and got out. I didn't want to leave Christian and go to bed, and apparently, he didn't either, because when we came inside; he started a fire. He told me to stay put and went upstairs. A few minutes later, he returned, carrying a colossal comforter, and laid it on the floor in front of the fireplace. I was about to give him crap for changing into comfy clothes, but before I could get all the words out, he smirked and handed me his black AC/DC shirt from the day I met him.

"Thanks," I smile, glancing at him lying on his back beside me.

His shirt engulfs me, stopping right above my knees. It smells like citrus and summer days and is now my new favorite scent.

"I like seeing you in my shirt," his eyes skim down my body and back up, landing on my lips before meeting my eyes.

'Electric by Alina Baraz Ft. Khalid,'
"You've got everything; you've got what I need. Touch me. You're electric, babe."

I feel my cheeks turning warm, and I already know I'm blushing. "What are you thinking about?" I ask.

"You don't want to know."

"Tell me."

He scoots closer to me and turns toward me. "I'm thinking about the night I first kissed you," his eyes roam over every part of my face, ingraining every feature into his memory, "and how I want to kiss you again."

"Kiss me then."

He cups the side of my cheek, pressing his full, soft lips against mine. Tingles shoot through my body, traveling to my toes. *This is exactly what I've been yearning for...*

Inhaling deeply, I open my mouth, gently exploring, running my tongue along his. He groans into my mouth, and my toes curl. He shifts his leg over mine, bringing himself directly above me, and spreads my legs apart just enough to slip one of his between them. I nervously run my fingertips through his hair. He growls, turning the kiss urgent, devouring my mouth, causing me to whimper. Our tongues search out the others as my hands drag up his back. The feel of his smooth skin under my hands shoots hot embers of electricity from my fingers throughout my entire body, landing as a raging fire between my legs. I had no idea something as simple as touch could ignite my soul in such a way.

He grinds into me, and I can feel his thick hardness underneath his sweats, pressing firmly back and forth against me. I draw a sharp breath, torn between unabandoned excitement and sheer terror. *I have no clue what I am doing or what he will do next...*

"Oh God," I pant, my body tensing slightly.

"You like that baby?" he asks between kisses and moans.

"Yes, Christian… God, yes!" pressing my hands into his back, I pull myself against him, trying to melt into him.

"Fuck baby." He groans.

I'm so turned on right now I can hardly think. I grab the hem of his shirt hesitantly, wanting to pull it off him. Sensing my timidness, he reaches behind his head with one hand and pulls the shirt over his head. Then immediately pulls his face back to mine, crashing our lips together. He crushes against me, his dick twitching. *Dicks twitch?* I think questioning everything.

He breaks our kiss, and I stiffen.

No. No. No. Not Again.

He's peering down at me with the flames from the fire reflecting gold in his eyes; God, he's beautiful. The wood crackles, and his gaze burns with desire.

He slowly brings his lips to mine in a delicate kiss. I relax, letting out a relieved breath. His hands touch the bottom of my shirt as he looks at me for approval. I nod. One hand holds himself above me, and the other removes my shirt.

"Fuck Rayne, you have no idea what you do to me." His eyes admire every single part of me.

"Show me," I say with a courage I didn't know I had. He kisses me slow and tender, trailing kisses to my neck. The action alone causes me to whimper in delight.

"God, I love hearing you whimper like that. I can come just at the sound," he moans, kissing above my breasts. My cheeks flame at his raw words, and I close my eyes. "Look at me." I open my eyes, doing exactly as he told me. "Don't ever hide from me." he runs his fingertips under the bikini straps on my shoulder. "Can I take these off?"

My heart pounds as I nod.

"I need to hear you say it, Raynie."

"Y... Yes," I stutter, trying to find my voice.

"We don't have to do anything you don't want to do, okay? I'm okay with only kissing, talking, or being next to you."

"No, I want to." I confidently say.

"Are you sure?"

"Yes."

Smiling, he brings the straps of my bikini down one side and then the other. Brushing my rib cage with his thumb before sliding his hand behind my slightly arching back and unhooking the clasp.

I can hear my heart thumping in my ears and my body trembles with nerves.

I can't believe this is happening.

He stares directly into my eyes while pulling my bikini top off, completely exposing my chest fully to him. My hands fist the blanket at my sides to keep from covering myself. His eyes trail down to my full breasts, and my already hard nipples harden even more at his gaze.

He wraps his mouth around my tit, twirling his tongue around my peaked nipples.

"Oh shit!" I gasp, gripping the blanket beneath me. I can't believe I'm laying here practically naked, baring myself to him. For the first time, he is taking me the way I've envisioned countless times since meeting him. I feel like this is all a dream, and the last thing I want to do is wake up.

With his mouth still wrapped around my breast, he moans, the vibration making me throb at my core.

He bites my nipple with perfect pressure, and I cry out in surprise and pleasure.

My fingers go to the back of his head, gripping it in place. He desperately kisses down my stomach, nipping at the side of my belly button before descending lower. My heart is hammering out of my chest, and desire is flooding my body and heart. He pauses, looking up through his thick lashes.

"It's okay," I say.

He slides down my legs, kissing my inner thighs, coming face to face with my bikini-clad pussy. He looks at me for acceptance before he slides my bottoms down and over my feet at a dawdling speed. Kissing his way back up, he stops to get one last reassurance from me before parting my legs.

This is so unreal. I feel so exposed, so vulnerable; this cannot be about to happen... I want to hide myself, but I don't want him to stop.

With two fingers, he opens my folds, finding my core with his soft tongue, lightly tasting my entrance before sliding it up to my clit, encircling it with his full lips and drinking in the hard little nub with a guttural moan. Without thinking, I move to pull away, and his eyes instantly move to my own. I groan deeply, nod, and relax my thighs, letting him know I want him to continue. He squeezes a hand on top of my own before releasing a hard tongue and fiery breath from his mouth and applying pressure to my sensitive clit. He flicks his tongue and gently sucks it into his mouth with a sigh of pure pleasure.

I throw my head back, my hips bucking off the blanket. "Christian," I groan loudly.

"Rayne, you taste so fucking good," he says before diving back in, lapping me with his tongue.

He wraps his hands around my thighs, grabbing my hips, bringing my ass back down to hold me in place.

"Do you like that?"

Whimpering a barely audible "yes." is the only word I can form.

He holds me in place, using one hand as the other kneads my breast and my body trembles as a tightness forms in my sex.

"Come for me," he growls.

His next move sends me over the edge. My body ignites with heat, tingles covering every inch of my skin. My pussy is extremely sensitive as it pulsates, and my legs shake. I lay there panting, my chest rising and falling as I try to catch my breath. I dazedly look at Christian; he beams at me, showing me his perfect smile before using the back of his hand to wipe my juices off his mouth and chin.

"That was... wow."

"I know," he chuckles, kissing my forehead.

My body is completely relaxed. I feel like I'm levitating as I come down from my euphoric state. Suddenly, I feel drained. I see Christian adjust himself, evidently still very hard, and I frown.

"What's going on in that pretty little head of yours?" he brushes my hair behind my ear.

"What about you?" I ask shyly, and he smiles.

"Not tonight. This was for you."

I smile, closing my eyes, exhaustion taking over me. I am too fatigued and can't even argue in such a blissful state. Christian cradles me in his arms, but I'm too tired to respond. I don't know how much time has passed, but I feel him gently place me in my bed, tucking me in.

"Sweet dreams, Raynie," he whispers before the darkness takes over and everything fades to black.

Chapter 18

Christian

The following morning, as I lay in bed, a light gust of wind seeps through my window, hitting my bareback. I hadn't gotten much sleep after my night with Rayne. It was better than anything I could have ever imagined. She is so fucking beautiful, and she is entirely unaware of it. Finally, telling her how I feel has lifted an immense weight off my chest. It wasn't easy to do, but seeing her with Tyler... the thought of losing her... I didn't expect things to progress as they did, but I wouldn't take any of it back. I've already made that mistake, and I promised her never to do it again.

Still, I can't fathom how I got so damn lucky to have her. I didn't expect her to forgive or trust me, but she did, and I'm not even surprised. She is good, and I don't deserve her. I've treated girls shitty, with no regard for their feelings, but with Rayne, it is different. I care about what she's thinking and how she feels. She looked breathtaking, lying beneath me, bared to me, completely vulnerable. Her trusting me that much means more to me than she will ever know.

She tasted as sweet as forbidden fruit—something I knew I shouldn't have, something my entire body craved. It was the hardest I have ever been. Last night, I took a cold shower, relieving myself at the thought of how she looked falling apart when she climaxed. Watching her reach her peak almost sent me over the edge.

    Like I said to her, last night wasn't about me; it was only about her. The last time she opened up to me that way, I stopped it, knowing it would hurt her. Most girls I've been with would get off whenever we fooled around, but I wasn't trying to. I didn't give a shit if they came; this was my way of showing her I'm in it for real, my way of showing her she deserves to be cherished and desired; this was me putting her needs before my own.

    I roll out of bed, stretching on my way to the bathroom to clean up before heading downstairs. Rayne and Laynie's door is wide open, so I assume they're already up. Ryker's door is shut, which I'm not surprised about; It would be shocking if he were awake right now. With the amount he drank last night, he will definitely feel it when he wakes up. I've been there and done that more times than I'd like to admit. I'm not sure what was going on with him last night, but I think I have an idea.

    Heading down the stairs, I can hear mumbled voices coming from the kitchen. I step off the last set of stairs and see Laynie sitting at the kitchen island as Rayne pours herself a cup of coffee. She hasn't noticed me approaching, and I take the time to admire her. She is wearing a black cropped top with tight black jeans, a gold chain belt, her signature Doc martens, and a long loose fitting beige cardigan. Her usual wavy hair is straight, making it appear longer than usual. She's. Fucking. Perfect.

    "Good morning, Raynie," she takes a sip of her coffee, eyes slightly rising in surprise behind her cup. "Good morning, Laynie." I smile at her as I walk toward Rayne.

    "Morning," Laynie says, giving me an extra-wide smile.

    Setting her coffee cup down, she says, "Good morning," and smiles shyly as she nervously fidgets with her fingers. "Coffee?"

A few hours ago, she was lying naked as I was between her thighs, and now she's nervous.

"Yes, please," I smirk.

She quickly turns to the cabinet, grabbing me a cup.

"How did you sleep?" Laynie asks, grinning at me.

"I slept great."

Her eyes move to Rayne and I follow. Rayne is shaking her head at Laynie with eyes wide. She catches me looking at her and masks her warning with a smile, as if I didn't just see her.

"Cream?" she asks, pouring coffee into my cup.

"Just a dash, please."

Laynie gags, "Might as well drink your coffee black." I chuckle. Sounds like someone else I know.

"That's the only way it works for me." I take a sip. "It's perfect, thank you."

"You're welcome."

The room fills with awkward silence. Laynie eyes Rayne and me. Rayne was again fidgeting with her fingers, avoiding looking in my direction. *What is going on with her?*

"Can I talk to you for a minute?"

"O... Okay."

With a slight nod, I set my cup of coffee on the island, walk to the sliding glass door, and wait for Rayne to pass through. Laynie stares at us, and Rayne stares at her feet, walking into the backyard.

I follow behind her, closing the sliding door behind me. "What's going on with you?"

"What do you mean?" she murmurs, her voice barely audible.

"Did I do something? You're acting," I pause, taking her hand in mine. "You're acting differently? Do you regret what we did last night?"

Her eyes focused on our hands, snap to me. "What? No, of course, I don't. It was everything, Christian. I'm just confused."

My stomach drops. Is she confused about me? About her feelings for me? Did I wait too long to tell her how I truly felt?

"What's going on in that pretty little head of yours? What are you confused about?" I gently kiss her on the forehead.

She leans into me, letting out a sigh. "I just don't know how to act around you."

Thank God it's nothing serious. I'm not used to caring so much. If she were any other girl, I wouldn't give a shit.

"Just be yourself. Be you. I like you just the way you are, and I never expect you to be anything else."

"Are we going to tell Ry? What about my dad?"

"Relax, Raynie." I rub my hands up and down her arms. "I was thinking we can just keep it between us for now, though."

She urgently moves away from me, stung by my words. "You want to keep us a secret?"

"Of course not!" I quickly grab her hand. "Of course. I don't want to keep us a secret. I plan on telling Jack when we get back. I'm not sure how I'm going to tell him, but I will." I look down at our hands, brushing my thumb along hers.

"And Ry?"

"I will tell him first. I just want to wait till after your birthday if that's okay? He asked me if we had anything going on between us, and I told him no."

Her eyes widen. "When did he ask you that?"

"The night of that fuck boy's party," I say, pissed at just the thought of him. "I told Ryker no, and now I have to tell him yes. I don't know how he will handle it, which is why I think we should wait till after your birthday."

"Yeah, I think you're right. I told Laynie about us," she tells me nervously, "but she won't say anything," she quickly adds.

Smirking, I wrap my arms around her shoulders, pulling her into a hug. "I kind of figured that," I chuckle. "I don't expect you to keep things from the people you care about.

Oh, and I almost forgot." I say as she leans back, looking up at me.

I brush a strand of her hair behind her ear before cradling the side of her rosy cheek.

"Happy birthday, Raynie," I whisper, kissing her on the corner of her mouth.

"Best birthday ever," she grins.

We walk back into the kitchen as Ryker walks in, looking like he was coming down from a binger.

"Good morning, bro. I've never seen you look so good."

Laynie looks up from her phone, and Rayne giggles as Ryker flips me the bird and sits next to Laynie on the island.

"Remind me never to drink again." He groans with his eyes closed.

"It's not like you'd listen," Laynie mumbles under her breath. When the doorbell rings, he holds his head and groans again. "I'll get it! It's Jamie," Laynie says, walking to the door.

A few minutes later, Jamie walks in with a backpack and a square box in her hands. Rayne squeals, running to her.

"I'm so glad you're here!" she grabs the box, sets it on the counter then turns to hug her friend.

Jamie laughs and embraces her, telling her she didn't make the cake herself because she isn't crafty enough for shit like that. They stand around talking about how they will get ready and what the plan is for tonight before heading upstairs so Jamie can get settled in.

Laynie stays behind, letting them know she will be up in a minute. She goes to the fridge, pulls out a water bottle, then walks into the pantry and comes out with a liquid IV packet. She pours the packet into the water bottle and gives it a shake, setting the bottle next to Ry.

"Here, drink this. It will help you feel better," she says, walking away, not waiting for him to respond.

He looks to the water bottle, then to the stairs where Laynie just was, and stares long after she's gone.

"You gonna stare at the stairs all day, or are you going to drink your water?" he whips his gaze away from the stairs as if he didn't realize he was staring.

"I don't know if I should drink this," he examines the bottle. "What if she poisoned it?" I laugh, throwing my head back.

"Just drink the damn water, will ya? I have a feeling tonight is going to be a long one."

Ryker grunts in response, and I laugh.

○ ○ ○

The girls have been in Rayne's room most of the day. I don't know what the hell takes girls so long to get ready, but I'm glad Rayne has her friends here, and she's having a good time. Getting dressed for me was quick. I have on a black blink 182 t-shirt, a denim jacket, and jeans that I bought shortly after meeting Rayne. She had that much effect on me that I bought a shirt because it reminded me of her, and I knew she'd like it. *God. What the fuck is happening to me?* I decided wearing layers was the best idea because it's fucking cold out here, and I don't want my balls shriveled all night.

I'm sitting back on the sectional when Ry walks in carrying a twelve-pack of IPA in one hand and a black bag in another.

"I come with gifts."

"What's in the bag?"

"Tequila." he shivers. "Man, just thinking about tequila makes me want to throw up."

"You staying away from the hard stuff tonight?" I smirk.

"What? Mama didn't raise no bitch. I'm drinking the hard stuff tonight. It's Rayne's birthday." I throw my head back and laugh. I swear he is something else. Coolest dude I know, but the shit that comes out of his mouth sometimes. He chuckles, grabbing a beer and handing me one.

"How did you get this shit, anyway?" I pop the cap off with my teeth.

"Let's just say the lady behind the counter liked what she saw." Biting down my smile, I roll my eyes.

"The lady behind the counter must have no taste," Laynie says from the stairs behind us.

Ryker turns around to face her, and his eyes nearly pop out of his head. Laynie and Jamie descend the stairs, and I draw a sharp breath and stare, awe-stricken. My reaction isn't to Laynie; it's who has my attention behind her—Rayne.

She looks fucking breathtaking wearing the same light pink dress with diamond tassels running up the side of her hip. My dick stirs awake, liking what I see. *Down, boy,* I remind the man downstairs. It's the same dress I saw her trying on the other day at the mall. I wasn't sure if she would get it, but holy fuck!

As she walks down the stairs, confidence radiating from her, I sit completely captivated.

"Aren't you guys going to be cold?" Ryker asks, taking me out of my hypnotic state.

"Not this again," Rayne says, rolling her eyes.

"I'm sure if I get cold, I will find someone to warm me up." Laynie smiles mischievously, and Ryker's jaw clamps shut.

"Happy birthday, sis."

She takes the bag and hugs him. "Thanks, big brother."

In the kitchen, Rayne grabs a shot glass for each of us, and then pops the cork, filling each of our glasses to the brim. Laynie raises her glass to the ceiling, and we all follow.

"Here's to love, here's to honor. If you can't come in her, come on her."

Ryker is in the middle of his shot when the clear liquid spills from his mouth as he chokes, realizing what she said.

"What the hell, Laynie?"

Laynie responds with a shrug, and we take our shot. It goes down smoothly, and I hardly notice the burn. Once upon a time, I looked forward to it. Rayne is the only one who scrunches her face and shivers at the taste. *So damn cute.*

"Uber's here!" Laynie shouts, grabbing the bandana stuffed in her bra. "This is for you." she smiles, turning Rayne around and covering her eyes.

"What's this for?" Rayne nervously asks.

"It's a surprise," Laynie grins, guiding Rayne as we all walk to the Uber.

"Would any of you want to connect your phone and play some music?" the driver asks as we pile in.

"Absolutely! thanks, man," Ryker says, connecting his phone. 'The Pursuit Of Happiness by Kid Cudi blares through the car.

"I'm nervous," Rayne whispers, leaning into me so I can hear her.

"Don't be." I take her hand, looking to make sure no one can see. "I'm right here." She smiles, and all I want to do is kiss her. I lay her hand over my beating heart and lean in, whispering in her ear, "Do you feel that?"

She draws in a sharp breath, and her whole body shivers.

"I do that to you?" she whispers, her hand steady over my pounding heart.

"Only you."

She grabs my hand, placing it over her chest. "Only you."

Her heart thumps, mimicking my own, and the action only causes my heart to beat faster. She removes my hand from her chest but hangs onto it, resting it on her lap.

"How much longer?" Rayne asks.

"Patience, sis, we will be there soon."

Ryker told me all about his and Laynie's plan for Rayne's birthday. I've never had friends or family do something like this for me. After my dad passed, I spent my birthdays with my mom and uncle Mav. I loved it and was glad to have them, but when I was a kid, a part of me longed for a birthday party all friends would attend, or at least just one. As the years passed and I got older, I didn't care anymore. It became just another day and hopefully a step closer to getting out of that town.

"We're here bitches!" Laynie and Jamie announce.

The driver parks the Escalade, and we all pile out. I turn to grab Rayne's hand, helping her out of the car so she doesn't trip in her sky-high heels. Even with her added height, she is still shorter than me, only coming up to my shoulder. I want to keep her hand in mine, but can't because I don't want Ryker to question anything. Guilt washes over me because I'm keeping a secret from him, but I will tell him once Rayne's birthday is over and we're back home. As quickly as the guilt came, it's gone. I let go of her hand, and we follow Laynie as she guides Rayne to the front entrance.

Rayne stands in front of the door, still blindfolded, with Laynie and Ry at her side.

"Okay, babe," Laynie says, removing her blindfold. "Surprise!" she wiggles her fingers, giving her jazz hands.

Rayne giggles, her eyes adjusting. "A door?"

Laynie bounces on her feet in excitement. "Open it."

Rayne looks nervous as she turns and glances at me, and I give her a reassuring nod. Taking a deep breath, she slowly opens it.

"Surprise!" multiple people shout at once from inside the packed cabin while the lights flicker on. Rayne jumps in surprise, moon-eyed, and covers her mouth with her hands.

"Oh my God. No way!"

Ryker shouts and sings, "Happy birthday to you!" and everyone attending joins in. She stands there with her mouth open, her eyes glistening. "Happy birthday, dear Rayne. Happy birthday to you." Everyone cheers and shouts.

"Thank you, everyone!" Rayne smiles and shyly waves to the crowd. She turns to Laynie, giving her a tight hug. "How the hell did you get this many people here?"

"When you tell a bunch of people, there's a cabin in the woods for you to party at and invite everyone. It's pretty easy, babe. Ry was a lot of help too, and he even came here earlier tonight and made sure everything was set up."

"Anything for my little sister," he says, pulling her into a hug.

"Thank you, Ry."

"Alright, let's get this party fucking started!" Ryker shouts, and everyone hollers as the DJ starts the music. We squeeze our way through the cramped living room and into the kitchen. Laynie grabs a bottle from the counter, pouring us a round of shots.

"Bottoms up, baby!" she shouts, and we all shoot it. "Another one," she says right away, pouring us all another.

"You think that's a good idea?" Ryker asks.

"Tonight isn't about thinking. It's about doing."

"Fuck it," he shrugs, taking his shot, and we join him.

"Let's go dance," he shouts over the music, walks into the packed living room and jumps onto a side table. "It's my little sister's birthday; let's make some fucking noise!" he howls, and the party erupts in screams.

Rayne, Laynie, and Jamie all throw their hands up and shout, joining the wild crowd. I push through the swarm of bodies, getting closer to Ryker. The walls are vibrating from the music, blurring with the beat. Ryker hops off the table and dances in sync with the song as a girl makes her way up to him and slowly turns around. He grins at me, his eyes a little bloodshot, and grabs onto her narrow hips as she grinds on him. Rayne is between Jamie and Laynie dancing the sexiest I've ever seen anyone dance. She moves as if the music has completely taken over her body and she has lost all control. She looks at me, smiling as she slowly rolls her hips. My dick stands in salute, and I groan, adjusting myself in my pants.

This is going to be a long fucking night.

Someone bumps into my side, drifting my attention to a tiny, petite blonde. She is cute with long hair and the bluest eyes I have ever seen. Unfortunately, they have nothing on

Rayne's emerald green. Her breasts are practically spilling out of the barely there dress she wears. She flashes me a suggestive smile, a blatant invitation to dance with her. Usually, I'd be all over an opportunity like this, but things are different now. I look back at Rayne and find her eyes already on me. Laynie looks over her shoulder, eyes landing on Ryker and the chick he's currently freaking with. Her eyes narrow into a glare, and she marches over to Ry as the blonde to my right pushes up on me. I take a step back, but Rayne was already there, grabbing her shoulder and moving her out of the way.

"This one is off-limits." She growls.

Surprised, my eyes immediately head over to Ryker, but he is paying no attention to me. Instead, he's dancing with Laynie, oblivious to everything but her.

"Off limits, huh?"

The DJ switches the music to 'Just A Lil Bit by 50 Cent.' Rayne looks at me glossy-eyed and sensually bites her lip.

"Definitely off-limits." she seductively turns, placing my hands on her hips.

My body immediately reacts, and I'm instantly turned the fuck on by her territorial behavior. I squeeze her hips as she moves. Leaning back against me, she brings her arm up and wraps it around my neck. Fuck! I had no idea she could move like this. She is the sexiest thing I have ever experienced. She feels my hardness pressing into her and gives me a seductive look.

"You like what you do to me?" I whisper into her neck. Her scent, mixed with the lavender she wears, invades my senses, and has a much bigger impact on me than the liquor does.

A shade of rose tints her cheeks, and she slowly nods her head. I can't get over how confident she is one minute and how nervous and shy she gets the next. She's shielded with innocence, but her chaos is ready to burst through the seams.

She turns to look at me with lust-filled eyes. Placing her hands on my chest, she slowly drags her body down mine, looking at me through thick lashes. *Fuck. Me.* Her confidence is so fucking sexy. Biting her lip, she glides her body back up into mine, wrapping her leg around my waist, and slowly rolls her hips. Damn, I can watch her forever. Gripping her waist with a light squeeze, I pull her toward me. She sucks in a sharp breath and leans forward, pressing a light kiss to my neck. A growl rips from my throat. I want her right fucking now. The music slows, and she steps away from me.

"The song is about to end, and we can't get caught dancing like that, can we?" she half smiles in a troublesome way.

"I really want to fucking kiss you right now."

"Then come and get it." Her green eyes darken as she pulls her bottom lip between her teeth.

My gaze flickers to where Ry was, but I don't see him. Fuck it! I smash my lips against hers as my hands get lost in her hair. My tongue dives into her mouth, exploring deeper, and she becomes putty in my palms. A shiver runs down my spine as Rayne moans into my mouth, pushing further into me. Her kiss is hard and hungry, and I give her back just as much.

The crowd roars when the song ends, and another begins. It's then that I remember we are in the middle of a packed cabin. A desperate whimper leaves her when I break our kiss.

Resting my forehead against hers, our breathing erratic, the corner of my mouth pulls upward. "What am I going to do with you?"

"Whatever you want," she breathes, her warm breath fanning against my lips.

Laynie steps up, informing us she has to pee, and we pull apart. Rayne shakes her head, snapping out of our bubble. With flushed cheeks, she asks where Jamie is, and at the same time, she appears. She's breathing heavily from dancing and fanning herself, telling us how good the boy she was with could dance. With Laynie focused on Ry, and Rayne focused on me, Jamie left. They both look at Jamie with a guilty expression and murmur a sorry.

"Where did you go?" Rayne asks Laynie.

"Um, I went to keep Ryker occupied so you can dance with Mr. Fine piece of a—"

"Okay, okay. I get it." Rayne says, covering Laynie's mouth, so she can't say more.

"What was that?"

"Nothing." Rayne quickly answers. "Where is Ry?" she eagerly changes the subject.

"He went to the bathroom," Laynie answers. "Which sounds really nice right now."

"Let's go. We should all go together."

"Aww, our own personal bodyguard," Laynie says, and I roll my eyes.

"Where is the bathroom, anyway?" I ask.

"Let's go that way." Rayne points to a hallway.

The music is blaring, and I can barely hear anything besides the thumping of the music and muffled voices cutting in and out as I pass people. I get to the bathroom and turn around to face the girls, but I don't see any of them. Shit. I must have lost them in the crowd.

"Hey bro, where is everyone?" Ry asks, stepping out of the restroom.

"I lost them. Let's go back and get them."

"It's a madhouse, man. I didn't expect this many people." He says, walking back toward the makeshift dance floor.

I'm quickly scanning the area, trying to find any of them, but I can't make out anyone with all the bodies.

"Let go of me!" someone shouts. *I would know that voice anywhere. Rayne.*

"It's Rayne. We have to find her!" I shout, pushing people out of my way.

"I'm right behind you!"

I can feel my heart pounding against my chest as I scan the crowd, looking for my girl.

Fuck. Where is she?

There are too many damn people here. I catch a glimpse of red and know right away it's Laynie. Thank God for that bright-ass colored dress she wore tonight. I make my way through the crowd and see her and Jamie take a step forward. *What's going on?*

"What the fuck are you doing here?" I hear Laynie say to someone now that I'm closer.

A crowd surrounding them makes it hard for me to see. I push more people out of the way.

"Watch it, bro," some dude snaps.

Shooting him a glare, he gulps and turns around, disappearing back into the crowd. *Good, because I'm not in the fucking mood.* I finally break through the bodies of people and see Rayne, Laynie, and Jamie standing side-by-side. Rayne looks like she has just seen a ghost, her olive skin drained of all color. I shift my gaze, following their line of sight.

Jackson. Fucking. Reed.

My heart thumps against my chest at an unhealthy speed, my fist clenched, and my jaw locked tight as my chest heaves.

"Come on, baby, don't be like that," he says, wrapping his hand around Rayne's arm, and I see red!

Without thinking, I grab his hand and throw it off her. Twisting his shirt at the collar, I use his body to push through the crowd and slam him against a wall.

"What the fuck are you doing here?" I shout, spitting in his face. The vein in my neck throbs as adrenaline invades me, making me lightheaded. His panicked eyes widen in terror. "Don't you ever fucking touch her!" I jerk him forward before slamming him back. "I already warned you, bitch."

I faintly hear my name being screamed from behind me, and I turn to look. Jackson head butts me, catching me off guard. *Fuck!* I stumble, my head already pounding from the blow. He lands a punch to my jaw, and I bend, dodging the other. I'm about to swing when Ryker's fist comes from the side and connects perfectly with fuck boy's jaw. It all happens in slow motion. He falls to the floor, going limp.

I pant, using the back of my hand to wipe the blood from my lip.

"I got your back, bro."

"Christian!" Rayne says breathlessly, running to me.

She captures my face in her hands as her eyes examine the damage. Feeling Ryker's stare, I gently remove them and put distance between us.

"I'm good."

She frowns, not aware of the eyes that are on us.

"I called an Uber, but there aren't any available big enough to take us all home at once. The first one will be here any minute." Laynie says, standing at Ryker's side.

"You go home and get cleaned up. I'll stay here with the girls and wait for the next one." He says.

"I'm going with him." Rayne blurts and looks to Ryker, "If that's okay? I'm tired anyway, and I can show him where we keep the first aid kit."

Ryker doesn't answer right away. His gaze bounces between us; questions burning in his eyes.

"I think that's a good idea," Laynie says, placing her hand on Ryker's arm.

He glances at her, then back to Rayne and me, hesitantly nodding his head and pressing his lips firmly together. "Yeah… alright, that sounds good."

"I'll see you back at the cabin. I'm going to take some Advil and knock out. I'm good, and if it wasn't for that cheap shot, he wouldn't have landed a punch."

"Yeah, I know. He's a bitch. I should have let you lay his ass out, but I had to jump in on the fun," he smirks.

"Fun?" Rayne asks sarcastically, "You guys are nuts."

"That was nothing." Ryker and I both say at the same time.

"Uber should be here. Let's get going," Rayne tells me. "Are you guys sure you're okay with taking the next one?"

"Yes, babe, go," Laynie flicks her hands, shooing her away.

"Alright," Rayne gives them all a group hug. "I love you guys."

"Ditto, babe," the girls respond.

"I love you too, sis," Ryker says as we walk away.

With every step we take, I can feel eyes following us, and I already know who it is.
Shit. I have to tell him soon.

Chapter 19

Christian

The twenty-minute drive back felt much longer with Rayne's scrutinizing eyes studying me. Her eyes are the window to one hundred questions. I'm sure she has. I didn't intend to lose my composure, but that flew out the window the instant I saw his hands on her. I didn't have a second to think; I just reacted on impulse.

"My feet are killing me," she groans.

In one swift motion, I pick her up. She squeals as I use my hip, shutting the car door.

"Put me down," she giggles. "You're hurt." I laugh, carrying her to the front door.

"The fact that you think that fuck boy hurt me hurts more than his cheap shot."

A crisp breeze blows past us, making her hair dance around her shoulders, and her scent fills the surrounding air.

"Fuck. I can't get over how good you smell."

"Lavender," she whispers, her eyes holding mine.

"Delicate," I whisper, kissing her forehead. "And sweet," I breathe into her hair, "Perfect."

She blushes and snuggles into me, warming up my entire body. I close my eyes and breathe her in, enjoying how she feels in my arms and against my chest.

I open my eyes as she looks up at me. "Citrus," she smiles. "You smell like lemons and oranges. You remind me of summer days and the warmest weather. You are warm and bright, and when I'm with you, I feel free. When I'm with you, it's always summer."

She gives me a smile that reaches her eyes, a smile so bright it outshines the darkness. The depth of her words draws me in. *I have always felt like a gloomy cloud, a storm brewing within, but to her, I'm bright and warm—I'm her summer. For once in my life, I don't feel so cold, I don't feel the darkness following me like a shadow—with her, I feel the fucking sun.*

In awe and lost for words, I kiss gently on her lips and love how her body shivers.

"Let's get you inside."

With Rayne still in my arms, I do my best to grab the key under the doormat and open the front door. She's giggling as I struggle, and I playfully scowled at her.

"Oh, you think this is funny, huh?"

"Yeah, I kind of do," she says between bursts of laughter. I stand to my full height and pretend to drop her, catching her before she hits the floor. "Christian!" she screams, holding onto me with a death grip.

"Not so funny now, huh?"

"I thought you were seriously going to drop me."

Using my foot, I kick the door shut before setting her down and cradling her cheek in my hand.

"I would never drop you."

She smiles and nods. "Let's get you cleaned up."

Rayne walks me to her room, and I can't hold back my smile. We've only been here for two days, but this room is all her. She has a light pink throw blanket she must have brought from home resting on a chair by the fireplace. The closet door is open, and I can see she has all her clothes hung up and organized. Her bed is perfectly made, not a single thing out of place. My eyes land on a pink book resting on her nightstand.

"What book is this?" I pick it up to inspect it.

She hastily runs over, grabbing the book from my hands and putting it behind her back.

"It's not a book," she looks down at our feet. "It's a journal..." I playfully try to take the journal from her, but she jumps on the bed before I can grab it.

I smirk. "Are all your secrets in there?" her mouth opens in an O shape, and her cheeks instantly turn pink.

"Umm, no, secrets," she nervously laughs. "It's just a stupid journal where I vent about pointless things. Nothing interesting."

"I'd love to read all about these *pointless* things."

"No," she says immediately. "I mean... not right now. Maybe one day." I wonder what she has in there to have her acting so nervous and embarrassed, maybe? I wouldn't invade her privacy, but I am certainly curious.

"I can work with one day," I grin.

Stuffing her journal in her drawer, she says, "We have a first aid kit in the master bathroom."

She opens the cabinet below the sink, pulls out the box, and places it on the counter beside the sink, patting the toilet for me to sit. I oblige and watch as she shuffles through the aid kit, pulling out everything she needs and lining them up neatly.

"I didn't know you had OCD," I tease.

"What?" she shrugs. "I like to be organized." With an antiseptic wipe, she bends down in front of me. "This might burn." She says, delicately dabbing the cut on my lip.

Her eyebrows knit together in concentration as she focuses on cleaning my lip before applying antibiotic ointment. Now and then, she will look into my eyes as if she wants to ask me something before moving her gaze back to her task.

"What do you want to ask me?"

"What did you mean when you told Jackson you warned him?" she casually asks, keeping her focus on the cut.

Fuck. I slipped up with him earlier. I blacked out and wasn't thinking clearly. To tell the truth, I wasn't thinking at all, and I should not have mentioned that night.

The night of Jackson fucking Reed's party invades my thoughts…

My blood boils as I pull up the long driveway I was in only a couple of hours ago. The place is still packed as if nothing awful had just taken place. Urgently exiting my vehicle, I slam my door shut behind me.

I'm fuming as I stare at the mansion in front of me. I hear laughter and cheers mixed with the thumping of the music as I try to get my breathing under control, but it isn't working. I open the large front door, not bothering to close it. This place is like a castle. Fucking rich pricks. My fists clench, and my jaw tenses as I scan the crowd, looking for only one person. I head for the backyard. It's as if I have flashing lights with the word danger written across my forehead because anyone who makes eye contact with me quickly shifts their gaze away from mine and gets the fuck out of my way.

Good.

In the backyard, I scan every face. I can't make out a group of people that stand around a blazing fire, so I make my way in that direction. As I look closer, I see just the person I was looking for—Jackson fucking Reed.

Just the sight of him makes me shake in rage. My forehead creases, my lips are tight, and my nostrils flare as I squeeze my fists tighter. He's laughing without a single care in the world. He's talking excitedly, just like he was the day I first laid eyes on him. I didn't like him then, but it's nothing compared to how I feel about him now.

As I get closer, I hear him speaking to a bunch of guys surrounding him.

"Yeah, bro, she was practically begging on her knees for me."

"Fuck yeah, man!" one guy says, taking a sip of beer as another adds, "You lucky bastard! Rayne is one fine piece

of ass." The guy says, slapping him on the back giving him praise.

I'm about five seconds away from wiping that smug look from his dumbass face. I should knock his ass out without warning and not give him a choice, just like he tried to do with Rayne. I won't be like him, though; I'll give him two options: step up and fight me like a man and get his ass whooped or be a scared little bitch and still get his ass whooped.

"Wow!" I sarcastically say, "Fuck boy, hear claims to have finally gotten his dick wet."

Jackson looks at me with surprise before creasing his brows, and his eyes turn to slits.

"I'd like to think you're a smart enough guy to know exactly why I'm here. You did some dumb shit earlier tonight," I smile, playing completely calm and in control.

He goes to speak, but I immediately cut him off. "Nobody said you could speak, bitch."

His eyes narrow even more, His jaw clenched tightly, and his fingers twitch. Good, he's pissed.

"Do you know why I'm here?" I ask, and he attempts to answer, "Don't fucking speak! Shake your head yes or no. Do you know why I am here?" He shakes his head back and forth, answering no. I laugh sadistically.

"You really are a dumb ass. Okay, let's try a different approach." I take a step closer to him and his posse. "You know why the fuck I'm here." I say, then look to his group, "Do you guys know he's a sick fuck who likes trying to take advantage of girls?" None of them say a word.

"Shut your fucking mouth. You don't know shit!" Jackson snarls.

"I know enough! I know you're the type of guy used to getting his way because mommy and daddy would rather give you money than give you their time."

His face contorts with rage.

"Shut the fuck up!" he shouts, his lip curling. "You don't know what the fuck you're talking about." He steps toward me.

"Let me guess... daddy is always away on business trips and has no time for his prodigal son? No matter how much you begged for his attention, he never gave it, so you started acting out in hopes of some attention, and even then, he wanted nothing to do with you." I grin, casually stepping closer toward him. "Oh, and you can't forget about poor mother dearest... does he take her with him, or does she get left behind and drink herself into oblivion because she'd rather be shit-faced than hang out with you?" I say, knowing I hit a nerve and have him exactly where I want him.

Jackson's fists are clenched at his sides, and he rolls his shoulders back, glaring at me. "I said fucking shut up!"

I give him my best smile. "Or what?"

He charges at me, taking a wide swing, but I am faster. I dodge his punch and throw a right hook straight into his ribs. He grunts, taking the force of the hit. He swings wildly in his rage, and I move as I feel the wind from his punch pass my cheek. I catch his forearm, pull him toward me and use my weight to toss him over my shoulder, slamming him onto his back. When he scrambles to his feet, I waste no time giving him a quick jab in the nose.

"Fuck!" he shouts, bringing his hand to his gushing nose, and I slap him with an open palm straight across the face. It rocks him as he draws a step back.

THWACK! I sock him straight in his eye, splitting his eyebrow open. THWACK! Connecting with the other side of his ribs. THWACK! I kick him right behind his knees. He crumples to the ground, groaning.

Setting my foot directly on his chest, pinning him down, I say. "This is your warning. Don't you ever touch Rayne again. Do not go near her. Don't even look at her." I seethe, peering down at him. I lean closer, making sure he can hear me clearly. "Don't even think about telling anyone about this. Rayne wasn't the first girl you've tried to assault. Imagine if others came forward..." He gaped. "You wouldn't last a day behind bars before you became someone's bitch. If you open *your mouth to anyone, I promise; you will regret it. Consider yourself lucky.*

"Christian, are you okay?" she softly pats my cheek, snapping me out of the memory. "Where did you go just now?"

"I'm sorry. What was your question?" I ask, hoping she wouldn't bring it up again.

I don't want to tell her. *What would she think of me?* I promised her I wouldn't do anything. I didn't mean to lie to her. I only wanted to protect her. He traumatized her and needed to be warned he couldn't get away without consequences. *I can't imagine how many others weren't as lucky. I don't have proof he's done anything else, but I have a nagging feeling in my gut he has. He was ballsy enough to do something awful during a full-blown party. There is no way this was his first time trying something like that. My threat obviously worked because he hasn't gone to the cops, and I'm still here, not behind bars.*

She looks at me, confused, tilting her head slightly to the side. "What did you mean when you told Jackson you warned him?" she repeats.

"The day I picked you up was the first time I'd ever seen him... but it wasn't the last," I confess, looking at her hesitantly. Her brows furrow as she thinks, and I watch her wheels turn as she pieces things together.

Realization dawns on her face, and she gasps, "Oh my God! It was you." She brings her hands up, covering her mouth. "His face... his face was demolished. You did that to him?" she meant it as a statement, but it comes off more like a question like she can't believe everything unfolding.

I slowly nod. I say nothing yet, giving her time to process this information.

"You lied... you promised me you wouldn't do anything."

"I am sorry that I lied to you," I say honestly, "but I do not regret what I did. I would do it again and again if it meant protecting you."

She runs her hands up through her hair. "It all makes sense now."

"What do you mean?"

"At school... the week after the party, he cornered me at my locker." My jaw ticks. "He said that I was the reason he was messed up. I didn't know what he was talking about, and I was confused. He threatened me... he said that he was going to bide his time and wait for the perfect opportunity to get even." She chokes with watery eyes.

Fuck! This was the last thing I wanted to happen, and now she is a target because of what I did. I'm worried about her, and I believe in his threats. He's bat-shit crazy, and can make all the threats he wants, but he won't fucking touch her!

"I'm scared, Christian... I'm petrified."

I pull her into my arms. "Don't be afraid, Raynie. I got you. Nothing is going to happen, I promise you. Have you told Ryker about this?"

She shakes her head against my chest. "No, I can't tell Ryker. He would kill him. I don't want anyone involved in my mess. Nobody can know."

Her mess? This is my mess and my fault. I should have thought this through; I shouldn't have reacted impulsively. Fuck! What do I do?

"I won't tell anyone. I promise." I thread my fingers in hers, walking us out of the bathroom.

I look at Rayne, her eyes still watery, and her pouty lips are pulled downward; she seems sad, which breaks my heart. I lay on her bed, leaning against the headboard. She lays her cheek on my chest, and I bring my arm around her.

"What is going on in that pretty little head of yours?" I ask, resting my chin on top of her head.

"I'm afraid Jackson will hurt me or harm someone I care about... I am worried he will hurt you." She uses her finger to draw patterns on my shirt.

"He isn't going to hurt me or anyone you care about, and he won't hurt you. Especially you."

"How do you know?" she whispers softly.

"Because I'll protect you, and when I say I will protect you, I mean it." She says nothing but instead squeezes me tighter.

I have no idea what Jackson has planned in that twisted fucking head of his, but I guarantee whatever it is, it isn't good. I'm not sure what game he is playing showing up at Rayne's party after I warned him not to go near her, but I need to figure it out.

"I better get to my room and let you get some sleep," I press my lips tenderly to the crown of her head. "Goodnight, Raynie."

"Can you stay with me for a little longer?" she asks, "please."

How could I possibly say no to her? I may be selfish, but I want her to only ever look at me like that—as if I were her lifeline.

"Yes." *and a hundred more times yes.* "I'll stay with you." *I'll always stay with you.*

Chapter 20

Christian

Knock! Knock! Knock! I slowly lift my heavy lids. Rayne was still lying on my chest. She looks so beautiful, and I can't help but smile. *Fuck, I feel happy.*

Knock! Knock! Knock!

Shit! I must have fallen asleep last night lying here talking to Rayne. For a second, I thought I might have been dreaming because waking up to her feels like that—a dream—a dream I never want to wake from.

This is bad.

"Rayne," I whisper, brushing her hair behind her ear. "Someone is knocking at the door." I'm trying to act calm; my forehead is broken out in sweat, and my heartbeat's a forceful thump in my chest.

"What time is it?" she mumbles into my chest. "It's probably Laynie." She says, still partially asleep.

"Rayne, I don't th—" The bedroom door swings open.

My head jerks to the door while Rayne urgently sits up. Ryker is standing there, his smile quickly vanishing as he sees me lying with his sister.

"What the actual fuck?" he rushes into the room, grabbing me by the collar of my denim jacket and pulling me up to him. "What the fuck are you doing in here with my little sister!" he shouts, looking from me to Rayne, then quickly back to me.

"Ryker!" she shouts in surprise.

"It's not what you think!"

"What do you mean, it's not what I think?" he says, pushing me against the wall. I don't fight back because he is my friend, and I understand why he is furious. "It's exactly what I think. I think you lied to me about anything going on between the two of you!" he yells, looking over to Rayne before moving his gaze back to me. "How long has this been going on? How long have you been lying to my face!"

"Ryker, calm down!" Rayne shouts, her eyes filling with tears.

"It's hard to explain… it wasn't like that," I say, and he punches me in my jaw. *Fuck!*

"That's bullshit, and you fucking know it."

"Ryker!" Rayne jumps off the bed and grabs him, trying to pull him off me.

"What is going on in here?" Laynie asks at the same time Jamie says, "Oh shit."

"What the fuck? Ryker, what the hell are you doing!" she says, storming up to him.

"Stay out of this, Laynie," he grits, not sparing her a glance. "I came here to see if Rayne knew where Christian was, since he wasn't in his room. Imagine my fucking surprise when I walk into her room and see them in bed together."

Laynie rolls her eyes and scoffs. "Were they naked? Were they having sex?" Our eyes dart to her, and Rayne gapes, her cheeks flushing.

"No, they weren't. If they were, Christian wouldn't be standing right now."

"Then what the hell is the big deal? She is seventeen, Ry… you were far worse at her age and have no room to talk." She hugs Rayne in comfort.

"It doesn't fucking matter. She is my little sister, and I thought he was my friend… he's nothing but a goddamn liar," he says, full of anger, but I can see the hurt in his eyes.

"I know you're pissed off at me and feel betrayed. You have every right to feel that way, but please hear me out and let me explain?" His jaw ticks and his brows crease together as he stares at me.

"Fine."

"Let's go for a drive," I say, adjusting my denim jacket. "We can get the girls some coffee while we're out. We have a long trip ahead of us."

"I can really use some coffee," Rayne whispers, looking at Ryker under her thick lashes.

Ryker looks at his sister, and even though he is full of anger, you can see nothing but love when he looks at her. His gaze flicks back at me, and that love vanishes.

"I'm driving," he turns and storms out of the room. Rayne runs up to me, wrapping her arms around my waist.

"I'm so sorry."

"You don't need to apologize," I brush my thumb over her wet cheek. "I should have told him."

"He hit you. I should have never asked you to stay with me last night, and none of this would have happened."

"I understand why he hit me, Raynie. I'm going to talk to him. You enjoy the last couple of hours here before we head home."

"Okay."

"Do you have your phone?"

"Yeah, it's right here," she says, grabbing her phone off the nightstand and unlocking it.

"I think it's about time I get your number," I smirk, adding my contact to her phone. "Text me what you guys want me to order for you at the coffee shop." A hint of a smile teases her lips.

I give her a slow kiss on her forehead, and she closes her eyes, letting out a long breath relaxing into me. "I'll be back."

"Thanks for waiting," I say, buckling myself in. "Look, I'm going to hear you out, but I don't want any bullshit from you. Keep it real with me and don't waste my time. If not, you can get out now." He says assertively.

"No bullshit," I agree. "I don't even know where to start."

"How about from the beginning? That would probably be a good place to start." *Right.* I pause, looking out of the window.

"When I first met you, you were the only person in years who I had things in common with, who was interested in me and my life. You are the closest thing to a friend I've ever had. When you invited me over to your family's breakfast, it surprised me. I never went to friend's houses to play video games, have dinner, or anything like that. I never had those types of friends, if that's what you want to call them." I look over at Ryker, and he glances at me. "Then I met your sister." His jaw locks, and he grabs the steering wheel a little tighter.

"She is beautiful, but that's not what caught my attention. Back home, I was used to girls throwing themselves at me. Girls back home were wild, and Rayne was different. She is calm and confident. She is pure and innocent; life hasn't tainted her with the fucked-up shit that happens. When she looked at me, it was as if she could see me… the real me that was hidden so deep under the surface. To tell the truth, it's easy to want to be that person with her. I realize I don't deserve her, and that's one reason I've tried to stay away from her. She deserves better, but then I realized I want to be better for her."

He is silent at my confession. We pull in front of a mom-and-pop coffee shop. It's busy with tons of people sitting out front drinking their coffee and eating breakfast. Luckily, we got here when we did because there wasn't a line inside. I look at my phone, reading Rayne's text.

"I'll take a large vanilla iced coffee with half and half, a large white mocha cold brew, and an everything cream cheese bagel, please."

"Okie dokie, will that be for here or to go?"

"To go," Ryker says. I hand her my debit card and pay, then walk to the side counter and wait for the order.

"Have you told Rayne about your past?" Ryker asks.

"Yeah, I have."

"And what did she say?" he arches his brow.

"She wasn't thrilled but decided to take a chance on me."

"Of course she did." He mumbles. "Rayne tries to see the good in everyone."

"Order up!" The barista calls, interrupting our conversation.

"I'm sorry," I tell Ryker as we leave.

"You getting mushy on me, bro?" he bites back a smile.

"Nah, I'm just a dude who can own up to their mistakes. I'm sorry for how you found out; I didn't mean to lie to you. When you asked me if anything was going on between Rayne and me, I was honest… there wasn't anything happening except a powerful attraction toward her."

"Dude," Ryker grimaces, cutting me off, and I laugh.

"When you asked me, there wasn't anything going on. I have this pull toward her I can't even explain. I have experienced nothing like it before. Right after I talked to her, I was going to tell you. I just didn't want to tell you until after her birthday because I wasn't sure how you would take it. I didn't want to ruin her birthday."

"Well, I kind of fucked that one up, didn't I?"

"Nah, like you said, Rayne likes to see the good in everyone. You know she will understand where you're coming from."

"You really like her, huh?"

"Yeah, man, I really do." I smile.

"This is so fucking weird," Ry chuckles. "So, what are you guys like, boyfriend and girlfriend?"

"No, not yet, but there isn't anyone else. I'm in this for real."

"We're bros, and this won't change anything, but Rayne is my sister, and if you hurt her—"

"I won't." I've done a lot of fucked up shit in my life, but hurting Rayne won't be one of them. "I plan on telling your dad soon."

"Good luck with that man," he says, pulling into the driveway. "I have something I want to say, though. Despite your past, it clearly isn't the guy sitting in front of me now. You may think you don't deserve my sister, but I think you're wrong. You guys are lucky to have each other. I had a suspicion, more so at the party, seeing how you went into beast mode on Jackson, and I know she is in excellent hands."

Tears sting the back of my eyes. *Fuck! When did I get so soft?*

"Go get your girl, bro," he holds out his knuckles, and I connect my fist with his.

I smile as we walk to the cabin. Even though I got punched, everything turned out better than I expected. I'm such a giddy motherfucker right now, but I don't care. For the first time in eight years, I feel like I belong.

"Honey, I'm home!" Ryker sing songs, opening the door.

The girls are all quiet and awkwardly standing in the kitchen. Laynie and Jamie look at Rayne anxiously fidgeting with her fingers as she bites her lip nervously, looking between us. *So damn cute*. I casually walk toward her as Ryker grins, and they watch my every move. I look at Rayne and she quickly shifts her eyes to her feet.

"What's going on in that pretty little head of yours?" I smirk, lifting her chin with my finger.

"He's talking to you, sis."

"What is happening right now?" she rubs her temples, perplexed. I chuckle, cupping her face in my hands.

"This is what's happening," I say and gently press my lips against hers.

"Fuck, this is so weird. I don't think I'll ever get used to it." I think Ryker says, but I can hardly hear him because it is only us when I'm with Rayne.

"Nice to see your bromance survived, and you guys are both in one piece." Laynie jokes.

"Bromance?" Ryker and I both question.

"Yeah, when Ry was in your face, I wasn't sure if he wanted to punch or kiss you."

"Ryker punched him, but clearly they kissed and made up." Rayne grins. "But seriously, I'm glad to see you guys worked everything out."

"Me too," Ryker and I both say.

"See... Bromance." Laynie teases.

"Yeah, yeah, whatever... let's get going. We have a long trip ahead of us." Ryker replies. "Rayne, you riding with Christian?"

She smiles, looking at me, "Yeah, I am."

And I grin.

Chapter 21

Christian

I have been on my feet nonstop at the shop since I arrived this morning. I'm still on cloud nine from everything that happened over the weekend. Admitting my feelings to Rayne and being honest about my past has made all the difference. Something about letting everything out that was buried so deep is refreshing, and I don't know how to explain the feeling; I feel... *lighter*. Rayne once told me I practically give her whiplash with how hot and cold I was with her, and I wasn't aware of how much of a toll it had on me, either. I was scared that I was too late, that she had enough of my bullshit, and I lost my chance with her. Seeing her with Tyler did something to me. It snapped me in place and made me realize I couldn't let her slip between my fingers and into someone else's hands. Seeing him touch her had my blood boiling, and at that moment, I felt nothing but pure fucking rage.

I was jealous and jealously is an ugly thing. I am a selfish bastard and needed to have her even then. When she touches me, she has no control; her body responds on its own accord before her mind can even process it, and I know this because it's exactly that way for me. She glanced at him, but *stared* at me. Her eyes told me everything her mouth wouldn't. Pick me, choose me, her eyes pleaded.

When I drove to Big Bear, I wasn't sure what would happen. All I knew was I needed to tell her how I genuinely felt, even if I was too damn late. She needed to know. It would eat me alive if she moved on, thinking I was playing games with her, thinking I didn't want her, or that she wasn't enough for me; when this entire time, I've felt I was never enough for her.

It hurt me when I saw Rayne with Tyler, and I knew I had no right to be. I was also scared. Afraid of losing her before I even got the chance to call her mine. I didn't have a plan or expectations. My only intention was to tell the truth… about everything, even if that meant losing her for good. She needed to learn the truth about my past before I could even think about a future with her.

I'm working on an engine with all sorts of problems. Worn spark plugs, check! Leaking engine coolant, check! Faulty sensors, check! Grabbing a hand towel, I wipe off my grease-stained fingers.

"Christian, a word?" Jack calls behind me.

"Of course, sir." I gulp, throwing the stained towel down and following him out of the car garage and into his office. Did he somehow find out about Rayne and me?

"I'm sure you know why I called you in here," he takes a seat behind his mahogany desk.

Shit, shit, shit! "Umm," I pause nervously, wiping my hands on the thighs of my work pants. "I'm not sure I do, sir."

"Relax, son. It looks like you're about to pass out. Do you need some water?" he asks, concerned.

I nervously chuckle. "Water would be great, thank you."

He grabs cold water from the mini-fridge at the side of his desk and hands it to me. I twist off the cap and chug the entire bottle, causing his brow to arch. *Get it the fuck together*, I think to myself.

"How do you like working here?"

"I love it, it's a very nice shop, and the customers are pleasant... mostly."

He chuckles. "That's good to hear. What about the staff? They treating you, right?"

"Everyone here is great. I have learned a lot already. Liam and Derek are cool dudes and always take their time to help me whenever needed. I feel like I fit in well here."

"I'm thrilled to hear that," he smiles. "I've been watching you, and I'm impressed. You know a lot about vehicles, especially for your age. You are great with the customers. We have had a few give some nice feedback about the service you provided, and happy customers are the chief priority here, so having that feedback is excellent. The guys here tell me your work is good, and you attain information well."

I give him a wide, toothy smile while mentally patting myself on the back because I am fucking proud of myself. It gives me more drive to continue pursuing what I love.

"Wow, it feels good to hear that kind of feedback from guys doing this most of their life."

"You should feel proud, son. I didn't know your father, so forgive me if I'm stepping out of line here, but I know he would be proud of you. Hell, I am proud of you."

"You don't understand how much that means to me. Thank you." I choke.

"I'd be honored to have you officially join the team. What do you think?" he says with a sparkle in his eye and a massive smile on his face.

I can't believe how lucky I am to have this opportunity. I want to jump up and scream yes, but I can't. Not yet. There is something I need to do first.

"I'd love to be a part of the team, sir, but there is something I'd like to tell you first," I swallow nervously, and his smile drops slightly.

"What is it you'd like to tell me?"

"It's about Rayne..."

He quickly stands. "What about her?"

I run my fingers through my hair. "I have feelings for your daughter." He stops pacing and turns to me. "I have feelings for your daughter, sir, and she has feelings for me, and I'd really like your permission to date her." He stands staring at me before returning to his seat behind his desk. "I have fought my feelings for her for a while now, but I can't fight them anymore. I appreciate how special she is to you, but I can assure you she is also special to me. I have nothing but the best intentions, and I promise you I will do everything possible to treat her the way she deserves. I will respect and protect her always." I tell him confidently, looking at him straight in his eyes. He is silent as he studies me, but I don't waver.

"I knew this day would come." He finally speaks. "Rayne is a true gem and my greatest treasure. Again, you have impressed me. It takes a lot of courage to look me in the eye and say the things you just did. I'll give you permission to date my daughter under two conditions."

"Yes, anything."

"One, your work life is separate from your dating life. Just because you date my daughter doesn't give you any special treatment, and I still expect you to work just as hard as you have been. You want to open a shop up of your own one day, so you need to stay focused."

"Absolutely."

"Two, Rayne is my baby girl, and that will never change. If you hurt her in any way..." he pauses, looking earnestly at me with a warning in his eyes. "Well, you get it. Don't hurt her, or you will see a side of me few people have."

"You have my word."

"I'll hold you to it. Now back to my question, how would you like to be a part of Davis Automotive officially?" he grins.

"Yes, thank you, sir, for everything." He walks around his desk, and instead of taking my hand, he pulls me into a hug, patting me on the back.

"Welcome to the team, son."

After talking with Jack, I returned to work grinning from ear to ear. I am so fucking happy, and the feeling is strange, but I like it, which it is something I can get used to. Being happy is much better than feeling angry all the damn time. I won't deny that a big part of me is terrified, and a part of me does not want to become used to it in fear of one day losing it.

○ ○ ○

My mom brings her attention to me, sliding her reading glasses to the top of her head. "You look nice. Where are you going?"

"I um… have a date," I tell her, sliding my hands into my front pockets.

"A date?"

"Yes, mom. A date. I'm going to surprise Rayne."

"The Davis's daughter?" she questions, and I nod my head. "You know I have heard a lot about this girl, but have yet to meet her."

"I know. It just took me a while to pull my head out of my ass and admit how I felt about her, especially with my past."

"You told her about your past?"

"Yes, she knows."

"Wow," she sighs. "Rayne must be exceptional."

"She really is." I don't even try to hide my smile.

"I realize I let things carry on too long with your behavior in the past, but I won't stand by and watch you self-destruct anymore. If this is just another one of your games—"

"It's not." I immediately cut her off. "Rayne is not a game, and she makes me want to be better, mom. The Davis's are special people, and I would never do anything to betray them."

"I am proud of you. I have seen so much growth in you since we have moved here, and it makes me happy. I thought I'd never see you truly smile again, and I am so thankful Rayne has brought light back into your life." She grabs a tissue and dabs under her eyes.

"Thanks, mom. I know moving here wasn't a simple decision to make, but I believe it was the best one." I smile, pulling her into a hug.

"Me too," she says into my chest. "When can I meet Rayne or the Davis's? I'd love to meet the people who have impacted my son's life so much."

"Soon."

After saying goodbye to my mom, I grab two blankets and a Bluetooth speaker before heading out. It hasn't even been a full day since I last saw Rayne, but I already miss her. The long drive back home was perfect We listened to music and laughed hard about stories she had growing up.

"When I was younger, Ry would always mess with me any chance he got, so, one day, I finally got my payback. Ryker hates mayo with a passion, and just looking at it would make him gag." She giggles. *"We were at this diner with our parents, and we were sitting at a booth all drinking milkshakes. My dad went to pay at the front counter while my mom used the lady's room. At the end of the table, I saw they had packets of mayo and other condiments next to the straws, and instantly an idea formed,"* she says, smirking mischievously. *"I carefully sucked the mayo into the straw, filling it entirely. When Ryker wasn't looking, I swapped the two straws."*

I see exactly where this story is heading, and I am already trying to stifle a laugh. I love how strong Rayne can be. She is shy at times, but I feel like there is a side of her I have yet to discover; a side I had only seen glimpses of when she was angry with me or lying beneath me, and all sense of rationality was nonexistent. I can tell she doesn't take shit from anyone and will dish it right back. She has a fight in her. I don't think she realizes, and she proved that with Jackson.

"Ryker took a sip of his vanilla milkshake, and his eyes turned into saucers, and he spits out the mayo that filled his mouth right back into his cup. His expression went from disgusted to sick right before he threw up all over the booth." She says, holding her stomach and laughing.

I throw my head back and laugh alongside her. The story is funny, and I could picture Ryker's reaction as if I was there experiencing it with them, but what really has me smiling is her.

For the entire drive, I had one hand on the steering wheel and my other hand in hers, and I wore a smile the entire time. This is a last-minute date, but after talking to Jack and getting his permission, I couldn't wait another second to see her. I quickly send Ryker a text, letting him know I have a surprise for Rayne and will pick her up from school. As I pull up to Raynes school, my phone vibrates with an incoming text.

Ryker: My sister already has you whipped… and this surprise better be PG-13!

Me: No promises…

Text bubbles immediately appear, but before he can respond, I send another text.

Me: I'm kidding, bro! You can put the guns away. I'm just taking her on our first legitimate date.

Ryker: If you were here right now, I would have punched you. See, told you whipped. (Laughing emoji)

Me: My jaw still hurts from the last time you punched me.

Me: I. Am. Not. Whipped.

Ryker: That was a love tap, and whatever you say man. Refusing to believe me, sounds a lot like denial.

Me: (Middle finger emoji)

Ryker: (Heart emoji)

I park in the same spot I had parked last time I was here. It is insane to think how much has changed since then. Rayne pushes through the doors of her school, looking down at her phone, and I send her a text.

Me: You look beautiful.

Rayne looks up from her phone with surprised eyes and a smile playing on her lips. Her eyes find me straight away, and she sprints toward me. Pushing off my car, I catch her in an embrace, twirling her in a circle as she giggles in excitement. My heart does this weird flutter, and I realize Ryker is right. I'm fucking whipped.
"What are you doing here?" she says, smiling.
"I came to surprise you, but I can go?" I tease, motioning my head toward the car.
"No, no, I am happy you're here."
"I have never been on a date before, so I don't know how this works, but I was wondering if—"
"Yes!" she squeals, answering before I can finish. "Where are we going?"
"You'll see." I say, placing a kiss on her forehead.
I hope Rayne likes what I have planned for us. I am nervous as fuck because I don't know the first thing about taking anyone on a date, and I need to get it right. In the past, I didn't give a shit about romance or impressing a girl; I just had one thing on my mind. With Rayne, everything was different. I don't care about any of that.
I make a quick stop at a nearby gas station, and Rayne looks at me questionably.
"Snacks," I smirk. "I'll be right back."
I am not sure what she likes to snack on, but there is only one way to find out. I walk to the front counter with arms full of options.

"That's a lot of snacks," she giggles as I struggle to get in the car. "Are we feeding the homeless?"

I chuckle. "I wasn't sure what you liked, so I got a little of everything."

"A little? You bought the entire store." She attempts holding in a laugh.

"Har-Har." I tickle her.

Rayne's eyes slam shut as she squirms underneath my touch, laughing hysterically.

"Christian!"

"That's my name, baby."

"Christian, please!"

"Please, what?"

"Please stop," she squeals, her laughter uncontrollable.

"Now you know not to tease me." I say, releasing her.

"You don't play fair." She says, out of breath. "I'll keep that in mind."

Rayne

"Well this is a first for the both of us," he says, giving me a crooked smile. "Wait right here." He takes his keys out of the ignition, hops out quickly, jogging to my side of the car, and opens my door.

I know it is a simple gesture, but it doesn't stop the butterflies from forming in my stomach.

"Thank you."

"You're welcome. I have to grab a few things from the trunk. Can you help grab the snacks from the back seat, please?"

"Yes, of course."

He reaches into the glove compartment, grabbing a medium-sized emerald green bag.

"I'll take these." he takes the snacks from my hands.

"I can help you know. You already have so much stuff to carry."

"Not happening, Raynie. Bring your backpack."

"Yeah, sure." I'm not sure why he wants me to bring it, but I'm too happy to question it.

We walk side by side along the hiking trail, strolling our way to the Hollywood sign. I tilt my head toward the sky and breathe in the fresh air. It is beautiful outside; the sun is getting lower, just about to fall below the horizon. Everything is silent; the only noise you can hear comes from the crinkling of the bags in Christian's hands and the rocky dirt crunching beneath our feet. I am relaxed without a care in the world. Talking to Christian comes easily, but I am just as happy being next to him in complete silence.

We reach a gate behind the Hollywood sign blocking our entrance. I am about to sit on a small area of dead grass when Christian speaks.

"Can you climb?" stopping my movement, I look at him with raised eyebrows.

"Why would I need to climb?"

"We're going to hop this fence so that we can sit in front of the sign." He shrugs his shoulders nonchalantly.

"Um, I don't think that is allowed."

"You're probably right, but that isn't going to stop us. We're so close, and the only thing stopping us from touching it is a metal fence." He sets the speaker and bags down, tucking the emerald green bag into the blanket before setting it alongside the rest.

He walks up to me, placing his hands on my tense shoulders. "You ready to live a little?" he gives me the biggest smile.

His smile instantly brings me comfort and helps me relax. I stare into his eyes that look like whiskey from the hues of orange reflecting from the setting sun. I am reminded of the warmth he brings—he's my summer.

"I'm ready."

His smile broadens. "That's my girl. I'm going to help you, and then I'll pass you the stuff, okay?"

I can't stop the blush on my cheeks from hearing him say, *my girl*.

"Okay." I timidly approach the fence, and Christian rests his hands on my hips. "Wait. I'm wearing a skirt."

He chuckles behind me, bringing his lips to my ear, and whispers. "I won't look."

My cheeks redden more. "Okay," I gulp, "on the count of three?"

"On the count of three."

"One," he whispers, and goosebumps break out like hives on my skin. "Two." his grip on my waist tightens. "Three." We both shout as I jump, and he pulls me up.

Grabbing onto the top of the fence, I swing my legs over and hop down on the other side.

"I did it!"

"I knew you could." He smiles proudly before throwing over the snacks and then grabs the emerald green bag before tossing the blankets to me.

He climbs the fence effortlessly, landing right in front of me. We grab our things and find a spot in front of the enormous sign.

I watch him as he lays out one blanket and pats it, signaling me to sit. I smile, taking a seat next to him, and he sets the other blanket over us, covering both of our legs.

"Want a snack?" he places multiple bags in front of me.

"Sure, I'll take..." I pause, searching through the bags. "This one." I smile, pulling out a dark chocolate candy bar.

"You know those who favor dark chocolate are problem solvers who are excited about the future."

"Is that true?" I ask, taking a bite.

"Honestly, I don't know. I read it in one of my mom's magazines once."

We're both silent before tilting our heads back and bursting into laughter.

"What is the verdict? Are you a problem solver who is excited about the future?"

"I would say that statement is accurate. I do like to problem solve or try to find a solution to things, and I am really excited about the future."

"What do you want to do after high school?"

"My dream is to attend New York School of Design."

His smile drops a fraction. "New York, huh? That is great, Raynie."

"What's wrong?"

"Nothing." He runs his fingers through his hair. "It's just really far from Los Angeles."

I know it is. Two thousand, seven hundred, and eighty-nine point four miles, to be exact. It's something I think about often. Before, my biggest worry was leaving my family behind, and now I worry about leaving Christian behind too. A light pain in my chest and an unsettling feeling in my stomach take place at the thought.

I didn't think of that. Before Christian, I didn't have anyone to consider when deciding, but now I do.

"It is, but a lot can happen from now to then," I grab his hand. "Let's just enjoy the now."

I try to give him a reassuring smile but can't tell if the reassurance is more for him or me.

"Let's enjoy the now." He agrees, squeezing my hand. "Do you have a pen and paper in your bag?"

I unzip my backpack and pull out a notebook and a pen. He opens the notebook flipping it to a blank page, writing 'The Journey of Living- R & C' across the top, then numbers the lines down the page.

"What's this?"

"This," he pauses. "This is living," he looks at me seriously. "It's our bucket list of things we want to do. No matter what happens between us, promise we will still do the things we put on this list?"

"I promise."

Christian doesn't know how much this list means to me, and it is like he knows exactly what I need. There is so much I want to do in life, and he's willing to help make it happen. Having him experience those things with me is everything; he may just be my greatest adventure.

"Number one, meet my mom." He casually says.

"You want me to meet your mom?"

"Of course, I want you to meet her... she is dying to meet you." He avoids my gaze.

My heart nearly stops.

"Your mom knows about me?" a smile plays on my lips as a reddish tint creeps onto his cheeks.

"Of course she knows about you. If you think it is too soon to meet her, we—"

"I'd love to meet her!" I rush out.

He stares at me with a look in his eyes, a look I can't decipher... adoration, maybe? He says nothing. Instead, he slowly brings his lips to mine and kisses me softly.

"Your turn," he says, bringing his attention back to our list.

"Number two, go to prom." He smiles, adding it to the list.

"Three, go skydiving."

"No way!" my palms sweat, and my heartbeat doubles in speed.

"What better way to truly live than jumping out of a moving plane thousands of feet in the air! The rush you must feel."

"I think you're crazy," I chuckle. "I might have a heart attack before I even make it off the plane."

"I know you can do it. How about we add it to the list, and you can think about it? Your mind might change one day."

"I can do that. Number four, go camping, but while we are there, go skinny dipping." He nervously drops his pen, and his eyes turn to saucers. "What better way to live than to go swimming in a lake in nothing but our birthday suits?"

He gulps, "Y... Yeah, I can do that."

I giggle at his surprised expression and shaky voice. For the next thirty minutes, we continue to add things to our list, watch the ball drop in New York on New Year, sneak into a movie theater, binge watch a show. Meet Christian's uncle, introduce our parents to each other, split a milkshake (hold the mayo), and take a picture in front of Christian's very own shop one day. Graduate high school and have an epic movie type of love. The list goes on and on, and I can't wait to check things off. The sun is long gone, and the only light is from the illuminated starry night sky.

"I have something for you." Christian grabs the emerald green bag and hands it to me. "I got this for your birthday and wanted to give it to you after I told you how I felt regardless of the outcome," he pushes his fingers through his hair. "But once we started fresh, I didn't want to give it to you until I told Ryker and your dad. I didn't want any secrets."

"But my dad still doesn't know?"

"I told him today."

"What! What did he say?"

"It shocked me, but he was okay with it. He warned me not to hurt you or else…"

My eyes water. He told my dad, and my dad was okay with it. I thought it would take a lot of convincing on his end, so to say I am shocked right now would be an understatement. For my father to be okay with this must mean he sees something good in Christian, just like I do. My dad may be highly protective, but he wants to see me happy more than anything.

"It wouldn't be like my dad to not threaten anyone about hurting me," I say, chuckling, wiping my eyes. "So… no more secrets?"

"No more secrets." I immediately feel lighter, knowing nothing is standing between us. I open the bag and see a black velvet squared box and a card. "Open the card last," he tells me nervously.

I open the delicate velvet box with shaky hands, drawing in a sharp breath at what's inside.

Oh. My. God.

I stare at the most beautiful deeply hued emerald green earrings, leaving me completely breathless. I am too stunned to speak. The color of the round diamonds matches my eyes perfectly. As I admire the striking earrings, my eyes turn glossy. It's an emerald green circled diamond secured in gold. With slightly shaky hands, I grab the card and read.

> When I first saw you, I knew it was true.
> Those eyes were made for me, not just you.
> They pierce me to the core,
> Making me want you more and more.
>
> They speak volumes without your lips ever having to part. I swear your eyes are like a work of art.
> You see me with just a stare,
> And in your reflection, I will always be there.
>
> I once felt lost,
> But in your eyes, I feel found.
> And on my darkest night,
> Your eyes will be my guiding light.
>
> Happy birthday, Raynie.
> Always yours,
> Christian.

I read his beautifully written card another five times and am completely captivated by the words in front of me. The earrings he bought me are beautiful, but his words are priceless. I never knew he could write like this, which proves I have so much to learn about him. The more I discover, the greedier I become to know more; he continues to both surprise and amaze me. Tears from my eyes fall onto the card, lightly smudging the ink on *'always yours.'* I quickly wipe it away, not wanting to ruin his beautiful writing. Even if it were to get destroyed, I already memorized it, and his words will be engrained in my memory forever.

"Why are you crying? Did I write something you didn't like?" the vision of him is blurry from my tear-filled eyes.

"I loved all of it," I say, quavering as tears run down my cheeks. "The earrings are beautiful Christian… but your words, I can't even describe how perfect they are. I never knew you could write."

He brushes his thumb under my eyes. "Writing is therapeutic for me. I don't always enjoy talking, and I am not always good at it, so writing is a way for me to get everything out."

"You are talented. I'd love to read other things you have written."

"I have never shown anyone my writing… not even my mom. I was in a dark place then, so my writing isn't pretty and can be kind of sad or twisted."

"I like you for you, Christian," I snuggle into him. "I want to know every part of you. It won't change how I feel about you."

"I'll show you a piece I wrote sometime, I promise." He kisses the top of my head.

"Thank you for the earrings. They are beautiful. The first set of jewelry I have ever owned, and I'll cherish them forever." He holds me a little tighter. "And thank you for the poem. It was *everything*."

"No need to thank me, Raynie." He tilts my chin toward him and rubs his nose along mine. "Thank you for helping me see the light." And presses his lips against mine.

He stands up and pulls me with him. Still holding my hand, he grabs his phone, and shortly after, the music flows through his Bluetooth speaker.

<u>'You And Me—Acoustic by Matt Johnson,'</u>
"It's you, and me and all of the people, and I don't know why I can't keep my eyes off you."

"Dance with me." He brings my hands up, places them around his neck, and lightly places his hands on my waist.

"O… Okay," I nervously reply. My heart hammers in my chest as we sway side to side. I awkwardly stumble on my own two feet, and he pauses.

"Focus on me," his eyes grip mine. "Just me."

I let out a breath, regaining my composure, and do exactly as he said. I focus on only him, and we fall in step, letting the rhythm control our movements. He gently draws me closer to his chest. My body is acting on its own, molded perfectly to him. I graze his wavy hair resting on the back of his neck with my fingertips. We aren't saying a single word, utterly content with the soft melody surrounding us and our strong, beating hearts. He spins me around in a slow circle, and my hair falls over my eyes. I move my hand to brush away my hair, but he catches my hand and carefully sets it back around his neck. With delicate fingers, he tucks my hair behind my ear.

I stand on my tippy toes, whispering softly into his ear. "You say you don't have experience with this sort of thing, but you know how to be romantic."

He grabs my hand, placing it over his heart. "Only you."

Wrapping my hand back around his neck, I close my eyes, resting my head against his chest. We continue to dance, lost in the music and each other to stop. We dance and time passes as our feet continue to move. I lazily open my eyes, bringing my head up to him, and lean in, planting my lips on his. He cradles the side of my face with one hand, holding me tight with the other as we continue to kiss.

I thought moments like this only existed in scenes of a movie. Dancing with him under the twinkling stars on the side of the Hollywood sign is like I'm in a film, and I smile, knowing this—is my reality.

Chapter 22

Rayne

"So, how was your date yesterday?" Laynie asks as I finish putting the last of my books into my locker. I smile; words from the poem he wrote me flood my mind.

"I once felt lost, but in your eyes, I feel found, and in my darkest night, your eyes will be my guiding light."

"It was perfect!" I say enthusiastically, not able to contain my excitement.

"I tried calling you like ten times and getting all the juicy details, but there was no answer." She pouts.

"Sorry, babe, I got home, showered, and knocked out." I purposely keep it short, knowing she is dying to find out everything that happened.

"Seriously," she whines.

"Yup." I say, dramatically popping the 'P.'

"Rayne Davis, you better be messing with me." I pause for a dramatic effect, and Laynie grows impatient and crosses her arms. "Spill!" she nearly shrieks.

So, I do. I tell her everything with a smile while she gaped at me.

"You lucky bitch! It sounds like one of those romantic movies we watch."

That is exactly what I thought. Laynie isn't much of a reader, but romance movies are our thing. We had sleepovers and painted each other's nails while we swooned over our favorite chick flicks.

"It felt like it, too," I admit. "Oh, here, you can have these back." I hand her the tiny little box with the earrings she let me borrow inside.

"Why do I need these?"

"Because I have these." I tuck a piece of hair behind my ear, showing her the emerald-cut diamonds resting in my earlobes.

She gasps, pulling my ear to get a closer look. "Where did you get these?"

Ow! "Laynie, can I please have my ear back?"

"Sorry, but these are stunning! Where did you get them?"

"Christian got them for me for my birthday."

"You're shitting me! Oh, boy, he's in deep." She shakes her head, amazed.

"What do you mean? What makes you think that?"

"He bought you fucking earrings! Expensive ones at that."

"How do you know they're expensive, and what does him buying me earrings have to do with anything?" she rolls her eyes as if I should know this already.

"What guy buys a girl jewelry if he's not super into her? And I have expensive taste. That's how I know these aren't cheap."

I know he likes me because he's told me, but also because it's clear by the way he treats me. Standing up against Jackson, always being gentle toward me, he is patient with me, not pushing me to do anything I'm uncomfortable with. Wanting me to meet his mom, his delicate fingers when he brushes the hair behind my ear, his forehead kisses. The freaking forehead kisses! I love when he does that, and his eyes... the way he looks at me. I can't describe it, but the way he looks at me is as if he can't look away because he's scared if he were to, I'd disappear.

"I know he likes me, Laynie Mae, but we're just getting to know each other. I wouldn't go as far as saying he's in deep." I try to downplay it, but who am I really trying to fool her or me? I'm in deep. I just hope I don't drown.

"I guess you're right. Do you know where I can find a Christian?"

"The fact that he is my neighbor, I'm going to say he's probably closer than you think."

She doesn't say anything right away as she ponders my words and gets a faraway look on her face. After a while of silence, she smiles, bringing her attention back to me and changing the subject.

"What are we wearing to the Halloween Bash next weekend?"

The annual Halloween bash, aka Devils' night. How could I forget? Oh, well, that's easy. I've never been. Every year, the night before Halloween, a text gets sent out an hour before sundown announcing the location of where this mysterious event will be held. It is never held in the city, and it's always in some remote area… well, so I've heard. Devils' night is for partying and pulling pranks in most places. Here in LA, it's both those things, but what really has people talking is the game. Every year there is a new game that everyone must take part in. Nobody knows what to expect, and what happens during Devils' night is a secret, so you're not supposed to talk about it. It sounds creepy to me. Laynie told me all about it. I mean, who would I tell anyway?

Laynie and Ryker have gone since they were freshmen. I, however, had my head in the books. Laynie begged me to go, but I never did. Instead, I spent those nights cooped up in my room, covered in my pumpkin pajamas, reading a romance novel with my good friend Ben and Jerry. Lame. I know. Last year there was a vast, scary maze that everyone had to go through and find their way out the other side. The first one to make it to the other side wins. Sounds kind of easy, right?

According to Laynie, some challenges and riddles needed to be solved throughout the maze to advance through. Rumor has it some never made it out.

This year will be different. I've missed out on too much, and I don't want to do that anymore. Christian asked me if I was ready to start living, and I wasn't lying when I said I was. I have always wanted more, and he is helping me by giving me the push I need to make it happen. He makes me want to experience everything, and with him by my side, I believe I can. I no longer feel like being the wallflower who stands outside looking in, the girl sitting on the sidelines living through my brother and friend's experiences. I want to create my own. I mean, doesn't everybody want to shine a little?

"I'm not sure, but I was thinking I can design our costumes." Laynie squeals and claps her hands.

"Oh my god, yes! I already know whatever you come up with will be perfect."

"You bet your ass it will." I bump my hip into hers.

"Whatever it is, make sure it's sexy."

I roll my eyes. "Of course, Laynie Mae."

I hate sexist bullshit. We should be able to wear what we want when we want to and not be deemed a slut. After my encounter with Jackson for a second, I blamed myself. I decided to get drunk and follow him into a pool house. I wore leather pants that squeezed my curves and a sheer cropped top. Then, when Christian said it wasn't my fault and I wasn't to blame for his appalling actions, I really thought about it. He was right. Who gives a shit if I wore tight pants? Does that make it okay to touch me? Who cares if I wear a cropped top? Does that automatically give consent or the idea that I *was asking for it?* Hell. No.

As we walk towards the front of the school, I get a text from Christian.

Christian: I'll see you soon. Ryker invited me over for dinner.

Me: Can't wait!

Christian: Me either... I miss you.

Me: Already? Even though you just saw me last night.

Christian: No amount of time is ever enough time spent with you.

Me: This whole time, you were a poet, and I didn't even know it... I miss you, too.

Chapter 23

Rayne

Laynie *dropped me off after school,* and I quickly changed out of my school uniform and showered. Once my hair dried, I threw it into a messy bun and added a light blush to my cheeks. I doused myself in lavender body spray and made my way downstairs.

My mom is at the stove wearing her cute apron I bought her for Christmas last year.

"Hey, mama, need any help?" she turns to me with a spatula.

"Can you throw the garlic bread in the oven for me, please?" I smile, giving her a nod. "You look cute!" she says.

I look down at my clothes. "Are you teasing me?" she playfully throws a kitchen towel at me.

"Oh hush, you look good in anything."

"Well, I got it from my mama." I throw the kitchen towel back at her.

"Now, who's teasing?" she blushes.

"Oh, please, I'm the mirror image of you. You're gorgeous."

"Damn right you are." My dad says, walking into the kitchen and kissing my mom on her cheek.

Damn them. They are the cutest. Is it weird to '*ship*' your parents? Honestly, I don't care. I so ship them. They have always been so effortlessly in love, and as the year's pass, I swear they only fall in love more, if that is even possible. Just watching them together, you can see their passion… you can feel it.

"You are the spitting image of your mother, so, of course, you're just as beautiful, baby girl." He kisses me on the cheek. "So, your boyfriend is coming over for dinner?"

I bow my head, my cheeks turning crimson. My heart does this weird flutter thing hearing Christian being referred to as my boyfriend, but I like it. It's strange hearing the word *boyfriend* fall from my father's lips. I thought hell would freeze over before I ever heard him utter those words.

"Pops, he isn't my boyfriend."

"Yet!" Ry cuts in, joining us in the kitchen.

I roll my eyes, trying to hide my smile. *Yet*. Before my dad can respond, the doorbell rings.

"I'll get it!" I smile, relieved to cut this conversation short. Opening the door with a wide smile. Christian stands with hands behind his back, returning my smile.

"Hi," I breathe out.

He makes simple clothing look good. My eyes shift lower, taking him in. He is wearing nothing but black. My eyes skim back up to his face, and he smirks, catching me checking him out.

"These are for you," he says, handing me a bouquet of lavender and light pink roses.

I gasp, "How did you know?"

"Know what?"

"My dad used to get me these whenever we would have our father and daughter dates, and he still does on special occasions."

"I pay attention. It's hard not to notice everything about you. Your favorite color is pink. I'm assuming based on the fluffy pink socks you were wearing the first time I had breakfast here, your journal, spiraled notebook, bedding, and you even brought a soft pink blanket to Big Bear. I added lavender because it smells like you, and that's my favorite smell."

How did I get so lucky?

I didn't know he noticed all those little details. The simplest things he does or says always make me feel special; he makes me feel seen.

I bring the bouquet to my nose. "Thank you, it's wonderful." I stand on my tippy toes, pecking him on the lips.

"Remind me to get you flowers more often." I playfully slap his arm, and I notice his other arm is still behind his back.

"What else do you have back there?" I try to sneak a look, but he moves, not allowing me to see.

He pulls his other hand from behind his back, showing me another bouquet. Only these aren't lavender and pink roses; they're just beautiful, red ones.

"These are for your mom." His cheeks pinked, and my smile widened.

"She's going to love them."

We make our way to the kitchen just as Ryker and my dad take their seats.

"What's up, bro!" Ryker lifts his head like guys do when they say, 'what's up?'

"Hey, Son." my dad says, giving him a welcoming smile.

Christian greets my dad with a handshake. "Hey, Jack." He then turns to Ryker, who continued to take his seat when we first walked in. "Hey, man," he says, bumping knuckles with Ry.

"Hello, dear." My mother says.

"Hello, Olivia. These are for you." He says, handing her the roses.

"How thoughtful, thank you." She blushes and takes them from him, immediately putting them into a vase. "Major brownie points," she adds, giving him a wink.

We sit at the table eating lasagna and garlic bread, talking about school, working at the shop, and my mom's big design project for a new publishing office built in Beverly Hills.

"So Christian, how are you liking LA so far?" My mother asks.

He looks at me when he says, "I'm really enjoying it, and it's much better than Oregon."

"I've never been to Oregon, but I've heard it's beautiful."

"It is. A lot of trees, mountains, and hiking trails. Much different from life in the city."

"Do you miss home? I mean, you grew up there. I can only imagine leaving after all this time." I tense at her question because I know how much he hates Oregon.

Ryker awkwardly shifts in his seat as my father looks at Christian, waiting on his answer. I'm about to cut in and deter this conversation, but Christian answers.

"Um," he clears his throat. "I miss my uncle Maverick. He is my dad's brother, and my uncle took on that fatherly role when he passed. We're close, and I respect the hell out of him." He smiles, but I notice the sadness behind it.

"I'm glad you have your uncle, son. Family is important, and your mother did a great job, judging by how you turned out." He chokes a little on his water.

"Y... Yeah. My mother is great, and my uncle was a lot of help. I'm grateful to have them."

Christian is hard on himself because of the guy he once was, but I wish he could see himself through my eyes. He should not allow his past actions to affect how he views himself now. His *friends* back home were shitty and awful and never deserved to have him in their life. He was too damn good for them; he *is* too damn good for them. It's hard to wrap my head around how horrible kids can treat a boy who lost his father. Nobody noticed he was feeling alone and how he acted out because of it.

"What's for dessert?" Ry asks, changing the subject. I look at him and smile, giving him a silent thank you.

"I'm full, and was wondering if Christian and I could go to my room and watch a movie?" I look at my dad, giving him a doe-eyed look. A look he could never refuse.

He leans back in his chair, removing his glasses. "Um…" He pauses, looking at my mom, slightly puzzled. She gives him a reassuring smile, setting her hand over the top of his.

Not only is dating a guy or having a guy over a first for me, but it's also a first for him as well. I can see the contemplation in his eyes.

"I guess that's fine." He sighs, then looks at Christian with an intensity. "The door stays open, and it's a school night, so you have until ten-thirty."

"Yes, sir. Understood." I grab mine and Christian's plates, setting them in the sink.

"Thanks for dinner, mama," I kiss her cheek.

"Thank you, Olivia." Christian smiles at her.

"Of course. You two go watch your movie."

"I want to watch a movie," Ryker says, and my eyes widen at him.

"Oh, stop it. You can help me with the dishes." My mother tells him.

He huffs, looking like he wants to protest but doesn't. *Thank God.* When we get to my bedroom, Christian nervously stands in my doorway with his hands in his front pockets. He surveys the room before his eyes land on me. I grab the remote to the TV on my nightstand, trying not to think about the last time we were here.

Taking a seat on my bed and leaning against my headboard, I say, "You're not going to watch the movie from there, are you?"

He chuckles, running his long fingers through his hair as he walks and sits next to me.

"What do you want to watch?"

"Whatever you want to watch. It doesn't matter to me."

"Alright, in that case, we're watching a chick flick." I look at him to see if he reacts.

"I said it doesn't matter, Raynie. I'll sit through a romance movie or some sappy tearjerker if it means I get to be next to you."

I smile coyly, not knowing what to say. His words always catch me by surprise, leaving me speechless. I search the romance section on Netflix and select a random one because it doesn't matter what we watch. I just want to hang out with him. The movie starts, and I turn off my side table light. Christian lifts his arm, and I snuggle into him. A mixture of citrus and lavender encircles us, and I smile, snuggling deeper into him. This is us, citrus and lavender… Christian and Rayne.

We watch the movie as he plays with my hair. I giggle in certain parts or sigh when the couple does something cute. His mouth lifts into a half-smile at my reaction, but he never teases me about it. The whole time we watch the movie, we never lose contact. He continues to play with my hair or run his fingertips down my arms, leaving a trail of goosebumps in its wake. I trace the harsh lines of his sculpted stomach with my fingertips over his shirt. He sucks in a sharp breath when I place my hand under it and make contact with his bare chest. My hands are curious as they explore, and my fingers glide near the waistline of his pants.

He grabs my hand, stopping my movement. "You have to stop that, Raynie." He says hoarsely.

I look up at him innocently through thick lashes. "Why?"

He nibbles his lip, letting out a hard exhale. "Because my dick is hard, and I don't know how much more I can take before I flip you onto your back and use my mouth to make you scream my name."

My eyes open in surprise at his admission, and my cheeks flush. His words instantly make me ache between my legs. My mind automatically wanders back to the night at the cabin and how good his mouth felt on my sex as he devoured me with his tongue. A moan almost escapes my lips, but I swallow it down.

"Fuck!" he groans. "You've got to stop looking at me like that."

"Like what?" I wet my lips.

"Like you're picturing my mouth on your pretty pussy."

My flush deepens, and I breathe in a sharp breath at his crude words. I'm insanely aroused, my panties drenched, and I feel like I could come undone just at his words alone.

I arch my neck, drawing him toward me, and he meets my lips in a kiss. It isn't rushed; we both take our time savoring each other's taste. His lips are warm and soft against mine. They part slightly, allowing my tongue to slip inside, and our tongues expertly mix. We both breathe into the kiss like our lips have been desperate to reunite.

Christian slides his hand up the back of my thigh, and I lean into him. I need more. I need to be closer. He turns onto his side, facing me, and I bring the leg he is still holding around his waist as we continue to steal oxygen from each other's mouths like thieves in the night, taking anything we can get.

An unexpected whimper erupts from my throat when I feel his full hardness against my sensitive bud, sending shock waves through my body. He groans into my mouth, gripping tighter behind my thigh. Our kiss is still slow as he traps my bottom lip tenderly between his teeth and gently sucks on it before releasing it. I moan, repeating his action.

Feeling completely aroused, I push my breasts against his chest till there isn't any space between our bodies, simultaneously rocking my hips and rubbing against him. We both pant as our kiss becomes hungry. He kisses the pulse on my neck while caressing my breast in his large palm.

Shit, shit, shit, I mentally chant, feeling like I'm about to burst.

"Rayne, it's time to call it a night." My dad's voice penetrates my ears as he walks up the stairs.

I urgently untangle myself from Christian and sit up, separating us. My chest heaves as I struggle to control my breathing. I look at him and his swollen lips from our kissing assault with wide eyes. As my dad steps into the doorway, a redness creeps up Christian's neck and onto his cheeks.

My dad's eyes jump from mine to Christian's, then back to mine. Trying not to be completely obvious about what we were doing, I look my father in the eyes and give him an innocent smile.

"Christian was just about to leave, pops," I say, sounding out of breath.

He watches us skeptically before he smiles. "I'll see you at work tomorrow, son. Have a good night."

Unable to respond, Christian gives him a tight-lipped smile and nods his head in acknowledgment.

"I guess I better get going," he says, traces of lust still lingering in his eyes and voice.

"I wish you could stay…"

He gives me my favorite crooked smile. "Me too."

With our fingers interlocked. We stop at my bedroom door, neither of us moving, not wanting to part. It's worse now that we're in a good place, knowing he's so close and just out of reach. The more my feelings grow, the harder it is to leave him.

His eyes are focused on our hands before he focuses on me. "I'll see you soon."

He kisses my forehead before pulling me into his warm embrace. We both breathe in, savoring each other's scent, memorizing this moment until the next time. I pull away from him but place my hand back in his. I give him a soft kiss on his mouth, then step backward.

He steps away, still holding my hand. "Bye…" his words linger between us as he continues out the door, only my fingertips in his grasp.

"Bye…" I softly whisper as he takes another step toward the stairs. He gives me a soft smile and takes one last step, my hand no longer in reach.

My hand drops heavily to my side, and I sigh. I feel silly to miss him already, but I do; I miss him. As he descends the stairs, I feel a sense of loss and no longer feel as warm. That warmth quickly returns when I remember we are no longer playing a push-and-pull game. We're in it for real. I smile and feel excited for the next time we get to hang out. We haven't discussed when that will be, but I have a feeling it will be soon. Ever since my birthday weekend and Christian telling Ryker and my dad about us, something has shifted between us in a good way. My feelings are stronger, our connection is more intense, and we're the closest we have ever been. I no longer feel like we're a lost cause. I feel hopeful.

I'm still worked up from our steamy kiss that ignited me at my core and made my toes curl just thinking about it. Even though I showered earlier, I take another one, this time a cold one, hoping to dim the burn in the pit of my stomach and the throbbing sensation still taking place between my legs. I stand under the icy water that feels like pins and needles as it hits my skin. Regardless of the coldness, it still does nothing to simmer the burn I feel at my core. Leaning my head against the cool glass, I sigh and turn off the water.

Snuggling into my bed, I'm hit with the smell of citrus still lingering on my sheets. My body instantly feels hotter, my cold shower doing nothing for me as the ache between my legs intensifies. I need a release. Feeling overheated, I throw my covers off my body. I close my eyes as I lay there on my back, thinking of Christian's lips searing my skin with his kiss, his rough hands leaving a burning trail everywhere they touch, and the twinge in my stomach feeling his hardness against my sex.

I let go of the comforter that I didn't realize I had gripped between my hands and bring them to my breasts. I palm them, picturing Christian's hands and not my own. My nipples are hard and sensitive, begging to be touched. I continue to caress one breast as I use my index and thumb to pinch my pebbled nipple on the other. Throwing my head back, I moan at the feeling, giving it another pinch as my stomach tightens.

I've never touched myself until now, but fucking hell, it feels good. I'm touching myself the way I'd want Christian to handle me as the build-up in my stomach and pussy forms.

Chapter twenty-three

I slide my hands into my panties and find my sensitive bud. Giving it a flick, I whimper, bucking my hips forward. Fuck. I continue rubbing and flicking as waves of heat build and a tingly sensation forms, making me hotter and hotter.

I'm about to explode when a tapping sound rips me away from the moment, and I freeze.

Chapter 24

Christian

"Bye," *she whispers* as I take another step toward the stairs. I give her a small smile, her hand no longer within my grasp. A longing takes place in my chest with every step I take away from her. Never in a million fucking years would I have thought it would be difficult for me to leave a girl at the end of the night. I was usually on my way out before I was fully dressed, not wanting to spend another second in their company. The more time I spend with Rayne, the less time I want to spend away from her.

Usually, I'd say goodbye to Ryker, but with a severe case of blue balls and still rocking a hard-on, I want to avoid him and get the hell out of here. Running into him would be awkward as fuck! After what just happened upstairs with his sister, I don't think I can look him in the eyes. Imagine, *"Oh, hey, Ry, the movie was great. I can't tell you what happened or how it ended because I was too focused on how your sister's mouth tasted and feeling her tight body against mine. Oh, and I was seconds away from busting in my pants.* See... Awkward as fuck.

Once I get home, I immediately strip out of my clothes and hop into a cold shower. I seem to take a lot of cold showers these days. Leaning my head toward the showerhead, I welcome the ice-cold water pelting against my face. Closing my eyes, I stroke myself, thinking about Rayne and how she was swirling her hips against my dick and the whimpers and moans escaping her lips.

I could tell she was aroused just as much as me, and if it weren't for Jack interrupting us, I would have had her legs wrapped around my head as I devoured her beautiful pussy. Fuck! This is torture. I'm so turned on right now. Stroking myself isn't even doing it for me. I need Rayne.

Quickly hopping out of the shower and changing, I head out the door. Using the trellis, I climbed up the same way I did the first time. *Trellis...* I smile.

As I approach her window, I hear soft moans and gasps coming from inside her bedroom. Sounds I could never forget. Is she touching herself right now? Fuck! My dick twitches at the realization. Giving her window a light tap, I wait for a few beats before I lightly tap again and this time, Rayne approaches wearing only a tiny lavender nightgown. Her nipples are hard, her face is flushed, and her chest deeply moves up and down.

Fuck, she's beautiful.

She slides it open, surprise on her face at seeing me. "Christian, what are you doing here?" she whispers as I step through.

Shutting the window before turning to me, she bashfully tugs at the bottom of her nightgown. I take a calm step toward her.

"What are you doing here?" she repeats.

I take another step, causing her to look up at me, our chests intensely rising and falling as we study each other. Her breath catches when I brush a strand of hair behind her ear.

"Finishing what we started," I say, crashing my lips against hers.

She yelps into my mouth before it twists into a needy moan. Standing on her tippy toes, she wraps her arms around my neck as our kiss becomes frantic. I slide my hands over her perfect ass, gripping under her thighs, and lift her. She instinctively wraps her legs around my waist as I walk her to the bed, gently setting her down, never breaking the kiss. Her legs stay wrapped around my waist as she swivels her hips and grinds into me. I moan at the feeling of her pussy sliding against my length, and she sighs breathlessly.

"Fuck, Rayne." I moan. "You feel so fucking good."

She bites my lip in response and claws at my back, pulling me closer to her. I move to her neck while every inch of our bodies rub against each other.

"More... please more." She moans, and I cover her mouth with my hand to keep her from waking anyone up.

"Shhh, baby... you're going to get us caught. If I let go of your mouth, are you going to be quiet?" she nods, still rubbing up against me, aching for more.

"M... More, please." She rasps the instant my hand leaves her mouth.

I smirk. "I'm only getting started, baby."

She looks me in the eye with a feeling of reckless, impatient desire before pulling my face back to hers, and once again, we crush our lips together, resuming our frantic kiss. I can feel her hard nipples pressing against my chest, and I notice she isn't wearing a bra.

"Fuck!" I groan, cupping her breast and giving her nipple a pinch.

"Oh god!" she hisses, throwing her head back.

Her nipples are sensitive, and the slightest touch sends vibrations through her body. After a long, hard kiss, we pause, trying to catch our breath as our hearts pound against each other.

"T... Touch me," she pleads.

"Touch you where Raynie?"

"D... Down there..." her throat bobs, and her cheeks turn a shade of rose.

She grabs the bottom of her nightgown, and I move, giving her space to take it off. I admire her sculpted thighs, toned stomach, and the way her bare breasts bounce.

I growl, bringing my mouth straight to her peaked nipple.

"Christian." My name escapes her lips. "Touch me, please."

With light pecks on her neck, I slowly make my way down her body, kissing and licking every inch. I pause at her tits and take my time, gently rolling my tongue around her nipples.

"Harder."

I pull one breast in through my teeth, and she groans loudly, grabbing my head. My free hand slowly slides down her body to her soaking panties.

"You're so wet, baby." I grind into her. "Do you feel what you do to me?" she squeezes her eyes tightly, arching her back.

"Oh… fuck." My dick jumps, hearing her fall apart beneath me.

I caress her clit from the outside of her panties, applying just the right amount of pressure.

"More."

I oblige, sliding my hands inside her panties, her juices instantly soaking my fingers. Carefully, I slowly insert one finger. She sucks in a sharp breath, biting hard onto her bottom lip.

"Is this okay? Am I hurting you?" she bucks her hips and rides my finger, telling me all I need to know. "God, you're so fucking sexy. Ride my finger, baby."

She pants, and I can feel her walls contract around me. She's close. I flick my index finger, hitting her g-spot while using my thumb to rub her bud.

"Oh god! I'm going to come, Christian." She bucks her hips, and I use my forearm to gently hold her down while I continue. Her legs tremble, and I know she's ready.

Giving her nipple one last suck before releasing it from my mouth.

"Come for me, baby," I demand.

"Christian," my name falls from her lips in a scream, and I quickly cover her mouth. She convulses beneath me, and her pussy tightens around my finger, releasing all over me. It is by far the sexiest thing I have ever seen. If I were to die right now, I would die a satisfied man.

I kiss her softly before climbing off her and heading to the bathroom. A few seconds later, I return with a warm, wet towel. I've never cared to do any of this before, but I don't want her feeling any discomfort tomorrow, so I gently clean her up before pressing a light kiss to her inner thigh and discarding the towel on the bed beside us. When I reach for her nightgown so she can dress, she stops me and stands up.

Rayne stands entirely naked, facing me. I've seen her completely exposed twice now, and I don't think I'll ever get used to it. Fucking. Perfect.

"What are you doing?" I swallow.

"It's your turn…" she nervously bites her lip.

Rayne looks so innocent standing in front of me, completely vulnerable. It's the opposite of how she looked, reaching her climax and letting go. Even after having me between her thighs and my fingers inside her pussy, the bashfulness she shows still catches me off guard. I expect nothing in return; I get pleasure in seeing her come undone. The way she whimpers and moans. The way her stomach clenches and her legs shake.

"You don't have to do anything for me."

"I want to."

The confidence I know she has peeked through.

"What do you want, Raynie?"

"I want to taste you." She steps to me and drops to her knees.

I groan, my dick jumping at her words. Looking down at her almost makes come on the spot. I've desired no one in my entire life as much as I crave her.

With delicate fingers and slightly shaky hands, she grabs the waistband of my shorts, pulling them down, and my erection springs free. She gasps as if my dick is the most intimidating thing she's ever seen. She looks up at me and swallows hard.

"You don't have to, Rayn—" she grips me in her hands, cutting me off. *Oh. Shit.*

Rayne

I can hear my heart beating in my ears. I'm scared I won't be able to fit him in my mouth. His cock is flawless. My mouth waters at the sight. I'm nervous and unsure what to do, but I want to do this. I want to make him feel just as good as he makes me feel. I may not be experienced, but I have watched porn before. So, I do exactly as I remember seeing.

I run my fingers down the length of him, admiring the smoothness of his skin under my touch. I press my lips to the tip of him, and his hands instantly go to my hair. I stare into his eyes when the firm tip of his manhood presses past my lips, and I take him into my mouth. His eyes never leave mine, and he watches me like he never wants to see anything else.

I circle my tongue around his tip before taking him as deep as I can. When he hits the back of my throat, my eyes instantly water, and his thighs shake. Pulling my head back, my hand follows, gliding back to his protruding tip before twisting my wrist and sliding back down his shaft. He groans, fisting my hair tighter, and I accept the pain. I hollow out my cheeks as he thrusts into me. With each thrust, his cock hits the back of my throat, forcing me to squeeze my eyes shut.

"Look at me." His husky voice demands.

Meeting eyes of honey that darken in hunger. I feel myself get wetter under his gaze. His hands tighten in my hair as his thrusts become rapid, his control gone. I can feel his cock swell between my lips, forcing me to adjust millimeter by millimeter of his thick girth. I twist and stroke, doing my best to take him fully. His thighs become stiff as a warm salty taste invades my mouth, and I welcome it.

"Fuck! I'm going to come."

I groan with him in my mouth, and he thrust harder and faster before quickly pulling out and stroking his length, ejaculating all over my chest. Spurts of milky white cling to my skin as his cock jerks in his hands. He scrunches his eyes shut and moans along with his last stroke, surrendering to his release.

Once he gets his breathing under control, he finally opens his eyes, looking down at me. He extends his hand and pulls me up to my feet. Saying nothing, he bruises my lips with a kiss. A kiss that makes me feel dizzy, and if it weren't for his arms wrapped around me, I'd lose all balance. He grabs the towel we used earlier from the bed and wipes me clean.

"Thank you."

He gives me a flirtatious smirk as he grabs my satin teddy. "No. Thank you."

I blush, thinking about what I had just done. He explored my body like a map with his lips. Only both of us got entirely lost in each other. I have never felt so alive. Christian makes me feel things I've never felt before. Something I've only ever dreamed of experiencing. He is a dream, and I fear that one day I will wake up and he won't be here.

Raising my arms, Christian dresses me, slipping my teddy over my head, and then we both get back into my bed, no longer aching to be touched. His arm automatically opens for me, and it's the most natural thing. It's as if we have done this our whole lives. We lie in comfortable silence as he plays with my hair.

"What's going on in that pretty little head of yours?" he asks, twirling my hair around his finger.

"That was amazing." I sigh, and he chuckles.

"Yes, it was." We're silent for a moment as my eyes get heavy. "Tell me a secret," he says.

"I was scared I wouldn't know how to do it right and that it wouldn't feel good for you."

"For one, don't ever be scared that it doesn't feel good for me, and for two, that was the best head I've ever gotten."

A pang of jealousy forms at the thought of him getting a blow job from other girls, and it pisses me off to imagine anyone touching him. They were most likely more experienced than me and knew what they were doing. Before I overthink the situation, I quickly remind myself that what we share is different and incomparable. Those girls meant nothing, and it was before I even knew him.

"Are you just telling me that so I don't feel bad?" I tease, but a part of me wonders if it's true.

He stops twirling my hair and lifts my chin, looking me in the eye. "Any touch from you feels good. It doesn't matter if you're holding my hand, kissing my lips, or unintentionally grazing my skin. I crave your touch, Rayne… I desire you."

How am I supposed to respond to that? Everything he said is exactly how I feel about him. Before I met him, I never knew what it was like to look at someone and smile for no damn reason. When I say I crave him, I'm not speaking in just a sexual way, but in the most innocent form. I yearn to hear his voice, crave to feel his lips against my forehead, desire to listen to his thoughts, but I crave him in ways where I just want to be next to him and nothing more and nothing less.

Laying in his arms and looking into his eyes, I realize two things. I am falling for him hard and fast; two, I am his, and I think I have been for a while now. I still remember when our eyes first met—an inconsequential second of almost nothing—yet the perpetual beginning of everything.

I kiss him slowly, telling him everything I am too scared to voice out loud. *I crave you too.*

We continue to lie wrapped in each other, not uttering a word. Only the sound of our steady breaths and the rhythm of our calm hearts fill the room. Exhaustion finally takes over, but I remember I wanted to talk to him about Halloween.

"What are your plans for Halloween?"

"That depends on what you want to do."

"Well, Devil's night is a big deal here, and I, of course, have never been. I was hoping you'd want to come with Laynie, Ryker, and me?"

"What's Devil's night? It sounds like trouble," he smirks.

"It is the night of mischief, after all." My lip tugs upward.

I tell him everything about Devil's night and why it's such a big deal. He wondered why I never went, and I told him I've always prioritized school above anything else, but I was also scared. I had never even been to a party, let alone a massive event where high school and college students from all over attend. It was intimidating, and once I learned about the game, it was a big hell no for me. Fear of the unknown is scary for most people, especially for a girl like me. I've had my future mapped out and knew what I wanted to do since I was little, and the thought of attending Devil's night and not having any idea what *game* would be held that year was enough to make me chicken out.

Since meeting Christian, I can feel something changing within myself, making me more curious now than ever before, and I want to try new things. I'm growing into this newfound person, this new version of myself that was always buried deep down within me, and I like who I'm becoming.

Venturing out of my safety bubble terrified me—all the unknowns and what-ifs were something I didn't like. I guess what really had me afraid was trying something new and failing. But now, I think it is better to try something and fail than never try at all. Being fearful of the unknown does nothing but limit yourself. It's when you test the edge of your limits that your limits expand.

Christian tells me he assumed we'd be together anyway, so of course, he's going with me. We won't know the location until an hour before it starts, so we will all meet and get ready at my house. He told me he doesn't dress up, but he will make an exception for me. Some guys go all out, but I told him when Ryker goes, he typically only wears a mask. Christian liked that idea and said that's probably what he will end up doing. Either way, I know he's going to look hot. He always does.

"What are you going to wear?" he asks.

"I'm not sure yet. I'm putting something together for Laynie and me. I just haven't figured out what."

"I'm sure whatever it is will turn out great. You'll look good in anything." I blush, snuggling deeper into him.

"Laynie insists it has to be sexy."

He chuckles. "Great, I'm going to be rocking a boner while fighting guys left and right for looking at you."

I giggle. "Who cares if they look at me? I'm yours."

"Damn right you are." He growls, flipping me over.

Lips and tongue etch my body as fingers trail with a soft, firm touch before giving me another earth-shattering orgasm.

This time, I can no longer keep my eyes open. Sleep comes instantly, and I fall asleep dreaming about him.

Chapter 25

Rayne

"Hold still, will you," Laynie says, grabbing my chin and angling my face exactly where she needs it.

"I'm sorry, but I've been sitting in this chair for almost two hours, and my ass felt numb."

"Have you ever heard the saying beauty is pain?" she smirks at me through the mirror, and I roll my eyes.

"Of course, I've heard of it doesn't mean I have to like it. Plus, the only reason we have a stigma around beauty is because of society's beauty standards, and I think it's all bullshit."

Laynie giggles at my little outburst. "I agree, babe. It is bullshit. However, it doesn't change the fact you still have to sit still. I'm almost done."

Yeah, she said that an hour ago. I was busy all last week making our costumes for tonight, and I decided on the purge. I thought it was perfect with my fashion skills and Laynie's makeup expertise. Since I didn't want to wear a mask all night, I thought it would be cool for Laynie to create a mask using makeup. My mask is pink, and hers is red. We have x's over our eyes, and our mouths look stitched. Whatever kind of makeup she's using makes it glow in the dark, and it's pretty badass. I didn't think it would take this long to do, but whatever we're going to look so good, it will be worth it in the end.

"Okay, you're done." She claps, wearing the biggest grin.

Wow, it looks incredible! I knew it would be based on how she did hers, but seeing it on myself is amazing. The way she created our mask using makeup looks way better than any mask you can buy. It's going to bring our costumes together perfectly, and the added touch of glow will have us standing out in the best way.

"Laynie, you have a serious gift and can do people's makeup for a living," I tell her, still examining her work of art in the mirror.

"Thanks, babe. I don't mind doing your makeup or doing it for fun, but I don't think I'd want to do it for a living. It would take away the fun, and I wouldn't enjoy it as much."

"I didn't think about it like that, but I would still give it some more thought because you have some real talent." Standing behind me, she puts her hands on my shoulders, looking at me through the mirror.

"Says the one who can make something out of nothing. You literally transform a piece of fabric now that's talent."

I scoff. "You literally transform faces! Give yourself more credit."

"That's true. I just wanted to hear you compliment me some more."

I turn around and playfully push her. "You ready to see our costumes?"

Laynie has been bugging me to send her pics throughout the entire process, but I told her she would have to wait and see. I already know she's going to love them. My favorite part of creating clothing is seeing the reaction it gets, and I can't wait to see hers.

"Fuck yes! I've waited too long, gimme." she holds her hand out, giving me grabby hands, and I swat her hands away.

"Close your eyes."

I grab our costumes hanging up in the closet, hidden behind some clothes, before walking back into the bedroom with our costumes in hand, setting mine on the bed but holding hers up.

"Okay, open," I tell her eagerly. She opens her eyes, and they almost pop out of her head. "Tada!" I sing, waving her costume from side to side.

Laynie runs excitedly toward me, trips over her duffle bag on the floor, hops to her feet, and grabs the costume out of my hands.

"Oh. My. God! This is so fucking perfect!" she shouts, walking over to the mirror and pressing her costume against herself.

"Put it on already!"

We both undress, discarding our clothes in a pile at our feet. I slipped on tiny white spandex shorts under my white tulle tutu that barely covered my ass and paired the skirt with a white lace corset top and matching thigh-high boots.

Laynie is wearing the same thing as me, but her costume is all black, and with her glowing, red-painted mask, she looks fucking stunning. I stitched the lace material to the corsets and added splashes of fake blood. Making the tutu was my favorite part. I used white tulle and sparkly tulle for mine and black and sparkly tulle for Laynie's. I even created our very own weapons. For Laynie, I created a bloody machete, and for me, I made a bloody barbed wired bat. I'm proud of myself and all my hard work. It was worth it.

My hair has gotten longer over the last month, so I'm keeping it in its natural dark waves that rest just above my ass. I curled Laynie's hair before running my fingers through it to give her that naturally messy look she loves so much. We look fucking phenomenal, and our costumes suit us perfectly. Laynie wearing black and me wearing white is exactly like us, night and day; the yin to my yang were opposites, but complemented each other flawlessly. We are a perfect balance.

"Damn Rayne, you outdid yourself," Laynie says, spinning around in front of the mirror.

I grin. "Thank you! Let's take a picture and send it to Jamie."

I'm bummed out Jamie couldn't be here with us. I asked her if she wanted me to make her a costume, but she told me she wouldn't be doing anything this year because of something about dealing with family things. She's been dealing with family things a lot recently, and I wonder what's going on. I've asked her multiple times, but she doesn't share much, and I don't want to force her to talk if she doesn't want to. So, I told her I was always there for her if she needed anything at all. I don't believe her when she tells me it's nothing to worry about.

The sad look she lets slip occasionally and how she flinches when we touch her, says otherwise. Maybe I should force her to talk to me about what's happening at home. Perhaps I can help?

We take a few pictures doing different poses. One is of Laynie and me puckering our lips, another is us making a silly face, and another of us just smiling. I send her one of us making a funny face. I'm crossed-eyed, giving duck lips, and Laynie is sticking her tongue out while holding her bloody machete.

Me: *Photo image*

Me: Miss you lots! Wish you were here with us. Xoxo.

Jamie: Miss you more. You guys look hot! Bummed, I'm not there to see you guys in person. Xxx.

Jamie: p.s. Careful with Laynie and that machete tonight… knowing her she'll try to cut Ryker's balls off at some point! ;)

Me: LOL!

"Is it safe to come in?" Ryker asks through the door.

"No, I'm naked!" I shout, walking in his direction.

"Ew! Thanks for the visual. I didn't need to know." I fling the door open, and his hands fly to his face, shielding his eyes.

"I'm just messing with you. Come in."

He drops his hands before slowly opening his eyes. "Holy shit. Your makeup is sick, and the costumes are fucking incredible!" he pauses, squinting his eyes, surveying Laynie and me. "A little short... but it's Halloween, so I guess it's alright." Laynie and I both scoff at the same time.

"As if you have a say," I lightly punch him in his arm. "Where is your costume?" I ask, looking down at his all-black attire.

"I have a red skeleton tactical mask in my room, and I'll get it before we leave."

Guys have it so easy.

Just as I'm about to ask where Christian is, he walks in. He's dressed similar to Ry, wearing a black hoodie and black skinny jeans with his black skeleton tactical mask resting on his head. He takes me in slowly, admiring me from head to toe, and I flush hot under his gaze. His eyes leisurely sweep back to my face, giving me his panty-dropper lopsided smile. I clench my thighs together to dull the ache forming between my legs. He notices, and his eyes darken. Laynie clears her throat, bringing my focus back to reality.

He catches me with ease when I smile and jump on him, wrapping my legs around his waist.

"I've missed you," I whisper into his ear. His arms wrapped around me grow tighter.

"I've missed you too."

Ryker groans behind us. I haven't hung out with Christian since the night he snuck into my bedroom window. That was over a week ago, and I've missed him more than I'd like to admit. Of course, we've texted, but it isn't the same as seeing him in person. He's been busy working at the shop and spending time with his mom because she found an opening for a teacher's position at an elementary school nearby and starts after Thanksgiving break. I've been busy creating these costumes for Laynie and me, staying up all hours of the night to get it done in time. Other than that, not much has been going on. Tonight is definitely needed time together.

We hang out in my room, listening to music and taking a few shots before we go. Ryker is the DD (designated driver), so he isn't drinking. He and Laynie receive a text an hour before sundown on the dot.

Unknown: We've been waiting for such a night to practice mayhem and other frights. If you're brave and don't take flight, you are in for a spooky night. The event starts at half-past eight, and don't you dare be a second late…
Location: 34.201580, -118.211148

"Well, this is a first," Ryker says, observing the text.
"What do you mean?" Christian and I both ask.
"They sent coordinates to the location, not an actual address like usual… I wonder what's going to happen this year?"
"Whatever it is, bring it on, baby! I'm so ready." Laynie says eagerly, rubbing her hands together in anticipation.
I, on the other hand, feel like throwing up. My stomach is in a knot, and instinctively I want to chicken out and come up with an excuse not to go. Of course, I won't, but it crossed my mind. Ryker said he would meet us at his car after he grabbed his mask. Laynie rushes down the stairs in excitement. Nerves take my excitement over, and I don't move; instead, I stand frozen in place. Christian notices and grabs my hand.
"What's wrong?" he asks, his face full of affection.
"Suddenly, I'm nervous… what if we have to split up for the game?"
"Hey, you'll be okay," he pulls me into his chest, comforting me. "I got you, and we aren't splitting up. The rules of the game are not something I give a shit about."
I relax into him. His touch makes me feel safe and suddenly not as nervous.
"Let's do this," I say.
"That's my girl."

In the car, Christian leans into my ear and whispers. "Did I tell you how sexy you look tonight?"

Goosebumps coat my arms, and the ache in my sex ignites. "I think you forgot to mention it."

He twirls a strand of my hair around his index finger. "You look fucking breathtaking, Rayne Davis," he kisses my collar bone. "Good enough to eat." He says in a husky voice that sends vibrations straight to my sex, and I clench my thighs.

"I bet you're soaking right now," he moves his hand up my thigh.

"Behave yourself," I tease. "My brother and Laynie are sitting right there."

He chuckles, taking my hand in his.

We drive listening to music for the next hour with the occasional bickering between Laynie and Ryker, nothing new there. Laynie flips the visor down to look at her makeup, and her eyes lock on mine in the back seat. We beam at each other because we look badass.

<u>'High Hopes by Panic! At The Disco,'</u>
"I was going to be that one in a million. Always had to have high, high hopes."

Laynie and I shriek at the song, rolling down our windows. We both hang out of the car shouting the lyrics, not giving a shit if our hair gets tangled in the wind. Ryker calls for us to get back in the car, but we ignore him, lost in the moment, and laugh. He eventually gives in and rolls down his window, throwing out one hand while he drives. Christian chuckles as his hands span the curve of my waist, holding me in place, so I don't fly out of the car. I feel fucking invincible.

He gives me a lopsided smile. "Your trouble, woman."

"No..." I pause, "I'm just finally living."

We arrive at our secret location, and I'm in awe. Our destination is in the middle of nowhere, bordered by tall, distinguished trees. Neon-colored lights make the evergreen forest look enchanted and illuminate the trees. The shots we took before coming here have finally hit me, and I'm feeling the perfect amount of a buzz as adrenaline courses through my body, making me feel exhilarated. Laynie is enthusiastically bouncing in her seat as Ryker parks. Christian and I are staring out the window, awestruck, as we take in everything. The secluded parking area is overflowing with cars. I knew a lot of people attended this event, but never in my wildest dreams did I expect it to be this crowded.

Before I start over-analyzing how many strangers are here, Christian gives me a reassuring hand squeeze, letting me know he's with me.

"Alright, you guys stay with Christian or me at all times," he looks at me before sweeping his gaze to Laynie in the passenger seat. "Understood?"

Laynie scoffs, rolling her eyes in annoyance, "Yes, sir," she says, saluting him.

"Don't worry about Rayne. I got her," Christian says to Ryker.

Before heading into total mayhem, we ask some girl passing by to take a picture of all of us.

"Can you take a couple of Rayne and me?" Christian asks, handing his phone to Laynie after our group photos.

"Alright, you two, show me how much you love each other," she says, smirking behind the camera.

Love.

My cheeks instantly heat, and I don't dare look at Christian. He chuckles nervously, but he doesn't deny it, and I don't know what that means. *Does he love me? Do I love him? What is the appropriate time to love someone?* Love is a big word, and I don't know the first thing about being in love. However, I know my feelings for him are deep-seated, and it's nothing I have ever experienced. I more than like him. That's a given, but I'm too scared to acknowledge anything beyond that. We both take notice of her comment but choose not to say anything about it and pose.

Chapter 26

Rayne

After putting my bat into Ryker's trunk, Christian and I walk deeper into the woods with his arm slung over my shoulder. A few girls stop to tell Laynie and me our costumes are sexy and that our makeup is killer. Everyone here is dressed to the nines, but I must admit I haven't seen anyone top our costumes. We look fucking phenomenal, and I smile, adding a little pep in my step. I gasp as we step into the center of the forest. There is a makeshift wooden stage with huge speakers on each side and an enormous teepee fire in the center. People have crowded around, dancing to the blaring music that shakes the ground below our feet. Alcohol-filled coolers are placed in line with a few wooden trunks for people to sit. The energy is high, and the crowd is getting more amped by the second. Christian pulls me deeper into his side as we all walk toward the alcohol-filled coolers.

"Buzz ball, anyone?" Laynie asks, digging into the cooler.

"I'll take one, please."

"Me too," Christian adds.

Ryker walks over and grabs a bud light, cracking it open, and I arch my brow at him.

He shrugs, "What? We aren't leaving this place for at least a couple of hours. Plus, I'm no lightweight. I'll be fine." Laynie holds up her fake machete.

"You bet your ass you'll be fine, or else I'll put this to good use." Using the machete, she pokes him in the dick.

He smacks it away and covers himself. "Get that thing away from me. Tell me why you thought it was a good idea for her to walk around with a machete, sis?"

Christian chuckles, and I full-blown laugh at Ry's reaction because I think back to what Jamie texted me earlier tonight. I knew she was right.

We chug our buzz balls as Ryker sips his beer. Laynie grabs another one before handing her machete to Ry and announces she wants to dance. Christian and Ryker stand off to the side, keeping us within their line of sight as we head to the massive fire pit.

Laynie and I walk hand in hand into the group of grinding bodies as 'Sexy Bitch Feat. Akon' plays. I spin her around, using one hand so her ass is facing me. She moves her hips from side to side, throwing one hand up in the air. The tequila from the buzz ball floods our senses and loosens our limbs, allowing us to move effortlessly. I grab her hand that's in the air and set my other hand on the curve of her waist. We are in sync with the beat as she rotates her hips, lowering us to the floor before slowly rolling our bodies back up. Laynie turns to face me with a smirk, teasing her lips. She pops open her buzz ball and tilts my chin up to the sky. She waterfalls the alcohol into my mouth, and I embrace the taste. Something about the way she pours it into my mouth is alluring. I take the buzz ball from her hands as she tilts her head back, opening her mouth, and I pour the rest of the tequila into it. A little bit of the alcohol slides down her chin, and she giggles, using the back of her hand to wipe it off.

I glance over my shoulder and freeze at Christian's penetrating stare. He is wearing his all-black mask, only allowing me to see the reflection of the fire burning in his golden eyes. I can feel his heated gaze from here warming me up better than the blazing pit ever could. With a flick of my finger, I call him to me.

He walks toward me dauntlessly, his eyes never leaving mine. Once he approaches me, he lifts his mask, allowing me to see him. He cradles the side of my face, brushing his thumb over my bottom lip.

"You are a fucking force to be reckoned with, and I can never keep my eyes off you," he says and sears my lips with a heated kiss.

The music abruptly stops, and a sinister voice echoes throughout the woods.

"May I have everyone's attention?" The faceless man wearing a grim reaper costume says, and everyone goes silent. I gulped, glancing at Christian, who wore a stoic expression.

"The events tonight are about to commence..." he announces, and the lights that once lit up the trees all go black along with the fire pit, leaving us in darkness.

What the hell is this? My heart beats harshly against my chest as beads of sweat form on my forehead.

A spotlight casts upon the grim reaper. "Out in the dark and under a tree, look for a graveyard skeleton key. Don't be afraid of guts and goo, for on that key is your next clue." He pauses, and even though you can't see his eyes, you can feel him surveying the crowd. "This game will require partners of two; you have ten minutes until the sound of boo."

Christian grips my sweaty hand, "Let's go find Ryker and Laynie." Thankfully, they were standing a few people behind us.

"Holy shit, that was intense," Laynie says, beaming.

"You think this is fun? I'm scared shitless."

"It's supposed to be scary, babe," she laughs. "Just remember, it's only a game and is supposed to be fun."

Walking into a dark forest looking for hidden clues is fun? Laynie and Ryker have been going to these events for years, and if they can do it, so can I. *Right?* I'm doing this whether I want to or not. How will I ever fully experience anything if I'm too scared to even try?

"Since your partners with Christian, I'll be partners with Laynie. I think it's best to have one of us with you guys, anyway." Ryker says.

"The scary-ass reaper was pretty damn vague. How many clues are there, and how do we know who wins?" I ask.

"There are way too many people here to have an entire list of objects, and I'm assuming there will only be a few. Look," he says, pointing to herds of people walking and grabbing natural-colored tote bags. "Whatever the objects are, they must be small enough to fit in those. Find the first object, and you'll get your first clue. Every object you find, put it into your bag." I nod slowly, and he must sense my trepidation because he adds, "You'll be okay. This is all fun and games. Follow Christian's lead and find as much as you can. A blow horn usually goes off when the game ends, and we will meet right back here when we are finished."

I nod as we walk to grab our totes and wait for the game to begin. Christian wraps his arm around me and reminds me he's with me. I know he would let nothing bad happen to me. *This is going to be fun.* I repeat inwardly. I'm being a little dramatic. Obviously, these events are safe, or they wouldn't have them. The more I think about it, the less nervous I become. This is going to be fun, finding clues and solving riddles. Ryker and Laynie let us know they will start from the outside and work their way to the middle. Christian and I think it's best to start in the middle and work our way out.

The word *boo* blares from the speakers, causing a few people to scream, including me. The game has officially begun, and ominous music plays. *Yeah... not creepy at all.* Christian laughs, takes out his phone, and turns on his flashlight, and I follow his lead and do the same. It is pitch black out here; the light from our phones only allows us to see a couple of feet in front of us. The wind slips through the leaves and undergrowth cracks beneath our feet with each step we take. The moon shines through a lattice of leaves, and I glimpse the patchy sky and stars through tree breaks. I can hear wolves howling in the distance and snapping twigs from others. It probably wasn't the best idea to wear heeled boots because my heel gets caught on a root, and I trip, falling to my knees.

"Shit!" Christian says, bending down next to me. "Are you okay?"

"Yeah, I'm okay. It's barely visible out here." He unhooks the root around my heel and helps me up.

"I know. Hold on to my arm, okay?" he kisses my forehead.

"Okay, thank you."

"Okay, so according to the reaper, we're looking under trees for a skeleton key. These trees are massive, so I don't think the key will be very far up, and it's probably at eye level. Look at the trees on your left; and I'll cover our right."

"Okay, good idea."

The air is fresh, and I can smell the rich earth. A slight scent of flowers mixed with tree sap surrounds us. I shine my phone on the tree trunks to my left, and my light reflects off something, causing it to sparkle.

"I think I see something," I say excitedly. Christian follows my lead to the trunk, and sure enough, there is a medium-sized skeleton key covered in fake blood dangling from an overhang.

"That's my girl," Christian smiles. I flip the key over and read the clue on the dampened paper on the back.

"They say bats come out at night but don't be overcome with fright. A bat hangs somewhere, and your next clue is hidden there." I unpin the golden key from the tree attached to twine, almost like a necklace, and place it in Christian's bag.

I don't trust myself in these heels, and I'll trip again and lose the key, knowing my luck. We head further toward the outskirts of the woods, looking for our next clue. It's hard to spot anything with all the overhanging limbs across our path. Occasional flickering of phone light breaks through between clumps of bushes from other people on other routes. It makes me feel better knowing we aren't the only ones out here doing something as crazy as this. We are in the middle of nowhere, using only light from our phones to guide us.

"Tell me a secret," he says as we continue our search.

"I'm afraid of being alone. I don't feel the need to have somebody, but I would like to, especially when I'm old and gray, and all my kids are grown up."

"You want kids one day?"

"I'd like to be a mother one day and love my children as much as my parents love Ry and me," I tell him honestly.

I'd love to be a role model like them for kids of my own and love them just as fiercely. My mother once told me I won't know how much I can genuinely love someone until I have a child. I wouldn't mind having one of my own and adopting one. I'd love to give a child a wonderful home and unconditional love.

"What is your biggest fear?" I ask.

"I don't fear anything."

Biting my lip to suppress my smile, I lightly bump him with my shoulder. "Come on. Everyone fears something."

He lets out a heavy sigh, and when he doesn't answer right away, I decide to drop it, but he breaks the silence and says, "I fear that one day when I have kids of my own, something awful will happen to me like my dad, and I won't be around to see them grow up."

My eyes immediately water at his confession. My biggest fear is being alone, and his not being around for his children. Growing up with his father for ten years, only to lose him, must have been hard. Scratch that. It must have been gut-wrenching, and it has clearly affected him. Who wouldn't be affected by losing a parent, especially at a young age? Of course, I know it isn't possible, but I wish there were some way I could bring his dad back. I know he will be a great dad one day, and it saddens me that his fear is not being around for them. I wish I could say something to ease his fears, but there aren't any words for that.

When I stop walking, he turns to face me. "I understand your fears, and they are valid. I hope nothing like that ever happens to you, but I want you to know regardless of the time they may or may not spend with you, they will remember you forever." I rest my palm on top of his heart. "Because you are impossible to forget."

He slips off his mask as a tear slides down his cheek, stopping above his lip, and I softly kiss it away. I may not remove all his pain, but I can take away his tears.

"Thank you…" he whispers, his voice cracking. He slides his mask down, hiding any emotion, and takes my hand as we resume our search.

I notice luminescent orange pieces of tape on certain tree trunks to help guide us in the right direction on our way out. As we walk, something brushes across the top of Christian's head.

"What the fuck?" he ducks abruptly.

We shine our lights up and see a rubber bat hanging with its large wings expanded. Christian pulls it off the branch and flips it over.

"Your last clue can be found next to something orange and round."

"We're so close it's our last clue." I bounce up and down in elation.

He smiles at my excitement. "I wonder if anyone has found them all yet?"

"I don't know, but I think we should split up."

"What? No way!" his head whips back and forth. "I'm not leaving you."

I smile at his protectiveness, placing my hand on his arm. "If we have eyes in more than one spot, we will cover more ground and have a better chance of finding it. We won't go far. I'll go further up the path, and you can go right here." I point. "We meet back here in five minutes."

He stares at me, but I can't see his facial expression because of his mask.

"I don't know, Raynie… I don't like the idea of splitting up."

Honestly, I don't either, but it won't be long, and I want to win. Although I appreciate Christian caring for me and not wanting to leave my side, I need to do things on my own.

I slide his mask onto his head before looking up at his eyes and wrapping my arms around him. "I'll be okay. I promise. Five minutes, that's it." He bites his lip and nods.

"Five minutes, that's it," he says reluctantly. "If you find anything before, then meet me back here. I don't want you wandering alone."

I nod. "I'll set a timer on my phone."

He gives me a lingering kiss like this will be the last time he'd ever get the chance to feel my lips against his.

"Okay, I'll see you soon."

We break apart, and I continue forward as he walks along the path to my left. *Your last clue can be found next to something orange and round.* I'm not sure what size pumpkins will be out here, but It's so much darker without Christian's added light. I search left and right, hoping to catch sight of a pumpkin, but don't see anything. It's ghostly quiet this deep into the woods, and I wonder how many others are around.

So many of us wildly ran into the woods at the start. Once the game began, we looked like Spartans charging our enemy. It was loud and chaotic, but the deeper we went into the forest, the more we all dispersed, putting distance between us. I laugh, thinking about Laynie and Ryker working together as a team, and wonder if they've found all their clues. I wonder how often Laynie has threatened to cut Ryker's balls off by now.

The sound of twigs snapping causes me to abruptly stop laughing. It sounds like it was close. I check my phone to see how much time I have left before meeting Christian. Three minutes and thirty seconds. Again, the sound of shuffling feet and snapping twigs creeps around me. I stiffen, and a shudder runs down my spine. *Stop overthinking, Rayne. This isn't some horror movie. There are hundreds of people out here.*

I'm about two minutes out, so I turn around and start heading back the same way I came. As I walk back, the hairs on my neck stand, and I get a menacing feeling someone is watching me. I turn around, panicky, shining my light, but don't see anything or anyone. Being by myself in the woods is getting to my head.

I look at the ground, surveying the bushes and trees at my sides in case I missed any pumpkins the first time around. When shining my light at the ground, making sure not to trip again, I run straight into something solid, almost knocking the wind out of me. I yelp, but hands quickly fly to my mouth to keep me from making a sound. Looking up, I come face to face with Christian's mask, and he lets go of my mouth.

"Oh, thank God! It's you." I sigh, relieved. He's holding his phone down, shining it directly on me so I can barely see him. "Did you find anything?" I ask, holding my hand up to keep the blinding light from hitting my eyes.

I can see the top of his black hoodie shake from side to side, telling me no.

"What's up with the light?" I say, turning my own off.

He does the same, and the darkness confines us. I can't make anything out, my eyes adjusting to the darkness. With feather-light fingers, he skims up my thighs.

I giggle shyly. "Oh… this is what you're trying to do."

He groans, spinning me around and backing me into a tree. His fingers brush against my shorts, rubbing my sensitive bud. I whimper as he applies more pressure. Well, he sure is eager. My stomach tightens, and the build-up forms at my core. Laughter emerges as a group of girls run by in the distance.

I stop his hands from circling my bud. "I want you, but there are people everywhere. Let's look for the last object we are so close to winning." He doesn't listen and continues to rub me.

I grab his hands again. "Down, boy," I tease. "We will continue this later, I promise." I wedge myself out between him and the tree behind me. "Let's go."

As I step forward, I see a dark figure with a phone light approaching just as the timer I set earlier goes off at the same time as the person in front of me. He mutes his phone and pulls off his mask. *Christian.*

The color quickly drains from my face, and I become paralyzed.

"There's my girl," he smiles, kissing my forehead. "I found the last clue. We need to get back and return the items so we can hopefully win."

My alarm from my phone rings in my ears, and I can no longer make out a single word Christian is saying. His lips are moving, but I hear nothing, just the beeping from my phone as my heart plunges to the floor. My body trembles as terror creep up my spine, and I can barely hold myself up as dread consumes me.

If Christian is here, then who... I frantically turn around but am only met with blackness and a sinister feeling in my gut. Christian touches my shoulder to get my attention, and I flinch at the contact.

"Woah, what's wrong?" he asks, concerned, turning me around to face him.

I want to cry when I see his face etched with worry. This night was another first for us, and I'm ruining it. I will tell Christian what happened because I could never keep something like this away from him, but now isn't the time. I want us to have this moment; we deserve this moment.

Putting on a fake smile to help ease his worry, I take his hand in mine. "Yeah, sorry, I thought I heard something." His eyebrows scrunch together as his eyes roam over my face, seeking the truth.

"Are you sure you're okay?" I kiss the corner of his mouth, hoping he lets this go for now.

"I'm positive that I'm okay. Let's go!" I smile, pulling his arm forward, heading back to where we started.

He chuckles behind me as we run through the woods hand in hand. My smile drops once my face is out of his view, and the feeling of dread returns. I'm taken back to moments ago when I thought I was with Christian in the woods. I feel sick to my stomach thinking about how whoever he was touched me and how I let him. How could I be so stupid?

How did I not recognize it wasn't Christian's hands that were touching me?

We continue to run, getting closer to escaping these woods. I can hear laughter from other groups, pant legs sliding against bushes, and breathing sounds from others running in the same direction. While everyone is energized with excitement, I'm suffocating. I urge my legs to move faster, my feet to dig deeper, getting closer to the clearing so I can finally breathe. Christian's long legs easily keep up with mine.

I have to get out of here!

The trees are closing in on me, trying to hold me hostage. We finally emerge from the wooded forest, but I don't stop running until we get to our designated spot. It's then that I drop my hands to my knees as I hunch over and struggle to breathe. My chest rises and falls in short, quick breaths, and I feel like I might pass out any second.

"We fucking won, baby!" Christian said enthusiastically. *We won.* Catching my breath and glancing around, I notice no one else has yet made it out of the forest. I beam at Christian.

"We did it!" I shout as he lifts me into his arms, and I wrap my legs around his waist as he spins us around.

"We did it!" he repeats, wearing a proud smile, setting me down on my feet. The blow horn that Ryker was telling me about goes off, and I leap into Christian, startled by the sound.

Flashes of the stranger in all black hit me at once, and I close my eyes tightly, but the visions don't go away. I'm pinned against the tree, and his hands are on my body. He groans into my ear and touches my sex. I clutch Christian's jacket in my hands, reminding myself I'm okay. I'm safe. He gently pries my fingers from his jacket before resting his hands on my shoulders and pushing me back enough for him to see my face. His eyebrows are again drawn together, and his lips are turned down in a frown. Just like he notices everything about me, he notices something isn't right.

"What's going on, baby?"

Chapter twenty-six

"N... Nothing..." I subconsciously start playing with my fingernails, drawing his eyes to my hands.

"We said no more secrets. What is going on?" he wraps his hand around mine to keep me from messing with my fingers.

High- and low-pitched voices followed by laughter catch my attention. I look in the direction of the woods and see groups of people making their way out. Scanning the crowd, I look for the stranger. With my body full of anxiety, I can't seem to focus on anything, and every bit of noise appears to be amplified. Every breath of wind is as loud as a blood-curdling scream in my terrified mind. I spot Laynie and Ryker exiting the woods. Even seeing them doesn't put my mind at ease. My vision is scattered, and I can't seem to focus on one thing. I feel jittery, my hands tremble, my legs shake, and everything around me looks magnified. I feel like I'm losing my damn mind!

"Rayne," Christian snaps, and I frantically snap my attention to him. "What is going on?" he asks, concerned but growing impatient.

"Noth—"

"Don't tell me it's nothing," he cuts me off. "Once we met back up inside the woods, something has been bothering you. You're on edge, skittish, and paranoid. You keep looking around as if you're looking for someone to appear. Please talk to me..."

"In the woods... I didn't know...." I close my eyes, trying not to cry.

"Didn't know what?"

"It wasn't you in the woods... he touched me," I whisper, barely getting the words out as the tears I was trying to hold back slide down my cheek.

Chapter 27

Christian

"He *touched me*..." those words linger between us, repeatedly echoing inside my head.

Everything slows down around me, and I feel like I've entered the twilight zone. *Who touched her?* Just as I'm about to speak, Ryker and Laynie approach and their smiles drop the moment they see Rayne's tear-stained cheeks and my pale face.

"What the fuck is going on?" Ryker looks at me before rushing to his sister. "Rayne, what happened? Why are you crying?"

"I… I don't want to talk about it."

She didn't want to involve anyone regarding what happened at the party with Jackson, and I get that, but something happened in the woods, and I have no idea what happened or who did it. I place my hand on the side of her cheek as she looks at me with watery eyes. The glowing pink makeup from her mask is smearing in her tears.

"Raynie, you need to tell us what happened?" I rub my thumb up and down the side of her face. "Please, let us be here for you." Laynie steps up to my side and sets her hand on Rayne's shoulder, confirming what I am saying is true.

"In the woods when we split up."

"What the fuck do you mean, you split up?" Ryker's rage springs to life.

I'm not sure what happened yet, but I'm confident that I. Fucked. Up. I should never have let her out of my sight. She looked at me with such confidence, and I couldn't deny her.

I go to speak, but Rayne beats me to it. "Ry, please, not right now." She sighs, defeated. "Let me explain." She closes her eyes for a moment, gathering herself before opening them and looking at each one of us.

She tells Ryker and Laynie how she planned our splitting up and how I refused at first. When she bumped into a stranger, my heart beats faster. The fucking creep was dressed just like me! Whoever he was made me think this was personal. They had to know who I was and what I'd wear, or worse; they'd been watching me. When she tells us he started touching her, she can barely speak the words. An icy wave enclosed me as the hairs on the back of my neck rose and my mouth went dry. I feel like I'm going to be fucking sick. If I had just found the pumpkin a few minutes sooner, I would have been back in time to catch that motherfucker.

Laynie bawls, and Ryker is pacing back and forth, pulling at his hair. My pulse beats in my ears, blocking out all other sounds. Somebody touched my girl when I was just feet away from her. Fuck! My sweet girl can never catch a break. At her very first party, that sick little bitch Jackson almost raped her. Her first time coming to Devil's night, she gets assaulted. Wait... *Jackson*. I try to make sense of everything. This could be a stranger, but my gut tells me otherwise; this was personal. After the his threats he made, it had to be him. He dressed the same as me, knowing she wouldn't think anything of it. He followed us into the woods without us knowing. His moves were strategic. This was fucking planned!

Without warning, I get my legs to move and instantly push through the costume-covered bodies, looking for Jackson *fucking* Reed. He's here; I know he is. That sick fuck wouldn't do something like this and not wait around to see the reaction. He has been a problem for too long now, and I should have done something a lot worse than beating his ass the first time. I should have demanded her to tell Ryker or Jack. How could I be so arrogant to think my threats would be enough to keep him away? I should have given her no choice but to say something. Even if she hated me after, at least she would be safe.

They shout after me, calling my name, but I don't stop, and I don't look back. There are so many people here you would think we were at a music festival. This is fucking ridiculous. Ryker runs up behind me, jerking me to a stop. I turn to him and glare. I'm too pissed to care. He's in the way of finding Jackson. Turning back and continuing my search, I only make it two steps before he jerks me back to him again.

"Why the fuck do you keep stopping me?" I grab his hand, throwing it off my arm. Ignoring my warning, he grabbed me again.

"Calm the fuck down!" he stares at me hard. "You look like you're on a mission to kill somebody." *I am.* "Talk to me, bro. What's going on?"

"Did you not hear what your sister just told us?" his nostrils flare, eyebrows pulled down.

"I heard every fucking word! We don't know who it was. Do you think we can find some faceless sick fuck in a crowd this big?"

"I fucking know who it was!"

He goes still, and his eyebrows deepen. "Who?"

"Reed."

His hand clutches my arm harder. "Are. You. Sure."

"Positive."

Letting go of my arm, he squares his shoulders. "Let's go."

We slide down our masks to cover our faces so no one can identify us if we find him. Molten anger rolls through me with each step I take. You can tell we are out for blood as we ram through the crowd, forcing people out of our way.

I came into this world kicking and screaming while covered in someone else's blood, and I have no problem with going out the same fucking way.

I'm not sure how long we hunt for Jackson, but we can't find him, which pisses me off more. Ryker suggests we take care of this later, but I want to keep looking and don't care if I'm out here all night.

"Let's get back to Rayne and Laynie."

"No. We have to find him."

"He's probably long gone by now."

No, he's not. I can feel it.

"We will find him, I promise. I won't let this go, and I know you won't either. We know where he goes to school, and he can't hide from us forever."

Knowing he is right and not arguing, I head back to my girl. Rayne sits on a tree trunk with Laynie, and as if she can sense me, she looks in my direction, her eyes landing on me right away. Without hesitation, she runs to me, and I open my arms.

"Are you okay?" she says, panicked and full of worry. I breathe in the smell I love so much. Lavender. *Rayne.*

"I am now."

The grim reaper steps to the podium and talks in riddles, announcing the winners of tonight. I don't give a shit about the game anymore and don't want to be here for another second. Rayne places her hand in mine, and without saying a word to each other, she tells me she wants to leave, too.

We turn to Ryker and Laynie. "Let's get outta here," I say, and they both nod, following us back to the car.

The walk back is silent as we process the events of the night. When we hear a manic laugh behind us, everyone tenses before slowly turning around. About twenty feet in front of us, I come face to face with Jackson *fucking* Reed.

Laynie gasps as Ryker pushes her behind him, and I shield Rayne instinctively. Her body trembles in fear, but I don't dare look back and take my eyes off Jackson. Ryker closes the gap between us, standing shoulder to shoulder with me and blocking the girls out of Jackson's sight. We stand there for what feels like hours as I take him in. Looking at him slowly up and down, I see an exact reflection of myself, and it shakes me to the core. He is wearing the same clothes as me and the same tactical skeleton mask. My nostrils flare, and I clench my teeth. He can't see my reaction because of my mask, which I want. He doesn't get the satisfaction of seeing me about to burst. I casually place my hands in my pockets to keep them from clenching, giving nothing away.

Ryker breathes raggedly as Jackson brings his hand to the bottom of his mask and drags it off, revealing himself. He wears a vile smile that would disturb anyone. Ryker and I take a step forward. Which only causes Jackson's smile to widen. He's a fucking psycho, but most would think I was with the things I want to do to him.

"Christian, don't."

"Ryker don't," both girls say.

My eyes are zeroed on Jackson when he slowly closes his eyes, brings his fingers up to his nose, and sniffs them. Sick fuck! I lose all composure and rush toward him, and Ryker follows. Jackson turns and makes a run for it. The girls scream after us, but we don't stop. We're gaining on him just as he hops into a ruby red range rover and locks the doors. My fist connects with his driver's side window.

"You motherfucker!" I shout, banging on the glass.

"Open the fucking door, you bitch!" Ryker snarls, pulling on the door handle.

"Get the fuck out of the car!"

The veins in my neck are ready to burst as I continue slamming my fist against his window. Jackson sits there calmly, safe inside the Rover, and smiles. Rayne and Laynie come rushing up to us. Rayne wraps her arms around my waist, trying to pull me away, but I don't move.

"Ryker, do something!" she says, panicked. Ryker ignores her, still pulling at the door handle, about to rip it off.

"Christian!" she shouts, still pulling me, and the whole time my eyes are on Jackson. His are on Rayne. I'm going to fucking kill him.

"You take your fucking eyes off her!"

"Christian, please!" she begs. "I'll go to the cops. I'll file a restraining order. Please, I beg you, just stop." I pause, but don't turn around. "I need you…" her voice cracks. "I need both of you. Please." She cries.

I close my fist, extending my arm back, giving one last swing at the glass, hitting it so hard it cracks. Rayne gives me another hard pull, and I let her move me. She drags me back to the car, and my eyes never leave Jackson's the entire time.

Chapter 28

Rayne

We're into the first week of November, and after the terrifying events last weekend, I'm glad it's behind me. After Laynie and I pulled Christian and Ryker away from killing Jackson, we drove home. As much as I'd like to say, Ryker didn't question it and that the hour-plus drive home was quiet. It wasn't. I wanted to keep him out of it all, but he was relentless. With the bit of information I gave him, he put the pieces together about what happened the night of Jackson's party.

    He was the angriest I have ever seen him, and after finding out this wasn't the first time Jackson assaulted me, he pulled the car over to get a hold of his composure. He trembled in rage and cried because of what happened to me and how he had failed as a brother. I can't recall when I'd ever seen him cry, so seeing him break down was hard to witness, and I cried with him. He felt like he had failed me, although none of this was his fault, and I made sure he knew that. I apologized profusely for keeping this away from him and explained why I didn't want to bring him into my mess, knowing how he would react. That wasn't an option; I had to protect him.

He cried harder, telling me, *"I'm your big brother Rayne. You aren't supposed to worry about if I get hurt or not, and you don't need to protect me. I am supposed to protect you… I'll always protect you."*

I'm afraid I still have to disagree with him. I understand his feelings, but I think the same way about him. If I can, I will always protect Ry. After calming him down, we returned to the car to head home. Yet, the mood remained hostile. Ry was furious with Christian for not telling him. Then Laynie was hurt with me for not telling her. Jackson was causing too much damage between all of us that it infuriated me. He held so much power. The psycho deserves what they wanted to do to him, but I will get a restraining order. I should have done it sooner.

Laynie and I stayed up the rest of the night talking about everything. She didn't stay mad at me for long. She was upset that I had to experience all of this in the first place and was hurt that I didn't tell her because she wasn't there to help me.

The next day, we all went to the police station. I made a police report and filed a restraining order against Jackson. I wasn't forthright with the police about the extent of things he had done to me because I didn't want to talk about my assault or the possibility of court. No one agreed with me, but it was ultimately up to me. Instead, I filed a restraining order for harassment, and Jackson can't come within one hundred feet of me.

Ryker was there to support me, but his anger toward Christian for the next four days was still brooding. It was brutal only talking to him if it was necessary. I wanted to tell Ryker to let it go, but Christian said Ryker had a right to be upset and would talk to him when he was ready. Ryker finally came around, but only after telling Christian that he was still upset about him keeping such a secret. Ultimately, understanding Christian didn't want to betray my trust. Everything returned to normal between us.

I was worried about going back to school and seeing Jackson, but fortunately, I haven't seen him. Christian thought it would be nice to check something off our bucket list. I'm finishing up getting ready, so we can head to the restaurant where I'll meet his mother, Sawyer, for the first time. I'm incredibly nervous and excited to meet the woman who means so much to Christian. If she is anything like him, I'm sure I'll love her. I just hope she likes me, too.

I'm wearing my long hair pulled back into a sleek ponytail with the emerald green earrings Christian bought me for my birthday. I haven't taken them off once, and I don't plan to. I slip into a black spaghetti strap dress that falls just below my knees and has a slit on the side, with black Steve Madden Carrson heels. Giving myself one last glance, happy with how I look, I grab a black clutch purse, spray my favorite body mist and make my way downstairs, where Christian awaits, sitting on the couch next to Ry.

Christian turns around and looks up in my direction. His eyes widen. A smile teases my lips at his reaction, and he quickly stands, adjusting his white button shirt. Meeting me at the bottom of the stairs, he holds out his hand for me to take, helping me with the last step. His white button-up is perfectly crisp, not a wrinkle in sight tucked into his slim black slacks. My smile widens when I see his shoes, all black converse. *Christian.*

"Wow," I say breathlessly. "You look good." I wrap my arms around his neck.

"I thought I better dress up if I'm going to be standing next to you." I blush, kissing him softly.

Ryker groans behind him, "We get it. You're in love."

Love... there's that word again. I feel my already pink cheeks burn at Ryker's mention of love. Christian's cheeks tint as he looks back and forth between my eyes as if searching for something. I don't break our eye contact, and it's as if he found what he was looking for within my eyes because he smiles, not just a tiny smile or his flirty lop-sided smirk I love so much, but a massive all teeth kind of smile. It's infectious, and I can't help but smile back.

We say goodbye before getting into the car. I love when we ride in his car because I'm instantly invaded by citrus and the rich smell of leather. My hands are clammy and only worsen the closer we get to the restaurant. I fidget with my fingernails and shift in my seat. Christian notices and reminds me there isn't anything for me to be nervous about. It still doesn't calm the ball of nerves bouncing around in my stomach or the wave of anxiety that floods my body. I want to make a good impression and want her to like me. I've never had a boyfriend; therefore, I never had to meet the parents, and it's nerve-wracking.

We arrive at an Italian restaurant called Little Rome. Carbs. I love carbs, but I think I'd throw up from nerves. I tell Christian I have to use the lady's room and that he doesn't have to wait for me; I can meet them at the table. He chuckles, kissing my forehead, telling me to relax.

Sighing, I make my way to the restroom to freshen up and look at myself in the mirror. Grabbing a paper towel, I place it under the faucet before dampening it and pressing it against my neck to help cool and relax me. Closing my eyes, I lean against the wall, focusing on my breathing. *Breathe in, breathe out.* Repeat. I'm counting my breaths before I'm interrupted by a knock at the door. I toss the napkin into the trash bin as the bathroom door swings open and Christian walks in.

"What are you doing in here?"

"Helping you relax," he says, locking the door behind him.

"Wha—" my words die when he grips my waist and lifts me onto the counter.

I yelp in surprise at the contact of my ass, hitting the cool ceramic countertop. He chuckles at my reaction, sliding the thin spaghetti straps down my arms, exposing my breasts, and groans. His breaths are heavy as his lips ghost over mine before pressing a light kiss to my mouth. Gently grabbing my jaw, he tilts my head and kisses down my throat before nibbling and licking my collarbone. His hands caress my breasts, and I moan in anticipation. I can fill his hard length pressed against my inner thigh, evidently turned on just as much as I am. My nerves are dissolving with each touch and quickly turning into desire.

The bathroom is well-lit and bright, and I can make out every perfect part of him. His cock is rock hard, tenting in his slacks, and the top few buttons of his shirt are opened, exposing his tan skin. I need to touch him. Urgently, I unbutton the rest, gliding my hands over every inch of his chest. Pressing a kiss over his heart, his body shakes under my lips. He's fucking breathtaking. He looks like a glowing sun under the bright white lights and his pale white button-up shirt. His mouth closes around my pebbled nipple, sucking me into his mouth.

"Oh, fuck!" my eyes slam shut and a deep growl rips from his throat as he pulls my other nipple into his mouth while using his hand to move my panties to the side. Juices from my dripping wet sex coat my inner thighs.

He rips his mouth away from my breast and drops to his knees, spreading my legs further apart, coming face to face with my smooth mound.

He intensely looks up at me. "Mine!" he says with a guttural moan before devouring my pussy.

I gasp, propping my legs over his shoulders and watching his every move. His skillful tongue licks between my folds from the bottom to the top, using it to apply pressure to my throbbing bud. Rocking my hips against the motion of his tongue, I fist his hair in my hands, letting out a throaty moan in sheer delight. My stomach tightens, a clear sign of my approaching orgasm.

"Your pretty pussy tastes so good, baby." He groans, and another moan rips from my throat. "And those fucking sounds you make."

Oh god. His tongue, his words, his fingers... fuck. He is invading all my senses; all I can see, feel, and hear is him. He adds a finger to my tightness, and it doesn't nearly hurt as much as the first time. It feels good. My body feels pure ecstasy, and I never want to come down from the high. I can feel the pressure of another added finger as my walls tightly wrap around them. He continues to lick and suck my pussy, pausing his finger's movement so I can adjust.

My legs shake, clenching tighter around his head, holding him in place. I can hear the bussing noise from employees and customers on the other side of the door, enjoying their meals while Christian feasts on me like I'm his. I secretly love the fact that they could catch us at any moment. *Who the hell is this girl?* A few months ago, if someone told me I'd be getting eaten out in the bathroom of a busy restaurant, I'd think they lost their minds, maybe even laugh, but here I am, and I fucking love it.

He thrust his fingers faster and faster, matching my moans. My chest is heaving, and every muscle in my body goes tight. He continues to push his fingers inside me while flicking his tongue over my clit, and I can't hold it in any longer. My legs lock around Christian's head, my sensitivity magnified as I throw my head back, screaming his name as I reach my climax and waves of pleasure wash through me.

My body goes limp after my release, and I close my eyes, leaning against the bathroom mirror to catch my breath. I don't move when I feel Christian lightly kiss my inner thigh before unraveling my legs from his shoulders. He slides my panties back over before pulling me to him. He holds me upright because I can barely feel my legs and slips my thin straps back over my shoulders. A hiss flees my lips at the silk material rubbing across my nipples, every part of me sensitive to the touch. He gently presses his lips against mine, and it's then that I finally open my eyes. I can taste myself on his mouth, and knowing it's me on his lips does something to me. His eyes search mine the same way they did when Ryker mentioned the word love, and I can't help but wonder what he's thinking.

I hold his stare the entire time I button up his shirt. I'm not sure if any of this is normal, but he is gentle with me as if I'm delicate glass. Every touch we make is intentional and only temporarily feeds the cravings. He fills me with butterflies and delicate fluttering that dance whenever he is near. We are intertwined, tangled, and tethered together, and I never want to unravel.

"How do you feel now?" he cups the side of my face.

I sigh, resting my forehead against his chest.

I feel like I love you.

"I feel like I can fall asleep right now."

He chuckles, kissing the top of my head. "We still have to sit through dinner with my mom."

"I'll check if the coast is clear." I nod to the restroom door. "Wait for me?" he smiles, following me to the door. I poke my head out, and thankfully, no one is there. "Coast is clear."

He playfully smacks my ass on his way out. "Hurry up."

I rush to the mirror, reapply my lipstick, run my fingers through my ponytail, getting myself together. Straightening my shoulders and running my hands down the front of my dress, I smile at my reflection; I'm ready.

Chapter 29

Rayne

Now that I'm much more relaxed than when I first arrived, and my mind isn't running a thousand miles per minute, I can take everything in. The restaurant is charming and makes you feel like you're actually in Rome. Linking my arm through Christian's, I followed him through the restaurant and passed the bar. Every table here is occupied and filled with chatter. At the end of the aisle, there is a booth to our left that sits a stunning woman with shoulder-length blonde hair and beautiful honey-colored eyes. I smile instantly, knowing this must be Sawyer, Christian's mother. He looks just like her, and I can't seem to pull my eyes away.

She takes a sip of wine, and her eyes land on us from over her glass. Getting to her feet, she greets us with the most welcoming smile.

"Hey, Ma." Christian smiles, giving her a peck on the cheek. Her smile widens when she turns to look at me.

"You must be Rayne." she beams, pulling me into a warm embrace.

"Hi." I smile shyly. "You must be Sawyer. It's lovely to meet you."

"Likewise, dear. I've heard so much about you."

"Ma," Christian bashfully warns, his cheeks turning pink.

"All good things, of course! Please, sit." She gestures toward the booth. The waitress arrives shortly after and asks us if we are ready to order. She fills our empty cups with water and takes our menu, clearing off the table before leaving.

"How are you liking LA so far?" I ask.

Her smile drops just a tad before quickly masking it with another. "It's a lot different from Oregon, but I love it so far." She takes a sip of her wine and clears her throat. "Oregon never felt the same after…" she pauses, "After my husband…" she pauses again, having difficulty getting the words out.

I place my hand on hers, and her eyes meet mine. What am I doing touching her? I wasn't thinking and just wanted to bring her comfort.

I pull my hand away, placing it in my lap and looking her in the eyes when I speak. "Christian told me about your husband." Her eyes widen in surprise and move to Christian's. "You don't have to talk about it, I understand." I smile, trying to show her I'm being sincere, as her eyes turn glossy.

"Thank you," she says, looking at her son as I do the same. He's looking at me with that look in his eyes. I've been noticing more and more lately. He says nothing, just smiles, setting his hand on top of mine under the table.

"Thank you for understanding, but it's good to talk about the hard things, even if talking about it sometimes brings you pain. Cameron was the love of my life, and it was very hard moving forward without him and even harder leaving Oregon behind because at least there, I felt like he was still with me."

My eyes water, but I blink the tears away before they can fall.

"The move was needed; moving here made me realize leaving Oregon didn't mean I left my Cameron behind because he is still with me… here," she taps her heart.

He is still with her, living in her memories as she carries him in her heart.

I feel a little guilty because when Christian slowly started opening up to me about his father and his life in Oregon, a part of me blamed her. I didn't understand how his mother couldn't see he was alone; he was hurting and needed someone. Talking to her now, I know she was hurting too and felt lost after losing her other half. Her words leave me speechless, and I don't know how to respond. Thankfully, I don't have to because she continues speaking.

"Enough about that." She waves her hand, taking another sip of her wine. "Tell me about yourself."

My hands clam up, and I feel nervous under the pressure. *Stop overthinking, Rayne. It's a simple question.*

I take a sip of my water, my throat suddenly feeling dry. "I have an older brother named Ryker, which you already know because he helped you guys move in." I awkwardly laugh. "I was born and raised here in LA and have never explored outside California. My parents, Jack and Olivia, are the best parents to my brother and me, and I'm close with both of them." She smiles. "I'm a junior at Huntington Prep High, and my dream is to get accepted into New York School of Design to study fashion and hopefully open my own shop one day, maybe even style celebrities."

"Very impressive, Rayne. Fashion isn't easy and not always as glamourous as it seems. It is hard work, but I'm sure you'll do great since it's your passion. I think it is wonderful that you have a dream and a plan."

"Thank you," I smile proudly.

"So, New York, huh? That's a big move." Christian tenses next to me.

"Yes, it is, but I've known I wanted to go there since I was a little girl. I'm just a plane away and will visit every chance I have."

"Your parents must be so proud of you! I'm sure they will miss you dearly. I know I'd miss Christian if he ever decided to up and move away."

"No need to worry about that, Ma. I'm not going anywhere."

I smile at her, but it doesn't reach my eyes—sadness cascades over me. I know I still have a year to spend with Christian, but the thought of being so far away from him feels wrong. *Could we do a long-distance relationship? Would he even want to?* I don't know what I expected, but hearing him say he isn't going anywhere definitely wasn't it. Of course, I would never expect him to give up on his dreams, but a hopeful part of me thought that eventually, he would come too. That glimmer of hope quickly burns out at his admission. He said it with such certainty.

Our waitress returned with our food, but I lost my appetite and didn't feel hungry anymore. Not wanting to be rude, I take a bite here and there, but I mostly push food around on my plate with my fork. Sawyer is wonderful, and everything is going great. I had no reason to worry. I'm trying to be present and enjoy our dinner, but it's difficult with the realization I only have a year left until I have to leave Christian.

"So, you've never been outside of California? Christian and I are going to Oregon during thanksgiving break to see his uncle Mav and take care of a few things. If you don't already have plans, I'd love it if you'd join us, and I'm positive his uncle Mav would love to meet you." I give her a genuine smile this time because I'd love to go. Plus, meeting his uncle is on our bucket list, so this is the perfect opportunity to cross it off.

"She's busy. She can't go." Christian answers for me, and my smile drops.

I look at him, but he doesn't look at me; instead, he scarfs down his chicken parm and avoids me. What the hell? First, he answers for me, then tells his mom I'm busy, which he made up because we haven't even talked about thanksgiving. My feelings are hurt that he doesn't want me to go. Does he not want me to meet his uncle Maverick? Is it too soon? I feel embarrassed. I know Sawyer doesn't know her son just lied to her, but I do. But why? Sawyer scrunches her brows, noticing my reaction, then shifts her gaze to Christian. I don't look at either of them. Instead, I keep my focus on my fingernails.

"Oh, okay, well, maybe another time." She suggests, giving me a sympathetic smile.

I keep my distance between Christian and me for the remainder of dinner, only engaging in conversation when Sawyer speaks to me directly. They both finish their food, but I've hardly eaten mine. Christian pays for our bill asking for a to-go box for me.

Sawyer gives me a tight hug, whispering in my ear. "It was truly lovely meeting you, Rayne. My son can be stubborn, but I assure you he cares about you deeply. I've never seen his eyes light up the way they do with you. Give him time to come around."

I nod. "I hope to see you soon."

"You will."

Christian and I walk back to his car in silence. As he drives, he sets his hand on my thigh, but I move my leg away and stare out the window. We remain that way the entire ride home, not uttering a word. I can feel his stare when he occasionally glances over at me; he never says anything.

He parks his car, and I quickly unbuckle my seatbelt, reaching for my door.

"Raynie..." he sighs, and I stop my movement, my hand gripped on the door handle. "Look at me, please?" I let out a long breath and turned to face him.

He runs his fingers through his hair, giving himself that sexy, messy hair I love. It's difficult to stay mad at him when he looks this good all the time.

"I'm sorry for the way I handled things at dinner."

"What part exactly?" I say with a slight bite in my tone, and he grips his steering wheel.

"All of it. I didn't mean to answer for you."

"Why do it? Do you not want me going to Oregon with you for thanksgiving?"

"No."

Ouch.

With watery eyes, I say, "Well, thank you for dinner. I'll talk to you later."

"Wait! That's not what I meant. My words aren't coming out the way I want them to. Of course. I want to spend thanksgiving with you. If I didn't think you'd get tired of me, I'd want to spend every second with you."

"And I'd like to spend all my time with you. What's the problem then?"

"I want to be with you on thanksgiving, and I'd love for you to meet my uncle Mav, but I don't want you going to Oregon. I don't want you around my old life. I was a different person then, and the people I hung out with aren't the best." He looks away, ashamed.

I softly turn his face towards mine. "I'm aware they aren't the best people. I'm aware you have a past and were a different person, but I like who you are now, and I accept who you were then. If you don't want me to go to Oregon, that's fine, and I'll have to deal, but if your reason is because of your past, that upsets me. You can't run from it, and with me, I promise you don't have to." I grab his hand. "We will face it together; you have me, and I'm not going anywhere."

His eyes golden eyes shimmer with affection.

"God, I l—" he stops suddenly, his eyes drifting over my face. "God, you're perfect, and I don't deserve you."

"You deserve everything, and I'll keep reminding you until you believe it." I kiss him deeply, giving him every part of me.

"Talk to your parents, baby," he cups my face, dragging his thumb along my jaw, "because we're going to Oregon," he gives me his notorious lopsided grin and the butterflies in my stomach flutter.

Chapter 30

Rayne

I haven't mentioned New York to Christian and how I hoped he would end up joining me, but with the realization that I only have a year left with him, I try to spend every moment I can get with him, not wasting any more time and enjoying the time we have together. He doesn't seem to mind because he is just as eager to hang out with me. If I'm not texting him to come over, he's picking me up after school, taking me on dates, and showing up at my house to watch the sappy movies that I love so much.

A week after having dinner with his mom, I invited her over to meet my parents, which is another thing we got to cross off our bucket list. My dad told Sawyer how great of a young man he thinks Christian is and how impressed he is with his work ethic. She probably thanked my parents at least one hundred times for accepting Christian into our family and giving him the opportunity he needed. She and my mother hit it off as if they had been friends their entire lives. My mother even invited her to a girl's night with her and Laynie's mom. It was amazing to see how well she blended with the people I love most, and I was thrilled to see the joy it brought her.

What I really loved was the permanent smile Christian wore the entire night. His smile didn't falter once; he was happy, and so was I.

Today is Laynie's birthday. Her birthday was technically Tuesday, but we can't do much on a school night, especially with a ten-thirty curfew. We had a relaxing birthday dinner with her parents instead, where they spoiled her with a two-hundred-dollar gift card to Sephora. I'm glad I don't wear too much makeup because that shit is expensive.

I thought about throwing her a surprise birthday somewhere, but I felt it was too predictable or wouldn't be very exciting because she did the same thing for me. If I'm honest, I think she would prefer to throw it herself, anyway. Party planning is her thing, and it's something she enjoys doing. Her parents went out of town a few hours ago for a business trip and thought Laynie was staying at my house for the rest of the weekend. Little did they know we were throwing a party here while they were gone.

She gasps. "What is this?"

I smile, "It's your birthday, and I couldn't have my bestie wearing some mediocre dress on her special day." I walk to her, pulling out the dress because Laynie is frozen in place. "I made you a dress."

"Are you fucking shitting me!" she screeches.

"Nope! now put it on." I throw it at her, and she catches it and starts stripping out of her clothes.

She looks sensational! I designed a lavender-colored ruched dress with thin spaghetti straps. It's slim-fitting, with a mesh cut out just under her breasts, exposing her ribs and the top of her flat stomach. The dress stops mid-thigh, showcasing her killer legs.

"You are seriously the best, Rayne Davis. I knew I kept you around for a reason."

"Watch it. As easy as it was for me to design the dress, destroying it will be just as easy."

"Seriously though, you're the best. This dress is amazing, and I'm lucky to have you."

"Me too, babe, me too."

She finishes getting ready before working her magic on me. She does my makeup naturally, giving me a radiating glow and adding my signature light pink lipstick. I lightly curl my hair into soft beach waves, keeping a few hairpieces in front to frame my face. I split my hair into two sections at the top of my head and French braid them into two pigtails wearing my hair half up, half down. I'm wearing a champagne-colored sparkly mini dress with matching heels.

Just as we finish getting ready, her doorbell rings, and my heart races. The party doesn't start for another fifteen minutes, and thanks to Laynie, I remembered nobody shows up to parties on time, so that means I know exactly who's here. Christian. We both walk together and answer the door, and Ryker walks in, carrying a bottle of tequila in one hand and a twelve pack in the other.

Christian steps into the doorway and pauses, looking me up and down, assessing me with his eyes, and I do the same. Why the hell does he have to be so hot? He seriously looks good in everything. He is wearing all black per usual, but damn, he wears it well.

"Eyes up, baby," he smirks, and I slowly drag my eyes away from his body and onto that gorgeous face of his.

"Sorry," I blush

"Never be sorry for checking me out. I check you out every chance I get, and I'll never apologize for it."

I gently grip his jacket, tugging him to me. "Well, that's good to know because I happen to like it when your eyes are on me."

"Is that so?"

Biting my lip, I nod, "Oh yeah. Why do you think I danced in front of my mirror? Do you think I give just anyone a free show?" He tilts his head, thinking before his eyebrows lift in realization.

"You planned that?" he groans. "I knew you were trouble."

I smirk, boldly rubbing my thumb along his bottom lip. "Only the best kind."

His golden eyes darken with lust. "Don't tease me, Raynie."

"Why?"

"Because I might just bite." He nips my bottom lip with his teeth, and I pull in a sharp breath. "We better join them in the kitchen before I take you to the bedroom. You don't want the birthday girl upset that we got her sheets dirty."

"Y... Yeah, you're probably right."

He chuckles, kissing the corner of my mouth before sauntering his sexy ass to the kitchen.

Well, that backfired. Damn him. I was supposed to be teasing him and somehow ended up soaking my panties and turned the hell on. *This is going to be a long night.* Walking into the kitchen, Laynie already has shots lined up, and honestly, I can use one right about now after that little stunt Christian pulled. Hopefully, the tequila eases the burn within me. We all make a toast to Laynie before knocking back our first shot. We take a few more before people start to arrive.

Christian brushes against my ass in the backyard, setting the chair he's holding next to mine. Raising an eyebrow, I turn to him. He raises his eyebrow back at me and smirks, then walks back to the garage to grab more chairs. He knows what he's doing; he's teasing me on purpose.

Laynie's backyard looks fantastic! A vast purple, white, and silver balloon arc is centered against the back wall lined with mermaid-colored metallic foil garlands. Giant lettered silver balloons that say 'Birthday Babe' are in the middle. Transparent multicolored LED balloons stand throughout the yard with twinkling string lights hanging above.

Her backyard is full of people. The group standing around the beer pong table erupts in cheers when some guy sinks the ball into the cup. The music is thumping, and everyone seems to enjoy themselves. Laynie is drunk dancing with some guy, and I can't hide my smile. Sitting on Christian's lap, I scan the crowd to see who's all here. I'm having a great time, but whenever someone walks into the party, my eyes immediately go to them, making sure it isn't Jackson. I still haven't seen him since Devil's night, and after my restraining order, I shouldn't feel worried, but he always seems to show up when I least expect it, so I'm a little on guard. At this point, I wouldn't put anything past him. He's bat shit crazy.

My eyes lock on Ryker, standing next to some girls I don't know. They are all over him, touching his arms, running fingers through his hair, wearing flirty smiles and barely there dresses. He isn't paying any attention to them. Following his line of sight, my eyes land on Laynie and the guy she's dancing with. Ryker's eyebrows are lowered, and his eyes are squinted in a hostile glare as he curls his lips. He flares his nostrils and clenches his fist at his sides. What the hell is his problem? Laynie has a flirty look on her face as she smiles over her shoulder at the guy behind her. He grabs her waist and leans into her neck. Again, I look at Ryker, and he's charging toward her. I quickly stand to my feet, rushing over to him.

I put my hand on his chest, stopping him before he could make it to the dance floor. "What the hell do you think you are doing?"

He looks at me, surprised. "Nothing."

"Why do you have a murderous look on your face, like you are about to explode any second?" His features relax.

"I don't know what you're talking about. I was going to get another beer." We both look down at his full cup.

He chugs it down before shaking it in front of my face to show me it's empty. "I need another." He brushes past me and heads straight to the coolers on the other side of the dance floor.

"What's wrong with him?" Christian asks, looking in Ryker's direction.

"I have no idea…"

He wraps his arms around me from behind. "I'll ask him about it later. For now, let's enjoy our night."

We return to our seats, sharing a cup of some mixed concoction. I have no clue what it is, but it tastes great.

Christian asked if I'd told my parents about Oregon, and I told him I did. They need some time to think about it, but I think they will let me go. He smiles, takes the mixed drink from my hand, and takes a sip. The party is in full effect, but Christian and I don't mind just sitting around and talking. He offers me the last of the drink before he gets us a refill, and I chug it down.

As I wait for Christian, I look out into the crowd, and someone sits next to me.

"Back already?" I smile, turning my head to face him. A guy around Christian's height casually leans back in the chair beside mine with a Bud Light in hand, and my smile drops.

"Well, that hurts the ego," he chuckles, taking a sip of his beer.

"What do you mean?"

"One look at me, and that beautiful smile of yours disappeared." I shift in my seat and fiddle with my fingers.

"I'm sorry. I was just expecting someone else."

"No worries." He gives me a kind smile. "I'm James," he reaches over, extending his hand.

I stare down at it for a few seconds. "Rayne."

"So, what brings you here? Did you come with some friends?"

"My best friend is the birthday girl."

"Who is the birthday girl exactly?" I point to Laynie, still on the dance floor.

"Her." He follows my finger and smiles. "Not to be rude, but if you don't know Laynie, why are you here?" his smile widens.

"I had to give my cousin a ride, and since I had nothing better to do, I stayed. I'm from New York, and I'm just here visiting."

"Who's your cousin?" he smirks and points. I follow his finger, and my eyes land on the guy grinding against Laynie.

I can't help but laugh at the odds. "Wow."

He chuckles, "I know."

"How do you like the big apple? I plan on going there for college."

"New York is fucking amazing! There isn't any place like it." His response gets me excited to experience it for myself. I grin just thinking about it. "You should take down my number, and when you find yourself in New York, text me I'd love to show you around."

"And you should get lost. She doesn't need a tour guide." Christian snarls from behind me. I turn, looking at him wide-eyed.

James stays seated entirely calm. "And who are you?"

I'm about to introduce Christian, but he speaks before I can. "Her boyfriend."

My head snaps back to Christian. *Boyfriend?*

James nods in understanding. "Well, I can respect that, and I didn't know she had a boyfriend." He glances at me. "Although I should have. A girl like her doesn't stay single for long."

"I'm aware. Now, you can stop looking at someone who isn't yours."

I stand up, no longer paying attention to James. Instead, I look at Christian, and his words replay in my head.

Her boyfriend.

"Boyfriend, huh?" the corner of his mouth lifts.

"When I tell you that you're mine, I mean it."

"It's about damn time." I tease.

He chuckles, skimming his lips over mine, but doesn't kiss me. The smell of pineapple fans against my lips, and I lean in to close the distance, but he pulls back before my lips can connect with his. My eyes widen before my brows furrow in confusion. He smirks at my reaction, and it's then I realize he's teasing me again.

Giving him no choice, I grab the back of his neck, pulling him closer to me.

"Don't tease me, Christian," I warn.

"Why?"

I smirk, "Because I might just bite." I crash my lips against his, feeling him smile into the kiss.

Mine.

Chapter 31

Christian

Life has been good, and it almost feels too damn good to be true. I got the fucking girl! She was officially mine. Who would have thought? I sure as fuck wouldn't have, but damn, am I glad. My life doesn't seem so dim anymore. I feel completely satisfied for once in my life and don't have a fucking care in the world.

Rayne once said I was her summer, but she failed to realize she was my sun. There is a fire in her eyes that can ignite my soul with a look. Her hands set fire to my skin, and her words set fire to my mind. She is the fucking sun, and I surrender to her flames. I have never felt something so powerful. It's fucking scary, but also the most exhilarating thing. Everything between us is hot and heavy, we can't get enough of each other, and there is so much passion. I want her in every sense of the word. She is mine just as much as I am hers, and it is incredible when you realize just how deeply in love you have fallen. I love her.

My mother does too, which isn't a shocker. What's not to love about her? We went to the Davis's so she could finally meet Rayne's parents, and she loved them just as much. Once we got home, my mother gushed the rest of the night about how she couldn't wait to go out with Olivia and Stacey for a girl's night. It made me smile and feel happy to see how well everyone got along and how happy my mother was. I'm thinking LA is feeling like home for her, too.

Rayne and I have been inseparable, hanging out any chance we can. We have been crossing things off our bucket list and adding some new things we'd like to do one day. Rayne texted me the other night to meet her on her roof. She wanted me to come over because she had an idea, and once again, I was climbing up her trellis. She wanted to check off camping from our bucket list, and of course, I was down for that. I asked her if we were all riding in one car, and she told me she wanted it just to be us. I know her dad would not be okay with that. Then she told me how Laynie said she would cover for her by telling her parents she was staying the night with her for the night. I wasn't sure if it was a good idea, but the best ideas usually aren't.

I pull up to Laynie's house and am about to get out of my car when Rayne rushes out of the front door with a duffle bag heading straight for me. I smile, seeing how eager she is to get to me, and quickly hop out. She drops her duffle bag and leaps into my arms as I close my eyes and breathe her in.

"Someone is happy to see me."

"You have no idea."

Oh, but I do.

"You guys make me sick," Laynie teases, scrunching her face as she walks toward us.

Rayne giggles, unlatching herself from my body, and I grab her bag, setting it in the back seat.

"Alright, you guys should be covered for the night, but tomorrow I need her back here bright and early, before my parents get up."

"We will be here first thing in the morning! Thank you for this," Rayne says, hugging her.

Laynie smiles and whispers something into her ear. When Rayne turns to me, her cheeks are pink, and she avoids making eye contact with me. Laynie, on the other hand, is smirking at both of us.

"You two have fun," Laynie wiggles her eyebrows.

I roll my eyes, and Rayne awkwardly coughs, giving her a wave before quickly getting into the car. I smile, shut her door, and make my way to the driver's side of the vehicle.

"Ahem." I pause, turning to face Laynie. Her playful demeanor is gone and replaced with a grave look. I'm not intimidated by women, but her look makes me falter in my movement.

"Yes?"

"You be good to her." She steps toward me. "I don't know what you have planned, but my friend better come back with a smile on her face."

"My plan is to camp."

She crosses her arms, "Mm-hmm."

"It is. I don't have any ulterior motives or expectations. I'm just taking her camping."

"Okay..." she squints.

"Okay..." I awkwardly repeat.

She smiles widely back to her playful self. "Have fun."

In the car, we head straight to the campsite. I've brought everything we possibly need so we don't have any reason to stop. I'm not wasting a minute of our time together. Our campground was only about an hour away because I didn't want to go too far just in case something happened and we needed to come back. God, I hope we don't need to come back. Besides me accidentally falling asleep with Rayne, this will be the first time we stay overnight together, and I'm a giddy motherfucker right now. A whole day spent with her, knowing she will be in my arms at the end, is just icing on the fucking cake. Already this is the best trip I've ever been on.

Setting my hand on her thigh, I glance at her. "You ready for the best camping trip ever?"

"I'm ready for it all."

An hour later, we pull up to Nestled in Nature campground. There are a few other campers, but not too many since we're in the middle of November, and it's getting cold out. Our camping spot is further down the crystalline lake, giving us more privacy. Parking the car, we both look around, admiring the scenery. Clouds blanket the sky in dark gray layers. A forest surrounds us with mixtures of greens merging with strong brown, showing fall is here. The smell of the earth is potent, and the lake is peaceful and still; it looks like glass, with no ripple in sight.

She smiles at the beauty surrounding us while I smile at her. Rayne turns to me, and I can't look away in time; she catches me staring.

"What?" she says.

"Nothing…"

"Tell me."

"I can't believe you're mine."

She blushes, leaning her lips closer to me. "Well, you better start believing it, Christian Hayes, because I'm not going anywhere."

Until you leave me and go to New York, just the thought makes my stomach ache. Not wanting to ruin our time, I kiss her instead.

As I grab the cooler from the back seat, Rayne grabs our fold-out chairs from the trunk and starts setting them up by the fire pit. We work side by side as a team, bringing things from the car and setting up.

"I can set it up." She offers as I set out pieces of the tent.

I chuckle, "I've got it. You sit down and relax."

She arches her brow. "What? You don't think I can do it?"

"There are a lot of pieces, and I don't have the instructions anymore."

"I don't need instructions; I can do it." She crosses her arms in a challenge, causing me to smirk.

"Okay then, let's see it." I take a seat while Rayne gets to work on assembling the tent.

She lays out the pieces and starts separating the poles into piles according to their size. Then grabs the nylon and polyester tent fabric and spreads it out. I reach for a grocery bag and pull out a bag of chips, casually snacking while I watch her quizzically stare at all the material in front of her. She looks up at me like she wants to ask me a question, and I raise an eyebrow, popping a chip into my mouth. My stubborn girl huffs, deciding not to ask for my help, and resumes trying to put the tent together. Thirty minutes later, she finishes and stands, wiping off her dirt-covered knees with a proud grin.

I nod, impressed, as I walk around, surveying the tent, and notice something inside the bag. The corner of my lips curl.

"Told you I can do—" I nudge the tent, and it falls over.

"What the hell?" A chuckle bounces off my chest as I grab some poles still inside the bag.

"You forgot these." I hold them up so she can see.

"I thought those were extra pieces."

"Nope, these pieces are needed."

"Damn it," she stomps her foot, "I thought I had it." *She's so damn cute,* I think, pulling her in my arms.

"You almost did it. I'm quite impressed."

She smiles at my words.

"It's an easy fix. I'll show you where they go, and you can help me stake it to the ground."

I showed her how to set up a tent properly and explained why it fell over without the missing pieces. She helps me hammer the stakes into the hard dirt and smiles in satisfaction once we're done.

"Next time, I'm doing it, and I'll make sure to do it correctly."

"Next time, huh?"

"There will definitely be a next time," she shrugs like I should know this already.

That's something I love about Rayne. When she talks about us, she says things like she is confident we will be together in the future. I'd like us to be, and it feels good knowing she is sure of us and what we have.

I grab our bags from the car, and Rayne takes them from me, stepping inside the tent. While she's in the tent, I open the case of wood and set the logs inside the pit so we can access it easily once it gets dark. She grabs the blankets and pillows from the car and heads back inside the tent to finish setting up. I continue to set up our spot, trying to push the thoughts of us wrapped up in one another all night out of my head.

"Want to walk by the water?" Rayne asks, stepping out of the tent. I'll do whatever she wants.

Hand in hand, we walk alongside the lake. Rayne tells me how she loves it out here and how peaceful it is. I agree with her; the silence is soothing. Being here is the perfect way to spend some quiet time together. We welcome the silence, fully content in the presence of each other. I still can't believe she's mine, and she's here with me. It's like I'm scared to blink, fearing she'll disappear or I'll miss something important if I take my eyes away.

Rayne slowly stops and smirks at me, a smirk that tells me she's up to something. She grabs the bottom of her graphic tee and pulls it over her head, dropping it at her feet. I'm utterly entranced as I watch her unbutton her jean shorts, shimming them down her toned legs. I swallow, taking in her perfect fucking body. She unclasps her bra, and her perfect breasts bounce freely.

"W... What are you doing?" I frantically look around, making sure nobody can see her. She giggles, removing her panties.

"Checking another thing off our bucket list." She flings her panties at me like a slingshot. "I'm going skinny dipping." With my mouth hanging open, I watch as she runs into the water, shrieking when the cold water hits her skin. "Are you going to leave a girl hanging, or are you going to get in?"

Fuck no, I'm not.

I drop her panties before eagerly pulling off my black tee and jeans. I'm pushing my pants down my legs when I realize I still have my Converse on. Rayne laughs as I hop around on one foot, trying to untie my laces, as my jeans are stuck around my ankles. Finally, I get my shoes off, my pants and boxers following right after. I charge into the water and its cold sting is like sharp needles against my skin.

"Fuck that's cold!" I hiss, making Rayne giggle.

"You will adjust; it feels absolutely amazing!"

My shriveled balls beg to differ.

We take our time floating in the water butt-ass naked. I seriously can't believe I'm doing this right now. Hell, I can't believe Rayne is doing this right now. She continues to blossom before my eyes, turning into a fearless woman. The confidence I've known she has is showing more every day. She's a fucking force to be reckoned with.

Rayne floats on her back, staring at the sky, lost in thought.

"What's going on in that pretty little head of yours?"

She smiles and angles to face me. "I'm really happy."

"Me too." I give her a crooked smile.

"What's that?" she points behind me. I turn to look and see nothing. Looking back at her, I am hit with a wave of water. Rayne laughs, then screeches when I leap at her. She disappears underneath the water, and I lose her. She comes back up behind me and splashes me again.

Oh, two can play this game.

"Rayne, what was that?" I glance down, looking at the water as if I'm searching for something. She suddenly stops laughing, frantically searching the water.

"What are you talking about?"

"I don't know. Something hit my foot." I shrug. "It was probably just a water snake."

"A what!" she shouts, jumping and wrapping her legs around my waist, and I toss my head back in laughter.

"Why are you laughing?"

"There aren't any water snakes, Raynie."

Her eyes widen before she grabs my head, trying to dunk me under the water. I don't move an inch as she struggles to dunk me, and her tits push against my face. It's a temptation I can't deny, and I suck her nipple into my mouth. Her fingers pull at my hair as she lets out a throaty moan, causing my dick to harden immediately. My mouth goes to her other nipple, and her grip on my hair tightens. I grip her waist, bringing her down, so she is face to face with me. Her green eyes gaze into mine as droplets of water fall from her long, dark lashes.

She slowly licks the water off her lower lip before closing her eyes and brushing her lips against mine. My hands cradle her face as our tongues tease one another. Heat rises from my stomach to my chest. She drapes her arms over my shoulder, pressing herself fully against me. We steal each other's breath with every sweep of our tongues while simultaneously breathing life into one another.

My hands travel down to her perfectly round ass, and I squeeze, groaning into her. She moans, rocking her hips, sliding her pussy against my solid cock. With a sharp breath, she pulls her lips away from mine. Her eyes roam over every inch of my face before slowly blinking, ensuring I'm not a figment of her imagination. My eyes are transfixed on every part of her. Her cute button nose, her sweet pouty lips, her high cheekbones, the way her ebony black hair is perfectly slicked back with water, and those beautiful fucking eyes that take my breath away.

Looking at her, I feel a rush of emotions. Nibbling my bottom lip, I watch the way her eyes follow. I cradle the side of her face, and she tilts her head, leaning into my palm. My chest rises, and hers falls as our breaths deepen. She is so fucking beautiful I could stare at her forever; I *want* to stare at her forever.

"Tell me a secret," she whispers.

Bringing my other hand to the other side of her face, I softly kiss her forehead before leaning back and staring deeply into her eyes.

"I love you, Rayne."

She holds her breath as her eyes sparkle, illuminating the green. Her face is full of emotion when she closes her eyes and gives me such a deep kiss that causes time to stand still.

"I want you." She says.

I gulp, "Are you sure? We don't have to do anything."

"I'm sure. Take me to the tent Christian."

Fuck. Me. This girl is going to be the death of me. She brings her hands around my neck and keeps her legs wrapped around my waist as I carry her back to our campsite. By the time we get there, Rayne's lips shiver from the cold. I quickly unzip the tent and gently set her on a perfectly made bed. The pillows are lined up neatly, and the comforter is laid out without a wrinkle. I smile when I see the two small stacks of folded clothes, one for me and one for her. She must have done all of this when I was setting up outside.

Rayne gets under the covers and pats the empty spot next to her, signaling me to join her. I smirk and get under the covers, pulling it over us. She instantly snuggles into me, bringing heat to our cool bodies, and presses her lips to my chest. Using a finger, I tilt her chin to me and gently kiss her full lips; we kiss slowly, savoring this moment. She rolls to her back, and I climb on top of her, placing my knee between her legs. Our kisses are soft and teasing as they come together before drifting apart, my tongue playfully gliding over hers.

I apply a pinch of pressure to her hard nipples, and she moans in surprise. I love the way her bare breast feels in my hands. I'm horny and hard, and I nearly come on the spot when she groans while rubbing herself against me. She is becoming more impatient, arching her back as I palm her bouncy tits up and down in awe of the way they move. She is my weakness, my living obsession.

I want her more than I've ever wanted anything. I'm so close to having her entirely, but I am battling within. I have to remind myself that I'm not the guy I once was, and she isn't like the others; I would never hurt her. I love her. She sees something in me I never once saw in myself; it's ironic, the boy with the dark soul making love to the girl full of light.

"Are you sure that you want this?" she takes a moment to realize that I'm speaking to her, and when she does, she grabs my face and looks into my eyes intensely.

"I want you. I'm sure."

I chuckle at the irony. Usually, I'm confident with things like this, and now the roles are reversed, and it's her who reassures me. I reach over into my duffle bag and grab a condom. Rayne's eyes widen when she notices what it is. Using my teeth, I tear the gold wrapper and slide the condom onto my swollen cock. Her legs open for me, and I align my tip with her pretty pussy.

Chapter 32

Rayne

The moment he told me he loved me, I was certain. It was the most vulnerable thing Christian had ever said to me. I know it must have taken him time to wrap his head around those feelings and come to terms with them. At least I know it's that way for me. I've loved Christian for a while now, and for most of that time, I didn't realize the emotions I felt toward him were love. I had an idea, but I think a stronger part of me didn't want to admit it because I was scared. What if he didn't feel the same way?

Hearing him say those three words was all the confirmation and reassurance I needed. That is why I am sure I'm ready. I wanted this for some time now but didn't want to give away something that meant so much to me unless I knew without a doubt that he loved me, too.

He stares at me intensely, making sure I'm confident about this. I want him more than I have ever wanted anything else. He has ingrained himself into every part of me, marking and taking little pieces of my heart. Tonight, I want to give myself to him entirely.

His eyes roam over my face, waiting to see if I'm going to change my mind, and when I don't, he bites his lip and slowly glides the head of his cock into me, filling me with pleasure and only a little discomfort. My hands fly to his shoulders, gripping them tightly, and he stops. After a moment, he pulls the tip out and glides it down my slit and back up. The action is torture having him so close, but not quite there. He grips his firmness, sliding it tediously down my slit before entering the tip of his cock again. He inches further into me, and I move, trying to adjust to the sting. My head collides with his, and he grunts, sliding out of me.

"Oh, my God! I'm so sorry." I brush his sandy blonde waves out of his eyes.

"I'm okay." He chuckles. "It didn't hurt," he pauses, "that bad."

I laugh at his teasing, blushing in embarrassment— *Smooth Rayne, real smooth*. I'm glad we can still be playful as usual, even in an intimate and serious moment, and it helps me feel less nervous about what is happening between us.

Using his elbows, he balances his weight above me. His expression is soft as he looks down at me, wetting his lips.

"Let's slow down, okay?" my eyes widen as I bring my hands up to cover myself. I'm so bad at this and totally ruined the moment.

"Did I do something wrong?" his eyes fall to my hands, tenderly removing them from my breasts and dragging them down my stomach. Without blinking, his eyes sweep back to mine.

"No, baby," his voice lowers, "Don't hide yourself from me. We don't need to rush. I want to take my time with you."

The tension in my shoulders releases. He's right. I want this with him so badly that I'm rushing this moment and not enjoying it as I should. I'm glad one of us is thinking clearly, and I love him more because of it. It means a lot to me knowing he wants to take his time and that this moment means just as much to him as it does to me.

"O... Okay," I stutter, no longer embarrassed but nervous.

"You don't have any idea how beautiful you are." Leaning in, he kisses me slowly, "I'm going to show you."

My body ignites at the feeling of his lips against mine while my heart warms at his words.

"How?" I ask, breathless from the kiss.

"I'm going to cherish every part of you the way it deserves to be." He plants a kiss on my jaw, causing fluttering in my belly. My lips part as he trails his lips down my throat, inching closer to my breasts. I hold my breath in anticipation, and he pauses, his warm breath fanning against my sensitive nipples, hardening them immediately. When his mouth covers my tit and he sucks my nipple between his lips, I let out a heavy sigh.

My fingers tingle to touch him. My hands go to the back of his head, running my fingers through his damp strands. His large hand palms my other breast, moving it in a circular motion as his tongue swirls around my nipple before lightly grazing it with his teeth. I draw in a sharp breath, and the hair on my arms rises.

"Does that feel good, baby?"

"Yes," I rasp.

"I love the way your body responds to me." Using both hands, he caresses my breasts as his mouth glides down my stomach. "Before I lay a finger on you, your body trembles and aches to feel my touch."

I feel lightheaded from his touch and his words. All of it is true. Before I can process what is happening, my body is already responding to his nearness. My body has always had a mind of its own whenever it came to Christian, and once I've experienced his touch, my body does nothing but crave it. I love how his hands fondle me, the way his mouth feels against my lips, and how they caress my skin.

He presses a gentle kiss to my belly button before lowering himself between my thighs. My breathing becomes quick, and my eyes fixate on him, his broad shoulders and all the hard lines of defined muscle. Keeping his head down, he gazes at me through his lashes, holding my stare as he sticks out his tongue and slowly but surely sweeps his tongue between my folds. I moan in pleasure, tipping my head back and closing my eyes.

"Look at me," his voice is low and demanding.

Snapping my eyes open, I do as he says and look directly at him. His golden eyes are now dark, his pupils dilated. I flush, and goosebumps break out amongst my skin. He resumes lapping me with his tongue, and I fight the urge to close my eyes and throw my head back—Christian circles my bud before sucking gently and entering a finger inside of me.

I gasped at the tingling surge starting in my chest and spreading throughout. My legs shake, becoming weaker with every flick of his tongue. No longer able to fight it, I close my eyes and throw my head back, concentrating on the pleasurable sensations taking over me.

Just as my body is about to surrender to its release, Christian withdrawals his fingers and mouth from my pussy, causing a desperate whine to flee.

"W... Why did you stop?" I stammer, trying to catch my breath. He chuckles, climbing back on top of me.

"I'm just getting started, baby. When you come, it won't be from my mouth or my fingers."

My throat suddenly feeling dry, I swallow. My insides are vibrating with excitement and nervousness at what's coming. I feel more relaxed thanks to Christian but needier than ever and slightly impatient again, thanks to Christian. I'm worried it will hurt or that I'll be awful at this and ruin the moment. It's my first time, it's *our* first time, and I want it to be perfect.

'loving you by Mahogany Lox,'
"The kind of love that never fades. I could just stare at you for days."

With a soft kiss on my forehead, he lets me know everything is okay, then tenderly kisses the corner of my mouth before pressing his lips to mine. The warm feeling of his breath is inviting, making my heart skip a beat. The smell of him is hypnotic. Our tongues slowly dance as I trail my fingernails up his back and into his hair.

His hardness presses against my abdomen, making me desperate to touch him. I reach between us and push my palm against his cock, only wanting to be closer. It twitches in my hands, and he groans. I smile at his reaction, loving that I can make him feel good. I squeeze him gently before stroking him. His mouth moves to my neck, and he drinks at my skin firmly, then slides his tongue over the sensitive spot to soothe the ache. My entire body is on fire, and I'm getting more turned on by the second. I want him right this instant!

He draws in a sharp breath, squeezing his eyes shut. Yes, I feel nervous and slightly afraid, but my love for him is more substantial and overpowers any other feeling. He is perfect. Using one hand to hold his weight, he uses the other, lining himself up to enter me. My heartbeat quickens, and my skin turns clammy.

"Are you ready?"

I look him directly in his eyes and tell him, "I'm ready." He kisses me softly as he presses into me. My eyes screw shut, and I fist the blankets, my body tense.

"Are you okay?" he pauses.

"Yes," I wince, "I'm just nervous, but it only stings a little. Keep going." He tenderly kisses my forehead, then my cheek, pushing deeper into me.

"Fuck." Christian groans.

He fills me completely, making us the closest we have ever been. The feeling is a little uncomfortable, but knowing he's inside me feels right. I wouldn't want to share this moment with anyone else but him—Christian moves in and out of me, and the stinging stops.

"Fucking perfect," he moans deeply, sending waves of vibration throughout our connected bodies.

Hearing the pleasure in his voice brings me comfort and confidence, knowing he enjoys this. I feel spellbound as I watch him, the smell of citrus invading all my senses. His eyes are tightly closed, and he throws his head back.

"Hey, look at me." I breathe, bringing his face to mine. He opens his eyes and his lips part. I stroke my thumb over the sweat above his eyebrow and down the side of his jaw. I want him to be in this moment with me. His eyes are bright and glossy, mirroring my own, and when I wrap my arms around him, his muscles contract beneath my fingertips. Our eyes never waiver: our only focus is on each other.

I can't believe this is happening. Everything about this... us... is perfect. It's better than I would have ever expected for several reasons. However, the main one is that I'm sharing this moment with him—my summer.

"I love you." He says, his breath staggered, hot and wild, fanning against my skin.

Those three words cause everything to slow. He kisses me again, and I can feel him wash over me like a wave of warmth. I've never felt so connected to anyone; our connection runs deep, making me feel things I never knew were possible. I do not know what our future holds, but this moment means everything; this moment is ours.

His eyes reflect my own, full of emotion; they radiate admiration and love. The way he looks at me makes it hard for me to breathe.

"You feel so fucking good, baby." He lets out a low moan. The feeling of him inside me is something I can't put into words. I feel so connected to him that he fills an inevitable part of me I wasn't even aware was missing. I feel complete.

His eyes still hold mine, and I'm overcome with so much emotion; I feel everything. The erratic rhythm of our hearts, our chests pressed against each other, and the constant tingle charging through our bodies. Filled with so much emotion, I tell him what I should have told him earlier.

"I love you, Christian." His eyes glisten, and his mouth parts as if he can't believe the words he's hearing.

"Tell me again."

I peck his lips, "I," then kiss the corner of his mouth, "love," my breath fans against his full lips. "You," I whisper.

"Oh God, I'm going to come," he thrusts faster. I move my lips to his neck, pulling on his sweaty skin, and he growls in response. I leave trails of kisses up his jaw and onto his mouth. My eyes never leave his as I brush his damp hair away from his forehead. His eyes never stray from mine as he comes; unspoken words are made as he releases inside me.

I'll love you forever. Mine.

Trying to catch his breath, he gently collapses onto me. The only sound is our hearts thumping. I kiss the top of his sweaty hair as a smile teases my lips. After catching our breaths and our heartbeat steadies, he pulls out of me, and I sense a sudden emptiness now that he no longer fills me.

I can't stop the doubt from flooding my mind. Was it everything he expected? He's more experienced than I am and has been with plenty of girls. Were they better than me? Did they feel better? I close my eyes and try to rid the thoughts of ruining this special moment.

"What's going on in that pretty little head of yours?" he lays beside me.

"Was it what you expected?"

"No, it wasn't. It was more."

"But what about the other girls? I'm not as experienced." His eyebrows pull down, and he frowns.

"I'm only going to say this once, okay?" his eyes are dark, his expression serious. "I've never made love to anyone. You are *it* for me." His expression looks hurt like my words caused him pain.

I kiss the bridge of his nose, then his chin. "I'm sorry. I promise I won't say things like that again." I say, and he wraps me in his arms.

"How was it for you?"

I smile, already thinking about the next time we do it. "Uncomfortable at first, but so good."

He chuckles, kissing the top of my head. "Are you sore?"

"A little bit, but I'll be okay."

"Good, I love you, baby."

I grin. I don't think I'll ever get used to hearing him say those words. We lay there for I don't know how long as we talked, and his fingertips languidly graze my arm. When I try to move, I wince, still feeling slightly sore. Christian notices and tells me to stay put as he puts on the gray sweats I had laid out for him and a blink 182 t-shirt that looks exactly like mine. He exits the tent, and shortly after, the tent lights up in warmth as colors of orange and red flicker, casting shadows throughout. He must have started the fire.

Smiling, I think to myself. I did it. I had sex; *we* had sex. Although I felt discomfort, it quickly turned into pleasure, and I'd go through it all again just to watch him fall apart because of me. I heard girls at school say they felt different after sex. Do I feel different? Not really. If anything is different, it's my connection with Christian. I feel closer to him, more connected, and my feelings for him are much stronger. I surrendered myself to him, heart, mind, body, and soul.

Stepping back into the tent, he smiles at me and drops to his knees. Watching him now, I see his face etched with worry about hurting me and feel the love that burns in his eyes. I don't care about the girls in his past anymore. I only care about the beautiful golden boy who just made love to me for the first time.

"I hurt you," he frowns, still observing my essence.

"You didn't hurt me, I promise. I'm okay." He places a warm kiss on my inner thigh before standing up and grabbing the pile of clothes I had laid out. I go to sit up, but he shakes his head in protest.

"I'll do it." He carefully pulls my soft sweats up my legs, tying them around my waist. I move to sit, and he gives me a stern look, telling me to stay still.

I giggle. "I have to sit up, so putting my shirt on is easier."

Once I'm sitting crossed-legged, I hold up my arms, and he slips the graphic tee over my head.

"Thank you," he whispers against my mouth.

"For what?"

"*Everything*. Thank you for giving me something so special and trusting me."

My heart skips, and my body warms at his words.

"It was perfect." I peck at his lips. "I love you."

His signature lopsided smile takes over his face. "I love you."

We made hot dogs over the fire and roasted s'mores for dessert. Christian teased, wiggling his eyebrows, telling me he would have me for dessert later. My first time was so special with him, and I can only imagine how good it will get the more we do it. Laynie was right; I have been missing out, and I get it now. Sex is amazing; however, I don't think I'd feel this way with anyone but Christian.

Gray clouds no longer cover the sky; instead, twinkling bright stars stretch across the velvet midnight canvas. As I gaze up toward the heavens, a streak of light shoots across the atmosphere.

I gasp. "Christian! Look, a shooting star," he tilts his head back, but it's already gone.

"Make a wish, Raynie." Closing my eyes, I do as he says. "What did you wish for?" he asks.

They say it won't come true if you tell what your wish is. Honestly, I don't believe it. I think what you speak into the universe is what you get.

"I wish you'd come to New York with me."

"I can't."

"But why?" my voice cracks.

"My life is here now, and I can't just leave my mom. What about my job?"

"I don't expect it to be right away. I was just hoping it could be a possibility. Maybe my dad can help you find a job in New York. He has tons of contacts."

"And my mom?"

Of course, I don't want him to leave his mom. At the restaurant, she made it seem like she'd be sad if he were to go, but that she would be okay. Now I feel selfish trying to get him to come with me when he's all his mom has. What am I supposed to do, though? Going to New York has always been a dream, and before him, nothing was getting in the way of it, but now that I have Christian, I can't imagine being in the big city without him.

I pick my fingernails, feeling defeated. "I thought she'd be okay with it, but I guess you're right..."

"We can do long distance. I don't want to give this up," he gestures between us. "You're only a plane ticket away, and we will visit each other as often as we can."

The irony is that he repeats words that I had once spoken. Thinking about leaving him makes me feel ill, and an ache forms deep within my chest. Sure, we can do long distances, but I'm selfish; I don't want to. I'll be in New York for years with school, and depending on if I get offered a good job, I may even be there longer. How long can we handle the distance? We barely want to be away from each other now, and he lives next door. We have had a night that I'll never forget, so instead of talking about something that only brings my mood down and hurts to even think about, I plaster a fake smile on my face and nod. He eyes me skeptically, as if he can see right through me, or maybe he doesn't because he drops the conversation.

The woods are pitch black, and I really have to pee. I asked Christian if he'd walk with me, and he chuckled, saying as if he'd ever let me go alone. *But you'd let me go alone to New York.* Whatever, there isn't any point in sulking over it now. Christian drapes his arm around my shoulder, and I welcome his embrace. We reach the bathrooms, and he walks into the restrooms with me.

"You don't need to come into the bathroom with me, you know."

"Why not?"

"Because I don't want you to hear me pee," I say, embarrassed.

"I've heard you scream my name. Hearing you pee is nothing." My mouth hangs open, and heat creeps into my cheeks. "Okay, fine," he dramatically sighs. "I'll be right outside." He pouts, stepping out of the bathroom.

Barely able to hold my bladder, I rush into the stall, layering the toilet seat with toilet paper because who knows how often these things get cleaned. As I pee, I wince at the burn. How long am I going to be sore? I finish up. Thankfully, the burn subsided, and I washed my hands. When I look in the mirror, my mouth falls open at my reflection. My lips are swollen from being kissed senseless, and my face is glowing. I move my hands over my cheeks, examining myself. My fingers brush over the fading red mark on my neck from where Christian marked me, and I smile. It's like I can feel his hot, wet mouth still against my flesh.

I am snapped from my thoughts at the sound of Christian's voice. "Rayne, are you alive in there?"

"Coming."

When I exit the bathroom, he is nowhere to be found. *What the hell?* I felt anxious; my skin is already clamming up, and my heart speeds up.

"Christian?" I whisper-shout, looking around.

"Gotcha!" he grabs me from behind, and I let out an embarrassing scream as I kick my legs, trying to break free from his hold. His grip loosens, and he gently sets me down. He walks in front of me and kneels.

"I'm so sorry! I should have known better not to do that after everything that has happened." He kisses me all over my face. "I wasn't thinking."

I'm instantly relieved and feel foolish for reacting the way I did. "It's okay, I'm okay. I can't be scared forever." He smiles, his eyes full of admiration.

"You won't be."

Placing my hand in his, we walk back to our campsite. The perfect idea comes to mind when I see a medium-sized branch lying on the path ahead of us. Just as we go to pass it, I trip over it, falling to my knees.

"Ow!" I howl.

"Rayne! Are you okay?"

"My ankle… it hurts." His eyes are wide and frantic as he tries to examine my foot.

"Gotcha!" I shout, jumping to my feet and sprinting away. I hear him shout you're going to get it, as I further the distance between us, and I laugh, running faster. Just as I'm about to unzip our tent, his firm hands wrap around my waist before he tosses me over his shoulder and spanks my ass, causing me to yelp.

"I'm ready for dessert," he growls.

I gulp, desire whooshing through my blood. Christian wasn't joking when he said he was ready for dessert; he ate my pussy as if it were cake on his birthday. My toes curled, my body shook, and my swollen pussy hummed. He unraveled me with his tongue, ravishing every part of me. My body became weak, and the weight of my eyelids was too heavy. I hear a sleepy *I love you* as Christian embraces me in his arms; I surrender to sleep.

Chapter 33

Christian

I'm casually leaning against my car when Rayne charges through her front door, running straight at me with a duffle bag around her shoulder and the biggest smile on her face. My mind automatically returns to last week when she was running at me full of excitement about going camping and getting a full night to ourselves, and I can't hold back the grin that takes over my face at seeing her.

Last week was by far the best week of my life. I know I've had sex before, but I have never given myself to someone in the way I gave myself to Rayne, but what means the most is how she gave herself to me. There are not enough words to truly express how much that meant or how much I love her. She's mine now and forever; Rayne Davis will always have me.

Just before Rayne reaches me, she drops her bag and leaps into my arms. I smile like a fool and can breathe easier now that she is in my embrace. She keeps her legs wrapped around me as I hold her for what feels like hours, but I don't give a shit.

It isn't until I see Jack and Olivia step out of their home that I finally set Rayne down. Jack has his arm wrapped around Olivia as they approach us. As if they coordinated a time to meet up, my mother came out and joined us.

"Hey, Sawyer," Olivia smiles and hugs my mom.

"Hey!" my mother beams.

"You guys have a long drive ahead. Are you guys planning on stopping?"

"We will probably only stop for gas and a bite to eat. The drive is long, but it's good that I have Rayne to keep me company. That way, I'm not just stuck with this guy," my mother teases, pointing her thumb at me.

Rayne and Olivia giggle, Jack smirks, and I roll my eyes, hiding my smile.

"Well, I don't want to keep you, and I just wanted to say bye before you guys left and wish you a safe drive. Please don't hesitate to text or call if you need anything."

"I won't," my mother gives her a reassuring smile before giving them space and putting her things into the trunk.

Rayne gives her mother a tight hug as Olivia's eyes water. I was happy when Rayne told me her parents agreed she could come with us to Oregon over Thanksgiving break, but I know it's the first time Rayne will be away for the holidays. I wonder how they will handle her being away for school in New York. How will I handle her being in New York? I never want to be away from her as it is. We will be okay, though we *have* to be, because New York isn't an option for me.

They say their goodbyes, Olivia wiping at her tears. Rayne teases her, telling her not to cry, or it will make her cry. Jack is stoic, kissing the top of her head before wrapping his arm back around his wife. They tell us both to have fun and stay out of trouble. Rayne smiles, giving them a nod and one last hug goodbye before getting into the car with my mom.

"Well, we're going to get going," I smile. "Thank you for allowing Rayne to come with us." Olivia smiles sweetly, and Jack shakes my hand.

"I trust you. Take care of her." I nod in understanding, then set Rayne's bag into the trunk and get into the driver's seat.

Rayne waves from the back and smiles as we drive away. Through my rearview mirror, I see Jack hug Olivia tighter and kiss the top of her head before they both turn and head back inside. It's refreshing to see and makes me sad at times. I can't remember the way my parents were together. I can't remember if my mom beamed when my father walked into a room or if my dad kissed her on the top of her head, as Jack does with Olivia. It's small minuscule things you don't think matter until you can't remember them, and you wish you could.

It's around eight p.m. when we pull onto my uncle's street, and all I can think about is how fucking weird it feels to be back here, not at my uncle's house, but back in Oregon. Pulling into his driveway, I see my mom's black Toyota parked. That's the main reason we made this trip because when we first moved here, I drove the U-Haul, and she drove my car, so we had to leave hers behind. Now that she starts at her new job after the Thanksgiving break, she will need it.

After parking, I look at Rayne to let her know we made it, but she's sound asleep in the back seat. Even when she's sleeping, she looks so fucking beautiful.

"Let's let her sleep a little, and we can grab the bags." My mother whispers.

We grab our luggage from the trunk and walk them to the front porch. Just as we reach the door, my uncle Maverick opens it with the biggest toothy smile I've ever seen on his face. I didn't realize how much I'd missed him until I had to blink my eyes to stop the tears from forming. Fuck.

"My boy!" he beams, spreading his arms and giving me a bear hug.

"Uncle Mav!" he lets me go and looks at my mom. His eyes soften, and I swear I see them shine.

"Sawyer," he says, like he's taking a breath of air.

"Maverick," she whispers.

He smiles, "Get over here."

She immediately goes to him. I smile because I know she has missed him just as much as I have. After a minute, my mom unwraps herself from his waist and takes a step back.

Maverick looks over our heads. "Aren't we missing someone?"

"Yeah, she fell asleep. I'm going to go wake her up now."

"I'll take these." He reaches and grabs our bags. "Should I set these in your room?"

"Very funny," my mother cuts in. "They will sleep in separate rooms."

My uncle chuckles, shaking his head, and my mom follows him into the house. I open the passenger side door and scoot the seat forward to wake Rayne. She stirs and slowly opens her eyes. I probably look like a fucking weirdo staring at her with a smile on my face.

"I didn't mean to fall asleep." She says.

"It's okay," I brush her hair behind her ear, "I'm glad you got some rest."

"We already brought our stuff in. You ready to meet my uncle?"

She swallows nervously, "As ready as I'll ever be. It's so beautiful here."

A beautiful place filled with ugly-hearted people.

Stepping through the front door, I hear my mother laughing at something my uncle said. It's good hearing her laugh like that, and I almost forgot what it sounded like. We pass the living room to our left and a door that leads to the garage to our right. My uncle and I have spent hours in that garage taking apart and putting together cars. It was always my place of solitude. When we reach the kitchen, Maverick fills a glass of wine and tops off my mother's.

"He's back," Maverick smiles. Rayne holds my arm a little tighter and shyly smiles at him. "You must be Rayne?"

"I am, and you must be Maverick?" she holds out her hand.

He looks down at it and smirks, "If your special enough for this jerk to bring home," he flicks his thumb at me, earn-ing himself an eye roll, "then you are already considered family, no need for handshakes," he hugs her instead. "I've heard so much about you."

Rayne looks at me and smiles.

"Not from him, from Sawyer. I can barely get a hold of him anymore." he glances at me before giving his attention back to Rayne, "but now I know why."

Her cheeks tint. "All good things, I hope," she smiles, looking at my mom. My mom returns her smile, taking a sip of her wine.

"Great things," Maverick says.

Grabbing her hand, I say, "I'm going to show Rayne to her room."

"You guys just got here. You can show her the room later. Hang out with us. Unless you're too cool for that now."

I chuckle, lightly punching him in the arm before Rayne and I take a seat on the kitchen island.

"So, how did the two of you meet?" he asks Rayne, and she chuckles at his question. "Now I have to know." He says, intrigued.

"Well, I paid for this *jerk's* order at a coffee shop, and he gave me a hard time for it."

Maverick looks at me, smiling. "Let me get this straight. You didn't pay for her drink, but she paid for yours, and instead of being thankful, you gave her shit for it?"

"As you said, I'm a jerk," I shrug, smirking, "I forgot my wallet in the U-Haul, but yes, she was nice enough to pay for my order," I look at her and smile, "that isn't the whole story though." He looks at me, waiting for me to continue. "She's my neighbor."

Maverick almost spits out his wine. "What are the fucking odds?"

"Maverick," my mom scolds him for his language, and he chuckles, holding up his hands.

"You know I can't help it. I have a filthy mouth." My mom's eyes slightly widen as she takes a long sip from her glass.

"I paid for his order and gave him a piece of my mind for not saying thank you. Eventually, he came around before he left."

"Good for you! I'm glad you put him in his place. Well, that's going to be one hell of a story to tell your kids one day."

Rayne's eyebrows lift as heat creeps up her neck and onto her cheeks, and I choke on air. Our reaction causes my uncle to laugh. He tells us he's only kidding but that we should have seen our faces. I love him to death, but I swear I feel like he's closer to my age and not pushing forty. We all continue to hang out for a bit longer, and my mom asks if I can run to the store to get a few things and pick up a pizza on the way home.

Rayne and I hop back into my car and head to Fred's grocery outlet. We pull into the parking lot, and I park my car at the end of the lot, away from other parked vehicles. My car is badass, and I don't trust parking near others. I'd be pissed if my baby got scratched or dented, and I really don't feel like fighting anyone tonight. As we walk toward the store, I see Rayne shiver, her arms igniting in goosebumps. She looks sexy as hell in denim shorts, a black Scarface tee she knotted around her waist, and her black Doc Martens, but the weather here is very different from the weather in LA. I unzip my black jacket and wrap it around her. She smiles, slipping her arms through the sleeves before grabbing my hand and kissing it. Going through my mom's list, we get sausage, pancake mix, eggs, bacon, and toast.

We're walking down the ice cream aisle with our shopping cart, searching for the best ice cream ever. Who doesn't like cookie dough? And who doesn't like ice cream? Now put both of those together, and you have yourself a deadly combo. Whoever thought of the idea is a fucking genius.

Rayne turns to me and pouts her lip. "I don't think they have it."

"They must have it. It's only the best ice cream."

"I know. It's my favorite!" I double check just in case we missed it, but she's right. I don't see cookie dough anywhere.

"You're right. They don't have any, but we can look for it at a different store tomorrow. Deal?"

"Deal," she smiles. "You know what I like more than cookie dough, though?"

"What?"

"Your mouth," she replies and gives me a kiss that goes straight to my dick.

With our cart full of everything on my mom's list, we head to the front to check out. Rayne stands on the front of the cart, and I push her faster down the aisle. She laughs and screams when I make sharp turns but never tells me to slow down, so I don't. I hit another corner fast, and her grip tightens on the shopping cart. She's looking right at me, smiling, and I smile back. I act like a child racing down aisles with my cart while Rayne hangs on, enjoying the ride. I don't care, though, because I've never been happier. Rayne and I can do the simplest things and always have so much fun. I don't think there is ever a time when we hang out that I'm not smiling. It feels good to be fucking happy.

"No fucking way!" A voice shouts behind us.

My happiness quickly fades at the sound of his voice. I slow down but continue forward, trying to get the hell out of here. Rayne scrunches her eyebrows, unsure of my reaction.

"Yo, Chris!" he hollers.

Fuck! I stop my movement but don't turn around. Rayne looks at me before glancing over my shoulder. My feet feel like bricks weighted in place as I stand here, hoping that maybe if I don't acknowledge him, he'll get the hint and leave us the fuck alone. That is wishful thinking because I heard his footsteps approach from behind me. My body stiffens, and I still don't turn.

"Chris, is that you?" I count to three in my head before I turn around and look at Josh.

When I turn to face him, I don't offer a smile or a response; I just stare at him blankly.

"Holy shit! It is you." He grins, bringing his tattooed-covered hand to his mouth in disbelief.

He looks the same as I remember, with only slight differences. He no longer wears his hair in a man bun; instead, it was shaved close to the scalp at the sides, longer and messier on the top. Half sleeve ink on his arm is now a chaotic, full sleeve. I don't know why chicks dig guys with tattoos so much, but they do. Josh looks like a fucking delinquent, and I don't get the appeal.

"Yup." I pull my lips together tightly.

"Are you back for good?" he takes a step closer.

"No."

"You have to come to my party tomorrow night. Lance and Ricky would love to see you, dude."

Lance was the most decent out of our group. He had his fair share of women but also respected them and was honest; he couldn't help that all he had to do was smile, and girls would flock to him. Ricky was worse than Josh, and I combined. Do you know how you get these terrible feelings, these gut instincts you can't ignore? Well, I get those feelings whenever I'm around Ricky.

Just as I'm about to respond and tell him I'm not interested in being nostalgic, a blast from my past makes an appearance. Shit! I can't even remember her name, but I can tell she remembers mine with the seductive smirk on her mouth and how she bats her fake eyelashes at me. I look over my shoulder at Rayne, but her eyes are zeroed in on the girl wearing the mini skirt, stripper heels, and some top that looks like a lace bra. This isn't good. I have to get the fuck out of here.

Quickly, I turn around to face Rayne. Her knuckles around the shopping cart are ghost white, but her eyes are curious. I can see the wheels turning in her head like she's trying to figure out who this girl is. *She's nobody.* Behind me, heels clack against epoxy floors as they approach, and tacky, over-the-top jewelry rattles against each other with each step she takes. Who the fuck needs that much jewelry?

"C, is that you?" long acrylic nails wrapped around my shoulder.

I almost laugh in her face. She doesn't know me well enough to call me some stupid ass nickname. Everyone always had another way of saying my name instead of just using my actual name. I've told them to call me Christian, but no one ever listened. They continued to call me Chris, C, and Hayes. Josh and Ricky loved to call me Christie or Hayley, but once Ricky earned himself a black eye, he never called me anything but Christian.

Turning around and facing her, I keep my mouth shut, looking at her expressionless.

"Oh my god, it is you!" when I don't respond, she continues, "It's me, Lexie."

Rolling my eyes, I remove her hand from my arm, shrugging, "Doesn't ring a bell."

She awkwardly laughs as if I'm joking with her.

"Most call me sexy, Lexie." She bites her lip and bats her fake long lashes.

She looks like she has bird wings on her eyelids, and I try my hardest not to bust out laughing. Also, who would want that as a nickname? Staring at her, all I can think of is what my nickname for her would be. It would be Laxa Lexi because she's trying hard to look sexy right now, but all she does is look constipated, like she could use a fucking laxative. She is a girl I fucked or a girl who wanted to fuck; I don't know. All of them just blurred together after a while.

"Nope. Don't have a clue of who you are."

Her nostrils flare as her gaze moves over my shoulder, and I try to step to the side to block her view, but it's too late. Her eyes land on Rayne standing behind me, and her eyes turn to slits.

"Who are you?" she snarls, placing her hand on her hip.

Rayne steps forward, "Um, I'm Rayne." she holds out her hand.

Lexie looks down at it but doesn't take it. Rayne quickly pulls her hand back and starts fidgeting with her fingernails. Josh's eyes flick to Rayne, dragging his eyes leisurely down her body. Not wanting them to notice my hands shaking in anger, I place them in my front pockets.

"Aren't you going to introduce us?" Josh stares at me, trouble dancing in his eyes. I don't want to, and I don't want them to know anything about her.

"Um, yeah." I gesture my hand to Rayne. "This is my friend Rayne; Rayne, this is Josh." I motion my hand back in Josh's direction.

Rayne's brows bunch together as she snaps her head up, suddenly looking pissed. I scrunch my brows, confused on why she seems pissed off suddenly.

"I've never seen you around here, and I would have definitely noticed." His eyes trail down her body again before landing on her breasts.

My nostrils flare as I clench my jaw, trying to keep myself from lunging at him. Rayne notices his stare because she crosses her arms over her chest, uncomfortable.

"I'm not from here," she politely smiles, "I live in Los Angeles."

"We're going to go." I take a step back.

"Come to our party tomorrow," Josh says, "and bring your friend." He looks back at Rayne and smirks.

He needs to take his fucking eyes off her. I'm struggling to keep my shit together.

Lexie darts her eyes to Rayne. "She doesn't really fit in with us." Her eyes drag up and down Rayne in disgust.

As if that's a fucking bad thing. I think to myself. They don't fit in with her! Rayne is better than all of us.

Rayne scowls. "We will be there."

My eyes quickly snap to hers, but she isn't looking at me. She is too busy shooting daggers at Lexie. *Fuck. Fuck. Fuck.* Lexie covers her shocked expression by dramatically rolling her eyes and scoffing.

"See you tomorrow night, same place as always," Josh smirks at me and throws his arm over Lexie's shoulder before turning around and walking away.

Rayne is still shooting daggers in their direction. She is staring so intensely at Lexie that I'm surprised she can't feel her gaze burning on her back.

"What the hell, Rayne?" I balk. "We aren't going to that party!" her deadly stare that once was pinned on Lexie shoots at me.

"I wonder why!" she stalks off angrily.

What the fuck just happened? Why is she mad? She was the one who agreed to go to this stupid ass party and didn't even talk to me about it. Women are so fucking confusing. I want to chase after her, but I need to check out first. Rushing through the self-checkout lane, I quickly bag and pay for the items and head back to my car. Rayne leans against the passenger door with her arms crossed.

"What's going on with you?" I unlock my car, and she gets in, not answering me.

Setting the groceries into the trunk, I leave the cart where it is and follow her. Closing my eyes, I lean my head against the seat, sighing. Usually, I find the silence peaceful, but in this case, it's suffocating. I'm not too fond of the tension I feel between us or the anger radiating from Rayne crashing into me like mighty waves.

"Talk to me." my head rolls in her direction. She still doesn't respond. "What did I do?" I grip the steering wheel in frustration. "You're the one who agreed to go to this party without talking to me first."

Her eyes snap to mine. "Why did you introduce me as your friend? Did you agree with Lexie? I don't exactly fit in with your crowd!"

I don't understand. Why would I agree with Lexie? She has it all wrong. We don't fit in with her; it isn't about her fitting in with us.

"What? Of course, I don't agree with Lexie. Why would you think that?"

"Why did you introduce me as your friend? The last time I checked, I was your girlfriend! I'm not sure what you're used to, but friends don't have sex!" her voice grows louder the angrier she becomes, "it didn't even seem like you wanted to introduce me at all! Then that girl Lexie insults me, and you didn't even stand up for me."

She's right. I should have said something to Lexie. She was being a bitch, clearly threatened by Rayne, but I was caught off guard at seeing them and just wanted to get out of there. I introduced her as my friend because I didn't want them to see how important she was to me. I don't trust them, and if they knew what she meant to me, they could use it to their advantage. They're miserable fucking people, and as they say, misery loves company. Rayne is leverage, something they can use to get to me. *It has nothing to do with her; it's me.*

"Rayne, it wasn't like that!"

"Take me back to the house," she demands.

Damn, she must be really fucking mad at me. I didn't think it was a big deal! She once called me a runner, but she is too. She storms off whenever we get into an argument, or she's upset. If we weren't in Oregon, and she was familiar with the area, I bet that's exactly what she would do. Fortunately for me, she needs me to take her back to my uncle's, and I'm not driving this damn car until we talk about this and resolve this stupid fight.

"No. I'm not taking you back until we talk about this."

"It was humiliating having her talk to me like that. To look at me the way she was, and you said nothing. What hurt me the most was having someone you love, someone who claims they love you, introduce you as a fucking friend."

"Damn it, Rayne!" I slam my hand against the steering wheel. "I didn't think it was a big deal! I was surprised and didn't realize that's how I introduced you."

Her eyes fill with tears as she digs her nails into her thighs. "It made me feel like you were embarrassed by me."

Fuck! "I would never be embarrassed by you. Never think that." I kiss her forehead. "We will go to this party if that's what I need to do to prove I'm not embarrassed by you." Using my thumb, I wipe her tear away. "I love you," I kiss her softly.

"I love you."

After hearing those words, I finally let out a breath I didn't realize I was holding. I don't want to go to this party and have her around my old life. I've already explained to her that they aren't the best people and that I didn't like who I became when I was with them, but I will go to this party for her, for her, I'll do anything.

Chapter 34

Rayne

After getting pizza and returning home, I was exhausted. I helped Sawyer put away the groceries while Christian and Maverick set plates. Once we finished with the groceries, we joined them at the table for pizza. I had eaten nothing all day and was starving. The pizza looked delicious; it was practically calling my name. Christian stacked two slices on my plate; shortly after, I added two more. Christian raised his eyebrow, smirking at me, and I shot him a look that said, "I'm on vacation; leave me alone."

Maverick had work in the morning, so he had to go to bed, but we were tired from the drive and called it a night. Sawyer said goodnight, giving us a warm hug but not without telling Christian to show me to my room and make sure he finds his way back to his. Even though I'd never been here, it somehow felt like home. It was a standard room with a queen-sized bed, two wooden side tables, and navy-colored curtains.

Walking to the nightstand, I pick up the picture frame and examine it. There are two guys in the picture, one I recognize as a younger Maverick, and the other looks a lot like him, just a little older, but not by much. They both have wavy, jet-black hair and stunning sea-blue eyes. Both are very good-looking. Their eyes crinkled, and the corners of their mouth were upturned into blinding grins. It's the type of smile that makes you feel warm; it's genuine. I take a deep breath and know the guy next to Maverick is his brother Cameron, Christian's dad. Christian looks a lot more like his mother, but there is no denying he gets his beautiful smile from his father. He even has his eye shape and full lips.

Christian's breath fans the back of my neck, causing my hair to rise, sparking tingles down my spine.

"I wish he could have met you," he whispers, pressing a light kiss to my neck. "He would have loved you."

Tilting my head, I shut my eyes and lean into him. His large hand gently wraps around my throat from behind me before he kisses the pulse under my jaw. His lips are soft, and his kisses are light, but I can feel their weight keeping me grounded.

"Christian," I try to speak, distracted by the feel of him everywhere, "We can't."

"Why not?" his other hand grips my waist as he continues assaulting my neck.

Why can't we? I can't think clearly with his hands and lips on me.

"Um, I... I don't know." He chuckles into my neck as his fingertips glide along the waistline of my shorts before he slides his long fingers into them. I pant as he takes his time, stroking his fingertips down my slit.

"Christian!" Sawyer shouts from the other room, "It's time to say goodnight." Christian groans behind me in protest.

"Impeccable timing," he mumbles, kissing me once more and stepping away from me. I giggle, setting the picture back on the nightstand, and turn to face him.

"We have plenty of time."

Well, until I go to New York, and we hardly see each other.

"I'll see you in the morning," he kisses my forehead.

"Goodnight." Christian turns, sulking to the door and stops before exiting. It's like he's battling with himself, fighting the urge to stay. He sighs, his shoulders relax, and he wills his feet to move, heading to his bedroom.

Today has me exhausted, and I'm ready to sleep. Sleep should come easy, but it doesn't. I lay in the bed, blankly staring at the ceiling, wondering if Christian had fallen asleep already. It's almost torturing with him being in the next room and unable to lie with him. I'm almost tempted to sneak into his bed, but that's probably a bad idea. Closing my eyes, I sigh; this is going to be a long week.

Light fingers brush my hair out of my face; I stir, snuggling further into my blanket. I hear a chuckle, and my heavy lids flutter open. A blurred body sits on the edge of my bed as I rub my eyes, trying to focus. Christian is sitting by my side, smiling at my sleepy state. What time is it? I'm not sure when sleep took over, but I feel like I've hardly slept. Christian is fully dressed. His hair still damp from his shower. He looks like he got better sleep than I did.

"How do you look so good this early in the morning?" I yawn, sitting up in bed.

He chuckles, "I haven't slept."

"What do you mean? You didn't get any sleep at all?"

"It was hard to sleep knowing you were next door, so I gave up on sleep after a while," he shrugs. "Besides, we're on vacation, remember? There is no time for sleep. Get dressed," he pats my thigh, "I want to take you somewhere." I'm about to ask him where we're going, "And before you ask where we're going, I'm not telling," he stands, kissing my forehead. "It's a surprise. Meet me downstairs when you are ready."

I shower quickly, put my wet hair into a braid, and then apply blush and lip gloss. Popping the cap off, I mist myself with lavender before making my way to Christian. My stomach growls at the smell of greasy bacon. He stands at the end of the hallway waiting for me, smiling when he sees me.

His mom is flipping bacon, and Maverick, dressed in his work clothes, hovers over her. They are talking in hushed voices. Maverick's eyebrows turn down at something she says, and her eyes look pleading. He shakes his head, upset, and takes a step toward her.

"What's going on?" Christian frowns in confusion, and they both snap their attention to us.

"Nothing," they both respond, and Maverick takes a step back, putting distance between them.

"I have to get to work," Maverick says, running his fingers through his tousled black hair.

"You don't want breakfast?" Sawyer asks.

"No," he says, grabbing his keys.

"We're going to get going, too," Christian says. "I have something planned for us." He walks to his mom, hugging her, "Thank you. We will be back later."

Christian stops at Starbucks to get us some coffee, and I'm grateful because I sure as hell need it with the bit of sleep I'm functioning on. He definitely needs it since he is running on no sleep. I don't know how he can look so good this early, like some GQ model or something.

"You ready to take a trip down memory lane?" he smiles, handing me my coffee.

"Memory lane?"

"I know I've told you how much I hated it here, but that's not what I want this trip to be about. So, I thought it would be nice to show you my few good memories."

Grabbing his hand, I put it on my lap and smiled in response. I'm afraid to speak because then I might cry happy tears. I know how much of a big deal this is for him. Not only did he bring me to a place he loathes, but he wants me to be a part of the few good parts that he has. He makes it so easy to love him. I wish he never had to endure the things he has, but I am grateful that all those things lead him to me.

At a red light, I glance at him, taking him in fully. He is leaning back casually with one hand on the steering wheel and the other resting on my upper thigh. His hair is now dry in beautiful waves flipping up around his ears. He looks content with a smile I don't even think he's aware of. At this moment, this is how I always want to remember him so carefree, comfortable, and happy.

We pull into a neighborhood not too far from his uncle's house. The homes are nice but not as new, and I can tell these homes have been here for a while. He parks in front of a light blue cottage-style house with a white picket fence. It's beautiful, and it isn't too big or too small. It's the perfect home for a family.

Christian looks out his window with a faraway look on his face. We sit in silence, admiring the house in front of us while I wonder who lives here. The corner of his mouth lifts as he turns to look at me.

"This was our home," he glances back at the house, "My dad and mom's room face the backyard, and that was my room," he points to the bay window upstairs.

I smile, picturing his mother sitting in the window reading him bedtime stories when he was little or his dad chasing him around his room. My smile widens, imagining him sitting there a couple of years ago writing.

"When I was little, my dad used to push me on that tire swing," he points to the swing hanging from the tree in the front yard as a smile forms on his lips, "In that garage over there," he points his chin, "I would work on cars with my dad I wasn't much help then, but I loved it," his smile widens. "We would be out there for hours until my mom would come out and force us to put down the tools and come in for dinner." He chuckles, reminiscing.

"My mother would garden in the front by the porch, and I would help her, but really, I just enjoyed playing in the dirt." I chuckle, picturing him out there with his mom making a mess. "After my dad died, I remember sitting on the tire swing all alone. Then, my uncle Maverick showed up and sat against the tree not saying a word but just being there for me. We sat in silence until the sun went down." My eyes water. "Even though I was sad, it made me happy that I had him."

I lean over and kiss his cheek, "I'm happy that you had him too."

We both sit there for a while, not speaking, staring at the house he grew up in, which held so many memories, both good and bad. He keeps me close, and I snuggle deeper into him, finding comfort in his embrace. Closing my eyes, I dream of the lonely boy on the swing who, at the moment, had no idea how much his life would change and how broken he would become. Opening my eyes, I look up at my golden boy, my summer, and smile. His damaged parts are stitched together, transforming him into beautifully broken art. He is a masterpiece, and I'll love him enough, turning those fractured pieces of him into barely their scars.

"Ready for our next destination?" he asks, into my hair.

"I'm ready."

He takes me to his dad's mechanic shop that his uncle took over once he passed. We don't go in, but he tells me that Maverick hasn't changed a thing, and it looks the way it did when he was younger. Christian tells me he didn't go there much when he was little, but sometimes his dad would bring him to the shop after hours while finishing up some paperwork. He smiled when he told me his favorite thing was coming here with his mom during business hours and having lunch with his dad. Seeing his dad in uniform, all greasy with oil-stained pants, made him smile as a kid. He knew then that he wanted to be just like him, dirty and covered in oil, but not giving a shit because he was happy doing what he loved.

After spending time outside the shop, he takes me to an elementary school. It drew the corner of his mouth down when he told me he didn't have a lot of good memories there and how awful kids were to him. He told me that when he has kids of his own, they will never be like the ones who bullied him about losing his dad, about being a loner, and only having a mom. He was angry with them for a while and even begged whatever higher power people believed in that they knew what it felt like. It wasn't until he was older that he realized they were just kids too, and who should be at fault were the parents for not doing a better job. The school should've been held accountable for failing him, not noticing, or not doing anything about it.

When he told me how he was treated and how everyone failed him, I felt sadness, and I thought this trip down memory lane was supposed to be happy. He told me how the school had a bring your father to school day one year. At first, he was sad about it and didn't mention it to his mom because there wasn't any point when his dad was dead, and he didn't want to make her feel worse than she already had. His uncle Maverick showed up and spent the rest of the school day with him; it was the most fun he had at school. Even though he would have loved his dad to be there, he was glad he had his uncle.

I think we're heading home until he continues driving, passing his uncle's house. I glance at him, wondering where he is taking me, but he doesn't look at me. His jaw is clenched, his shoulders are tense, and his grip is tight around the steering wheel, completely different from his demeanor a few minutes ago. We pass tall metal gates and a sign that says Sanctuary of Peace. Following the long stretch of road lined with trees, we pass a decrepit white building in the shape of a church to our right, with hundreds of headstones throughout. Christian parks, turning off the ignition but doesn't move. He briefly closes his eyes tightly, gripping the steering wheel tighter, before releasing a breath and hopping out.

He opens my door. "Ready to meet my dad?" his eyes shimmer, and I'm not sure if he is ready to be here.

Giving him a reassuring smile that tells him everything will be okay; I take his hand. "I can't wait."

As we walk deeper into the cemetery, Christian stares at his feet. I don't recall ever being at a cemetery before, which means I'm lucky I have never lost anyone close or important to me. I'm not sure what I expected to feel about being here. I've heard creepy stories, but I don't feel the presence of any spirits of the dead. It's quiet, aside from the fluttering wings from a flock of crows dispersing as we approach.

Christian stops at a grey headstone with a written inscription.

Cameron L. Hayes
A dear husband, father, and brother.
His absence is silent grief;
His life is a beautiful memory.

"Why doesn't he have a date?" I nervously ask, not wanting to be rude but not able to help my curiosity.

"We didn't want him to be remembered with a tragic date, a date that took away someone as special as him. We carry the weight of that date with us forever, and my mom didn't want us to be reminded of it every time we came to visit."

I swallow, biting back tears. "That makes sense, and I never thought about it that way."

Cameron's headstone is well maintained with freshly planted flowers, and the grass above where he rests is crisp and green compared to the plains surrounding us. Examining the other headstones, I notice a lot of patchy dry grass and frown. Were they forgotten? Do they get visitors, or are they alone? Seeing the dead grass makes me feel like nobody comes to visit them, that when life moved forward, they were left behind.

My parents aren't highly religious, and we weren't the type of family to pray before bed or at the dinner table, but I'm sure there is something much greater out there, something far more powerful than anything here on earth. At least, I hope so. It's depressing to think that we become nothing once we finish existing here on earth, leaving us alone in blackness.

"Mav still comes here to clean up his gravestone and spend time with him," Christian's voice interrupts my thoughts, "His inscription says his absence is silent grief and his life a beautiful memory. Those words couldn't be truer. All I will ever have of him are memories; I don't remember what his laugh sounded like; I just remember the way he would tilt his head back when he did. I can't remember the way he smelt or the way it felt to be hugged by him," he kneels, rubbing his palm along the headstone, "I may not remember all the tiny details, but I remember how much I loved him and how his presence always made me feel safe."

I kneel beside him, resting my head on his shoulder, trying to bring him silent comfort.

He leans his head against mine. "Hey, dad," he pauses, his voice quivering, "Remember when I was here last time, right before mom and I moved? I told you I wouldn't ever bring a girl here to meet you because she would never be special enough, but if I found someone by some miracle, I would. I also told you not to count on it," he chuckles before pausing again, then looks at me.

"I told you that if I were to bring someone here, it was because I knew she was the one."

Our eyes both filled with tears, and as I went to wipe his away, he reached for mine at the same time. He offers me a small smile.

"You would have loved her," his smile widens, "probably just as much as I do."

Another tear escapes from my eyes and I quickly wipe it away, trying not to be a blubbering mess. Once again, his words get to me, leaving me speechless. I pay close attention, absorbing his words, not wanting to miss a single sentence that falls from his mouth. The emotion clear in the glitter of his eyes is utterly compelling.

Pecking the corner of his mouth, I turn and face his dad's headstone. "Hey Cameron," I say, avoiding Christian's stare.

"I may have never met you, but after hearing so much about you, I feel like I have," I smile, "I would have loved to meet you; I would have been honored to meet you." I glance at Christian as a tear slides down his cheek. I rapidly look away before I choke up, unable to form the words I want.

"I wanted to say thank you...." I rub my fingertips over the inscription, "Thank you for loving Christian as much as you did and being the role model you are. I know you must be so proud of him, and you should know that I am, too." I close my eyes, "Your son wishes you got to meet me, but honestly, I think you have. In your special way, I think you have been here alongside Christian for all the important moments, including this one."

As the words leave my lips, out of nowhere, a sharp gust of wind transpired in the still air, blanketing us. When Christian chokes out a sob behind me, I turn and wrap my arms around his shoulders.

"I know I've been rambling, but I have one more thank you." I lean on my knees as Christian's sparkling eyes meet mine. "Thank you for sending your son to me. Some people search their whole lives to find what I have found in him."

The tears I have held finally fall as Christian squeezes me tighter, encasing me in his powerful arms. I brush my fingers through his wavy strands, repeatedly kissing the top of his head.

"I don't know what I ever did to deserve you, but I never want to lose you," he says, voice hoarse from crying.

"I'm right here; I'm not going anywhere." He cups my face in between his hands, staring at me with wet cheeks.

"I love you, Rayne Davis."

"I love you, Christian Hayes." I smile before giving him a deep kiss that can cause the ground to melt below us.

Chapter 35

Rayne

Examining my black sheer long sleeve in the bathroom mirror, I can't help but wish Laynie was here. I've tried calling her, but she hasn't answered. I needed her to talk some sense into me about going to this party. Is it a good idea or not? I believed Christian when he told me I didn't embarrass him, despite how he made me feel in front of his friends. What's pushing me to go is that Lexie girl. She was openly flirting with him right in front of me, and how she was looking at him. I have a feeling they have been together before. I tried being nice and introducing myself. Even so, she acted like a total bitch! And then had the nerve to say I didn't fit in with them, as if I would even want to! Which only fueled the fire burning inside me.

How do I not fit in? She doesn't even know me! I'm going to this party, and I won't allow some girl with stripper heels and wings for lashes to decide where I belong. After slipping my belt through the loops of my skinny jeans, I give myself one last look over. My tits look fabulous in a simple black bralette under the sheer blouse I tucked into tight denim jeans. My belt with its gold clasp, and small dangling gold chain, emphasizes my natural curves, and matches the gold on my clutch and my dainty heart-shaped golden necklace. Of course, I topped it off in comfort and style with my signature, Doc Martens.

Happy with the way I look, I flick the lights off and meet Christian in the living room.

Sawyer walks over to me, "Oh honey, you look great!" she hugs me. "I wish I were young enough to wear things like this," she smiles, eyeing my attire.

"Please! I can only hope to look as good as you when I'm older."

"Have you seen your mother?" she smirks. "You have good odds."

My cheeks warm at her sweet comment.

"You better watch this one," Maverick teases Christian, nodding his chin toward me. "Make sure not let her out of your sight." Christian tenses, giving him a tight-lipped smile.

Maverick notices, "I'm just giving you a hard time," he pats his shoulder. "You guys have fun, and if you need anything, call us."

He responds with a forced laugh and walks to me. "Ready to get going?"

"Yeah, let's go."

Christian and I agreed neither of us would drink. We are going to stop in for a little, then head home. The drive is silent, and the tension in the car is high. He usually rests his hand on my thigh as he drives and steals glances at me; this time, he didn't. He doesn't even look at me, not once. He stares intensely at the road, a death grip on the steering wheel.

"Are you okay?" his jaw ticks, and he doesn't respond right away.

"I'm fine."

The words *I'm fine* never actually mean what they imply. Usually, it means the opposite. I want to push and get him to tell me what's going on, but I decide against it. I'm not trying to argue or ruin the night before it's started.

We arrive at a front lawn with drunk people everywhere, the front door wide open as party-goers stumble in and out with red solo cups in hand. People are making out on the porch and dancing right in the front yard. Meeting at the front of his car, he hangs his arm over my shoulders, protectively pulling me into him.

A few people recognize Christian saying "what's up," and a few "Yo, where have you been," but he never responds as we continue walking through the wake of people. Stepping onto the threshold, I have to quickly close my mouth to keep from choking on clouds of smoke. I spot the guy from the grocery store right away. Josh, I think his name was? He sees us simultaneously, and his brows raise; a smirk traces his lips. A petite girl is sucking on his neck, his arms hanging by his sides as if he would rather be doing something else. He leaves her without saying a word and approaches us.

"Well, well, well, look who the fuck decided to show up," he smirks, lifting his fist and dabbing it against Christians.

He wears a plain white t-shirt, but it looks like he ripped off the sleeves showcasing his black ink tracing up his arms. I've never met anyone with so many tattoos. It's different and intriguing. I can't seem to pull my eyes away until he notices me staring, and I snap my head away from examining the art. His grin deepens, and my cheeks heat with embarrassment that he caught me checking him out, but not in the way he must think.

"Glad to see that bitch Lexie didn't scare you off," Josh says, and I stiffen at the mention of her name.

Squinting my eyes, I lift my chin in confidence. "She doesn't scare me, and isn't that bitch your friend?"

He chuckles. "I have known her since we were kids. Calling her a bitch isn't mean when it's the truth. She is a bitch, and she knows it."

"Yeah, so, you saw me. I'm going to show Rayne around, and then we're leaving." Christian says, sidestepping Josh.

"Woah, Woah, Woah," Josh places his hand on Christian's shoulder, "You just got here. Let's go outback. Lance and Ricky owe me twenty bucks."

"Twenty bucks?" we follow Josh to the back.

He glances back over his shoulder with a sly grin, "Yeah, when I told them I ran into you at the store and invited you, they bet me twenty bucks you wouldn't show."

Christian's jaw ticks and he pulls me in closer than before. We step through a sliding glass door, entering the backyard just as packed as the rest of the house. The smell of marijuana is strong, lingering in the air, but at least out here, I can breathe. Josh leads us to a group of people hanging around a small fire. They use plastic buckets flipped upside down for chairs and a worn-out couch with rips along the sides. I've seen patio furniture in backyards, but not a sofa like you would find inside your house.

My eyes land on Lexie, and my body tenses. She smiles at something the guy next to her is saying, but it becomes a nasty scowl when she sees me. I straighten my back and raise my chin at her, not letting her intimidate me, and just when it looks like she is about to say something, the guy beside her follows her gaze.

"I can't believe my eyes," the guy with olive skin smiles, rising to his feet.

I follow his movements as he approaches us. He is good-looking with hazel eyes and a buzz cut. His smile is broad, lined with straight white teeth; however, there is something wicked about it. I can't quite put my finger on it, but nothing is inviting about his expression. A glimmer on his lip catches my eye, and I notice it's a thin silver lip ring.

"Christie," he says, and Christian's brows lower.

"What did I tell you about calling me that?"

He holds up his hands. "Okay, okay," his eyes sweep over to me. "And who are you?"

"Her name is Rayne." Christian replies taking a small step forward, so he is partially in front of me. "My girlfriend." The guy looks at me questionably before he gives Christian a skeptical smile.

"Girlfriend, huh?" Christian doesn't respond, but I can tell he's losing his cool by his tightened jaw, creased brows, and intense stare.

I step forward, "Yeah, girlfriend."

He looks at me, trouble dancing in his eyes, "Well, nice to meet you, girlfriend. I'm Ricky." I give him a tight smile just as a tall, lean guy with light brown hair approaches.

"Fuck!" he says, digging into his front pocket, pulling out a twenty, and handing it over to Josh. "I didn't think you'd come."

Josh smiles in victory, snatching the twenty out of his hands, then holds out his palm to Ricky. "Pay up."

Ricky slaps his hand instead. "I'm not paying you shit. You're at my party. That's your payment."

What a dick, I think to myself at the same time I hear Josh mutter dick under his breath. I cover my mouth to hide my laugh.

"I'm Lance," the guy with the fohawk says, holding out his knuckles.

Now that he's talking directly to me, I look at his face. He is good-looking too and looks a lot nicer than Ricky. His canine teeth are sharp and pointy, resembling a vampire with his porcelain skin. He doesn't have a lip piercing but a nose ring. These are Christian's old so-called friends? I wonder if Christian ever had any piercings?

"Rayne," I say, bumping my knuckles with his.

"Come sit," Ricky motions, walking back to the couch. "We're about to play a game."

Lance and Josh follow, but Christian hesitates. He stares at the group, then shifts his gaze to me, contemplating whether we should join them.

"Ten minutes, then we leave." Anxious, he runs his fingers through his hair, then takes my hand and guides me to the others. He sits on one of the plastic buckets, pulling me down onto his lap.

"Where is your drink?" Lance asks.

"I'm not drinking." Christian replies.

"Oh, come on, one drink, that's it," he grabs a beer from the cooler and hands it to Christian, "What about you?" he looks at me.

"I'm okay, thank you."

"Of course, she doesn't drink," Lexie snickers. "What a buzzkill."

"You know what?" I blurt to Lance, arching a brow at Lexie. "I'll take one."

"Rayne, you don't have to." Christian whispers into my ear. I love that he cares and is only looking out for me, reassuring me I don't need to do anything that makes me uncomfortable on his account. We both said we weren't drinking tonight, but since he is, why not? One beer won't hurt.

Turning to Christian, I kiss him. "I know."

Lexie's lip curls in disgust and I smile at her. *He's mine.* Ricky tells us that the game we're about to play is called never have I ever. Each person goes around saying something they have never done, and everyone who has done it has to take a drink. Seems easy enough. There are a lot of things I haven't done.

Lexie starts, "Never have I ever gotten dumped." I look around the group, and nobody takes a sip.

"Never have I ever beat the shit out of somebody so bad they had to be rushed to the hospital," Josh says.

Ricky and Christian glance at each other before taking a sip of their beer. I knew Christian had been in multiple fights, but I never knew he had hospitalized someone. It's hard to wrap my head around because I can't picture him being that type of guy to hurt somebody that badly. Well, besides, Jackson Reed. Even I want to hurt him.

Lance pauses on his turn, thinking of something he hasn't done. "Never have I ever," he smirks, looking between Ricky and Christian, "shared a girl with one of my friends."

Ricky chuckles, taking a sip. Christian's jaw ticks before taking a drink, avoiding my gaze. I knew he'd had his fair share of girls, but sharing one with his friend? Thinking it was most likely Ricky makes me feel nauseous. Not wanting to think about him being with anyone other than me, I take a large gulp of my beer, trying to wash the thoughts from my mind.

Lexie laughs, "Oh my god, remember that one time that girl... what was her name?" she taps her sharp acrylic nail against her chin, "oh right, Addy. Remember when she got so wasted, she stripped completely naked in front of Ricky and Christian?" her eyes fleet to me, and my stomach churns. "Ricky wanted her, but she wasn't willing unless Christian did it, too."

"Keep your mouth shut!" Christian snaps, and Lexie responds with a contemptuous smile and continues.

"What was that you said to Ricky again?"

Ricky responds with a triumphant grin. "Who would I be to pass up on an easy piece of ass? There are two holes for a reason."

"Ahh, that's right. Christian can never pass up on a piece of ass." She looks at me sadistically.

My heart is thumping, anger welling up in my chest. Christian already told me about his past and how he had little to no regard for girls or how they felt. Hearing actual conversations about it makes me sick, and I keep reminding myself that this isn't who he is anymore. Lexie is a bitch, and she knows exactly what she is trying to do. Cause problems between Christian and me.

"That's it. We're done here." Christian growls.

"Never have I ever been known for being a complete bitch." I smile, casually chugging my beer to smolder my anger. Everyone stares wide-eyed between Lexie and me. Lexie is gripping her solo cup so hard it folds.

I'm too pissed to care, so I continue, "Never have I ever been so fucking desperate for a guy's attention who clearly didn't want me." She snarls, quickly stands, and rushes back into the house. I got little satisfaction from throwing insults at her, but she started it.

Christian chuckles behind me, hands gripping my waist, "You, Rayne Davis, always surprise me." He grazes his lips against the top of my head. "Seeing you stand up to her was so sexy."

Ricky claps, "I didn't think you had it in you."

"You don't even know me."

He smirks, "You didn't seem like the type."

"Ricky," Christian warns.

"No, it's okay." I lightly squeeze his thigh. "What exactly is my type?" he eyes me tentatively, roaming over my face like he's trying to figure it out.

"Good," he smiles, "Innocent." He adds. "Too bad we never met you back then. You would have been perfect." he glances at Christian, and he tenses beneath me. I scrunch my eyebrows, confused by what he is trying to imply. Perfect for what? Before I can ask, Lance interrupts.

"Ricky!" he hisses, subtly shaking his head.

"Listen to your boy Ricky," Christian encourages. "You wouldn't want another hospital visit."

Ricky's smile quickly fades, his top lip curling into a sneer as he stands, his hands shut into fists. Before I can process what's happening, Christian swiftly grabs me by my waist, sets me on my feet, and stands. Shoulders squared, head lowered, looking through his lashes at Ricky, challenging him to do something.

"Alright ladies, settle down," Josh teases, trying to lighten the mood. Neither of them moves or breaks their stare-off, so I gently place my hand on Christian's arm to calm him down. I regret ever coming here.

"Ricky!" Lance warns again. Ricky glances at Lance, and a silent conversation passes between them.

"Chill, I'm just joking." He grins at Christian.

"Let's all take a shot," Lance says, grabbing a bottle of vodka from behind the cooler and a smaller bottle of whiskey. "You guys need to loosen the fuck up already." He passes the whiskey to Christian, "Your favorite, for old time's sake."

"To old times," Ricky lifts the bottle of vodka, his grin still displayed on his face.

Christian surveys the whiskey for a moment, hesitation clear on his face, then shoots it back. Ricky never takes his eyes off Christian as he gulps. It isn't until Christian wipes his mouth that Ricky smirks, glancing between Lance and Josh, who wears the same expression, then takes a small shot of vodka.

After a while, the guys continued to stand around talking about girls, and I quickly blocked it out. I don't care to hear about their sexual endeavors. Christian doesn't participate in the conversation, but I'm thankful the tension has lessened and he is much more relaxed. He lightly sways side to side, his eyes low as if they were too heavy to keep open. "Christian," my hand wraps around his, "Let's go home."

He looks at me, squinting one eye, trying to focus. "No. I want to stay."

"Um, I think you've had too much to drink." I laugh nervously.

"What are you, his mom?" Ricky says. "Damn, Christian never pegged you the type to wear a Goddamn leash."

"Excuse me?" I say.

"I," Christian blinks, trying to open his eyes wider to keep them from drooping, "I'm nobody's beach," he chuckles, "I mean bitch, and he's right. You aren't my mother. We're staying."

All his friends laugh, and I fight back the tears. I'm embarrassed and upset. He was the one who didn't want to stay long. We have stayed longer than planned already. I don't like the way he's acting or how he is speaking to me. He never talks to me this way. I'm taken aback by his behavior; I don't even recognize him. He lifts his hand sluggishly, intending to wipe away my tears with his thumb, but he rubs my chin, not my cheek.

"Aww, are you cwying... crying?" Christian pouts his lip, taunting me. "So damn sensitive."

My lip quivers. "What the fuck is wrong with you?" I step back, holding my chest, his words and actions physically hurting me.

He chuckles, shrugging, "The only thing wrong with me right now is the fact that I have to piss." he taps my nose with his finger. "So, on that note, I'll be back."

"You're just going to leave me here?"

"You'll be fine," he stumbles away from me, bumping into a few people on his way into the house.

My mouth hangs open in disbelief, watching him enter the house, not looking back at me once. Who is this guy? I feel sick. I almost feel like I'm in some sort of nightmare, but this is real. I quickly wipe at my face before turning back to the guys. Ricky and Josh are grinning ear to ear. Lance is the only one who looks somewhat sorry for me.

"Shot?" he asks.

"No thanks."

"Dollface, lighten up." Ricky says, "Christian is usually a lot worse."

"That was before he moved away from here," I wave around the place. "He isn't like this anymore, and he has never been like this with me."

My eyes well with tears again.

"Or," he holds up his index finger, "You just never knew the real him."

"I'm the only one who knows the real him! You guys call yourself his friends? You guys aren't friends, and honestly, I feel sorry for you all." I look at each one of them. "When Christian comes back, we are leaving. I don't give a shit what he says because I actually care about him. You guys are pathetic." Ricky sneers, and Josh and Lance sit quietly. "We will work through whatever the hell this is, and when we return to Los Angeles, we will return to our lives and continue following our dreams and making something for ourselves. While you guys will be still sitting in this small ass town, fucking miserable with nothing better to do but drink your lives away and do whatever the fuck else you guys do on this disgusting sofa in this shitty little yard." I laugh like I've lost my mind. "Which newsflash isn't much!"

Straightening my shoulders, pulling myself to my full height, and lifting my chin, I turn on my heels and storm away from them before any of them can speak. I've had enough of listening to their bullshit. Where the hell is Christian? Taking in a deep breath, I step back into clouds of smoke and search for the restrooms. He's drunk and probably fell into the Godamn toilet! I'm scanning the room just in case Christian is on his way out, but don't see him anywhere. In the hallway, there are four doors. One must be a bathroom.

There are three doors on the left and only one on the right, so I go for that one first. I knock, waiting for a response. Nobody answers, so I open it and am met with an empty bathroom. Did I pass him on my way over here and not realize it? Maybe he used a restroom inside one of the rooms. Closing the door behind me, I open the first door on the left, once again empty. Opening the next door, a guy leans over, holding up a girl's hair who is crying as she throws up into a trashcan. I murmur a sorry and quickly shut the door. I reach the handle for the last bedroom but decide to knock just in case someone is throwing up in this one, too.

My knuckles are centimeters away from hitting the door when I hear soft moans. Shit! Thank God I didn't just walk in. I turn around, and as I'm about to step away, I hear a female voice whisper, Christian. I freeze; panic instantly sets in. My heart throbs in my ears, loud and irregular, but I can barely hear it. My mind was clouded with fear.

Closing my eyes tightly together, I whisper, "This isn't happening."

Christian would never do that to me. I'm silly even to think of such a thing. Besides, it's a common name, and probably someone else. Still, I have to look and know for sure. I'll go in, and once I see it isn't my Christian, I'll awkwardly laugh, apologize, and get the hell out of there.

I reach for the doorknob with trembling hands. Taking a deep breath, I slowly turn the handle, pushing the door open. My hands fly to my mouth as I try to fight the bile from climbing up my throat. Tears instantly fall from my eyes as I stand frozen, trying to comprehend what I'm seeing.

Christian is lying shirtless, jeans hanging low as a girl in nothing but a tiny skirt and bra straddles him. Her fingers run through his hair as she grinds against him, licking and sucking on his neck. A sob escaped my lips, and the girl turned her head to look at me. *Lexie.*

My heart freezes right then. Squeezing my eyes closed, trying to wake myself up from this nightmare because that's what this is, right? A fucking nightmare. When I open my eyes, I'm still in this tiny room staring at Lexie on top of Christian, almost naked.

"Are you going to stand there and watch?" she snaps in annoyance. I can barely speak. All the oxygen stole from my lungs.

"W... What are you doing?"

She huffs dramatically, rolling her eyes. "What the fuck does it look like?"

"He's my boyfriend."

Tilting her head, she laughs, "Yeah, and the sky is green. Christian doesn't date."

"What the fuck Christian!" I yell. "How... How could you?" I choke. He tries to lift himself, but he's too drunk.

"W... Waynniie," he mumbles.

"You can't even say my name," my voice cracks, "you got so drunk you can't say my fucking name! H... How could you?" I cry again. "You were different. We were supposed to be different!" he doesn't respond. "Look at me!" I plead.

Lexie huffs, climbing off his body. "Look," she places a hand on her hip, "Guys like him never change," she looks over her shoulder at Christian, "Once they have you, they get bored and find someone else to play with." She looks back at me, but I can barely see her through my tear-filled eyes. "You're just boring," she shrugs with smugness, "but don't take it personally because Christian hardly finds anyone interesting."

Pulling my hand back with a sureness I was not sure I possessed, I fling it forward and slap her across the face.

"Fuck. You." And then I turn and run out of there with quivering lips and no oxygen to breathe. I smack straight into someone solid. Looking up through blurry eyes, Ricky smiles down at me.

"Dollface, why are you crying?" looking over his shoulder, I see Josh and Lance. Josh is smiling; Lance stands with his hands tucked into his front pockets with a frown on his lips. Pushing off his chest, I run, and hear "Dollface come back," followed by a laugh.

I'm pushing through bodies of people furthering my distance and hear Lance shout, "Dude, enough! She did nothing. She's got nothing to do with this."

Finally getting to the front door, I pick up my speed. Everyone is too drunk to notice, or they don't care. I've passed multiple houses, most dark and quiet like everyone is asleep when my legs give out from underneath me, and I drop to my knees on the sidewalk. It hurts. Everything fucking hurts! I grip my chest, trying to ease the pain in my heart, but nothing can subside it. I sob and weep, then sob some more for so long until I have no more tears left inside me, until the pain vanishes, a fog settles in, and I become—numb.

My body reacts on autopilot, and I don't know what I'm doing, but I hear Laynie's voice on the other end of my phone. *Did I call her?*

"Hey babe!" she chirps.
Silence...
"Babe?"
Silence...
"Hello, Rayne?"
Silence...
"Rayne! Are you okay?"
"I need an Uber." I pause... "And a plane ticket back to LA."

The Road To Oblivion

Chapter 36

Rayne

"I'm *at baggage claim*. Meet me at terminal four arrivals." I say, holding my phone in the crook of my neck. "Okay, babe, see you soon."

I just landed in LA, and this is not how I imagined spending Thanksgiving. Misty-eyed, I think about everything that has led me to this moment. I'm supposed to be having Thanksgiving dinner with Christian and his family; instead, I'm crying in the middle of a crowded airport. Wiping my eyes, I grab my bag and search for terminal four. I will tell Laynie everything, but I'm not ready to face her right now, especially when I'm still trying to come to terms with everything myself.

There is a naïve part of me that's hoping Ashton Kutcher pops out with cameras shouting, "you got punk'd," and this is all some sick joke. It's a lot easier to think about that than accept what really happened. How could Christian do this to me? What's worse is once I got to his uncles, I had to wake them up because I didn't have a key, and they both had to see me distraught. Maverick left Sawyer and me alone to talk. I didn't plan on telling her anything, but one sympathetic look from her, and the mother-like comfort she gave me, was enough to have me sobbing and telling her everything that happened.

I had to tell her. She wouldn't have been okay with me catching a flight back home without good reason. She rubbed my back and let me cry into her shoulder. Once the tears stopped, she quietly gathered my belongings and took me to the airport. I felt terrible for lying to her and telling her my parents were meeting me once I landed, but it was the only thing I could think of not to have her call them herself.

There weren't many words exchanged between us, just sad glances from her, and she offered me to stay as planned, regardless of her son's actions. The gesture only made me cry again when I realized I wasn't just losing Christian; I was also losing her. Even if I wanted to stay, I couldn't. I cannot look at Christian without breaking down. The hurt, betrayal, and anger I feel are too much right now and just simmering within me. I want to slap him in the face for everything he's done.

He warned me of the guy he was and tried staying away from me for that reason, but I believed he had changed. I thought what we had was different. I feel like an idiot for how wrong I was.

Spotting Laynie's red BMW, I walk in her direction, bracing myself for all the questions she's going to ask me. I don't want to answer them, but it's the least I can do since she bought my plane ticket and picked me up on such short notice. Laynie flips her hazards on before jumping out of her car and jogging toward me. The second I'm within reach, she wraps her arms around me, knowing exactly what I need.

Pulling away, she studies my face, giving my arms a light squeeze. "You look like shit."

I chuckle, playfully pushing her. She takes my bag and throws it into her trunk, meeting me inside the car. Now that I'm here, I don't know where I will go. I can't go home because I don't want to face my parents or Ryker and ruin their Thanksgiving. I can't go to Laynie's because her parents will call mine.

"I'm sorry I interrupted your Thanksgiving," I tell her, staring out of my window. I can feel her looking at me, but I don't turn to face her. "I can't go back to your house or my parents."

"Already got it covered."

"You do?" my head snaps in her direction, and the corner of her mouth lifts.

"Duh. We will go to Jamie's and talk. She said it was cool for you to stay with her, and once my parents fall asleep, I'll come back and get you."

"Thank you," I smile, not knowing what I'd do without her.

I can spot Jamie's wild curls as we drive down her street. She is sitting on concrete steps leading to her house's metal gated door. Laynie and I have never been here before. She is very private about her home life and never seems to want to be here either.

"What's up bitches!" Jamie smiles, walking over to us.

"Hey Jay, are you sure it's okay for me to stay here for a little while? I don't want to interrupt your Thanksgiving with your family."

"I'm positive!" she turns around, gesturing us to follow. "We aren't doing anything for Thanksgiving."

Laynie and I both share a look and a frown. The metal door creaks when Jamie pulls it open, and we follow her inside. Her home is tiny, with a small kitchen and a smaller living room. A little girl no older than three comes running toward Jamie wearing the biggest toothy smile with chocolate-stained lips.

Jamie smiles and sets her down on the couch. "This is my niece," she looks back at us, grabbing the remote to the TV, "I watch her sometimes while my older brother Leo works."

She puts on Mickey Mouse Clubhouse, and Adriana jumps up and down on the couch in excitement. She is so cute I can't help but smile. Jamie tells her something in Spanish, and Adriana nods, her eyes trained on the TV. We follow Jamie to her bedroom, where she sits at her vanity while Laynie and I take a seat on her bed. They stare at me, waiting for me to tell them what happened.

Huffing, I fall back onto the mattress and tell them everything. I started from the beginning, how we ran into Josh and Lexie at the grocery store and how Christian acted. They listened quietly, letting me get everything out. I told them about our trip down memory lane and how perfect everything was. They still didn't say anything and listened intently, even when I couldn't hold back my tears and cried. It took me a while to get through everything that happened at the party, not only because there was so much to tell, but because I still can't believe it happened in the first place. It all seems surreal, like a bad dream I cannot escape.

Before telling them about walking in on Christian and Lexie, I take a long pause as Laynie angrily started pacing back and forth while Jamie sat, brows furrowed, trying to make sense of the whole thing.

It's bad enough to experience and see it, but it's almost worse to retell and relive it. I can picture her face now, how she devoured his neck and ground against him, making me sick all over again. You know I expected stuff like this from Lexie, but I never expected anything like this from Christian. He willingly allowed her to touch him in that way while I was waiting for him at the party with his *friends*.

"That's it!" Laynie's pacing intensifies. "It isn't too late. We can catch a flight back to Oregon and have another round with Lexie because a slap to the face isn't enough!"

"It doesn't make sense…" Jamie finally speaks.

Our heads snap to her. "What doesn't make sense?"

"You said he didn't drink that much. It doesn't make sense for him to act that way from a shot of whiskey and a beer."

"Yeah, and that's what makes everything so much worse," Laynie throws her arms up, "He wasn't that drunk. He acted like a total dick in front of his friends and then had the nerve to cheat on Rayne!"

I cringe at her words, and hearing them out loud physically pains me. She notices and apologizes while wrapping me in her arms. Jamie joins, wrapping her arms around me in support. My best friends bring me comfort, but there is a small ping in my chest at the loss of solace that only Christian can give me. It's a weird feeling needing the one person who makes you the happiest but also brings you the most pain.

"Have you talked to him?" Jamie asks.

I shake my head, "No. I turned my phone off and haven't looked at it since I turned it back on to call Laynie at the airport."

"Maybe you should check your phone?" Laynie suggests.

Pulling my cell out of my pocket, I freeze. My finger hovers over the four red notifications on the phone icon and five red notifications on my messages. I click the missed calls first and sure enough, they are all from Christian. Thankfully, no voicemails because I don't think I have it in me to hear his voice right now, but I also don't think I have it in me to ignore it either. Clicking on my messages, I select his name at the top of the screen.

Christian: Raynie, please answer your phone.

Christian: I need to talk to you, please.

Christian: You left me...

Christian: I love you.

Christian: I'm sorry. Please forgive me.

My vision blurs as tears fill my eyes, making it challenging to see the texts on my phone. I'm reading his text repeatedly, feeling the pain and anger rise in me. I quickly wipe them away to read his words once more. *"You left me. I love you. I'm sorry."*

Laynie carefully takes the phone from my trembling hands and locks it. "What are you going to do?"

I look at her, then at Jamie, and see nothing but anguish on both their faces. I'm hurt, and they hurt for me. "I... I don't know…" He hurt me, betrayed me, and I don't know if I can forgive him.

Laynie leaves shortly after, and Jamie and I talk a little more. It's nice hanging out with her, and I wish we did it more often. My mother once told me I'd be lucky to count five genuine friends on one hand, and I smile, knowing I can count two. Without a doubt, I know I will have them forever.

Jamie's parents still aren't home by dinner time, but I don't question it, and she doesn't mention anything. Her niece Adriana sits at the small wooden table devouring mac n cheese as if her life depended on it. The front door swings open, and a tall, tan older guy steps in.

"Papá, Papá!" Adriana shouts with a mouth full of mac and runs to him.

"Hola pequeño," he smiles, lifting her with ease. "I made a new friend," she beams, looking at me, and he follows her gaze to me.

"Hi, new friend. I'm Leonardo, but I prefer Leo," he grins, holding out his hand.

"I'm Rayne. Your daughter is adorable and smart."

His smile widens. "Yeah, she gets that from me."

"Continue dreaming, brother." Jamie taunts, and we both chuckle.

Leo sits at the table with his daughter, and Jamie and I stand at the counter eating. It's nice watching her and her brother banter back and forth. They remind me of Ryker and me, making me miss him. After eating, we sit comfortably watching Mickey Mouse Clubhouse. I'm staring at the screen as my mind drifts to Christian. I wonder what he's doing right now? Has he thought about me? Is he with Lexie? Frowning, I close my eyes, trying to get their images out of my head.

"Who hurt you?"

My eyes snap wide open, darting to Leo, "W... What?"

"Mierda," *shit*. He murmurs, "I'm sorry. I didn't mean to say that out loud." He shakes his head. "You don't have to tell me. I'm a stranger."

"What makes you think someone hurt me?" his eyes tentatively roam over my face.

"It's a certain look in your eyes. It isn't the look you get when someone dies..." he pauses, holding my stare, "It's the kind of look you get when you lost someone who is still living."

"B... But how do you know someone hurt me? What if I hurt them?"

He shakes his head. "When someone hurts someone, they hold a different kind of look. They carry remorse, sometimes regret. They don't look as if they are in total agony and are seconds away from crumbling to the floor."

A tear falls from my eye. "You're good."

"No, pain recognizes pain. I don't know what happened, and it's none of my business, but if you are going to listen to anything, I say, listen to this..." he pauses, pinning me with his hazel eyes. "Love would have no meaning without pain."

What does he mean? Isn't love supposed to be painless and easy? I'm about to ask him when Jamie walks into the living room, joining us. He and Jamie get back to shooting the shit and playing with Adriana while I watch, Leo's words replaying in the background. I feel everything I thought I knew about love is all wrong. Perhaps it isn't as black and white as I made it out to be. Maybe love is messy.

His words follow me as I watch him pick up his sleeping daughter a little while later, taking her to bed, they follow me after he says goodnight, and they continue to follow me long after Laynie picks me up and brings me back to her house.

Leo's words echo in my head as I lie beside Laynie, who has been passed out for some time now, and continue to resonate when my phone lights up at a FaceTime call from Christian.

His words, *"Love would have no meaning without pain,"* taunt me as my thumb hovers over the green accept button, and I release a breath, hitting decline.

Pain is all I feel, and I'm not ready to face him.

The Road To Oblivion

Chapter 37

Christian

I woke up to a fucking shit show! Everything hurts. My head, my muscles, my fucking heart. Rayne didn't know anyone here, so there was only one place she could be. My uncles. Driving to Mavericks, I keep glancing at the clock; every minute is agonizingly slow.

"Hurry, hurry up!" I pound my hand against the steering wheel.

Pulling into my uncle's driveway, I park the car and hop out, not bothering to turn it off. Barging through the front door, my eyes fall onto Maverick's disappointed face, sitting at the table, before drifting to my mother's saddened eyes beside him. I don't have time for this shit. I sprint down the hall, pushing open Rayne's cracked bedroom door. The smell of lavender crashes into me, and I let out a breath, relieved she's here, until I scan the room and see her bed is perfectly made. Her duffle bag no longer sits on the chair by the window, her favorite pink blanket isn't folded, resting at the end of the mattress, and aside from the lavender that still lingers throughout the room haunting me, there isn't any trace of her.

In hysteria, I rush back out to the kitchen. "Where is she?" I look between my mom and Maverick.

My mom's eyes shimmer gold as she looks at my uncle Mav. Neither of them looks at me or answers.

"Mom?" I croak, "Mav? Please tell me where she is."

My mom's eyes drift to mine as a tear runs down her cheek. She goes to speak but pauses, a pause that's so long and scrutinizing I can hear the clock ticking on the wall in the living room.

"Honey…" she rasps, "Rayne is gone. She left on a plane back to Los Angeles an hour ago."

Rayne is gone…

"I thought we were past this Christian. I… I thought you changed?" my mother wipes at her eyes.

"I have!" I assure her, "I've been doing my best, I swear."

"Based on your actions last night, I beg to differ!" she raises her voice in frustration. "How could you do such a thing to Rayne?"

"It's not what you think!" I slide both my hands through my hair, resting them on my head. "How could you!"

"What do you mean? How is this my fault?" she looks taken aback.

"You let her leave!"

Maverick leaps to his feet. "Don't you raise your voice at your mother!"

"Who do you think you are? You aren't my father!" he takes a step back, feeling the blow from my words.

"Christian Hayes!" my mother scolds. "You apologize right now."

"No," I retort. "Why the hell would you let her leave? You know how much she means to me. Why would you let her go?"

"What was I supposed to do?" she throws her hands up. "I couldn't hold her hostage. If you had seen her face, you would have let her go, too. She looked broken, Christian." Her eyes glisten. "You made your bed; now lie in it."

Damn it! Something snaps inside of me. Pure, undiluted rage sweeps through me like a wildfire. I swing at the wall, my fist flying through the drywall. White residue dusts my knuckles. I rear my arm back and punch the wall again as my mom breaks down, bawling.

"That's enough!" Maverick roars. "You will not disrespect your mother, and you will not disrespect me or my home!" he grabs me by my shoulders, spinning me around. "I may not be your father, but I raised you like a son." he wraps his arms around me, holding me in place.

I try to fight my way out of his hold, but his arms tighten around me.

"Let me go!" I push against him, but he doesn't budge. "Let go of me now." I push against him again, and he squeezes me tighter in his embrace.

"Let it out, son... let it out." He repeats those words softly. I wrestle in his hold, thrashing around, trying to escape. Rayne was gone. I messed up, and she left me. *How am I going to make this right?* Will she ever forgive me? I need her. *Let it out, son...* rings in my ears. All the fury I feel dissipates. I let it out, I stop fighting, and I let go. My shoulders shudder as I cry into Maverick's chest, gripping the back of his shirt. No longer fighting, I surrender. Rayne is gone, and I have nothing left.

After letting everything out, I feel drained and empty. I can't wrap my head around how everything went from amazing to shit overnight. I can't believe she's gone. Pulling out my phone, I call Rayne, but it goes straight to voicemail, and I try calling again. My mother steps up, putting her hand over mine, stopping me from hitting the haunting green button.

"Honey, she is on a plane. She isn't going to answer. Rayne is extremely hurt right now, and I know you want to get a hold of her and talk to her, but she needs space, and you need to give her."

"Go take a shower, try clearing your head, then meet me in the garage. I have a car that needs to be fixed by tomorrow, and you can help me with it." Maverick says.

My mom is right. Rayne is on a plane right now, even though I want to call repeatedly until she answers so I can tell her everything. How all of this is a huge misunderstanding and beg for her forgiveness. She needs time, and I need to give it to her. It's the least I can do. Looking down at my bruised knuckles, I can see them crusted with blood, but I'm not sure if it's from punching through the drywall or punching Ricky's face.

"I'll go shower," I look at my uncle, "I need to turn off my car first."

"Don't worry about it. I'll do it. You go get yourself together." My uncle squeezes my shoulder and walks outside.

I stood in the shower taking deep breaths while focusing on the feeling of expansion as I inhaled and the tension relief I felt when I exhaled. I continued to do this until there wasn't any hot water left, and even then, with the freezing water pelting against my skin, it didn't faze me; I felt nothing—all I felt was numb.

Maverick is leaning over the hood of the car, inspecting the engine, when I step into the garage. Hearing the door open, he looks up at me and smiles. He tells me what needs to be done to the car, and we both get to work. Typically, working on cars is the perfect way to clear my mind and escape reality for a short while; however, this time, it's doing nothing for me. All I can do is think about Rayne. She should have already landed by now. Did she make it okay? Did she cry some more? Do Ryker and her parents know what I've done?

She was always going to end up leaving me, anyway. I laugh out loud at the irony, and Maverick looks at me skeptically, as if I've lost my mind.

"What's going on with you? What's so funny?" he wipes the sweat off his forehead, smudging oil as he does.

"I guess it's not funny. It's actually kind of sad..." I use my shirt and wipe my face, "I didn't expect it to happen like this, but either way, Rayne was always going to end up leaving me."

"What do you mean?" he scrunches his eyebrows, confused.

"She's going to New York for school. I said we could do long distance, but you've seen her. She's beautiful and will live in a huge city with endless opportunities to follow her dreams. Any guy who comes across her is going to want her. They would be stupid not to. I would have lost her at some point."

Frowning, he shakes his head.

"What?"

"You don't get it, do you? That girl loves you, and you're being an idiot."

"It's true, though."

"No, it's not, and you know it. That girl looks at you with so much light in her eyes you'd think she was staring at the sun." he pauses, "Why can't you go to New York with her?"

"I can't leave mom. You know that."

"Why not?" he looks at me, holding no judgment like there aren't any wrong or correct answers. He's just curious.

"Because I'm all she has. We just moved to LA, and I can't just leave her." He's silent for a moment.

"Your mother wouldn't be alone; she has me. She is also a grown woman and doesn't need her teenage son looking out for her for the rest of her life. Her job is to look after you. Your mother wants to see you happy, Christian, and if you think being with Rayne in New York will make you happy, then you should do it; you'd be a fool not to."

Will going to New York make me happy? I'm not sure, but will I be happy away from Rayne? Absolutely not. I'm happy wherever she is. I never gave New York much thought, but I haven't been giving the idea of being away from her much thought, either. I've been dreading the day I would have to say goodbye. My uncle is right. Maybe I won't have to say goodbye. For the first time today, I smile, but it quickly fades when I realize it's too fucking late. I'll never go with Rayne to New York because I've lost her.

"It's too late…"

"Maybe so, but we're Hayes' men, and we don't give up without trying." The corner of his mouth lifts. "You have two options. You can either sit around and brood about the massive fuck up you made, or you can try to fix it and go get your girl."

My girl... I smile in response, because once again, he's right. Rayne Davis is mine, and I'll do whatever it takes to get her back.

Chapter 38

Rayne

Laynie *wakes up,* but I shut my eyes, pretending to be asleep. I don't want her to worry about me or know I haven't slept all night. Instead, I've been lying next to her, staring at nothing but thinking of everything. At one point, I did close my eyes and tried to listen to Laynie's calm, steady breaths, hoping it would help lull me to sleep, but every time I closed my eyes, I saw her; I saw him; I saw them. Once the sun started peeking through her bedroom blinds, I gave up. Christian tried calling me again last night. It wasn't FaceTime, but I still didn't answer. I let it ring until it reached my voicemail.

"Wake up, buttercup!" Laynie shouts, hopping out of bed. "We're going to get into bikinis, go out front, and wash ladybug."

"It's probably freezing outside," I yawn, sitting up. She slides her window open and sticks out her hand to feel the temperature outside.

"It's a little nippy, but we will live," she pulls the blankets off me. "A little sun is bound to cheer you up." She pins me with a look, letting me know this isn't up for discussion, and

I smirk, rolling my eyes, and head to her closet to pick out a bikini.

Her parents aren't in the kitchen when we head downstairs to get me my daily dose of caffeine, which I'm glad for because it will make it more believable to tell them Ryker dropped me off if they ask. We walk through her garage with my coffee in hand to grab everything we need.

Laynie sprays down the car while I chug the rest of my coffee. I grab a sponge from one of the soapy buckets and start wiping down Ladybug. We're wiping down the car, getting it nice and soapy, when a few guys I recognize from school ride by on skateboards and bikes. Laynie turns around to face them, their attention already on us. Tilting her head, she squeezes her sponge above her chest, letting the soapy water mixture fall onto her skin.

I stifle a laugh at the little act she is putting on. It looks like I'm watching a slo-mo scene in a music video. One of the guy's mouths hangs open, and he's too busy paying attention to her. He doesn't see the trashcan before him and crashes right into it. All his friends laugh as the guy quickly recovers, embarrassed, getting back onto his bike.

Laynie grins, "Eyes on the road, boys," she says as she rolls her fingertips in a flirty wave.

"You're such a tease!" I throw my sponge at her, chuckling. She gasps when it hits her in the back of the head.

"You're gonna pay for that bitch," she smiles, throwing my sponge back to me, and we resume wiping down her car.

'Car Wash by Rose Royce' plays, and we both stop our movements looking at each other. A slow smile forms on both of our faces.

"Ooo, yeah!"

"This song couldn't be any more perfect right now." She says.

"I know!" I agree, swaying my hips side to side, cleaning the driver's side window.

We both continue wiping every inch of the car, giggling and dancing around each other. This is exactly what I needed, some fun in the sun with my bestie. I extend my arm, pointing it at Laynie, and she grabs my wrist, singing into the sponge as if it's a microphone. She holds out hers, and I do the same. We bump our hips, and I turn around to the soap-filled bucket.

"Hey, Rayne. Remember when I said..." she pauses.

"Said what?" I turn to face her and get drenched with water as she sprays me with the hose, laughter spilling from her lips.

"You're going to pay for throwing a sponge at me!" she shouts in between laughs.

Turning around, I reach for the bucket before pouring all the water on her. She shrieks, and I bust out laughing, and with my luck, right on cue, my sandal slides perfectly over the soapy water, causing my feet to fly out from under me, landing me on my ass. Laynie's eyes widen as she runs to help me, and she slips too. Now her ass is on the ground next to me. We both stare at each other wide-eyed in shock before bursting into tears of laughter.

It feels good to laugh. I've been doing so much crying these last twenty-four hours I almost forgot what it felt like. Our laughter gets swallowed by the rumbling of an engine, both of us turning our heads to look. My smile fades when my eyes connect with Christian's white Mustang stopping in front of Laynie's house. He hops out of the car, not bothering to turn it off as he walks urgently toward me.

"Raynie," he says in a panic, trying to get to me.

I jump to my feet, backing away from him, "What are you doing here?" he pauses, looking at Laynie, and she turns to me, face traced with guilt.

"You knew?" she shifts her gaze to her feet, giving me my answer. "Unbelievable," I take another step back.

"Rayne, I've been trying to call and text you. Can we please talk?" I try not to acknowledge his disheveled hair, the light stubble growing on his chin, or the prominent bags under his eyes.

Chapter thirty-eight

"Usually, when someone doesn't respond to text or calls, it's because they don't want to talk." I take another step back.

"Please?" he pleads with the saddest eyes I have ever seen, and all I want to do is go to him.

Where the hell was he for me when I needed him?

Looking at his insistent eyes, I tell him, "No." then turn around and walk into Laynie's house before I change my mind and go to him.

Shutting the door behind me, I lean against it, clutching my chest, fighting for air. Being in his presence gave me oxygen to breathe but walking away from him nearly suffocated me. I rush into Laynie's bathroom to splash water on my face. When I realize I'm already soaked thanks to her, I look at my reflection in the mirror and start laughing before my laughs quickly turn to sobs. Damn it! I feel like a crazy person laughing one minute and sobbing the next.

The sound of light tapping on the other side of the door fills the room, and I wipe my eyes, pulling myself together.

"It's me," Laynie says, "If you don't open the door, I'm going to break it down." Rolling my eyes at her dramatics, I open the door, knowing damn well she would bust through the door if I didn't. "I'm so sorry!" she rushes out, wrapping her arms around me. "I know you don't want to talk to him, but I think you should hear him out."

I pull away from her, feeling defeated. "Why?"

"He called me yesterday before I picked you up at Jamie's." My eyes grow wide, and I try to speak, but she cuts me off, continuing, "Don't be mad. I didn't tell you because you wouldn't have agreed to see him, and you would have wanted to know what he told me."

"You're right, Laynie. I don't want to see him, and I want to know what he told you."

She shakes her head. "Look, I'll tell you if you want me to, but I promise you, I think you should hear it from him, Rayne. He's hurting in all of this, too."

Grabbing a towel, I step around her, walking out of the bathroom. "I can't."

Of course, he's hurting, but not for the same reasons I am. He's hurting because he got caught. He is the one who fucked up, not me, and I can't face him. Not yet. I'm trying to be strong, and being around him does nothing but make me feel weak. Before he betrayed me, being around him made me feel invincible, but now I feel like glass, like one wrong move, and I'll break.

She doesn't argue and turns on the TV sitting next to me on the bed. We usually binge-watch romance movies, but she puts on a comedy instead. Probably scared I wouldn't be able to handle watching anything about love. The sad thing is, she's probably right, and I feel pathetic. We watch the movie, neither of us moving or talking. Laynie laughs at a few scenes, but I can't even muster a smile.

My stomach growls just as the movie credits roll, reminding me I haven't eaten since the small bowl of mac n cheese at Jamie's. Laynie makes us a sandwich, and we take them to the couch to eat. She walks over to the window, looking out front before taking a seat next to me.

"He's still here, you know?" she takes a bite of her sandwich. "He told me he would not leave until you talked to him." I freeze mid-bite.

"You're just now telling me this?"

She shrugs. "Would it have made a difference?"

"Yes!" I say a little louder than I expected. "I would have been out there sooner to tell him he's wasting his time." Setting my sandwich onto my plate, I go to him to tell him exactly that.

He's parked directly across the street, and when I approach, he's reclined back in his seat, his arm resting over his eyes. With delicate fingers, I use my knuckles to tap on his window. He sits up quickly, startled, all his muscles tense, but his body relaxes once he sees me. He gives me my favorite crooked smile, and his golden eyes glisten.

I look away momentarily because looking at him is too difficult. It's hard to see the pain in his eyes and not go to him. It's hard to see his notorious smirk and not want to kiss him, and it's hard to be around him and not want to be in his arms. His car door opens, and I close my eyes, trying not to cry.

"Rayne," he whispers, setting his hand on my shoulder, and tingles rupture down my spine. "Look at me, please."

I'm not sure if it's how his voice cracks when he asks me to look at him or how my body responds when his hands are on me, but I don't fight the force pulling me toward him. Keeping my eyes closed, I slowly turn to face him. His fingertips trail from my forehead and down my cheek, leaving a path of goosebumps in its wake. I gradually open my eyes as a tear escapes, and he instinctively brushes it away with his thumb.

"Please don't cry, baby." He speaks the words so gently that the dam behind my eyes bursts, and he pulls me into him, and I let him.

My shoulders shake with each sob that rakes through me, and he squeezes me tighter, rubbing my back. His touch immediately comforts me, his arms around me a safety blanket. I cry, letting out all the pain, sadness, and betrayal I feel until I'm left with nothing but anger.

"How could you?" I choke, pushing away from him, and I already crave his warmth.

"I know I'm sorry." His voice shakes.

His sorry only makes me angrier.

"Sorry fixes nothing! You hurt me." I poke him in the chest.

"I know," he says, barely audible.

"You betrayed me! You embarrassed me!" my voice rises with each word, and a tear glides down his cheek.

"I know."

I push him, "Don't you cry! You did this." I shove him again, but he doesn't budge.

"Let it out, Raynie, go ahead." So, I do. I push him again and again until he's pressed against his car.

"How could you do this to me? How could you do this to us?" I slam the sides of my fist against his solid chest, and he takes it. "Come on, say something!" I yell, repeating my action, "I begged you to say something that night, and you just laid there shirtless with h... her on top of you," my voice cracks, and I hate how it makes me sound weak.

I go to slam my fists against him again, but he grabs my wrists, his nostrils flaring. "Listen to me," he pins me with a soft yet stern expression, "I love you, and I know that's hard to believe right now. You can hate me all you want but hear me out first. Listen to what I have to say, and if you still hate me by the end, then I promise I'll leave you alone." He struggles to say the last part like he doesn't believe his own words.

Christian let's go of my wrists, and I wrap my arms around myself. "I'm listening."

He shakes his head, frowning, "Not here. Let me take you somewhere with a little more privacy, and I'll explain everything."

I look down at my feet, trying to think clearly. Should I go? A part of me wants to, but the other doesn't want to be around him right now. What's there to talk about? I saw everything I needed to see, but then I remembered what Laynie told me in her room, and I can't help but feel like there was more to what happened at that party than what I saw. She wouldn't insist I hear him out if she didn't believe or agree with whatever he told her. I'm terrified for two reasons: I'm hopeful. I'm hopeful that whatever he has to say can fix this, and two, I'm scared whatever he has to say *won't* fix this, and we will be done for good.

Now that I have calmed down a little, I can think more rationally, and I know we need to have this talk regardless of what he tells me can fix or tear us apart. So, I walk to the passenger side without a word and get in.

The hour-long car ride feels like torture mixed with bliss. Being in this car like we've been so many times before is lovely and feels like paradise. I always feel that way when I'm with him—on the other hand, being in the small confines of his car, leaning against the door to put as much distance between us as possible, is my own personal hell. We are maybe four feet apart, but it feels like we're galaxies away from each other.

I have been counting my breaths, too busy noticing every movement Christian makes without even looking at him. I didn't realize where he was taking me until he exited the highway and turned down a dirt road. Nestled in Nature campground. The place we spent our first night alone together and the first place we made love. *Why did he bring me here?* Tears brim my eyes and I blink, wiping them away. I'm so tired of crying. When is it going to stop?

He pulls to a stop at the same spot we parked the last time we were here. *Things between us were so different then.* It's tough being here, being reminded of everything we've shared. Even with the way I feel right now, I don't regret what happened that night between the sheets in our tent. It was by far the best night of my life. It was special and perfect. I sneak a glance at Christian, and he is staring out at the campground we shared. Is he thinking of the last time we were here?

"What are we doing here?" his eyes move to mine.

"Talking."

"But why here?" he looks down, frowning before lifting his gaze back to me.

"Because the last time we were here, we were happy, and I think we can both use a little happiness right now." I look away because looking at him is too damn hard.

"What do you have to tell me, Christian?" I sigh. "I saw everything I needed to see."

"It wasn't what it looked like." My head whips in his direction as anger flares inside me.

"So let me get this straight. You weren't shirtless with your pants unbuttoned and halfway down your legs, and Lexie wasn't on top of you in nothing but a bra and a fucking mini skirt?" he flinches at my words.

"I didn't know what was happening. You know I would never hurt you."

"Are you really using alcohol as an excuse for you cheating on me?"

"I didn't cheat on you," clenching his jaw, he runs his fingers through his hair, "This is what happened…"

Chapter 39

Christian

48 hours ago...

I groan, rolling over in my bed. My body feels weighted down. My limbs are hard to move. Blinking my eyes, I slowly open them, moaning in pain when the beaming sun hits me. Fuck! My head is killing me. My head throbs; it feels like my brain has a pulse vibrating inside my skull, mimicking my heartbeat. When did we get home? I don't remember ever leaving Josh's yard. It feels like I was on a binger, but I know I only had a beer and a few swigs of whiskey. Everything is fuzzy, and I can hardly think straight.

Dragging my body up the headboard, I attempt to open my eyes again. It takes a minute for my eyes to adjust, but I'm more confused than ever when they do. Drifting my eyes over the pale-yellow sheets, I realize this isn't my room. Did Rayne and I spend the night here? My shirt is off, and my belt is unbuckled, but I'm still wearing my shoes. How the fuck did I get so wasted I fell asleep with my shoes on?

I grab my phone off the bedside table, smiling at my screen saver. It's a picture of Rayne and me on Devil's night.

It was right after I tilted her backward and kissed her. Laynie had made a joke about us loving each other, and even though neither of us had said it yet, I knew I loved her already. Rayne has the biggest smile on her face, and I'm smirking, looking down at her. Fuck, she is beautiful.

Swiping my notifications list down, I scrunch my eyebrows.

(3:00am) **Mom**: 10 missed calls.

(3:40am) **Mav**: 3 missed calls.

My heart races, my dry throat scratchy as I try to swallow. I need to find Rayne and get home. Adrenaline kicks in, and I drag my heavy body, which feels like dead weight, off the bed. Buckling my belt, I see my shirt crumpled on the floor. I pull it over my head and walk toward the kitchen to find Rayne. Music resonates throughout the entire house. I bring my hands up, rubbing my temples, the music reverberating inside my head, knocking brutally against my skull.

A few people are passed out on the couch, a couple on the floor. Red solo cups are littered throughout the house. It looks like complete shit, but honestly, it isn't the worst outcome I've seen from these parties. Ricky is sipping a corona while casually flipping his omelet when I step into the kitchen.

"Fuck," I grumble, staggering into a chair at the table.

"Rough night?" Ricky smirks over his shoulder just as Lance and Josh enter, joining me at the table.

"My skull feels fucking broken. I don't remember drinking that much last night." I scrunch my eyebrows, still confused about why I feel so shitty. "Where is Rayne?"

Josh snaps his head to Ricky, and Lance briefly closes his eyes, keeping his head down.

Ricky chuckles, "Man, after last night, Dollface is probably long gone by now."

Dollface? "What the fuck are you talking about?" he turns off the burner, taking another swig of his beer.

"You really can't remember?"

"No shit."

Giving me a knowing smile, he brings his fingers up, tapping the side of his neck, which only pisses me off more. Everything is a fucking game for him. Why can't he just tell me what the fuck happened last night? I bring my fingertips to my neck and hiss at the slight sting. I rush to the bathroom, his laughter following me. Leaning over the sink, I tilt my chin to better view my neck. There is a purple bruise-like mark right at my pulse. It's not a bruise; it's a hickey. What. The. Actual. Fuck?

Did Rayne give me a hickey last night? Why can't I remember anything? Closing my eyes, I try to replay the events of last night. Rayne and I arrived at the party. We met up with Josh, and he took us to the backyard. We ended up playing some stupid ass game, and Lance gave me a beer, and Rayne took one too. Lexie was being a bitch, saying shit that she had no business saying. Anything to piss off Rayne. Rayne came back heavily, upsetting Lexie so much that she stormed off angry as fuck. Lance brought out the hard liquor, and they all had vodka, and I took a big shot of whiskey. A little while later, I remember feeling buzzed, and everything was fuzzy. Ricky's words echo in my head "After last night, Dollface is probably long gone by now."

Storming back into the kitchen, I slap Ricky's plate off the table, and it shatters into pieces.

"What the fuck did you do?" he shoots up from his seat, his chair screeching against the tiled floor.

"What you should be asking yourself is what the fuck did you do?" he shouts. "You had some alcohol and started acting like an asshole to Rayne. She wanted to go home, but you insisted on staying. You were such a dick and didn't give a fuck if you made her cry or not. You left her while you stumbled your way into the house like a drunk mess."

No, no, no. I pace back and forth, gripping my hair. What did I do?

"After you left, Rayne went looking for you," he continues. "The next thing I know, she's running into me, bawling her eyes out before running off. I tried to get her to come back, but she wouldn't listen."

I feel sick. Why was she so upset? Why did she run, and what was she running from? The better question is, who was she running from? Me? She was running from me!

"I went to the room she came running out of, and that's when I saw you lying on the bed shirtless with your pants halfway down your legs. Lexie was hunched over in nothing but a bra and skirt, holding her face," he chuckles like all of this is funny, "Dollface has one hell of a swing because she slapped the fuck out of Lexie, leaving the imprint of her hand on her cheek."

Rayne slapped Lexie? This is so fucking bad. Why was I in the same room as Lexie? Why was she only wearing a goddamn bra? Rayne hit her, which means she saw us together. Fuck! My mind is reeling a hundred miles a second, and I can't wrap my head around anything. Nothing makes sense. I would never hurt Rayne like that.

"I would never do that to Rayne! And I would never get into the same bed with that bitch."

Josh and Ricky laugh, "Well, dude, you did." Ricky counters. "Why do you seem so surprised? You would do shit like this all the time to girls. Make them believe you gave a fuck about them, then set them up to find you in bed with someone else."

Feeling sick, I swallow down the vomit, trying to escape my mouth. He's right. That is something I would do, but that was the old me. He's wrong about me now. He doesn't know who I really am, and he never did. None of them knew me. Only Rayne sees the real me. I would never betray her like that, and I sure is fuck wouldn't get into bed with another girl.

"Something isn't adding up." I shake my head, gripping at my hair again, resuming my pacing.

I know how to handle my liquor. This isn't my first time drinking. I used to drink every weekend, sometimes even during the week. There is no way one beer and a few swigs of whiskey will make me forget everything. Stopping dead in my tracks, I look at all of them. Ricky and Josh glance at each other as Lance keeps his focus on his feet. They all had vodka. I was the only one who drank whiskey, and I'm the only one who can't remember shit.

I'm the only one who had whiskey...

At that moment, I had an epiphany: the fucking whiskey! Molten anger rolls through me, my hands reacting before my brain can process it. I curl my right hand into a fist, aiming straight for his nose. I swing with all my might, connecting perfectly. The bridge of his nose crunches underneath my knuckles, and he wails out in pain, his blood splattering all over the tile.

"You set me up!" I attempt another swing, but he ducks, dodging my fist and landing a punch to my lip.

I recoil in pain, the taste of blood coating my tongue, but I quickly get over it, welcoming the sting and bite of my blood.

"You set me up," I repeat in a chilling tone. "You guys all set me up." My cold gaze sweeps to Josh and Lance before fleeting back to Ricky.

"You had it coming!" Ricky booms, "Do you honestly think you can act all big and bad, and I would not retaliate? This is my house and my fucking town! You came here acting like the broody fucker you are and made a fool of yourself to your precious Rayne." he rolls his eyes, curling his lip in disgust. "All we did was supply you the alcohol. You took it upon yourself to get shitfaced and show who you are... who you've always been!"

Letting out a growl, I lunge at him, wrapping my arms around his waist and taking him to the ground. He grunts from the impact. Using my body weight to keep him pinned down, I fist the collar of his shirt with one hand, drawing my other arm as far back as I can before I let loose, bashing his face over and over, enraged.

"You're going to kill him, man!" Lance shouts, pulling me back.

Turning my head to Josh, his eyes are wide in shock as he inspects Ricky's bloody face lying on the floor, moaning in agony. His face is pale, drained of color like he might be sick.

"I know you were behind this shit too! What the fuck did you do? Own up to what you've done!" panicked eyes dart to mine. "You would've been next!" I try to break out of Lance's hold. "Come at me! Come on, you bitch!" he doesn't move; he doesn't blink; he just stares, watching Lance pull me further away.

Lance drags me out of the house and I break free from his hold. I throw him a hard look, burning with outrage, my body a violent red hot solar flare of rage.

I see a glint of disappointment in his eye that I can't decipher. Is he disappointed in how I reacted or in himself for having a part in all of this? None of them need to admit anything when I already know the truth. I take a predatory step forward.

Lance holds out his hands in front of him, "Wait..." Ignoring him, I continue to invade his space, "Wait!" he panics, "I'll tell you everything." I stop, then pace, unable to stand still as my blood boils. "You're right; we set you up." My jaw clenches, "Josh told us he saw you at the grocery store, then he told us about Rayne," My nostrils flare hearing her name come out of his mouth, "he told us he could tell she meant something to you even though you tried your hardest to act like she didn't. I'm glad you found someone, man."

"I don't give a fuck!"

"Okay, Okay," he says, "It was Ricky's idea to drug you if you came to the party. We honestly didn't think you'd show. At least I didn't, because I knew how much you despised being here and how much you despised us. You were a ticking time bomb every second of every day." He takes a small step away from me. "Ricky didn't like the idea that you moved on with your life, and he didn't believe you really cared for this girl. He purposely played the game so that we can all say shit we knew would piss you off and hopefully make Rayne question you." He looks at me full of guilt. I don't give a shit about his guilt! "It didn't make Rayne falter, which surprised me. That's when I knew she was different and wasn't some game. You must have opened up to her about your past because she didn't act surprised. She stood by you. Ricky and Josh told Lexie to push Rayne and make her uncomfortable. When Rayne snapped back, it surprised us all, even Lexie, which is why she stormed off all pissed. Ricky or Josh must've texted her once you went inside to use the restroom. You were hammered, dude, and I didn't know the drugs would affect you the way they did."

I figured I was drugged, but I'm concerned about what the hell happened to Rayne. I'm trying to avoid ending Lance right here, but I need to know, so I stand deathly still, not making a sound.

"Josh texted Lexie, letting her know to find you. She did, and she brought you to the room, took off your shirt, unbuckled your pants, and started stripping. We hoped Rayne would go looking for you and find you guys, so it looks like you were cheating on her. At this point, I regretted ever going through with the plan, but it was too late. Rayne went looking for you, and she found Lexie straddling your waist and kissing you."

I feel fucking sick. No longer able to hold anything in, I hurl over and throw up. Rayne thinks I cheated on her with Lexie. Fuck! I hate all of them. I want to go back inside and have another round with Ricky and Josh, too, but I need to find Rayne.

"Look, man, if you want to punch me, I understand. If it means anything, I'm sorry." I punch him straight in the jaw, dropping him to the floor.

"I was going to punch you regardless, thanks for the understanding," I peer over him, ringing out my hand, "and you're sorry doesn't mean shit. Have a miserable fucking life, Lance. Pass the message on to the two bitches inside."

The Road To Oblivion

Chapter 40

Christian

"It was a setup. Everything was planned before we even got there."

"H... How could they do something so awful?" her voice quivers as tears stream down her beautiful face. "You told me they weren't good people, but Christian, this is something else entirely. We need to do something. They can't get away with this."

I hesitantly reach for her hand, and she lets me, "I already handled it."

She gives me a tired laugh. "I'm not talking about beating them up. What about the police? You were drugged and not to mention taken advantage of."

My body still feels sluggish and not completely normal. I could have gone to the police and probably should have, but Ricky got what he deserved and Lance, too. Hell, Lexie even got a nice bitch slap from Rayne. If anything, Josh was the only one who got off the hook. I believe in karma, and he will get his one day. It's not fair what happened to Rayne or me, but it's done.

I rub my thumb over hers. "All of this is fucked up. I'm exhausted from my past having a hold on me. I want to let it go and move forward." She brings her hands to her face and cries.

"Hey, don't cry, baby. What's going on in that pretty little head of yours?" I gently pull her hands away from her face.

"This is all my fault," she chokes. "None of this would have happened if I didn't agree to go to that stupid party, and you would have never been drugged."

It breaks my heart that she is blaming herself for what had happened. I knew they were scum, but even I never expected them to drug me. None of this is her fault.

"Look at me," I say softly, and her eyes find mine. "You didn't force me to that party, and you didn't force them to drug me. No one is to blame here besides them."

She nods her head, sniffling, "Tell me a secret."

"I was scared I was going to lose you."

"Me too."

A smile immediately forms on my face, causing one to creep on hers. I've missed seeing that smile so much; I've missed everything about her. The past forty-eight hours have been hell, but as I said before, I'd walk through the gates of hell for her.

I brush her hair behind her ear, and she draws in a sharp breath from my touch. Her eyes fall to my mouth, and the corner of my lips lifts at her reaction to me. I was so terrified of losing her and needing to explain the truth about everything, I didn't realize she was only wearing an oversized graphic tee. My eyes leisurely sweep to the soft skin on her perfect thighs, my fingers itching to touch her.

With her index finger, she nudges my chin up. Wetting her lips, she leans in, pressing a soft kiss to the corner of my mouth before moving to my lips. My dick stirs awake, pressing uncomfortably against my jeans. She moans into my mouth, and my lips part, letting her in. Her tongue glides against mine, and I lightly suck it into my mouth.

We kiss slowly, taking our time and exploring each other's mouths like we've done so many times. Rayne stops kissing me, leaning her forehead against mine. Her warm breath fans against my lips as we both pant heavily, trying to come down from our euphoric state. After a moment, she leans back into her seat, fidgeting with her fingernails.

"What's wrong?"

"N... Nothing." A blush creeps into her cheeks. "It's embarrassing."

"Tell me anyway."

"I can't stop thinking about the last time we were here..." her blush deepens.

"Is that so?" I smirk, tucking a strand of hair behind her ear. "What about that night are you thinking about?"

"The way you touched me."

"Like this?" my fingertips skirt up her thighs teasingly.

Drawing in a sharp breath, with wide eyes, she hums, "Mhm."

"What else?"

"How you made me," she pauses nervously, unable to look me in the eye, her cheeks burning with heat.

"Made you what?"

"Made me wet," she swallows.

Fuck! "If I stick my fingers inside your pussy right now, will you be soaked?"

I already know the answer. I can tell by her shallow breaths, how she clenches her fists in an attempt not to move, and how she occasionally squeezes her thighs together. She is turned on, craving my touch the same way I'm craving hers. It's an indescribable feeling of wanting someone and having them want you back.

"Yes," she rasps.

My dick jumps at the need I hear in her voice. I move her bikini bottoms to the side and slide two fingers down her slit. Her pussy is dripping wet, giving my fingers the perfect lubrication to glide into her. Rayne throws her head back, breathing heavily.

"Does that feel good, baby?" I continue rubbing my fingers up and down her crease, teasing her. She moans in response as her hips slightly buck forward, needing more. "Tell me what you want." My thumb circling her swollen clit.

"You. I need you."

"Do you want my fingers inside your pretty pussy?"

"Yes."

Giving her what she needs, I glide my fingers inside her, feeling her walls tighten around them. Her hand flies to my arm, and she moans, rocking her hips, and I smirk—*my eager girl*. I push my fingers further into her before sliding them back out and entering her again. Rayne thrust against them, matching my movements. With each thrust, her pussy responds to me, getting wetter.

I still can't believe no one has ever touched her like this before. It makes me feel more territorial about her, knowing I'm the only one who has ever made her feel this way. Her pussy is drenched because of me. She is so responsive to my touch, and it's fucking hot. *Mine.*

"You're so fucking wet, baby."

She moans, sending shock waves to my dick. Pushing deeper, I curl my fingers like I'm trying to pull her to me. Her breathing gets faster, her legs stiffen, and I know she is close. Watching her come undone, shaking beneath me, is my favorite fucking thing. I flick my fingers while rubbing her sensitive bud in small circles with my thumb.

"Oh my God!" she groans in ecstasy.

"That's it, baby, let go." I quicken my speed, applying more pressure to her clit, sending her over the edge. Rayne arches her back, lifting her ass off the seat, calling out my name repeatedly as her entire body trembles.

A whimper falls from her lips as I drag my fingers out of her. I lean my forehead against hers, inhaling her scent that I was afraid I'd never get to smell again.

"I love you," I whisper against her lips.

"I love you." she runs her hands through my hair, lightly gripping the ends.

Fuck. I can't describe the feeling hearing those three words brings me. It's frightening when you're so close to losing someone who means everything to you. When I thought I had lost Rayne, it felt like my world was ripped out from underneath my feet, and I wasn't sure where I would land. I always knew she was important to me, but I don't think anyone realizes just how important someone is until they lose them.

Rayne kisses my forehead, places her hands on my chest, and gently pushes me back against my seat. Before processing what she is doing, she straddles my waist. I bury my face in her neck, my lips finding the spot below her ear.

"My golden boy," she whispers, "I thought I was going to lose you for good. What was I going to do without my summer?" she rubs her thumb along my jaw.

"Good thing you never have to worry about that. I will always be here."

I mean it. I'll fight for her, and I will fight for us, always. Rayne was worth it. I will do whatever it takes to prove myself worthy of her. That's the thing about Rayne. No matter how undeserving I feel of her, she makes me believe I am. I'm not an easy person to love. Maybe that's why a part of me always felt unlovable. Rayne didn't judge or try to pick me apart. She tries to understand and see the good in me the same way she sees the good in everything around her.

She loves me with so much passion and intensity I forget what my life was like before she came along. Rayne is a lot of things—honest, compassionate, kind; she is light, she is love. She deserves everything. I may not be the easiest to love, but I will work my ass off loving her.

"Promise me I will always have you," she says.

"I promise you will always have me."

As the last word leaves my lips, she crashes hers against mine. With her kiss, she tells me so many things. *I'm sorry about everything. I love you, I believe you, I want you.* She resumes burying her fingers into my thick, messy hair, and I recline my seat back a tad to give us more room. My car may be badass, but there isn't a lot of space.

<u>"I Ain't Ever Loved No One by Donovan Woods, Tenille Townes,"</u>
"I guess before I met you, I didn't know better, but you swept in out of nowhere, and I thought I'd never go there, and you set the bar for this stubborn heart."

Her shirt is bunched around her waist, exposing her smooth thighs. I trail my palms up her thighs, not able to avoid the temptation. Grabbing the hem of her tee, I pull her shirt over her head, tossing it somewhere in the back seat. Her white bikini top against her olive skin makes her look like a glowing goddess. I hold the side of her face with one hand, and with the other, I pull the string of her top undone. Her perfect tits bounce freely, begging to be touched.

I caress her breasts, and she whimpers in pleasure, arching her back. I smile, knowing what she needs. Taking one breast into my mouth, I knead the other, giving it the same attention. She moans my name in approval, taking her lip between her teeth. My cock is so hard it hurts. Rayne swivels her hips, and I hiss in half agony from how hard I am and half pleasure from how good she feels rubbing against me.

"Can I touch you?" she asks shyly.

"I told you before. You don't even have to ask."

A modest smile teases her lips as her hand moves, gripping me through my jeans. I moan at the contact, and Rayne smiles at my reaction to her touch. She knows what she does to me. I glide my tongue over her breasts, and her eyes roll to the back of her head.

"I want you," I rasp.

She eagerly nods, fumbling with my button, desperate to set me free. I lift my hips as she pulls my jeans and briefs down my thighs. My cock springs free, standing at its full height. Her eyes widen as she wets her bottom lip, and I fist myself. Giving my hard length a slow stroke, Rayne's eyes stay captivated by my movement. Grabbing her hip, I lift her and rub my protruding tip along the slit of her wet pussy.

"C... Condom," she groans.

Shit! I'm so engrossed in her that I almost forgot. Popping my glove box open, I reach for a condom. She arches her eyebrow at me, and I chuckle.

"I bought them shortly after we made it official," her cheeks flush, "Just in case..."

"Can I put it on you?" I nod, kissing her forehead. Tearing the wrapper with my teeth, I pull the slick latex out and hand it to her. She brings it to my tip with shaky hands and pauses, uncertainty clear on her face. She is so confident and sexy without trying that I forget how new all of this is to her. I place my hand over hers, lowering the condom to the head of my cock.

"Like this." I glide her hands down my hardness.

Biting my lower lip, I draw in a harsh breath. Watching her hands slide down my hard skin turns me on more. Something about helping her put on a condom is intimate, almost as personal as making love to her.

She smiles proudly, and I can't help but do the same. *So damn cute.* My hands move to the curve of her waist, and I lift her above me. Her hands tighten on my shoulders as I lower her onto me, and we both share a pleasurable moan.

"Fuck baby. You feel good." She swivels her hips in response, and my cock jerks inside her. Fuck!

Rayne lifts herself slowly before easing herself back down onto me. I love watching her take control. Sliding my hand through her thick hair, I gently grip it and kiss her. I lap my tongue around hers, enjoying the feeling of her pussy gripping my length and the control she has over me.

"Never leave me again," I breathe against the crook of her neck before gently sucking.

"I won't leave you," she groans, her hips quickening their movements.

A gruff sound rips through me. Holy fuck, I'm already going to come. Reaching down to where our bodies are joined, I bring her swollen clit between my fingers, lightly pinching it.

"Christian," she pants, tightening her grip on my shoulders.

"I love hearing my name fall from those pouty fucking lips." Her nails dig into my shoulders as she slides up and down my cock.

I rub her sensitive bud steadily, both of our breathing erratic. I lick her bottom lip before pulling it between my teeth. Rayne moans, her pussy gripping me tighter, and I almost come on the spot. Not breaking our kiss, I grabbed both of her hips, guiding her up and down. As the pressure builds deep inside me, my cock is getting harder by the second.

Rayne pants my name, her legs growing stiff. I grip her waist, giving her one hard thrust, and our names fall from each other's lips. Her pussy squeezes all around me, my balls tighten, and I burst. Her head falls to my shoulder, and we fall apart together.

I wrap my arms around Rayne, stroking her back, not wanting to leave this moment. She leans back, her eyes slowly lifting to mine. She flushes, and I give her a crooked smile. After what we shared, it amazes me; that she still manages to get shy around me, I delicately grab her chin, bringing her swollen lips to mine, and kiss her softly.

Rayne smiles into the kiss before inching her way off me, and I already miss the feel of her. Leaning over into the back seat, she reaches for her shirt, and her perfect round ass is in my face. I smirk, unable to resist, giving it a playful slap. She yelps in surprise, falling back into her seat. Rayne gives a playful scowl because we both know she liked it.

As she puts on her shirt, her phone vibrates against the dashboard. She tells me it's Laynie before taking the call. While she is on the phone, I give her some privacy to talk and tuck myself back in, discarding the condom in a nearby trashcan.

When I get back into the car, Rayne says, "She was just making sure you were alive."

"Me?"

"I was really mad at you." She shrugs, and I shake my head, chuckling.

"That's a fair point. I should probably thank her for letting me come over and see you."

"How did you get a hold of Laynie, anyway?"

"I texted Ryker, saying I needed her number because I wanted to surprise you with something." She arches a brow at me.

"What?" I shrug. "I was desperate."

Rayne giggles, leaning over the console to kiss me. "I should probably get back."

I frown, I just got her back, and I'm not ready to leave her yet. Who am I kidding? I'm never ready.

"Did you maybe want to hang out with us?" she fidgets with her fingers. "I know it's just us girls and might bore without Ryk—"

"I want to be wherever you are."

She pulls her bottom lip between her teeth. "Good. Me too."

Rayne

When we arrive, Laynie is already waiting outside for us with crossed arms and a mischievous look.

"You're welcome," she says to Christian. He scrunches his eyebrows in confusion. "For telling you where Rayne is."

"Right," he laughs, "Thank you."

"Mhm, I'm just glad to see Rayne have a smile back on her face," Christian frowns. "If I didn't believe what you said,

I would have never been okay with you seeing her. I believe you, though, and I'm sorry you had to go through that." She bumps her shoulder with his.

"Thank you. I'm happy we worked everything out."

"Me too. Rayne is insufferable when she's depressed."

"Laynie!" I push her lightly, and she laughs.

"You two bumped uglies, didn't you?" she whispers. "You're glowing." My cheeks instantly turn pink.

"Laynie!" I hiss, turning to make sure Christian didn't hear. His eyes are already on me, wearing his signature panty dropper smirk. *Kill me now.*

"It's normal, Rayne. I'm glad one of us is getting laid because I'm dryer than the Sahara Desert." I give her a full belly laugh and hear Christian chuckle behind us.

Chapter 41

Rayne

"Do you think he will like his gift?" I ask Laynie, rubbing my fingertips over the flexible leather.

"Rayne, that boy will love anything you give him," she walks over, sitting next to me on the bed, "You can give him a sack of potatoes, and he would still look at you as if you were holding the sun."

"A sack of potatoes?" I giggle.

"A turtleneck. Shit, even a kilt."

Now I laugh, "You're crazy!"

"Oh please, you're the same way. He could gift you a card with a drawn stick figure, and you'd still look at him, ready to jump his damn bones."

"Laynie!" I squeal, a blush creeping onto my cheeks.

"What?" she shrugs. "You guys are so in love it's sickening."

"We're not that bad…" She tilts her head to the side with an *are you serious right now* expression. "Okay, maybe a little. I can't wait for you to find your person." I lightly bump my shoulder with hers. Her smile fades, replaced with a sullen look.

"Yeah… me too."

My bestie is a total catch. I know her person is out there waiting for her. She has guys lined up for her but doesn't give most of them the time of day. The ones she does are never anything serious. Laynie is a hopeless romantic like me, but she has never gotten into a relationship with a guy for whatever reason. When I ask her why, she says she isn't looking for anything serious, or they don't do it for her.

I can understand that because a few guys caught my attention, but none of them ever did anything for me either. I've never had a connection like the one I have with Christian. With him, it was immediate from the moment we met when we were just two strangers inside a coffee shop. Our connection is strong, and I am drawn to him in every way. I've always been someone who loved the idea of love and believed that movie types of love existed. However, I never knew it was possible to find it, but now that I have, I can't ever picture not being loved this way.

"Do you think it's always going to feel this way?"

"What do you mean?" Laynie rests her head on my shoulder.

"I don't know… from the inside looking out; it's hard to explain. Do you think I'll always feel this rush with Christian? It's like whenever he is near, my heart accelerates, and I get anxious but not in a nervous kind of way, but I can't wait to talk to you or touch you way."

She is silent for a moment, processing my words. "I'm not sure, babe. Remember when we used to go to the state fair every year, and we would stand in line waiting for the biggest ride there?"

"Yes!" I smile at the memory.

We would wear shoes with a thicker platform to help make us tall enough to ride. It was so much fun. At the time, it was the only place our parents felt comfortable enough to let us go alone. It was the only place Ryker wouldn't follow us, and I think it's because he was a chickenshit and was scared to ride the rollercoasters. He will never admit it, but he didn't have to. Laynie and I both knew.

"We would stand in line, bouncing on our feet in excitement and full of nerves. Other rides weren't as exciting and didn't give us that rush, but every year we would go back and ride that one big ride that did because we remembered the feeling."

"I'm confused."

"What I'm trying to say is there are so many people out in this world, and not all of them will make you feel that rush; however, Christian does. So, to answer your question, I think Christian is one big ride for you. No matter how many others you may have encountered, none of them compared to him, and as long as you have him, the rush will never go away."

"So, are you saying that it isn't so much about the rush itself, but the person and Christian is that person for me?" she looks at me, smiling.

"That's *exactly* what I'm saying."

"Wow, that was beautiful, Laynie Mae. When did you become so wise?" I tease, wiping under my eyes.

"Boobs aren't the only big thing I have." I arch my eyebrow. "I have a big brain, too."

We both bust out in laughter. *God, I love her.*

We finish wrapping our Christmas gifts and head downstairs to meet the rest of our family. After turning ten, we no longer celebrated Christmas in Big Bear and instead started celebrating it here. It was easier for Laynie and her parents to join, since we only lived up the street. Celebrating holidays without them feels like a part of our family is missing. Now, on Christmas Eve, Laynie and her parents come to our house every year. We spend the whole day together watching movies, playing games, having dinner, and giving presents at the end. Christian and his mom will be here this year, and I can't wait.

After explaining everything that happened when we visited his uncle during thanksgiving break, we made up and returned to normal. We see each other almost every day. Even Sawyer comes over often to spend time with my mom. I go over to his house for dinner a couple of times out of the week, and he does the same. They even join us for our Sunday breakfast, and I love it.

I never felt like anything was missing, but I guess that saying, "You never miss what you've never had rings true." It's always been Ryker, me, and our parents, sometimes Laynie, but now that I have Sawyer and Christian, I can't picture having our Sunday breakfast without them. Everything feels right, like it was always supposed to be this way.

As we descend the stairs, there is a knock at the door. "I'll get it!" I shout to no one opening the door.

Sawyer stands with a casserole dish in her hand, with Christian beside her holding an arm full of gifts.

"I come bearing gifts," He smiles down at me. I giggle, taking him in. He is wearing a dark gray sweater with black jeans, his hair put in place but still has that natural messy look like he ran his fingers through it.

"Come in," I give them a welcoming smile, taking the dish from Sawyer. "Mm, it smells delicious."

"It's a secret recipe of mine. I'll have to show you sometime," she winks.

"I'd like that."

Christian gives me a tender kiss. "Merry Christmas Eve, Raynie."

"Merry Christmas Eve." I blush, slightly embarrassed, kissing him in front of his mom. "You can set the presents under the tree. I'm going to set this at the table." Sawyer follows me into the kitchen, and my mother's face lights up when she sees her.

"Hey girl!" she says like a teenager, making me smile.

"Would you like a glass of wine?" she asks, holding up a bottle of Chardonnay.

"I'd love a glass, thank you."

"I know it's still kind of early, but—"

"I'm not complaining, and I won't tell if you won't," Sawyer cuts in, making my mom laugh.

"My kind of woman," Laynie's mom says, stepping into the kitchen.

On that note, I set the casserole dish down, leaving them laughing behind me. See what I mean? Everything feels right, like it was always supposed to be this way. It makes me happy to see how much my mother likes Christian's mom; I know Stacey will, too.

Walking into the living room, I pause, leaning against the wall. A piney aroma radiates off our large, illuminated tree resting in the corner of the living room, and there isn't a blank space underneath. The area is full, surrounded by presents. The smell of cooking turkey and freshly baked pie seeps from the kitchen, making my stomach growl.

Christian sits on the couch with Ry and my dad talking about something I can't hear from where I stand. Laynie is seated beside them on a love seat, pretending to listen but is engrossed in her phone. Hearty laughter reverberates from the kitchen, our mothers enjoying each other's company. My heart warms from the combination of everything. I have my family here. These are my people, and they are perfect.

This is my favorite time of the year. It's winter break, so there is no school, and I get to be surrounded by the people I love most in the world. My parents and Ryker have time off from work, allowing us to hang out and spend quality time together. I love passing by houses and seeing the decorations and tall trees lit up through neighboring windows.

As a child, I loved all things Christmas and would always be excited to decorate the tree and wrap presents. My parents would do elf on the shelf with Ry and me, and we were very into it. We didn't dare touch the elf for fear he would lose his magic. I think Christmas is my favorite holiday because it's the only time everyone believes in the impossible for a little while.

Christian's eyes find mine, and his smile widens. I flick my index finger in my direction, telling him to come to me. His eyes never leave mine as he approaches.

"Did I mention how beautiful you look?" he twirls a dark strand of my hair around his finger.

"Hmm," I nibble my lip, pretending to think, "I don't think so."

"Well, I was most certainly thinking it."

"Do you want to know what I'm thinking?" my voice pitches in flirtation as I softly dance my fingers up his chest. His eyes follow my trailing fingers before slowly lifting to me.

"What is going on in that pretty little head of yours?" Tucking my hair behind my ear, I smile coyly, looking toward the ceiling. He follows my direction, and his mouth turns up on one side when he sees it—a mistletoe.

"I think you should kiss me, Christian." I wrap my arms around his neck, bringing his attention back to me. He leans in close to my mouth, so close all I had to do was tilt my head, and our lips would touch.

"Hmm, I think you're right." His minty breath teases my lips, making me feel dizzy.

Anticipation floods my senses as I wait for his lips to touch mine. He slowly inches closer, closing the space between us, and presses his soft, plush lips against mine. He pecks my lips with the perfect pressure, opening his mouth just enough for my tongue to enter. Our tongues stroke each other once before he pulls back.

A whine almost escapes my lips at the sudden loss, desperate to feel his lips again. He chuckles at my reaction, kissing the corner of my mouth. His cheeks are flushed, and his golden eyes glow with desire. Christian glances over his shoulder, and I follow. My dad and brother are still immersed in their conversation, and Laynie is typing away on her phone.

My heart warms: he was being respectful. We both get so caught up in each other, utterly void of our surroundings. I wanted more, and so did he, but he pulled away out of respect for family, out of respect for me. It was an innocent kiss, weighted with so much passion it could have anchored me to my knees. Kissing him is like losing the ability to breathe for a brief moment until we open our mouths and all our oxygen is returned—the kind of kiss that can take your breath away but at the same time give you air.

Christian's attention returns to me, and he gives me a look. A look that tells me we will finish this later. Biting my lip, I smile. *Yes, we will.* Taking my hand, he guides me over to the couch, joining the others.

For the next hour, we all played charades in the living room. We aren't keeping score because it isn't about that. We're having fun spending time with each other, laughing, and creating memories. A timer goes off in the kitchen, and we all but cheer because we are starving, dinner smells phenomenal, and we finally get to eat.

We all sit around the dinner table and feast. Laynie's dad, Charlie, joined us and filled us in on how business is booming. Sawyer talks about how she loves the school she now works at, making Christian smile. My mom talks about the publishing house she designs for and our dinner continues just like that.

"I can't believe our kids are growing up," Stacey says.

"I know," my mother's eyes water, "Next year will be Rayne's last year until she is off to New York." Christian stiffens next to me.

A lump forms in my throat, and everyone turns their focus to me. "I don't know for sure just yet. I haven't applied."

"Sis, we all know you're getting in. You've only worked for this your whole life. This is what you want."

A part of me is happy and proud because he is right. I have worked hard and long for this. I can live in New York studying fashion and hopefully interning at a major fashion company. New York was always about stepping out on my own, away from my comfort zone, and doing what I love. Now, when I think of leaving, I don't feel as thrilled knowing who I'll be leaving behind. I'm going to miss them terribly when I go off to college. It's all approaching quick, and I am not ready to say goodbye. I'm starting to wonder if being so far away is really what I want.

Looking over at Christian, he gives me a small smile, squeezing my leg under the table. For the first time, his touch didn't bring me comfort in the way he intended it to. All I feel is dread. I will miss my family so much, but I think I will miss Christian the most. I've gotten used to him being there, making me feel brave and confident, loved and comfortable. He helps put my mind at ease when I'm in my head. We spend so much time together that I can't picture not spending time with him like we do now. I will be in a vast city alone, and I don't know how I feel about that. I thought I had everything figured out, but now I feel more lost than ever.

"We will just have to wait and see," I say, mustering a smile.

After dinner, we gather around the tree and hand out presents. My mom hands us all our gifts, setting them in a pile in front of us. We all start opening them at the same time. I got a friendship bracelet from Laynie, a Barnes and Noble gift card from her parents, and a lavender-scented candle from Sawyer. Saving Christian's gift for last, I open it, and my mouth hangs open. I leap into his arms, telling him thank you over and over.

He chuckles. "I'm glad you like it."

"What is it?" Laynie tries to peek inside the box. Grinning, I hold up a pair of white and black doc martens.

"You lucky bitch."

"Laynie Mae!" Her parents scold.

"Sorry," she winces. "Those are so cute! Thank God we're the same shoe size."

Christian opens my gift, a smile instantly forming on his lips. He holds up a pair of black and white Converse, and everyone smiles at the fact that we both bought our favorite pair of shoes.

He pecks me on the cheek, "Thank you, baby."

"Alright, we have one more gift," my parents announce. I look at them, wondering who missed a gift. My parents walk over to me, handing me a small, squared box. Slowing, lifting the lid, I drop the box, my hands flying to my mouth.

"No way!" I gasp, my eyes filling with tears. "Are you guys joking right now?"

"You're welcome, sis," Ryker smiles, leaning back against the couch.

"Oh hush, all you did was drive the thing over here." My mother says.

"Rayne got a car!" Laynie shrieks, jumping to her feet. "Let's go! What are you waiting for?" she bounces eagerly.

Laughing and just as excited as she is, I grab the keys and run out the front door. Sitting in our driveway is an all-white Kia Optima with black tinted windows. It's beautiful! I unlock the doors using the key fob and hop into the front seat, Laynie joining me on the passenger side.

"You got a car!" she squeals.

"I got a car!" I bounce in my seat, rubbing the leather steering wheel.

It's perfect! I wanted to save and buy my car, but I'm not complaining. It's not super expensive but not cheap either. They couldn't have picked out anything better if they tried. My parents do so much for me, and I would have been grateful for anything. Quickly getting out, I run to them, standing in the driveway.

"Thank you." I wrap my arms around both of them. "You guys didn't have to get me a car!"

"Baby girl, you have worked hard and never ask for anything. You deserve it." My dad squeezes me a little tighter, and tears spring to my eyes.

"Plus, we bought one for Ryker. It's only fair we get you one too," my mom adds. "Your father and I are very proud of you, Rayne. Merry Christmas."

"I love you guys. Merry Christmas!"

"Ready to give us a test drive, sis?" Ryker asks, Christian and Laynie standing next to him, all smiling.

Once we got back from driving around the neighborhood in my new car, Laynie and her parents headed home. Sawyer and my mom were tipsier on wine than when we left, so Sawyer called it a night and went home to sleep, and my mom and dad went up to their room. Ryker, Christian, and I watched *"The Nightmare Before Christmas"*, but Ryker passed out ten minutes into the movie.

"I'm going to head home to grab your other gift," Christian tells me.

"Another gift?" I grin.

"Mhm," he hums, kissing my forehead.

"I have another gift for you, too." He grabs my hand, pulling me to him.

"You do?" he gives me a lopsided grin, his hands drifting to my ass.

"Not that kind of gift," I playfully push him away.

"Meet me on your roof in ten?"

"Okay," I nod, kissing him before running upstairs to grab his present.

This gift was something I wanted to give him in private, and I hope he loves it. Ten minutes later, Christian is climbing up the side of my house with an envelope between his teeth. He hesitates, looking down at the envelope. His thumb brushes over the pale paper before looking at me. His eyes are filled with so much love; I feel it at my core.

"This is for you." he hands it to me and then nervously places his hands into his pockets.

"Thank you."

"You don't even know what it is yet."

"That's true, but I know whatever it is, I'll love it. This is for you." I hand him his gift wrapped in matte black wrapping. "You go first."

I take a small step back, suddenly nervous about what I got him. He wastes no time ripping off the paper, and I hold my breath, praying he doesn't hate it.

"I love it," he rasps, tracing his fingers over the words engraved in the black leather. I wasn't sure what to get him for Christmas. All I knew was I wanted it to mean something. The words engraved on the journal say, *'Tell me a secret.'* It's something we say to each other and thought it was perfect. Ever since he wrote me a poem for my birthday, I have been captive by his words and crave to hear more.

"Your words are always so beautiful. I figured you can write your secrets in there or any thoughts you may have because I want to hear them all." His eyes glisten, and I swear I can see the stars reflecting in his pools of gold.

"This is perfect, and the meaning behind it is perfect," he holds the side of my face. "You are perfect. Thank you." His eyes flutter shut, and he steals my breath with a kiss.

Feeling weak from the kiss, I sit, pulling him down next to me, and I open his gift. There are two plane tickets—one with my name and one with Christian's for a round trip from LAX to New York. I suck in a harsh breath, my mouth gaping open.

"We leave for New York in five days," he says.

I don't move, I can't move. I'm frozen, staring at the plane tickets in my hand.

"We both know you will get into the New York School of Design, baby. I want to take you for your first time, and we can check out your dream college in person." My vision becomes blurry as my eyes well with tears. "Then we can see what the Big Apple is all about and bring in the new year in Times Square."

Tears stream down my face, and I let them fall. I am overwhelmed and flooded with so many emotions. How did I get so lucky to end up with him? I'm not sure he understands how big of a deal this is for me. From the moment I met him, he changed my life without even trying. This is exactly what I needed, especially with my recent doubts. I've always planned to visit New York before making such a serious commitment, but it's happening, and it's all because of him. There isn't a single person I'd rather experience this with other than Christian.

Maybe being there in person will give me answers to the questions I have swirling through my mind. Is this what I really want? Can I leave my family behind? Will I be happy being away from them? Can I do this on my own? Without them, without Christian.

"Christian," his name shakes as it leaves my mouth, "This is… this is," I stumble, trying to form words.

"I know, baby, I know," his thumb feathers my cheek, wiping away my tears.

"Thank you."

"You don't need to thank me. I wanted to do this for you."

"Every day with you feels like a dream. You are everything I have ever wanted, and I fear sometimes blinking, thinking if I do, all of this will disappear, and none of it would be real."

"I know the feeling," he tucks a strand of my hair behind my ear, "but this isn't a dream, baby; this is our reality."

"We're going to New York," I smile.

"We're going to New York," the corner of his mouth lifts.

This is our reality, his and mine. I don't care where I go or where I end up as long as I end up with him—my golden boy, my summer.

Chapter 42

Rayne

You can do this, Rayne Davis. You're going to New freaking York! I chant to myself, studying my reflection in my bathroom mirror—the feelings of angst, exhilaration, and anticipation brew within me. I'm ecstatic and fearful of seeing the big city for the first time. What if I hate it, and everything I thought I knew feels like a lie?

On the other hand, what if I love it, and it was more than I could ever have imagined, only making the decision to leave everyone I love behind that much harder? I'm grateful to experience these firsts with Christian, but if I end up loving New York, I'm scared it will become spoilt with the memories he and I create together when he doesn't come with me. Either way, this needs to be done, and I can't back out now. I have a flight to catch in a little over two hours.

Sighing, giving myself one last pep talk in the mirror, I grab my suitcase and meet Christian and my parents out front. His face lights up when he sees me, and I do my best to imitate their expression. He must sense my apprehension because his light dims a fraction.

"What's going on in that pretty little head of yours?"

"Um," I pick at my nails, glancing at my feet, "It's nothing, really." He looks at me with probing eyes, seeing straight through me.

"Tell me a secret." He rubs his hands up and down my arms, pulling the tension from my bones.

"I'm scared for this whole New York thing. It's what I've always wanted, but what if what I want isn't what I need?"

"Or what if what you always wanted is exactly what you need? Trust in what's in here," he taps on my heart.

Only if it were that easy. What if my heart wants it all? The fact of the matter is, its just not possible.

"It's okay not to have all the answers right now," he cups the side of my face. "A wise girl once told me *to enjoy the now.*" I smile at the repeated words that I once spoke to him. I'm not quite sure what my future holds, but I decide at this moment to embrace the uncertainty.

My mom and dad talk about their excitement for us to experience New York. She fills us in on all the touristy spots we must visit. Her excited energy reverberates throughout the car, tunneling straight to me. Christian beams. His leg bounces in eagerness, clearly feeling the effects of my mother's words just as much as I am. My dad pulls to the curb, following everyone else, getting ready to depart. He helps Christian unload our bags while my mom and I stand off to the side.

"Okay, honey, did you pack everything you need? Extra sets of clothes. Lots of warm attire because it's going to be freezing. Thermal to wear under your clothes. Beanie. Scarf." My mom lists without catching a breath.

"Yes." I try to stifle my laugh.

"Do you have your ID? Your plane tickets? The card we gave you with money?" she continues.

"Yes, mom."

"Darling, she's fine," my dad chuckles, wrapping his arm around my mother's waist. Then he looks at me, his forehead slightly creased. "You are fine, right?"

I giggle, "Yes, daddy, I'm good." He nods, giving me a tight-lipped smile and pulling me into their embrace. My mother kisses me on my cheek, and my father kisses me on the top of my head.

"Get over here, son." Christian holds out his hand, and my dad takes it but wraps one arm around him in a hug.

"We trust you to keep an eye out on our daughter."

"Yes, sir." He pats his back, releasing him, and my mom swoops in, wrapping her arms around him, too.

"You guys both be safe and have fun. You know the rules. Check-in with us twice a day, and if you need anything, do not hesitate."

"Will do." He assures.

On the plane, Christian hesitates, staring at the two empty seats before deciding to take the seat at the end of the aisle, not the window. Squeezing between him and the chairs in front of us, I plop down next to him, opening the window shade immediately. The window seat is my favorite.

He closes his eyes and looks away. It isn't until the flight attendant gives an in-flight safety briefing that he snaps his eyes open, as if startled by the sound of her voice. He studies her every move as if he is expected to take a test on all this afterward. The overhead lights start beeping, informing us to put on our seatbelts. I calmly click mine in place, looking over to make sure Christian clicked in his.

He fumbles with the belt, growing impatient by the second. Placing my hands over his, he tenses before letting out a long sigh, trying to relax. I swiftly click his buckle in place as the pilot informs the flight attendants and crew members to prepare for takeoff. A light layer of sweat coats his forehead. Once the plane propels down the runway, his hands tighten on the armrest, his knuckles turning white.

"Hey," I softly say, setting my hand atop of his, "Are you okay?"

"Yeah. I'm fine."

"Have you flown before?" he subtly shakes his head. "And you thought jumping out of a plane would be something to add to our list?" I smile, trying to distract him. He let out a forced chuckle, side-eyeing me, scared to move. Pulling out my headphones from my hoodie, I connect them to my phone.

'Young Forever by Jay Z,'
"Let us die young or let us live forever. We don't have the power, but we never say never."

Leaning closer to Christian, I gently caress the side of his cheek, turning his face toward me.

"Look at me," he slowly opens his eyes. "Breathe, I'm right here, okay? Focus on me and only me." I place one earbud in my ear, adding the other to his.

His eyes hold mine as the plane ascends toward the sky, the music faintly playing in the background. Once we are in the air, he shuts his eyes, pressing his lips to my forehead, telling me *thank you* without having to utter a word.

I face forward, adjusting in my seat until I'm comfortable, and he rests his head on my shoulder. The melody hums in our ears, and after a while, I can feel the weight of his body against me as he fully relaxes, succumbing to sleep. Light snores escape his full lips, and I smile, his long lashes fanning against his cheekbones. I brush his hair back away from his eyes before turning my gaze out the cabin window. I am wide awake, staring out at the ocean below, still trying to process the fact that I'm on my way to New York. It feels like a dream, but then again, every day with Christian feels like that.

He stirs next to me about two hours later, slowly opening his eyes. The corner of his mouth lifts when he sees me.

"So, I wasn't dreaming. We are on a plane," I giggle, nudging him with my shoulder, "Sorry I fell asleep."

"It's okay. How are you feeling?"

"A lot better, thanks."

"Good. Did you want to watch a movie? I paid for Wi-Fi while you were sleeping."

"Sounds good."

"I'll let you pick the movie."

"An action movie then?" he side-eyes me, failing at hiding his smirk.

"I don't care what kind of movie it is as long as I get to sit next to you." I return his crooked smile, thinking of when he told me the same thing about my romance movies.

His mouth curves ear to ear as he scrolls through the movie options. He settles on Fast & Furious, stealing another smile from me. My mind immediately goes back to the night we sat on the couch as Fast & Furious played in the background while he comforted me. It was also the very first time he kissed me. Despite how angry, hurt, and confused I was at how the night ended, I'd go through it all again to end up at this moment, to end up with him.

Landing in New York is something I will never forget. It was absolutely surreal; it almost took my breath away. We got a clear view of the Statue of Liberty, Central Park, and One World Trade Center. I'm positive I missed so many other things, but I couldn't focus on one thing. Instead, my gaze darted around, trying to see as much as my eyes would allow. I couldn't sit still and bounced in my seat as I begged Christian to look because I did not want him to miss out on the view of New York City lit up at night. He was initially reluctant, but the city below held him captive once he looked. His eyes widened in awe, and his lips slightly parted, forming a small 'O.'

We catch a taxi from JFK airport and get dropped off at Hard Rock Hotel. Again, I am in awe. I'd imagine Las Vegas is like this but on a tremendous scale. Stepping out of the taxi, Christian grabs our luggage as my feet are planted on the busy sidewalk, looking up at the lofty building illuminated with purple lights, completely stunned.

"It has 36 floors." Christian stands beside me, looking up at the towering building.

"Wow," I say in an astonished breath.

"Pretty amazing, right?"

"I'm not sure if that word gives it justice."

He grins. "Imagine what the inside looks like."

The thought causes my heart to beat wildly in my chest. Not wanting to waste another minute, we grab our bags and head to the front desk. The lobby is massive, with white and gold marble flooring with a matching staircase leading up to the second level. The walls are warm brown with gold accents throughout. Its bright white luminescent lighting makes the hotel feel alive. This place feels expensive, and I wonder how much all of this cost.

"Christian," I gasp, slowly twirling in a circle, burning everything into my memory. "How much was this place?"

"That doesn't matter."

"Tell me, please." I'm not working right now, but eventually, I will. It may not be soon, but once I have my own money, I want to pay him back.

"Why? So, you can pay me back?"

"Ye—"

"Not happening." He kisses my forehead and turns to the desk before I get a word out.

The lady behind the front desk watches his every step as he approaches, but he doesn't notice because as she watches him, his gaze is locked on me over his shoulder, giving me my favorite crooked smile.

When he turns to face her, she flushes, flustered, and quickly looks away. He hands her his credit card, and she gives an exaggerated smile. She hands him back his card along with the keys to our room, but she extended her arm, resting it on his forearm as he attempts to turn around. I clench my fists; she needs to get her hands off him before I rip them off myself. Scrunching his brows, his eyes fall to her hand before giving her a kind smile, taking a small step back. She giggles. Over what? Who the hell knows?

Her cheeks are rosy as she asks him a question. He runs his hands through his hair as she slides a piece of paper and pen towards him. What the hell? He writes what I assume is his number down and hands it back to her. I march in their direction, pissed the hell off, but Christian turns toward me with a grin, stopping me in my tracks.

"What was that about?" I look over his shoulder at Malibu fucking Barbie.

"She asked for my number." He shrugs, grabbing our bags and walking to the elevator. My mouth gapes in disbelief as I rush after him and hold his shoulder, stopping him as he presses the elevator button.

"And you just gave it to her!" he grins as my phone buzzes.

Why the hell does he keep smiling like this isn't a big deal? Pulling out my phone, I scrunch my eyes at the unknown number that texted me.

Unknown: Hey, it's Mallory. <3

Christian lifts my chin. "She asked for my number, and I gave her yours." My mouth hangs open. "I love when you get all territorial like that."

"Well played," the corner of my mouth lifts. "You're going to pay for that." The elevator dings open behind him, and Christian walks backward, stepping inside.

"I'm looking forward to it, baby."

Yup, my panties are now soaked.

We get off on the thirty-fourth floor and make a right, stopping at the last door on our left. Christian pulls out our key card, scans it, and our door clicks open. I'm so excited I can scream. When we step inside, my mouth all but drops to the floor. Just when I think it can't get any better, it does. This room is to die for! There is a large king-sized bed in the center of the room, large open windows giving you the perfect view of Times Square, and a large flatscreen TV hanging on the wall.

Christian sets our things on the bed, surveying the room. His smile is huge as he walks toward me.

"Do you like it?"

"Are you kidding me? This is unbelievable! Everything about this place is perfect."

"Come, let's check out the rest of the room." He takes my hand, guiding me to the bathroom.

"This is a bathroom?" I look around the massive room. "It's huge!"

"That's what she said," he smirks.

I laugh playfully, pushing him, and he chuckles, catching my hand and kissing me. The bathroom has a walk-in shower and a tub that I can't wait to soak in. I take a bunch of photos and send them to Laynie.

Me: 6 photo images.

Laynie: Eeeek! I'm so fucking jealous right now! Have fun, babe, and make sure to put every inch of that room to good use. ;) Love ya!

Me: LOL! Ditto babe. xoxo

My stomach rumbles, echoing throughout the large bathroom, and Christian shoots me with a look, arching his brow.

"What? A girl needs to eat." His stomach growls just as the words drift from my lips. I arch an eyebrow at him, the corner of my mouth curving around the edges.

"What?" he shrugs. "A guy needs to eat." I giggle. "What do you think about room service for dinner? It's getting late, and we have a long couple of days."

Wrapping my arms around his neck, I say, "I think it sounds perfect."

This room is out of this world, and I don't mind staying here at all. Christian ordered our food and surprised me with dessert; both were by far the best food we had ever tasted. We changed into pajamas and cuddled up in our bed that felt like we were lying on a cloud. Nothing compares to hotel beds and their cozy sheets. It's my favorite part of the room. I haven't even explored New York yet, but I'm already having the best time. My smile never leaves my face throughout the rest of the night because I'm happy, and this is only the beginning.

Chapter 43

Rayne

Letting *Christian sleep,* I showered, applied light make-up, and quickly dressed. When I step out of the bathroom, he is still in a deep sleep, lying on his side with his arms stretched out around a pillow. I smile, walking over to the small table in the room's corner, my smile expanding when I click a button and the drapes spread apart.

Even this early morning, with gloomy skies, the city is wide awake. From way up here, the people look like a colony of ants quickly overpowering city sidewalks. Yellow cabs fill the bustling streets as my mind drifts off, wondering if I can picture myself living in such a busy state. Christian groans behind me, breaking me from my daze.

"It's so bright," he murmurs. "Sleep. Need more sleep." I giggle, jumping onto the bed.

"Time to get up. The city awaits!" he pulls my legs out from under me in a flash, and I yelp, landing on my back. He is immediately on top of me with my hands pinned above my head. Drawing in a sharp breath, my eyes widen at the hunger flaring in his.

"We aren't going anywhere until I've had my breakfast." I swallow, my throat suddenly dry. He moves to the crook of my neck, planting a kiss on my collarbone, causing a shiver to rake through my body.

"What are you doing?" he nips at my tender flesh before easing the sting with his soft tongue. Goosebumps appear, and he smirks at my responsive body.

"I'm ready to eat, baby," he says in a husky tone.

My core aches at the need I hear in his voice; my pussy instantly becomes wet. He releases his hold on my wrist, pulling me around my waist in a sitting position. Grabbing the bottom of my sweater, he takes it off in one swift motion, gently pushing me back against the mattress. Reaching over his shoulder with one hand, he removes his shirt, tossing it on the floor. His chest heaves as he sits on bent knees, his teeth digging into his bottom lip. While he burns me with his heated gaze, I let my eyes roam over his broad shoulders and golden chest.

He kisses the side of my belly button while simultaneously pulling down my leggings. My heart beats out of my chest, and my insides ignite. He nips, licks, and sucks, making his way down to my essence, dragging my panties till they hit my ankles.

"Fuck baby! You smell so good." He stops at my sex, looking up through his thick lashes, "But I know you taste even better." He growls, pushing his tongue between my folds.

I let out a sweet cry as my hands fly to the back of his head, gripping his hair. He lets out a guttural groan that sends vibration against my sensitive bud. I moan in response, arching my back and lifting my ass off the mattress. Without removing his mouth from my sex, he pushes me back down with his forearm, pinning me in place. It's so hard to lie still; naturally, my body wants to squirm, my hips begging to buck forward.

Being touched by him is something else. I didn't know what to expect when he first touched me, but I never expected it to feel so good. The more intimate we become, the better everything feels. The way he handles me drives me insane, the way he drugs me with just his fingertips.

My legs tremble as he quickens the strokes of his tongue.

"That's it, baby," he purrs. "Come for me." And I do. I never knew in the midst of an orgasm that I could feel so alive. "Now we can start our morning."

After Christian quickly showered, we headed out, stopping for an actual breakfast. We walked the lively sidewalk in Times Square, stopping at Starbucks for my daily dose of caffeine.

As we walked the streets, it reminded me of a zoo. It's wall-to-wall people, and you have to pay attention to weave through pedestrians constantly. All my senses are assaulted with sound, color, people attempting to entice you into their stores, and folks dressed in costumes as people stop to take a picture with them. I also notice many people talking or texting on their phones. The majority look in a rush, not wanting to be bothered.

The absurd number of people and the thousands of things going on at once make me feel dizzy, but in the best way. The energy is high, and there is so much to see. I'm too busy looking up and not what is right in front of me that I almost crash into a few people. None of them spared me a glance as they swerved around me. If I end up living in New York, I know it would never be boring, that's for sure.

The Broadway show signs really catch my attention. It would be a dream to style clothing and see it advertised on billboards around New York City.

"This place is crazy." Christian shouts over the blaring horns and people chatting as they pass.

"I know, right? It's kind of awesome."

He smiles, grabbing my gloved hand. "The school is a few miles from here. Maybe we should catch a cab?"

The thought of seeing my dream school brings a smile to my face. I'm nervous to see my dream so close but at the same time anxious. What if attending NYSOD isn't my dream anymore? It's crazy to think when this is all I've ever seen in my future. I was always so sure, but now I'm not. The closer it gets to deciding, the more complex the choice becomes, and the more confused I feel.

I like to think I'm confident, but lately, I'm realizing I feel secure surrounded by the people I'm the most comfortable with, the people I love the most. Would I still feel as confident on my own without them?

"I'm okay with taking a cab."

Christian kisses my frosted cheek and steps toward the sidewalk, waving his hands for a taxi. A gust of icy wind sweeps by, and I shiver, adjusting my beanie lower onto my forehead. While Christian waves his hands, trying to catch a cab, I pull out the visitor's map offered at our hotel to see what is around here. There are museums, and shows, and Central Park is relatively close. Scanning the map, my eyes land on a club called. I squint, trying to read the name of it just as the wind picks up, blowing it straight out of my hands.

I bend urgently, trying to grab it as it dances in the wind. Just as I'm about to catch it, a shiny dress shoe steps on it, holding it in place. Long, thick fingers wrap around the map before their hand lifts. I step back, still staring at the ground. My eyes leisurely trail the polished shoe up to long legs that seem to go on forever and muscular thighs. I know this is a man in front of me by the build. When I look up, I'm face to face with a solid chest. I crane my neck further, getting a better look at this stranger.

"Thank y—" My words lodge in my throat as my skin prickles, and I lock eyes with this mystery man.

His eyes are as gray as thick, prowling clouds in a thunderstorm—eyes with a grilling gaze that can cause hell to freeze over. I look at his hair, jet black, the color of a raven.

It's shorter on the sides, and longer on top, combed over to perfection. This man is all business, and by the looks of his light gray Armani suit, he's wealthy, too. He towers over my slight frame, not saying a word, and grins. My eyes widen at his perfect set of teeth. Everything about this man seems to be flawless.

What the hell am I doing?

Straightening my spine, I take the map from his hand, giving him a tight-lipped smile.

"Thank you."

He doesn't respond, just continues to pierce me with his stormy eyes. I turn on my heels, returning to my spot a couple of feet away. What the hell was that? And why the hell didn't he speak? Oh my god, maybe he's deaf! I glance in his direction, and his eyes are still pinned on me. Nope, definitely not deaf. He just chose not to talk to me. *Asshole!*

Christian approaches me. "I can't hail a cab. I swear they are purposely ignoring me."

"We can just walk."

"We're getting a cab, baby. I'm not giving up." He takes my hand, guiding me to the curb. "Maybe if they see an attractive woman, they'll stop." He smirks.

"Are you using me for my sex appeal?" I tease.

"Never," he grins, kissing my forehead.

My skin tingles in awareness. Not able to help myself, I glance over my shoulder. The mystery man is still staring, no longer on his phone. What is this guys deal?

"Hey, asshole, you got something you want to say?" Christian snaps, startling me with his tone. I look at him, but his eyes are locked on the strangers—his jaw ticks.

"Christian, what are y—"

"You going to speak or what? If not, turn the fuck around."

My eyes bulge, and I look back at the unknown guy behind me. The corner of his mouth lifts into a crooked smile as he casually walks toward us, radiating confidence. Christian squares his shoulders, asserting his dominance. Oh no, this is not good. I place my hand on his chest, hoping my touch will calm him, and he relaxes for a moment until I feel a strong presence behind me. Looking over my shoulder, the stranger doesn't look at Christian. He continues to look at me as he brings his index and thumb to his mouth, letting out a shrieking whistle.

A cab immediately pulls to a stop, and the mystery man walks away without a word. What the—"Who the fuck does that guy think he is?" Christian cuts off my train of thought.

"I don't know, but at least we got a cab," I smile, trying to bring his attention back to me and lighten the mood.

"I don't want to take the cab that asshole got."

"Come on. Don't let whoever the hell he is ruin our day." He looks down at me, his hard eyes softening.

He takes my hand, letting out a long exhale, leading me into the taxi. I feel eyes on me, and I don't glance back until we drive away. The mystery man is still watching me as a blacked-out Range Rover pulls up, and a man dressed in black and white emerges, opening his door. I roll my eyes, turning back in my seat—*a chauffeur.*

Maybe *we should have just walked* because the three-mile ride took over thirty minutes. I thought LA was hectic, but it doesn't compare to the traffic here. Pulling up to NYSOD, the parking lot is empty. The building itself is around five stories high with all glass windows. I grin, imagining myself in one of those rooms, working hands on and being taught by some of the most established names in the fashion industry. Working hard on upcoming fashion shows, building my resume, and editorial shoots to create a killer portfolio.

"I don't think it's open," Christian says, pulling on the front door handle. Disappointment sneaks in.

"Yeah, I didn't even think about it being winter break."

"Me either. I thought of everything else besides that." He frowns, "I'm sorry."

"It's not your fault you've done so much for me already. Just being here and seeing it up close is enough."

"Campus is closed," comes from a gruff voice. We turn toward the source. A shorter man with a pudgy belly wearing all black with the word security written on his chest approaches us. His heavy set of keys clipped on his belt loop jingle with each step he takes. "Do you guys go to school here?"

"Um, no, sorry." I look down at the ground.

"That's her plan," Christian says. "We are visiting from California and were hoping to check out the campus."

"Sorry. You guys can try again after winter break."

I look up to the man, frowning in disappointment, "Alright, thanks…"

Christian grabs my hand as we turn around. "Wait." The security guard says, stopping us, "I know California isn't close, so I'll let you guys in to have a look." My frown lifts into a smile. "It has to be quick, and I'll be staying with you guys on your tour. I can lose my job for this."

"No problem, thank you!" I beam in excitement.

The security guard, who we now know as Ben, lets us in. He stands a few feet behind us, giving us space. The halls trail on for days, and although all the doors to the classrooms are closed, each room has a wide glass window allowing you to see straight inside. Some classes have runways, and some have long rectangular tables with chairs. It filled other rooms with whiteboards with cut-out fashion pieces from magazines, but my favorite classrooms are the ones with stations littered with sewing machines and every fabric imaginable.

"Imagine when you're in one of these rooms."

I imagine myself in one of these rooms alongside others that share the same passion. My first reaction was to feel happy and excited about my future, but it wasn't long before

I felt apprehensive. Why can't I have everything figured out? I always knew I would eventually have to say goodbye, so why is it such a big deal now?

The truth is, I'm terrified. I've always had everything figured out, and this is the first time I don't. I've lived with my family my entire life. Attending NYSOD, I'm going to be over two thousand miles away. I'd like to believe I will be fine on my own, but what if I'm not? Since I was younger, I have always been with Laynie and Ryker. Yes, I made friends, but none that I hang out with outside of school aside from Jamie. What if I don't make a good impression on my classmates and don't make any friends? School has always come easy, but with college, that's different. What if it's a lot harder than I expected, and I fail?

I look at him, mustering a confident smile. "Yeah, imagine?" he frowns, but before he digs deeper, I change the subject. "Where do you want to go next?"

His brows deepen, "Um, did you want to look around more?"

"No," I shake my head, "Ben said we had to be quick. I've seen everything that I need to."

I already know I love it here, but is it enough to leave everything and everyone behind? Christian glances at Ben, who leans against a wall, scrolling through his phone, paying us no attention.

"Alright, let's go."

Thanking Ben, Christian calls a taxi, and we leave, heading to our next spot. I'm not sure where we are going because he wanted to keep it a surprise. It's sweet how thought out this trip has been. He has done everything to make it perfect for me and succeeded. This is a trip that I will never forget, and it is all thanks to him. He is perfect.

Christian had purchased tickets to Ellis Island in advance to see the Statue of Liberty. The ferry ride there was breathtaking. Being in the middle of the ocean and seeing New York's skyscrapers reaching toward the sky mesmerized me and made me realize how small we were. The Statue of Liberty is my favorite New York City landmark. What she symbolizes is powerful; she represents freedom, democracy, hope, and the American dream. The tour itself was around three hours, but was worth every minute.

After our tour, we caught a ferry back and then a taxi to take us back to our hotel. We both changed into something warmer because it would be dark and cold when we finished dinner. Virgil's authentic BBQ was near our hotel in Times Square, so we shared a rack of ribs, mac n cheese, and mashed potatoes, there. New York has some of the best food and will surely be a positive on my list of reasons that New York is the right choice.

Walking the streets of Times Square at night is something else. It's incredible during the day, but at night it's magical. It somehow becomes more alive and isn't something words could justify. You would just need to be here to experience it for yourself.

Christian and I weave through seas of people, taking in our surroundings. It's already insanely loud from the mixture of chatter, laughing, yelling, horns blaring, and occasional cussing, but it doesn't compare to the deafening music across the street. Despite the frigid temperatures, at least a hundred people stand behind a red rope dressed to the nines. Three large and intimidating security guards in suits stand in front of two open doors with arms crossed over their broad chests.

By the men's and women's attire, I can tell it's an upscale club that would probably cost me a kidney to get in. This must be the club I was trying to look at on my map before the wind carried it away. The word Knight is luminously displayed in bold grey writing, drawing attention to the club. Captivated by the gleaming grey sign, flashes of stormy eyes hit me like lightning—the same grey-colored eyes of the mystery man from earlier today. I squeeze my eyes tightly together, forcing them out of my head.

"I want to take you somewhere." My eyes fly open at the sound of Christian's voice.

"What?"

"I want to take you somewhere."

"Take me wherever," I smile.

Back at the hotel, he takes me to the elevator and up to the thirty-fifth floor. I give him a quizzical look, and he chuckles.

"We're going to the roof. We need a special key to reach the top floor, so we're taking the stairs."

My heart raced at the idea of being caught. We aren't supposed to go up there, and I don't want to get in trouble. However, I ignored the feeling because I trusted him. We reach the top of the roof and are met with a metal door cracked open by a rock. He leads me to the ledge, only stopping once the tips of my Doc Martens hit the wall. I zip up my coat as the condensation of my breath floats in front of me.

Christian stands behind me, wrapping his arms around my shoulders, resting his chin on the top of my head. I lean into him, enjoying his warmth and the view in front of me. Being up here feels like being in another world; I feel free. All the uncertainty dissipates, swirling with the wind.

"What's going on in that pretty little head of yours?"

"It's so beautiful." I peer over the edge, barely able to make anything out. "This city is immense and makes me feel so small."

"Baby, this city is yours if you want it," his lips press against the back of my head. "LA is too small for all of your big dreams."

"I'm scared." I turn around and face him.

"If your dreams don't scare you, they aren't big enough."

"But what about my family? What about you?" His glowing amber eyes sweep over my face before he speaks.

"Just for a second, don't think about your family or me. Can you picture yourself here? Do you think New York can give you everything you're looking for?"

"Yes," I tell him without hesitation.

"Then choose New York, Rayne."

My eyes glisten. "What about you? What about us?"

Using both hands, he cups the sides of my face. "You will have me always."

I look back and forth between his eyes and know without a doubt he's telling the truth. I don't think I'll ever be completely ready, but I firmly believe I'd regret it if I didn't try. If I go for it and it doesn't work out, it will still be a win for me. At least I had the guts to head straight into something that frightened me. I won't make it anywhere without that kind of courage. Would I be okay not choosing New York? Probably, but okay, isn't thrilling. It isn't passion. It's not life-changing or unforgettable. I'm unwilling to risk a simple okay for everything I've worked so hard for.

I choose New York.

Chapter 44

Rayne

I see the city in a new light. I don't look at it as an *if* I live here, but *when* I live here. I don't know what's going to happen between us, but he's reassured me time and time again that long-distance won't change anything. We will both visit as much as possible and FaceTime every night. He seems confident in us and my choice, which helps put my mind at ease. What is that saying? *"Distance makes the heart grow fonder."* With us, I'm hoping that is the case, and I'm choosing to believe that it is true.

Christian went to grab some things for tonight since it's New Year's Eve, and we're going to Times Square to watch the ball drop. I'm dancing around in the bathroom while I get ready for tonight. I can't stand still; I am full of energy. Moving my hips from side to side, I unravel my braided hair. I chose a sparkling champagne two-piece pantsuit with heels. I'm no makeup expert, but I made it work and love the way it turned out.

"Sweat by ZAYN,"
"Damn, I could get lost in a heartbeat. Damn, I can't get over your body. Can't take my eyes off you, baby."

Running my fingers through my hair, I sway and roll my hips to the music, feeling confident as I watch myself in the mirror. Closing my eyes, I lean my head back, letting the beat take over my body. I am lost in the moment when I feel hands on my waist, stopping my movements.

"Keep your eyes closed," Christian says in a sultry voice.

A sudden warmth charges throughout my body as he squeezes my waist. He slowly slides his hands up my sides, brushing my hair to one side, exposing my neck's curve. My body shudders at the caress of his breath against my skin. Anticipation and desire flood my veins as his lips lightly brush against my rapid pulse.

"You look sexy, baby." He whispers into my ear. Goosebumps erupt along my arms, and my back arches, pushing further into him.

He nibbles my shoulder, and I bite my lip, trying to suppress a moan. His touches are innocent, but his tone is anything but. Giving my waist another squeeze, he pushes into me, his hardness pressing against my back. Not able to hold it in, a moan escapes, causing him to smile against my neck before kissing it. His hands are hot against my skin. My breaths are shaky as he trails his fingers to the waistband of my pants. I open my eyes, but Christian grabs my chin, making sure not to hurt me, and tilts my head back.

"Keep those pretty eyes closed," he demands. My heart pounds against my chest as his fingertips glide from my waistline before he inserts them into my pants, dragging them closer to my sex. "You're not wearing any panties." He says in surprise with his finger pressed against my sensitive bud, and a throaty moan escapes. "So soft," he kisses my neck, "So wet."

I let out a pleased hum. His words, his voice, his touch, all of it is driving me crazy. He invades all my senses, and I can feel, smell, and hear him everywhere. His finger moves faster; my legs tremble, feeling weak.

"Christian…" He pinches my clit, and I let out a surprised squeak. He chuckles, pushing his finger inside me and giving me what I want. I rock my hips against him as his fingers work my pussy. His lips touch and taste my neck. My breathing grows faster. With my eyes still closed, my focus roaming from his nips and licks and the way his thumb presses against my clit while his fingers fill me.

"Open your eyes." They flutter open, finding him in the mirror. "Look at yourself." He says.

I observe my reflection, cheeks flushed, giving me a natural blush, my eyes dilated with a far way dreaminess.

"Fucking perfect." My eyes move to him. His cheeks are flushed, rose just like mine, with his mouth slightly parted.

"I need you." I rasp.

He rubs faster against my clit, "What do you need?"

I whine, growing impatient, "You know what I need."

The corner of his mouth lifts. "I want to hear you say it." I can hardly think with his hands on my body. It's one thing to think about what I want, but saying it aloud is different. "Tell me what you need, Rayne." he pushes.

"I want your cock inside of me." He growls, flicking my clit and my legs almost give out from under me.

He quickly grabs a condom from his pocket, glides it down his hardness, and pulls my pants down. Using one hand, he pulls off his shirt before placing his hand under my thigh and lifting it. He slowly pushes into me, and we both share a relieved moan. He pinches my nipple and slides in and out of me faster.

I watch him in awe of how his stomach is tight and his sculpted abs glisten in sweat. He looks like a fucking masterpiece, a beautiful chaotic art that I want to admire forever.

"You feel so fucking good, baby."

"Yes," I groan.

Tilting my head back, he crashes his lips against mine. Opening my mouth, he slides his tongue inside, stroking it against mine as he pumps in and out of me from behind. I pull his bottom lip into my mouth, sucking it hard. He thrusts into me harder and faster in response. A clapping sound echoes throughout the room, intertwined with our heavy breaths and moans. It's a beautiful sound; our appetites being deepened and fulfilled.

"Look in the mirror. I want to watch you fall apart." My grip on the counter tightens, watching as he feverishly pounds into me. My core tightens, and my pussy tingles. Fluttery sensations erupt in my stomach and chest. Eyes transfixed on his tight jaw, the way he grips my shoulders as he drives into me, his stomach flexing with each thrust, and the way his eyes never leave mine.

"Christian, I'm going to come." He brings his hand around and rubs my swollen bud, thrusting into me forcefully.

"Come for me." He commands.

I let out a pleased cry shared with Christian's shaky grunt, both of us reaching euphoria, falling over the edge, and falling apart together. I close my eyes, my body weak. He wraps his arm around my waist, helping me stay upright, and kisses in between my shoulder blades. He pulls out of me, and I whimper at the loss.

"Keep making sounds like that, baby, and I promise we won't leave this room."

I snatch my pants from his hands, and he chuckles, grabbing his off the floor before walking out of the bathroom.

I can already hear the rowdy crowd and music filling the streets just outside our hotel. The energy is high, my heart pounds in anticipation and excitement. What looks like hundreds of thousands of people are in the streets. There are so many people that I can't make out the ground. The sea of heads bob and dip, and flickers emerge throughout the crowd, reflecting off beaded necklaces, glittery New Year's hats, light-up glasses, and sparkly attire.

The crystal ball is set high in the distance, but I have no idea how we can make it through the herds of people who have been camping out here since this morning.

"This is insane!" I shout over the noise. "How are we going to get over there?"

"With these," he grins, holding up two tickets. "The tickets will get us past the barricade but in order to get close to the ball we are going to have to push our way through," I gulp, suddenly nervous. "I've got you, baby. Do you trust me?"

Swallowing the lump in my throat, I nod. Christian holds me in a tight grip as we sandwich our way between bodies, trying to get closer to the ball. We reach a metal barricade that comes to my hip, keeping the crowd from entering. NYPD and security stand by surveying the crowd. Christian hands over two tickets and they let us through.

Passing through the barricade, my hand tight within Christians grip. He pushes his way through hundreds of people before, we make it to forty-third street. I can't believe we made it! Being out here amongst the crowd is a rush. Ryan Seacrest walks onto the stage, and my mouth falls open. I squeeze Christian's hand, trying not to fangirl over the man I grew up watching on American Idol. Waves of excitement burst through Times Square. After the crowd settles, Ryan calls X Ambassadors to the stage, and I lose my shit. Tilting my head back, I cup the sides of my mouth and holler with the crowd.

"Come on, baby, it's the X Ambassadors!"

He whispers in my ear so I can hear him, "Did you just call me baby?"

"I sure did."

'In Your Arms' (with X Ambassadors) plays. Christian holds out his hand, offering me a dance. I blush, resting my hand on his, and he quickly pulls me flush against him.

My hands wrapped around the back of his neck, his resting on my lower back, and we sway side to side as everything around us fades. I rest my head on his chest, letting the sound of his heart relax me. He turns us around elegantly, his body in tune with the slow music. Looking into his eyes, I'm hit with so much emotion. His touch warms me, and his eyes whisper sweet nothings to my soul. He is by far my favorite. My favorite pair of eyes to look into, my favorite way to spend time, my favorite voice to hear. *He is my favorite everything.*

The song ends, and X Ambassadors wishes their fans a happy New Year and exits the stage. Ryan comes on, and the sixty-second countdown begins. What looks like powdered gems falls from the sky. The icy flakes land in our hair, and we both look up toward the stars—an onslaught of white flutters through the air, blinding, freezing, and magical.

"I want to tell you something." his eyes glow softly as he stares at me.

"Tell me." I grab his hand.

Ten...

"I love you."

Nine...

"And I love you." I say.

Eight...

"I can see you here. You're going to do so many big things, and I want to see you achieve every single one of them."

Seven...

"I'm glad you chose New York," he squeezes my hand.

Six...

"But..."

Five...

My heart races and my legs suddenly feel heavy.

"But?"

Four...

"You chose New York."

Three...

"And I *choose* you."

Two...

"I'm coming to New York with you."

One...

"Happy New Year, baby."

Using both hands, he cups my face, and I can no longer breathe. He kisses me the softest he has ever kissed me before. Slowly opening his mouth, he delicately moves his tongue across mine, and every sweep of his tongue makes it easier for me to breathe.

"What do you mean?" I whisper, not sure if I heard him correctly.

He doesn't blink as he speaks. "I don't want to be away from you. I want to see you every morning before I go to work. I want to kiss you every night before I go to bed. I want *everything* with you, and I can't imagine staying in LA when my heart is in New York."

My lips part as I take large, deep, and savoring breaths. I don't realize I'm crying until he leans in and kisses my tears away. *He chose me,* and I can't even think straight. Christian is coming to New York with me, and we will start this next chapter together. He doesn't want to be parted from me the same way I don't wish to be parted from him. I can't picture my life without him, and now I don't have to.

"Say something..." he says, his eyes shimmering with emotion.

"I... I don't know where to start. I'm still trying to figure out if I'm dreaming or not."

His thumb glides along the side of my face. "This is real. What we have is real."

Biting my lip, I nod, blinking away my tears. "You changed my life without even trying, and I don't think I could ever find the right words that would come close to explaining how much you mean to me. I can't imagine what things would be like if I hadn't met you." I cover his hands, resting on my face. "It's amazing how you walked into my life one day and changed everything. My universe shifted on its axis, and I can't remember what my life was like before you. I don't know how I ever lived without you."

A lone tear falls from the corner of his eye.

"I'm so in love with you, Christian. I love you today, tomorrow, and the day after that."

Before he can speak, I steal his breath with a kiss. I kiss him, leaving no doubt about the way I feel about him.

He held me close in his arms and whispered, "I love you."

In that whisper bellowed so many promises.

Chapter 45

Christian

One year later...

Ten... Nine, Eight, Seven, Six, Five, Four, Three, Two, One. "Happy New Year!" everyone roars. Confetti fills the air, and noisemakers go off at once. Rayne sets down her cup of apple cider and wraps her arms around my neck, playing with the wavy ends of my hair.

"Happy New Year, baby." She whispers against my lips, smiling.

"Happy New Year, Raynie." I kiss her, and her mouth parts, accepting my invitation.

The taste of tequila and sweet apple charge my senses. A year later, every kiss is still as if I'm feeling her lips for the first time. Only better.

"Mmm, that doesn't taste like apple cider."

She grins, "It's spiked."

"Let me guess, Laynie supplied the tequila?"

"Damn right I did," Laynie grins, throwing her arm around Rayne.

"And who do you think she got it from?" Ryker joins, "Where's my thank you? A New Year's kiss will do." He teases, puckering his lips.

"Oh, fuck off!"

"Ew," Rayne gags.

I punch him in his bicep, unintentionally giving him a dead arm. "Ow!" he groans, rubbing the spot I hit. "What was that for?"

"Not offering me any."

"Yeah, and when was I supposed to do that? When you guys were sucking face in the backyard or sneaking up to her room doing God knows what." He grimaces, and Rayne's cheeks instantly flame in embarrassment.

Fuck. I never knew it was possible to love someone so damn much.

"I don't know what you're talking about. I was helping her pack." My lip tugs upward, and I shrug.

Laynie's smile drops slightly at the mention of Rayne packing. It's going to be hard on everyone, even my mother. Her bond with Rayne has only strengthened, and I don't doubt that she will miss her as much as she'll miss me.

"Dude, you guys have like five months left before you leave." Ryker counters.

"You know I like to be prepared, big brother."

"I don't want to think about how much time we have left. It is flying by. We graduate in five months, then all we have is summer." Laynie says, her tone laced with sadness.

Grabbing Rayne's drink off the table, I take a sip because I might as well catch up. Laynie is right. Time is flying by. It's weird to think how much has changed since last year, but it all feels the same. My mother and I still come over here for Sunday breakfast, and I still work at Davis Automotive. We spent Rayne's birthday in Big Bear just like we did last year, and if it wasn't Rayne and me together, our days were spent with Laynie and Ryker.

Rayne applied to NYSOD, and of course, she got in. She was stressed for no reason, because there was no way she wasn't going to get accepted. Rayne worked at The Hideout over the summer, saving money for our move to New York. I told her she didn't have to because I've been saving every penny I make, but she's stubborn and didn't want me paying for everything.

Our parents wanted to celebrate New Year's together since it will be our last one for a while. We have already discussed coming home for as many holidays as possible. New Year's in New York was an experience, but this year we are exactly where we want to be.

"Let's get a picture," Olivia says.

She sets her phone on the mantle, and we all huddle in for a picture. Everyone smiles as the flash goes off, but I keep smiling long after. I'm fucking happy. I am blessed and grateful for where I'm at and excited about where I'm going.

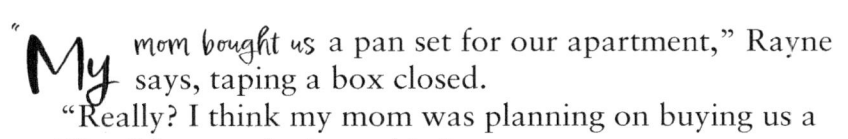

"My mom bought us a pan set for our apartment," Rayne says, taping a box closed.

"Really? I think my mom was planning on buying us a set. I'll tell her we don't need it."

"No, it's okay. She already got it."

"She did?"

"Her and my mom went together, and they figured we could never have too many pots and pans."

"Man, I can't wait to see you cooking in the kitchen."

"Who says I'm going to be the one cooking?" she quirks a brow.

"I can cook, if you don't mind our first apartment burning to the ground."

She laughs, walking over and wrapping her arms around my neck. "Fair point. Let's leave the cooking for me."

"I'll do the dishes."

"Sounds perfect." Standing on her tippy toes, she lightly pecks my lips and pushes me toward the bed. Rayne smiles, climbing on top of me. "I can't wait to live together."

"What are you most excited about?"

"Being able to do this anytime I want." Her mouth immediately covers mine.

"Mmm," I hum.

I'm looking forward to being able to kiss her, touch her, and love her whenever I want, but it's more than that. I'm more excited about all the other things, like lazy Sunday afternoons and seeing her smile during the romance movies she loves so much and writing while she reads, going out on Saturday nights, doing laundry, cooking dinner, kissing her goodnight, waking up next to her each morning, and not getting out of bed until I tasted her lips.

Rayne stops kissing me and climbs off. She grabs an empty box and returns to her packing, a smile teasing her lips.

"You give me the worst case of blue balls," I groan.

"We can fix that later," she gives me a one-sided smile. "Right now, we pack."

"You're still trouble, woman."

"And I'll continue to tell you, only the best kind."

Facts.

Chapter 46

Rayne

You know that saying. *"time flies when you are having fun?"* well, I agree. However, time doubles in speed whenever I'm with Christian. Months went by like a dream, and before we knew it was prom.

Salon appointments, dinner reservations, and flashy car or limo rentals are the norm for most on a night like a prom, but we did things differently. Having a nice lunch together was the best idea, and I didn't want to rush when getting ready since we were doing our hair and makeup ourselves. Plus, who wants to eat and be bloated wearing a tight dress? Not me. The one thing I wanted to keep traditional was being asked to prom, and Christian did that perfectly.

I was hanging out in his room when he opened his journal and told me to read it before disappearing into his closet.

I read the journal entry, and it said,

Your dad said that I could take you to prom when pigs fly. Well...

Then he emerged from his closet holding two helium-filled pig balloons.

When I didn't answer right away, he said, "I don't do this shit, Raynie. I'm holding up two flying pigs. Help my ego and say yes."

Of course, I said yes.

Laynie asked Ryker to prom, which surprised me, but I guess she wanted to go with him so we could all spend time together since we try to spend as much time together as possible before we leave for New York.

"**Not** so fast." Christian stops me. "Where is my kiss?" I giggle, turning around to face him.

"How could I forget?" I peck his lips.

"I'm going to head home and get ready. I will be at your place early because you know my mom will want at least twenty pictures."

"Between your mom, my mom, and Laynie's mom, I think we should expect much more than that before we make it out the front door."

"Great," he says, his tone was full of sarcasm. "I know Maverick is excited to see you."

Maverick flew in while we had lunch, because he wanted to see Christian attend his first prom. We haven't seen him since our trip to Oregon, and I know Christian has missed him. It makes me happy knowing the people we love the most will be here.

"Tell him I'm sorry I didn't stop by, but being a girl is a lot of work." I wrap my arms around his neck, "and that I can't wait to see him."

"I will, baby. Get ready. I will see you soon."

"Bye, neighbor."

"Soon to be roommate," he shouts over his shoulder. I blush, smiling the whole way to my room; *roommate*.

When I enter my room, Laynie is half naked, putting her hair in curlers. "I can't believe it's already prom!"

"I know! We are going to look fucking stunning."

"Damn right we are."

"I'm going to miss you." She says.

I sigh, hugging her, "I'm going to miss you too, Laynie Mae."

We only have a little time left. Even though I'm excited and ready for New York, I am not prepared to leave her. I don't think I will ever be ready for that.

"Alright, babe, enough of this sad girl shit."

Letting out a half laugh and half cry, I say, "Okay, you're right."

I know exactly what we need. I grab my phone and play 'Best Friend (feat. Doja Cat).'

"Now that's what I'm talking about!" she smirks, swaying her hips from side to side.

The next three hours were spent dancing, laughing, and talking while we got ready. Smiling, I grab my garment bag that hangs on the back of my closet door before stepping into my emerald green dress.

"Rayne," Laynie gasps. "I knew the dress was stunning, but it doesn't compare to how you look in it!"

"Thank you. You look beautiful, Laynie. Seriously, this dress is perfect for you." I walk around her, examining her strapless black mermaid-style gown that falls to the floor.

"Thank you," she twirls.

Running my hands down the soft satin of my dress, I ask, "Do you think Christian will like it?"

"You look elegant and sexy! He will come in his pants at the sight of you."

"Laynie!"

"What? You look that good!"

Perfect, I'm hoping to get that kind of reaction from him, and later I am hoping he wants to rip this dress right off me. Christian loves my eyes, so I designed a dress that matches them exactly, pairing it with my favorite pair of earrings he bought me for my birthday.

"Picture time!" Laynie squeals.

We pose, taking a few pictures together before I take some of just her. She takes the phone from my hands, telling me it's my turn. I am glad to get some full body pictures because I have spent the last five months working on this dress. It's beautiful and classy, with the right amount of sexy. Tiny straps go over my shoulder, and it's tight against my skin, cascading to the floor. I created a slit for my right leg that turns into the lace at my hip bone, wrapping around my lower back. As I examine the pictures, Laynie took of me. My heart races, and my skin tingles, thinking about Christian's reaction when he sees me.

"I'm so nervous," I admit.

"I can help with that." she grabs a bottle of tequila from her duffle bag.

At this point, I don't know if the tequila will help calm my nerves or make me feel sick because of how anxious I am. Laynie hands me the bottle, and I bring it to my lips. Guess there is only one way to find out. Passing the bottle back to Laynie, she moves it to her lips. Her cheeks expand, and her hand clutches her stomach as she runs to the bathroom and throws up.

"Oh my god! Are you okay?"

"I'm fine," she heaves, hanging over the toilet, trying her best not to vomit again. "I don't know what happened. The smell of tequila made me feel sick."

She has been talking about prom since Junior high school, so that's a possibility. I felt nauseous myself.

Ryker shouts from downstairs, telling us to hurry, and Laynie rolls her eyes, purposely making him wait as she takes her time, ruffling her hair and reapplying her lipstick. Popping my lips together, satisfied with how I look, I glance at her, and she grins, linking her arm through mine. We stop just before reaching my door, and I close my eyes, taking a deep breath.

I don't know why I'm nervous. Hearing excited voices and laughter downstairs causes heart palpitations in my chest.

"You ready?" she asks.

Nodding, I grin, "Ready."

The moment we reach the top step, gasps echo throughout the room. My eyes instantly find Christian's, and everything fades around us. His eyes stay locked on mine as he meets me at the bottom of the stairs, his smile growing wider. Taking his hand, my skin prickles at his touch, warmth spreading throughout my chest. My face feels stretched from smiling so much. Redness trails up his neck, creeping into his cheeks. Neither of us speaks as our eyes leisurely sweep over one another, leaving trails of heat with our gaze.

He looks incredibly sexy in an all-black tux. His dress pants are tight around his muscular thighs, his button-up black shirt tucked into the waistline of his pants, and his black vest taut around his broad chest and narrow waist. My smile widens, noticing his all-black Converse. *Perfect.*

His eyes drift to mine, and I gulp under his searing gaze. Those seductive eyes tell me he is hungry and I'm what he wants to eat. My stomach flutters when he lifts my hand, and I shyly bite my bottom lip, giving him a little twirl. Taking his time, his eyes steadily sweep up and down my body as I do, darkening when he notices my bareback.

"You. Are. Breathtaking," he drawls.

"Wow, just wow," my mother says, placing her hands on my arms. "You look very beautiful, Rayne. Doesn't she, Jack?" my father's throat bobs as his eyes shimmer.

"Yes, she does."

Smiling, I hug my dad. I'm going to miss this. My mother's warmth, my father's hugs, and being around my family daily.

Sawyer wraps me in her embrace next. "You are stunning, and this dress!" she steps back, taking me in.

"Thank you, Sawyer."

"And you, my boy, look so handsome. You remind me so much of your father."

"He does, doesn't he?" Maverick places his arm around her.

Christian swallows, holding back his tears, and I quickly dab under my glistening eyes, not wanting to ruin my make-up. Ryker, Laynie, and her parents join us for a group photo. Moments like these are what I love the most. Our families joined together and were happy. I look up at Christian and find him looking at me with a genuine smile reaching his eyes. My favorite.

Since Christian has been in my life, I've looked forward to this night. This is the last night we all attend a high school event together before moving over two thousand miles away. Yes, we still have summer, but we only get prom once. It feels like a special event moving us into adulthood. It gives us girls the chance to dress up and have a night that we will remember long after high school is over.

Christian and I laughed when realizing we had forgotten to exchange our corsage and boutonniere. I pinned his to his jacket pocket, and he slid the emerald green and black corsage onto my wrist with delicate fingers. The simple touch had my heart erratic, but it wasn't just his touch; it was the way his eyes never left mine as he did it.

The corner of his mouth lifts, knowing his effect on me. "Ready to get out of here, Raynie?"

I'm ready for a night I'll never forget.

Chapter 47

Rayne

Prom *is at a luxurious venue* called The Legacy in Calabasas. The fucking Kardashians live here, so that should tell you something. A massive balloon arch is in front, with a navy-blue carpet leading into the entrance. There is a banner high on the front of the building that says, "A night under the stars." Cameras are flashing one after another. Photographers stop everyone to take their picture in front of a beautiful starry backdrop before they enter.

"Do you see this shit, Rayne?" Laynie says.

"Uh-huh."

Everyone looks incredible! All the boys are so dapper in suits, and the girls are gorgeous in their dresses. Limos line up to drop off students like celebrities attending a famous award ceremony.

"Bro, this shit is wild. I don't remember my prom being like this." Ryker says to Christian.

"I have nothing to compare it to, but this is insane."

"Well, what the hell are we waiting for? Let's get our asses in there!" Laynie says excitedly.

Before entering, Ryker pulls out a flask. "Alright, guys, you ready to party or what?"

"Hell yeah!" we all shout.

After our photos are taken, we reach the dance floor, moving to the beat of the music. Laynie bounces her hips from side to side, and Ryker dances beside her. He pulls out his flask, taking a swig before passing it to Christian. He takes a sip, hands it to Laynie, then lightly grabs my face and tilts my head back. His lips find mine, and my eyes widen when the potent taste of tequila is transferred into my mouth. If I were wearing panties right now, they would be ruined. That action alone caused pools of heat in my stomach. Feeling dizzy from the tequila and the warmth of his lips, he smiles down at me before planting a chaste kiss on my exposed neck.

Thankfully, I wore my hair up because it is hot in here, crowded with people, and we can barely move without bumping into someone. The room is dimly lit with dark blue lighting, making it feel like we're outside as hundreds of twinkling lights mimicking stars dangle above us. It could not be more perfect. I've always loved the stars, but now I love them more because they remind me of Christian. The first night he almost kissed me on the roof under a star-lit sky, the night we first made love, we sat by the fire, and I saw a shooting star.

The music ends, and Christian's hands move to my waist. I close my eyes, breathing in the citrus aroma that wafts through the air, encompassing me entirely.

"Dance with me, Raynie."

'Iris—Acoustic by The Goo Goo Dolls,'

"And I'd give up forever to touch you 'cause I know that you feel me somehow, You're the closest to heaven that I'll ever be, and I don't want to go home right now."

He trails his fingertips down my arms. I pull in a breath, leaning my forehead against his chest. My throat feels thick as I squeeze my eyes tightly together. I love him so much. We have come so far together and haven't even reached the surface. He is the sweetest feeling I know, something indescribable.

"What's going on in that pretty little head of yours?"

"I'm happy, and this night is perfect. Thank you."

Tilting his head to the side, he cups the side of my face. "Why are you thanking me?"

"For everything... you let me know what real life is, what this world is about. Without realizing it, you have made me stronger and more confident. I thank you for how you love me, the memories we've made, and the way you have changed my life."

"You never need to thank me for loving you the way you deserve to be loved. I'm the fool lucky enough to get the chance to love you in the first place." his thumb strokes the side of my face, and my eyes sparkle with unshed tears. "I'm much more me when I'm with you."

He kisses me long and intensely, setting my skin ablaze. The kind of kiss that I will never forget... with a fire and an intensity that will burn into my memory for the rest of my life. His kiss lingers and seems to last forever, and I want it to.

Laynie shrieks when "Yeah!" by Usher plays and pulls me away from Christian. We dance for the following few songs as Ryker and Christian dance beside us. When Ryker and Laynie go to get some punch, Christian pulls me back into him.

"I'm stealing you back." His fingers skim to my lower back. "You're mine for the rest of the night."

"Only for the rest of the night?"

He growls, "You're forever mine."

"Mmm," I hum, playing with the hair at the nape of his neck, "I like the sound of that. As much as I'd like to stay here with you, I have to use the lady's room. Wait for me?" he nods, kissing my forehead.

Weaving through the crowd, I exit the banquet hall. The moment the door closes, I'm met with silence. Quickly using the restroom, I fix my slightly smeared lipstick. I grin as I exit the bathroom when my phone pings with a snap from Laynie.

I'm looking down at my phone and not paying attention when I smack into a chest, almost knocking the wind out of me.

"I'm sor—" My words get stuck in my throat when I see Jackson fucking Reed standing before me.

I quickly step back, looking around, hoping that we aren't alone, but we are.

"Jackson, what are you doing here? You aren't supposed to be near me."

"I know. I wanted to apologize for everything that I've done."

"You aren't supposed to be near me," I repeat, stepping around him.

"Don't walk away from me when I'm talking to you!" he grabs my arm, stopping me. "I've been going to therapy ever since I was served papers. I needed help, and I got it. I'm a better person now and just wanted to say sorry. Please forgive me." I clench and unclench my fists, trying to prevent my hands from shaking as I try to think of a response. "Where is your boyfriend?"

"Don't talk about him."

"You are too good for him, you know."

There's the Jackson, I know. My panic quickly dissipates, replaced with pure rage.

"I said not to speak about him. You don't know me, and you sure as fuck don't know Christian. You're insane for speaking to me after everything you have done!" he takes a step toward me, and I take a step back.

"You're so defensive over Christian..." he takes another step, "but where is he when you need him to defend you?"

I stare at him, unable to blink. Jackson slowly takes another step toward me, and I wrap my arms tightly around myself to keep my body from trembling.

"Don't take another step," I warn.

My heart beats wildly as I dart my eyes around, trying to figure out a way out of this. He smirks smugly as he continues to approach me, and I want to slap it right from his face. I back away but feel the coolness from the wall pressed against my back. My pulse races, and I feel like crumpling to the ground, realizing I'm trapped. Despite the terror running through my veins, I refuse to cower to him. I will not let him hold any power over me anymore. He takes a final step, stopping when the tips of his loafers touch my heels.

Lifting my chin in confidence, I look him directly in the eyes when I speak. "I don't give a shit about your apology, and I don't fucking forgive you." He stares at me through squinted eyes. "Stay the hell away from me."

I push against his chest, and he stumbles back, caught off guard. Quickly moving around, I make a run for it, only making it a few steps before his arms come around my waist, pulling me back. I let out a primal scream before his hand covers my mouth, silencing me. My heartbeat thrashes in my ears as I attempt to kick free out of his hold.

No, no, no!

Stupid, stupid, stupid. How did I get myself into this situation again? I haven't heard from or seen Jackson since Devil's night, and I wasn't thinking about the possibility of running into him here or the possibility of him violating the order of protection.

"You look fucking divine in this dress." He whispers into my ear as he drags me further away. "But without the dress..." his fingers dig into my waist, and I let out a muffled cry from the pain.

He pecks my neck as I swallow down the vomit creeping its way up my throat.

"Raynie?" tears spring to my eyes at the sound of Christian's voice. With all my might, I wildly thrash my body, trying to break free from his hold. I can't see him, but I know he is close.

"Stay still and don't make a fucking sound." Jackson's threatening tone sends chills down my spine. I stop fighting, relaxing my body as I mentally count my breaths. "Good girl."

"Where the fuck is she?" Ryker asks.

"She isn't in the restroom," Laynie says. "Maybe we missed her, and she came back inside."

"Let's go back inside and check."

No! Don't leave!

"You guys go back inside," Christian says. "I'm going to look around here."

Relief washes over me, but it doesn't last long when Jackson tightens his grip, warning me to keep quiet.

"Rayne?" he calls for me, and my heart cracks at the worry I hear in his voice. He pauses his movement before I hear his feet getting closer to the end of the hall where Jackson currently has me pressed into a darkened corner.

My body shakes in anticipation the closer he gets as my heart nearly thumps out of my chest when I hear his phone ring.

"No, she isn't out here. I'm going to head back and meet you guys."

My legs feel weak, giving out from underneath me, knowing he's about to leave and I will be left alone with Jackson. Any hope I feel vanishes with each step he takes away from me, but then his movement stops. Suddenly, my ringtone blasts as it vibrates in my hands.

"Rayne!" he shouts.

I use this moment to fling my head back, connecting with a part of Jackson's face, and he grunts in anguish, his hands no longer holding me prisoner.

"Christian!" I don't stop running until his arms are wrapped around me, lifting me off the ground.

The instant I'm in his arms, I can no longer hold back the tears I've been fighting to hold. I instantly feel relief and safe now that I'm with him, but still shaken about my encounter with Jackson.

"What's wrong, baby?" he sets me down, cupping my face. His eyes roam over me before quickly looking past me.

"It was Jackson."

His eyebrows lift to his forehead, the whites around his eyes showing. The muscles and veins strain against his skin as his nostrils flare to life.

"I'm going to fucking kill him!" he pushes past me, sprinting in the direction I came from.

"No! Christian, wait!" he doesn't stop. I quickly dial Ryker's number as I chase after him.

"Rayne! Where the hell we—"

"Ryker! It's Christian. Please come to the front!" I end the call before he can reply.

When I reach Christian, he is flinging open doors and searching rooms. I've seen him angry before, but nothing like this. Stampeding footsteps come from behind me and the next thing I know I'm being pulled into strong arms.

"Rayne, what happened!" Ryker pushes me back slightly to get a better look at me.

Before I can get a word out, Christian roars, "I'm going to kill that motherfucker!" Ryker tenses, and Laynie's eyes turn to saucers.

"What is going on?" Laynie asks.

"What the fuck happened?" comes from Ry.

"He isn't fucking here!" Christian paces back and forth, gripping the ends of his hair.

"When I was stepped out of the bathroom, I wasn't paying attention and ran into Jackson. He came out of nowhere."

Ryker lets go of my arms, clenching his fists, his knuckles turning white, "Where the fuck is that bitch?"

"Not fucking here." Christian retorts.

"Did he do something to you?" Laynie whispers, her eyes sparkling with tears.

"Not in the way you're thinking. He didn't get the chance. He pulled me far into the corner at the end of the hall when he heard Christian call for me."

"It doesn't matter if he didn't get the chance. He knows better than to even look at you. I promise you when I get my hands on him—"

"When *we* get our hands on him," Ryker interjects.

I hate this. I hate that they are involved and will get in trouble for retaliating. Once again, he managed to ruin another night. A night that was meant to be full of fun and firsts for all of us. I'm sick of it, and I will not let him affect me or the people I love.

"No." They all turn to look at me with surprised expressions. "Neither of you will do anything. He is scum on the bottom of my stilettos, and I will not allow him to tarnish any more of our memories. I won't let the both of you guys do something that will put you in jail."

"Like hell we aren't going to do anything." Christian snaps. Damn, I love him and his protective behavior. He watches my every step as I walk over to him. Pulling him into a kiss, I can feel the tension in his body slowly release. Good. I'll take it all.

"You aren't going to retaliate. Especially over a guy who wears fucking loafers." He chuckles into my lips, and then I turn to Ryker. "And neither are you." His eyebrows rise. "Christian and I are going to the police station and reporting what he did and how he violated his restraining order. We're sending his ass to jail."

Ryker and Christian speak. "But—"

"But nothing. We have less than four months before we're living in New York away from him. Less than four months before we're away from you guys." I look at Laynie and Ryker. "It isn't worth it... he isn't worth it."

Laynie smirks, "Atta girl, you tell them."

Ryker rolls his eyes. "We're coming with you."

I shake my head. "No, you're not big brother. You guys have fun and enjoy tonight." He looks at me, perplexed. "I'm fine, okay? Christian has me."

I glance at Christian, and he gives me my favorite crooked smile, instantly causing my cheeks to heat.

"I love you," Laynie says, hugging me. "We will catch a uber home. Text me once you get to the police station, okay?"

I nod, "I love you too, Laynie Mae."

Chapter 48

Rayne

<u>"Wait by M83,"</u>
"There's no end. There is no goodbye. Disappear with the night."

"I'm sorry," Christian glances over at me, turning right onto the empty two-lane road. "Why are you apologizing?"

"Because of Jack—"

"Don't ever apologize for him," he grips the steering wheel, pressing harder onto the gas. "You did nothing wrong. Do you understand me?" exhaling a deep breath, I nod.

"I hate that you are involved in my mess. He has caused too many problems to count, and I feel like everything is all my fault."

"I hate that you feel that way," he shakes his head, glancing at me before bringing his attention back to the road. "Don't you get it? I love you, Rayne. Anything that involves you has an affect on me. I will always protect you, no matter what. I *want* to protect you."

"I love you. Do you know that? God, I love you so damn much." I say, blinking back my tears.

He and his damn words always get to me. They pass my heart and reach the depths of my soul. As much as I try to be perfect at everything I do, I never believed perfection existed, but Christian makes me believe because if he isn't perfect, then I don't know what is. I feel safe with him, like no one can hurt me. Under his strong embrace or his heated gaze, the feeling is indescribable. It's a feeling I have never experienced until him, but I can only hope everyone is lucky enough to experience it one day.

He pulls his eyes to mine. "I know, baby. We're putting that bitch in jail, and then we will live our life in New York, where he will never be able to hurt you." The warmth of his hand reaches mine, sending me waves of relief and hope. "We will do so many big things because together, we are fucking unstoppable." He squeezes my hand with an amorous touch that I can't help but melt under his love and confidence. "I'm going to open a shop of my own, and you will kill it in school and become some high-end fashion designer. We will walk the streets of New York and see your designs on billboards everywhere! Everyone will know who Rayne Davis is, and I will be the lucky bastard by her side." He pulls his optimistic eyes from mine, glancing back at the road, gaining speed now that we are going downhill, "You. Will. Always. Have. Me."

I lean over, kissing him hard. He squeezes my thigh in response, sending pools of desire swirling around my stomach. His crooked grin and sultry voice only fill me with anticipation.

The light ahead turns red, and his expression turns solemn. Christian pumps his leg vigorously up and down. His eyebrows are drawn together as he looks bewilderingly down at his feet and then at the red light—his gaze darts to me, then back to the road. The light is coming up fast, and panic sets in. Why isn't he slowing down?

"C... Christian. Please slow down." I look back and forth between him and the red light.

"Baby..." He clenches and unclenches his hand on the steering wheel, wildly looking at his feet, to the light, then over at me. "No, no, no, no." He chants frantically.

The terror in his voice causes fear to set in, and I feel like I'm choking. His crazed eyes roam over my face before falling to my seat belt.

"Put your seatbelt on, Rayne!"

My fingers tremble as I attempt to click the buckle struggling to get it in place as panic overcomes me. The red light reflects in his eyes, lighting up the side of his face. Before I can process what is happening, he bolts across me. A horn blares, tires screech, and then the crushing sound of metal giving way, followed by glass shattering. My head slams into the side window with a loud crack. *Was it glass or my skull?* I'm not sure.

Suddenly, the car is spinning out of control. Images flash across my mind. Ryker and Laynie. My parents. Moments Christian and I had together. Clips of my life flash past like a sped-up slideshow. Then it all slows down.

One... Two...

A massive blow to the back of the vehicle.

I don't think I felt the hit, but I know I screamed Christian's name. The last thing I see is him flying backward through the windshield, a waterfall of glass cascading around him. His fingertips grasp onto mine, but the impact is too strong. Our locked hands rip apart, and I'm flung forward. Raging pain shoots right through me, making me feel crippled with agony.

This isn't real.

This isn't real.

This isn't real... is all I remember thinking before everything fades.

A piercing ring echos in my ears. *Where am I?* Everything was very quiet for a few seconds, or at least I thought it was, but I'm not sure, I'm not sure if any of this is even real. The sharp smell of burnt rubber assaults my nose, and smoke invades my lungs. My head pounds, making it difficult to open my weighted eyes. Everything is a blur, like waking up groggy from a deep sleep. *Am I dreaming?* The ringing intensifies as my eyes flutter open and shut.

"Are you okay?" someone asks.

Pushing through the agony, I uncover a man pacing back and forth. He stops when he notices me stir.

"Oh, thank God! I thought you died."

Shards of glass scratch against my cheek, bringing me back to reality, and I hiss at the sting. My eyes land on a lone Converse shoe in the middle of the street. Slamming my eyes shut, I clench them tightly, trying to convince myself that this can't be true. When I muster the courage to open my eyes, they instantly lock on the shoe that lies in the intersection. My heart stops as a horrendous sob breaks free from my throat.

No!

No!

No!

Empty. The panic, pain, fear—none of it mattered because, at this moment, all I felt was emptiness.

"Christian," I whimper before everything goes black.

In an instant, it all changed. And then there was only before and after.

To be continued...

Chapter forty-eight

About Author

Born and raised in Southern California, Jessica Voll has always had a love affair with words. You can often find her getting lost in the pages of a great novel or listening to some moody music on a gloomy day. She reads a book a day and has a song for everything!

Her true love is her amily, her two young boys, Carter and Chandler, and her high school sweetheart Cody. They are the driving force for all her hard work and dedication. Setting an example for her boys to look up to and know possibilities are endless when you don't give up.

Jessica is a hopeless romantic who enjoys writing and reading all things romance—the type of books that make you feel things even when it hurts. She always admired storytelling and the author's ability to capture you emotionally into a new reality; within the pages of a book. Telling her own was never a thought. Who has time with two kids under five? The idea of writing wasn't of interest. Until one night, she had a dream that stuck with her, and she had to tell it. That's when Rayne Davis was born, and The Road To Oblivion came about. Now, storytelling is something she can never go without.

When she isn't writing or forming bonds with the characters within a novel, she enjoys creating memories with family and friends, cooking, drinking coffee (all the coffee), and obsessing over true crime.

Books By Jessica Voll

The Oblivion Series

Book One
The Road To Oblivion
Now Available On Amazon
Available in Print August 2022

Book Two-
Oblivion
Coming Spring 2023
(Excerpt included in this book)
Book Three- Coming Winter 2024

Contact Jessica Voll
AuthorJessicaVoll@hotmail.com
Social Media
Facebook Author Jessica Voll
Instagram @authorjessicavoll
TikTok @AuthorJessicaVoll
Goodreads Jessica Voll (Personal & Author)
Webpage AuthorJessicaVoll.Wixsite.Com

Sneak Peek

Book Two

My Story Is Not Over

    Denial, anger, bargaining, depression, and acceptance. I don't think there is a specific order you're supposed to go through them, but what I do know is my experience has been hell.
    Denial came first... there was no possible way that he wasn't with me, especially when he promised me forever.
    Second, was bargaining... if I had just paid attention, then maybe I would have noticed Jackson lurking before it was too late. I could have avoided him and the need to flee. Then we would have never had to get in his car and leave prom early. If we had just taken a stupid limo, he wouldn't have had to drive at all.
    Depression consumed me in my third stage of hell... nothing I do feels the same without him. There is nothing to fill the void of emptiness that I feel. I hardly eat or sleep, and all I ever seem to do is cry. Ryker, Laynie, and my parents keep telling me everything will be alright, and I won't feel like this forever, but for the first time in my life, I think they're wrong. Without my summer, everything is cold and dull. Nothing is bright and warm anymore.

Acceptance sneaks in every now and then, but honestly, it's hard to wrap my head around this part... he really isn't here. I don't see him working outside on his car, and he no longer comes over for Sunday breakfast. The smell of him that used to linger inside my bedroom is fading, and I'm scared I'll forget it once it's gone.

Then came the anger... he left me! He broke his promise. I hate that I'm angry at him for something he had no control over, but I'm even angrier at myself because I feel like I'm to blame. There are so many things I could have done differently... things that I should have done differently, but none of that mattered anymore because what's done is done, and there isn't going back.

Each day I can't wait to go to sleep so I can dream of him. That's the only time the pain subsides. In my dreams, it's just us—Christian and Rayne. Then I wake up, and I'm knocked so hard by the reality of it all that my heart breaks all over again.

I wanted a movie type of love story, and I got it, but nobody tells you what happens once the movie ends. I used to think once you got your happily ever after, that's all there was, happily... ever... after...

I was very wrong.

My name is Rayne Davis, and I thought my story was over, but it's only begun.

Chapter 1

Rayne- Rather be alone.

I'm dragging my feet through campus as if trudging through mud. One more class to get through, then I'm done for the day. NYU isn't a terrible school; ranked ninth in the U.S., but just another thing on the lengthy list of reminders of how everything in life is nothing I expected it to be. I am glad to have Laynie here. She surprised the shit out of me when she told me she would come with me. As far as I was concerned, her plan has always been to attend UCLA, just another thing to feel guilty about. Giving up her dream to follow me to New York, and she will never admit that, but I know. Honestly, I have no idea what I'd do without her.

Walking into math class, I'm always the first one here and I have nothing better to do. I'm not meeting up with friends in between classes or standing outside the classroom till the last-minute chatting. Plus, it allows me to call dibs on a seat in the very back row. It's less likely for someone to try to have a conversation, *as if anyone would try, anyway. A freshman in a junior-level class.*

Students file in as I grab my notebook for today's lesson and a few colored pens. The professor begins to speak. I am counting the minutes until I can leave.

With fifteen minutes left of class, I hear "Psst." coming from my right.

I don't acknowledge because it isn't someone trying to get my attention. Then I hear it again, this time louder.

"Psst." Turning my head just enough to see what's going on, I freeze at the culprit. Beside me sits a guy who must be at least six two by the way his legs are crammed underneath the desk. He's extremely good looking, and the boyish smile tells me he knows.

My eyes travel from his long legs, past his long fingers that rhythmically tap against the desk. His jaw is sharp, and his lips are — "Are you done checkin' me out yet?" he asks, smiling smugly—The New York accent thick between his lips. I drop my pen as my eyes snap to his, cheeks instantly flushing in embarrassment. His eyes are one of the prettiest I have ever seen. Deep pools of glacial ice glittering against tan skin. He smirks, drawing attention back to his mouth. Shit! I shake my head, snapping out of my daze, and he chuckles at the fact I'm blatantly checking him out.

"I was not checking you out." The curve of his lip turns into a full-blown grin.

"Mm hmm," he drawls.

"I wasn't."

"I'm Riley." My focus sweeps to his offered hand, but I don't move.

"Did you need something?"

"Can I borrow a pen?"

"What's wrong with that one?" I ask, glancing at the pen on his desk.

"You have options, and I like options." *Insert eye roll.*

"I'm sure you do." With the way he looks, I'm sure he has plenty.

"What's your name?" he asks, just as the professor ends his lecture, dismissing us. *Thank God.*

"Gotta go," I stand, grabbing my notebook and pens before tossing them into my bag. His hand goes to my arm, stopping my movement.

"Hang out wit' me," he says, towering over me.

"I don't even know you."

"I already told you, I'm Riley."

"Yeah, and I am Megan Fox." He chuckles, amusement dancing in his eyes.

"Now that you mention it, you do sort of look like her." Tilting my head, I stare, my expression blank. "Look, we can hang out in a public place here on campus. Nothing more than friends, I promise."

Not only is he easy on the eyes, but his accent only adds to his appeal. I've never heard one like it. It would be nice to have a friend other than Laynie out here, and he's not asking to go back to his dorm. I don't know, though; I hardly know him and only exchanged a few words. The last person I trusted was Jackson, and look how that turned out.

Grabbing his hand that's still on my arm, his smirk deepens.

"No, thank you," I drop his hand. His eyes widen in shock, and his pompous smile falters. Giving him my back, he calls after me as I walk away.

"I'm persistent, Megan Fox! It's in my blood, and I'll getcha to hang out." My lips twitch as I try not to smile. Holding my arm above my head, I give a thumbs-up. *Good luck, buddy. You may be persistent, but I'm stubborn.*

NYU differs from most campuses. Most colleges I've researched have a massive quad in the center, and NYU has a public park with a variety of campus buildings surrounding it. It's different from what I expected, making it a unique compared to other colleges. Laynie loves New York and fits right in here. She didn't care what college we went to, she just wanted to get out of Los Angeles. It was confusing at first and had me worried about why she wanted to get away so much when that was never the plan, but she said that aside from parents, she didn't have anyone keeping her there and wanted to be wherever I was. Laynie wanted to experience college life with her best friend.

I take a seat on a bench in the park, where Laynie and I meet after class. It's awful that Laynie came here expecting to have the college experience with me, and I've done nothing but left her alone. We've only been attending classes for a month, but I have done nothing I did not have to. Fortunately, that hasn't stopped Laynie from experiencing all that college life offers. She has made many friends, which is not surprising because she's outgoing, even found herself a boyfriend she met the first week of school. Laynie denies that they're together, saying they're only good friends who occasionally have sex. Whenever I point out that not only is there sex, but he's over at our apartment at least half of the time, and when he isn't at our place, she is at his, her cheeks turn pink, and she rolls her eyes not denying it.

I never expected to see her in a relationship, but it warms my heart to see her happy because she deserves it. She is cautious when they hang out around me, worried that I wouldn't be able to stand seeing her in a relationship or getting to do the things Christian and I had planned, but I'm just happy she's happy. Yes, it hurts sometimes, but I never want to take away her happiness to appease mine. I still try to hold on to hope that one day I will be happy again and that this isn't the end. The only thing difficult is it's hard to be hopeful when there is nothing but hopelessness.

Grabbing the leather journal out of my purse, my fingers trace the engraved letters. *'Tell me a secret.'* Sawyer gifted me the journal before I left for New York. Eyes brimming with tears, I stare at the leather-bound journal with blurred vision. That was a year before the accident when I had no idea how much of a hairpin curve life would take. Our last night in NY, he said he chose me, and wanted to be wherever I was. That's all I've ever wanted — to be next to him.

I imagined nights in our apartment cuddling up on the couch after a long day of school and work. He'd watch my cheesy romance movies as he played with my hair, missing half the movie because he was too busy watching me. I'd dance in the kitchen as I cooked, and he'd give my favorite lopsided grin before I grabbed his hands and made him dance with me. He would refuse at first, but ultimately give in because he never could deny me the same way I could never deny him. We would dance until he kissed me. We'd go to the bedroom and make love. Once we were done and finally able to pull away from each other, we'd warm up now cold food and have dinner on the balcony overlooking the city.

If I had only known, I would have held Christian tighter, kissed him more, and loved him as if I'd never get to love again. Life is finite and fragile, and just because someone is there one day doesn't guarantee they'll be there the next.

Sawyer thought he'd want me to have the journal, that it belonged with me. Four months have passed, and I still haven't opened it. I know I should, but I'm scared. Afraid that I'm not strong enough and won't be able to handle reading his words. There have been too many times to count that I held the flexible leather in hand, repeatedly telling myself to open it and read the secrets he never got to tell.

"Boo!" I yelp, almost falling off the bench.

"Shit!" Laynie hisses, helping me right myself.

"Jesus, Laynie, are you trying to kill me?" Her eyes drop to the journal on the floor, and I snatch it up, putting the journal back in my purse.

"No, it was a stupid thing to do. I'm sorry."

When did I become this person who can't take a fucking joke or laugh with my best friend? Hudson, her *boyfriend*, gives me an empathetic frown, putting his arm around Laynie. There's that look again — pity. He knows about the accident. Laynie told him after I had a nightmare a couple of days ago. He spent the night, and when she ended up sleeping in my room, she had to explain why. I didn't expect her to lie, but it's embarrassing.

Using the back of my hand to wipe my eyes, I pull myself together.

"Don't apologize, please. I'm the one who should apologize, I overreacted, and I'm sorry."

"It's okay," she nods, worry still etched on her face. "Hudson and I are going to meet with friends at the bar on campus. Want to come?"

"Maybe next time."

"Come on, it will be fun!" she says with enthusiasm and hopeful eyes. "We can finally put our fake I.D.s to good use."

"Um," I shift on my feet, picking at my nails, "maybe next time, okay? You two have fun! Take a shot of tequila for me." Her shoulders sag, giving me a clenched half-smile.

"Y... Yeah, okay, I will." I do my best to give a convincing grin and a small wave goodbye. "Hey, Rayne?"

"Yeah?" she runs to me, wrapping her arms around me.

"I love you." Tears spring to my eyes as a heaviness settles in my chest.

"Ditto, babe."

Chapter 2

Rayne - Finding hope

Thankfully campus is in a main section of the city, and it's ten minutes away from our apartment and eight minutes away from Times Square when taking the subway. I don't know what made me walk past my apartment and into the metro station, but I did. Maybe because I missed Christian and thought it might bring him closer, or maybe it was the fact that Laynie was out right now making memories and I didn't want to go home to drown in mine.

    Times Square is exactly how I remembered. The energy is high, the streets swamped with people, and the noise is non-stop. Walking down forty-second street, taking everything in, is refreshing. Nobody knows me or my story; they aren't looking at me with pity in their eyes. I'm just a girl in a big city. I am nobody.

What am I even doing here? I should have gone home. Coming here was a mistake. We filled Times Square with nothing but memories and it only makes me miss Christian more. Just as I turn around and head back to the subway station, my phone rings with an incoming call from Ryker. I hesitate to answer or not, but I can't avoid him forever.

"Hey Ry," I try to sound cheerful.

"Wow, she's alive!" guilt washes over me. Not only have I been a shitty friend, but I've been a shitty sister, too. Ryker has tried to call multiple times, and I never answer, only reply to texts. My throat tightens, and eyes instantly water. I miss him tons, and it feels good to hear his voice.

"I'm sorry. We've been settling into our place, and I've been busy with school." The lie slips off my tongue with ease. He's silent for a moment, causing me to shift on my feet uncomfortably. Can he tell I'm lying?

"I get it, I do, but I miss you, and it would be nice to hear your voice every once in a while," he pauses, and a tear slides down my cheek, "Shit, do you hear me right now? Don't tell anyone about this because I'll deny it."

I chuckle. "Your secret is safe with me, and I miss you, too. I promise I'll do better and check in with you more."

"Okay, good because you know I'll fly out there if you don't," I laugh, because that is the truth. "How are you?"

This is why I didn't answer the calls. He asks how I am and what am I supposed to say? I'm awful? I'm a shell of the person I once was. I feel lost. How one moment, one second, one instant changed me forever, and I'm mentally grasping at proverbial straws. I'm terrified. I don't know how to get better and get out of this dark place, and it only gets worse, day by day. Everything feels too much, and everything is pounding in my head. It hurts, all of it fucking hurts. Physically, mentally, and emotionally, I'm drained.

"I'm good, Ry. How are things going back home?"

"Things are..." he pauses, clearing his throat, "Things are good. I've been busy with work, and mom and dad are still the same. Everything is different now that you aren't here, but I'm happy you're out there doing your thing. We are proud of you, Rayne."

"H... How are..." I pause, trying not to lose it over the phone. "How are you dealing?" he's silent. The only sound is our breathing, and with each passing second, I know the answer. "Never mind, stupid to ask."

"Don't do that," he sighs, and I don't need to see to know he's running his hands through his hair. "It isn't stupid to ask, and you should ask. I'm taking things one step at a time. Each day is different. Sometimes I hardly think about everything that has happened, and other times, it takes residence in my head."

I nod. The silence between us is interrupted by the sound of clanking and raised voices in the background.

"I have to get back to work. Don't be a stranger and call once in a while or answer the phone. We've lost so much, and I can't lose you, too. I wouldn't survive it." His words stopped me because Ryker was never one to show vulnerability, because it hurt to hear how selfish I'd been in my grief. In the months following the accident, I neglected to notice my mother's watery eyes, which she wiped away the instant I entered the room, and the forced smile plastered on her face. Of Laynie's wary looks, given whenever she spoke or tried to comfort me. One night, I faintly remember hearing sobs from across the hall in Ryker's room, followed by a loud crash. The following day when he came to check on me, I hadn't noticed his eyes were rimmed red or the fact his hair was in disarray, as if pulling at it all night.

Closing my eyes tightly, I repress the sob threatening to break free and rub at the ache in my chest. We have always been close, but now not only are we thousands of miles apart, but I also feel a massive disconnect between us. It isn't because of him, but because of me. These past few months have been insurmountable, and all I've done was push everyone who loves and cares away, creating acres of distance between us.

I have been selfishly drowning in my self-deprivation. Not acknowledging the loss and pain those who matter most have endured. All they wanted to do was be there for me, and I couldn't even give them that. God, we lost Christian and felt a gaping hole in our chest, felt the coldness creep into our ribs and up our spine because my golden boy, my summer, was no longer shining. I wasn't the only one struggling to find the light through the sudden darkness.

"Rayne?" Ryker says when I don't speak.

"Yeah?"

"You know you can come to me for whatever, right?"

"Yes, of course." The sound of clanking tools grows louder.

"Okay, good. I have to go now before this new trainee gets us a lawsuit. I love you, sis."

"I love you too, brother."

After getting off the phone with Ry, instead of going home as originally planned, I decide to continue roaming the streets of Times Square. I could not let them be there for me, but I can try to live the way my brother wanted me to, the way he *thinks* I am. Continuing my walk, my attention locks on the club called Knight. The outside of the club is just how I remember it, except it doesn't have a line of people waiting to enter and given that the sun is still out, the word Knight isn't luminously displayed in bold gray writing. Even though it appears not open, I still can't pull my eyes away.

While in line at the grocery store one day, I read in a magazine that they voted it New York's most successful club of the year. It's a spot Laynie would love, and also something we couldn't afford. We decided we didn't want to stay in a dorm on campus. We wanted our own apartment. It made the most sense because going to NYU was a last-minute decision and we would have ended up in whatever dorms they had left. I never planned on staying on campus once Christian said he wanted to come to New York with me. We had a cute two-bedroom apartment picked out with an open floor plan and the perfect balcony on the eighth floor. Thankfully, the landlord didn't charge us to cancel our lease once my parents explained what had happened.

When I ended up deciding to come here without him, it didn't feel right if Laynie and I stayed in an apartment that was meant to be mine and Christians, so we looked around and found one that was perfect for us. It isn't the biggest, with a decent sized living room, an enclosed kitchen with a bar top big enough for two barstools. We qualified for many grants, so we used that to afford the place with extra money to spare if we manage our money. Not counting the bit of money I earned working at The Hideout.

My attention drifts to the blacked-out Range Rover that pulled up to the curb in front of the club. Tilting my head, my brows lower in curiosity as I watch an older man dressed in black and white walk over to the other side of the car. The man looks oddly familiar. I can't pinpoint where I've seen him. Intrigued, I watch him closely as he opens the door and takes a slight step back with a brief bow of his head. From over the top of the car, a tall man with wide shoulders and silky raven hair, dressed in an Armani suit, steps out. He squares his shoulders, giving a curt nod to what I assume is his chauffeur as he adjusts his tie.

His back is facing me, so I can't see who he is or what he looks like, but from how he stands and how the man responds to him, I can tell he is respected and holds power. My feet instinctively take a step forward, hoping to get a better look. His chauffeur says something causing the powerful man's shoulders to shake, and I wonder what he said to make him laugh. My eyes never leave him as he walks toward the club. Before he reaches the door, he stops, and I hold my breath as he turns toward me.

"Um, miss?" an older lady with graying hair says, drawing my attention to her. "You are standing in front of the door, and I am going to need you to move."

"I'm sorry," I mutter, my eyes drifting back to the club. The Range Rover pulls away and the man no longer stands there. With pursed lips and slumped shoulders, I bring my attention back to the lady.

She studies me and I awkwardly shift on my feet.

"Why don't you come in and have a cup of coffee?"

It's then that I realize I'm still blocking the door of a coffee shop called The Roast. The older woman's brows deepen when I don't respond, wondering what the hell my problem is or possibly because I still haven't gotten my feet to move and am still standing in front of the entrance.

"Oh, I'm sorry. Sure, I'll come in for a minute. I'm always in the mood for coffee."

She smiles, happy with my answer or the fact that I finally said something and stepped out of the way. The sweet aroma of roasted coffee awakens my senses. The invitingly warm smell filled the atmosphere, making my taste buds ache. A smile graces my lips as I take in my surroundings. The place reminds me of The Hideout back home. It has an industrial style with touches of farmhouse, making it inviting.

"So, what can I get for you?"

"I'll have a vanilla iced coffee, please." I dig inside my crossbody bag for my wallet.

"Don't worry about that," she waves her hands, "It's on the house."

"Oh, thank you." I smile kindly, and when she turns around, I drop a ten-dollar bill into the tip jar.

Waiting at the side counter, I watch as a girl with long dark hair like mine sits at a table typing away on her laptop. She has a smile on her face that widens when a guy approaches her. He kisses her forehead and from where I stand, I can see her cheeks turn crimson. She scoots over and he takes a seat next to her, throwing his arm over her shoulders as if he can't stand the idea of not being able to touch her. A sad smile takes over my face as the ache in my chest intensifies.

They remind me of how Christian and I once were, and I wonder if that's how we would still be. I'd come to this coffee shop and work on digital designs on my computer, and he'd meet me here on his break. He'd give me his signature crooked smile before kissing me on the forehead and wrapping me in his arms. No work would get done when he was there, but I wouldn't care because I'd be wrapped up in him, hanging onto every word that left his charming full lips.

She catches my stare, and my cheeks heat with embarrassment as I avert my gaze.

"Excuse me, miss? I forgot to get your name, but here is your drink."

"My name is Rayne," I smile, taking the coffee. "Thank you."

"What a lovely name. I'm Margarette, but you can call me Mar. My husband, Robert, and I own this place."

"It's a beautiful place. You guys have done well with it." She grins proudly.

"It wasn't always this, but it was a dream of mine, and with plenty of hard work and dedication, I think I did alright." She winks, wiping the counter. "Are you in college?"

"I am."

"Do you happen to be looking for a job?" she asks, and that's when I notice the looking to hire sign on the counter.

"Oh, I don't know. I have a busy schedule. I'd have to think about it." She holds up her finger, signaling me to wait, and leaves before returning with a paper in hand.

"Give it some thought, and if you decide you are indeed looking for a job, bring back the application. The position is for part-time now." I smile, slipping the paper into my bag.

"Thank you, Mar."

Leaving the coffee shop, my mouth curves as I bring the coffee cup to my lips. I'm not sure if it's the conversation I had with Ry or the potential possibility of a job, maybe both, but for the first time, I feel optimistic. I don't know how long this feeling will last, but for now I'm hanging onto it and enjoying it. Not only does the little seed of hope that has blossomed inside my chest fill me with promise, but I welcome it. I need to be better for the people that I love the most.

Taking my seat on the subway, I release my grasp on the leather journal, exhaling a long breath.

Then... I open it.

Printed in Great Britain
by Amazon